*A
Harlequin
Romance*

OTHER
Harlequin Romances
by WYNNE MAY

Many of these titles are available at your local bookseller,
or through the Harlequin Reader Service.

For a free catalogue listing all available Harlequin Romances,
send your name and address to:

HARLEQUIN READER SERVICE,
M.P.O. Box 707, Niagara Falls, N.Y. 14302
Canadian address: Stratford, Ontario, Canada.

or use order coupon at back of book.

A PLUME OF DUST

by

WYNNE MAY

HARLEQUIN BOOKS   TORONTO
WINNIPEG

Original hard cover edition published in 1975
by Mills & Boon Limited.

© Wynne May 1975

SBN 373-01875-4

Harlequin edition published May 1975

Printed in Canada

1875

For
Marie
with love

CHAPTER ONE

THERE had been a sweeping tile-paved driveway, past white obelisks bearing lanterns, to a wide parking area and garages and, to Michelle Abbott, there was an Eastern palace look about the mansion.

'Within the last few years,' Laney, her brother Peter's wife, had said, 'there've been several films made in the Drakensberg. This house was built by a film company for that very reason. You should see it *inside*. Lyle Cunningham rents it, by the way. Before *he* decided to lease it, an artist used to live in it. I understand that the house is being put on the market soon. Pete, I wonder if Lyle will end up buying it?'

Shrugging his shoulders, Peter had replied, 'Who knows? He has the kind of money to buy it.' There had been a kind of impatience in Peter's voice, Michelle had found herself thinking, as the car came to a halt in the parking area.

They were in the ceramic-tiled, high-ceilinged entrance hall now, which was like the inside of an oriental palace, and they stood near a wall covering of a repetitive sun design in colours of pale gold, shocking pink and orange. A handsome black man in a cool white suit told them to take a seat on the long, low divan which had a back rest of gold-braided cushions in olive green, shocking pink, purple and orange, but Laney said, 'It's quite all right, thank you, Usef, we'll wait here.'

As the man went in the direction of heavily carved doors which led to the lounge Laney said, 'Now you can see why I was grateful when he offered to have your welcome party *here*.' Fairly tall with short blonde hair, parted simply on the side, Laney patted her bulge and grinned. 'He suggested that it might be too much for me to have a party at this stage. We did want you to meet everybody and so Pete and I agreed. I made out lists, and things, of course – about invitations and food.'

'I can see what you mean about the film people having

7

built it,' Michelle answered softly. 'It's – well, what I've seen of it – absolutely fabulous, Laney.' Her blue eyes flickered towards the brass candlesticks with their pink candles and then to two tremendous hand-carved black elephants standing at the foot of the burnt orange carpeted stairway which curved elegantly past an exotic indoor fountain set in the midst of huge green leaves. 'Tell me, do you always have to wait here, like this, before Lyle Cunningham decides to show himself?'

Laney laughed. 'No, of course not, but this is a special occasion. Listen to the voices in there.'

At the far end of the hall the carved doors had been left slightly ajar and the glimpse Michelle had of the lounge was absolutely breathtaking – all honey-gold carpeting.

'I thought that we were going to be the first,' Laney said, 'but as usual, I seem to have made us late.'

Even while Laney was talking, Lyle Cunningham, tall, with dark hair and eyes which looked blue-green even at a distance, was coming towards them. Tanned, loose-limbed and handsome, he created instant excitement and Michelle felt herself blink – once, twice. As their eyes met there was a silent and unexpected communication between them.

'I'm sorry,' Laney was saying, 'I didn't mean us to be late, Lyle. This is Pete's sister, Michelle.'

'But you're never late, Laney,' Lyle answered, before he gave his full attention to Michelle, and Peter laughed outright.

'That's the understatement of the year, and you know it,' he said, glancing at his wife.

Lyle Cunningham held out his hand to Michelle and the physical impact caused a shock to pass through her. She told herself that this was foolish while their eyes linked for one more moment before he greeted her. Afterwards, she wondered what he had said and whether she had answered.

Peter and Laney appeared to be on good terms with Lyle Cunningham, but Michelle was aware of a certain tension in Peter's attitude as Lyle led them to the carved doors and through to the lounge.

Michelle felt her feet sink into the honey-gold carpeting as she was being introduced around. 'You look a lot like

Pete,' one of the men said, 'only beautiful.' Glancing at Peter, Michelle laughed.

'That's a very sly and subtle way of telling you that you've got him interested,' said Lyle.

Although the party in Michelle's honour was in his house, Lyle, with a careful dignity, allowed Laney and Peter to do most of the talking while the introductions went on.

More people were arriving. Drinks and snacks were being passed around.

'Where do all these people *come* from?' Michelle whispered to Laney once, thinking of the vast spaces and mountains outside.

'Some of them are farmers, others people we've got to know. A few of them are, strictly speaking, Lyle's friends. A party is a party here. We don't have them often, but when we do, *we do*!' Laney laughed.

Finally Michelle was free to look around the room – not that she had been unaware of it. It was plain that the house had been built as the setting for a film. There was a conversation pit which included an indoor garden, vibrant with huge exotic leaves, but at the moment, everybody seemed to be keeping to the lounge with its copper and brass artwork above a six-seater honey-toned leather sofa. In front of the sofa there was a long, low coffee table which resembled a casket, but got away with it, upon which stood a gleaming gold Turkish coffee set. There were deep leather chairs to match the sofa.

Michelle sipped her drink contemplatively and listened to that clinking, rustling and murmuring noise which goes along with a party. Everybody seemed to be involved in 'clever' talk.

When Lyle Cunningham spoke, cutting into her thoughts, she almost jumped. 'You're a long way from home.' He gave her a long, direct look. 'Let's get this straight, are you here to settle?'

'I don't know,' she answered, 'it – depends.'

For a seemingly endless moment their eyes remained locked. 'On what?' he asked.

There was a little pause before she said, 'Well, on whether I like South Africa, for one thing.' She gave him what she hoped was an easy smile.

The soft lighting in the room was turning her hair the colour of golden grass at sunset. Michelle Abbott was a girl who would look coolly elegant in an English twilight or sultry and exciting beneath a South African sun or sub-tropical stars – a girl who claimed her right to be even more beautiful by the kind of fastidious taste she had and the way she wore her clothes.

'And of course, it's too soon for you to have formed an opinion. Is that it?' There was an almost frozen moment as Lyle Cunningham waited for her reply.

'Well, yes, of course, and then – there are other reasons . . .' she broke off.

He took a sip of his drink, his eyes still on her face. 'I see,' he said. Then he smiled and his smile started somewhere at the corners of his mouth and ended up in those fantastic eyes. 'In that case,' he lifted his glass, 'here's to liking South Africa and – other reasons.'

'Thank you.' She had finished her savoury, which left one hand free, and she felt the fingers of her free hand tighten on the wrist of the hand which held her glass and glanced down at them, surprised.

'I – I like your house,' she looked up at him.

'Not mine – not yet, anyway. Like you, I'm not sure yet.'

'I see.' She looked down again. 'And yet it's a house that – that seems to suit you, somehow, if you know what I mean.'

'For all its lavish luxury, it's a very livable-in house,' he answered. 'I suppose Laney or Pete would have told you it was built by a film company?'

'Yes.' She thought for a moment. 'I didn't think to ask – what was the film called?'

'It was called *A Plume of Dust*.'

Her blue eyes showed surprise. 'Why? Why *dust*? Everything seems so lush.'

'Not everything,' he said, smiling, 'as you'll soon find out for yourself. But in any case, it was something to do with a happening on the Sani Pass. You'll be going up the Pass, I take it?'

'I don't know whether I'm going to have the courage.' She

smiled at him. 'From the little I've heard up to now, it takes a Land-Rover several hair-raising manoeuvres to get round a bend. Is that correct? Or are Peter and Laney stringing me along?'

He laughed, regarding her appreciatively. 'That's perfectly correct, I can assure you. They weren't stringing you along.'

'Have you ever driven one up?' she asked seriously.

'Yes.'

'Aren't you nervous?'

Suddenly he grinned. 'All the time. Especially when the brakes suddenly go out of action.'

'You shouldn't talk that way,' she laughed a little. 'Isn't it bad for publicity? I mean, Peter tells me that apart from the hotel you have a business and that your Land-Rovers take people – tourists – up all the time.'

'Talk like that makes some people just that much more determined to go, as a matter of fact.' He mocked her with his eyes and the corners of his mouth.

'Now I think you're mocking me,' she murmured, her mind becoming hostess to chaotic thoughts about Lyle Cunningham. 'Laney's been up and she says once was enough.'

'Laney's a baby,' he said, laughing, 'but anyway, she didn't go up with me. Who took her up, do you know?'

'I don't know – I just know that she's been up. I'm longing to go for walks, of course, and to do a little harmless climbing. I'm no mountaineer.'

'In that case, we'll have to turn you into one.' He gave her a humorous glance.

'At the risk of spoiling your amusement, I don't think so.'

'Are you afraid of heights?' he asked.

'Not heights, exactly, but of losing my footing. I'd try not to look down, of course, not to be aware of the heights. I wouldn't mind a stiff climb.'

He was laughing at her again and so she said, 'I mean, I don't mind a gradual climb, but I have no desire to hang on to ropes and use axes and . . .' she hunted around in her mind for a word and couldn't find one, 'things.'

'Well, you never know until you try, do you?' he asked.

'I suppose not. Do you climb?'

'Not unless I have to.' He grinned. 'I've been on the odd rescue party, of course.'

'Why *of course*?' She gave him a puzzled look.

'People do unpredictable things,' he said, 'such as getting hurt.'

At that moment a girl came across the gold carpeting to them, walking with a grace that was the hallmark of self-confidence. Despite the long gown she was wearing it was obvious that her legs were long and superb. Her eyes were almost black, like her hair.

'Hello there,' she said, looking at Lyle. 'I've been looking for you.'

'You've already met Liza, I think.' Lyle looked at Michelle.

'Yes, I have, but you'll have to forgive me,' said Michelle, looking at the girl, 'I wasn't able to catch your full name. I get like that when I'm being introduced to people. I either get the first name or the last – seldom both. It's a bad fault, I know.' She shrugged charmingly.

'Liza will do, but in any case, it's Monatti, and if there's one person who has the knack of making the name sound great that is Lyle.' The black eyes slid round to Lyle Cunningham.

'I notice that Peter gets called Pete,' said Michelle. 'I can see I'll have to get used to it. Laney has also started calling him Pete.'

'What is Laney short for?' Liza asked.

'It's Laney – just Laney.'

'How long are you staying for?' Liza asked. She sounded openly hostile, Michelle thought.

'It depends,' said Michelle.

'On what?' Liza's voice was frankly abrupt.

'For one thing,' Lyle cut in, and there was that mocking look about him again, 'the climate.'

'Well, let me fill in for you,' said Liza. 'It's freezing cold in winter and as hot as Hades in summer, and apart from all that glamorous talk about golden-tanned South Africans and long golden semi-tropical days and moon-shadowed nights, it all boils down to what it really is – harsh and bad on the skin. That golden tan finally gives way to dried out wrinkles and brittle hair. You just have to look around. You won't keep that skin of yours for long, let me tell you that. Neither will Laney, if Pete keeps her here much longer.'

'Well, your skin certainly looks beautiful,' Michelle said with sincerity. 'As a matter of fact, it's the *one* thing I *have* noticed, up to now. South Africans do seem to have golden tans and it's no exaggeration.' She tried to keep her eyes from going in the direction of Lyle Cunningham's rich tan. 'Besides, you get neglected skin anywhere, Liza. It's only natural that one has to look after one's skin. I didn't just come here for a tan, though.' She laughed lightly.

'What *did* you come here for?' Liza asked, with open rudeness.

'To be with Peter and Laney, for a while.' Michelle was surprised at the spurt of anger she felt towards this dark girl.

'I see ... so you're going back, finally?' Liza sounded more than just a little interested.

'Well, as I say ...' Michelle began, and then Lyle Cunningham put in, 'Liza, how is your glass?'

Holding it out, she said, 'Empty.' She tipped the glass upside down.

'In that case allow me to do something about it.' His eyes went to Michelle. 'Michelle?'

'Thank you,' she murmured, 'but mine is not.' Lyle Cunningham, she found herself thinking, had succeeded in making her own name sound great, as he used it for the first time with ease.

'But you've been nursing it for a long time,' he said. 'I'll get you a fresh one.' He took the glass from her, and when he had gone Liza looked moodily around. 'What do you do?' she asked, not looking at Michelle. 'What kind of work, I mean?'

'I'm a hair-stylist.'

Liza swung round quickly. 'Are you kidding or something? A hairdresser?' Her eyes were suddenly narrow.

'Why should I be kidding?' Michelle showed her surprise. 'I hope to have my own salon one day.' Gone now, she was thinking, was that hope. When she had inherited the money from her mother's oldest friend, the ambition seemed about to be materialized. Instead, however, she had used a big lump of the money to come to South Africa to see Peter and Laney. Peter's letters, lately, had contained an element of despondency in them. The farm was not paying and she gathered also that he was in debt from borrowing money – well, *more* money – to keep things going. Into the bargain, Laney was in the first trying months of pregnancy, and because of the heat not feeling at all well. There were constant trips into the small town of Thabana to visit her doctor and more and more accounts to meet. His letters always ended up on a note of cheer, however. Apart from everything, he and Laney were happy on their farm under the Berg and they were determined to try and keep it. They had made some wonderful friends and had the baby to look forward to.

Although Michelle was not in a position to offer much help financially, she felt that during Laney's first months of pregnancy she would be able to be of some help during those times when Laney felt wretched in the mornings. The ironical part of it all was that, almost overnight, Laney had begun to feel better.

However, there was one other very good reason for her coming to South Africa – and that was to get away from her loneliness in London. She and Peter had lost both parents in a motor accident, soon after he and Laney had left for South Africa. Peter had flown back to be with her, and that had also set him back financially, and then, at her insistence, he had gone back to his farm and Laney beneath the Drakensberg Mountains, not to sell and go back home but to try and make it pay.

'In that case, when you get back to England, I suppose you'll be doing just that – opening your own salon?' Liza was saying, now, still in that same abrupt voice.

'It's all so vague,' Michelle replied, 'I just don't know. You see, I've spent a lot of money getting here.'

'But in any case, you'd have to go back, wouldn't you? You haven't resigned your job, have you?' Liza made Michelle feel vaguely disloyal to Salon Juliet.

'I have, actually, but they would always take me back,' she said.

'But, apart from that — you must have left most of your possessions over there, surely? I mean, you can't take much with you on the plane — and you did come by plane,' Liza answered.

'I left everything with an aunt — all packed, as a matter of fact, in case I wanted her to send it on here.' Michelle was trying not to feel ruffled.

There was a little pause and then Liza said, 'I see. In fact you worked everything out with a foolish kind of speed, once you got going, didn't you?' Her tiny laugh sounded forced.

'Why foolish?' This time Michelle couldn't control the irritation in her voice.

'Well, you have almost committed yourself, haven't you? This will be awfully dull, after London, I should imagine.'

'My life wasn't all that exciting. London can be lonely.'

'No man in your life?' Liza widened her black eyes.

'No.' Michelle kept her voice light and slightly mocking. She seemed to be getting all involved with this dark girl — but suddenly there seemed to be nothing to say. She breathed a sigh of relief as Lyle Cunningham came back carrying two glasses. He gave one to Liza. 'I couldn't find a tray,' he said, handing the other to Michelle.

Several people closed in on them and Michelle found herself the centre of attraction. When she looked again it was to see Lyle walking away, with Liza's long fingers clutching at his elbow.

'What do you think of Lyle's house?' Laney asked, joining the party but looking at Michelle. 'I'm going to take Michelle away, for a few moments,' her eyes flickered from face to face. 'I want to show her Lyle's fabulous bedroom. I feel jealous every time I see it.'

'That sounds bad,' someone said, 'does Pete know about this?' There was a burst of good-natured laughter.

'As a matter of fact, he does,' Laney answered promptly. 'I go up there every time we come here — just to look at it. I provided the pot-plants for his bathroom, as it so happens, and I go to check up that he isn't neglecting them. Come on, Michelle. Lyle won't mind.'

Lyle Cunningham's bedroom was nothing short of stunning.

'Whew!' Michelle found herself saying, as she gazed across plush ruby-red carpeting to the huge bed which looked lost in the tremendous room. 'What a magnificent bedspread!'

'It's shaggy white goat-hair,' said Laney. 'Isn't it superb?'

Oriental chandeliers were suspended low above twin bed-side tables. Michelle's eyes went to the spacious, black-louvred cupboards which formed the wall between the bed-room and dressing-room, and to the gold bouclé shantung curtains.

'The carnations are from the farm,' Laney went on, going towards a low table which stood before a ruby-red sofa. There were chairs to match. 'In fact, all the flowers you see here tonight come from our farm. In fact, we're tempted to start a nursery – or should I say, we're being tempted.'

'I suppose the heroine in the film had close-ups taken of her as she relaxed there in bed,' said Michelle.

'I haven't seen the film,' Laney said. 'It was showing when Pete flew to London to be with you after—' she broke off. 'I believe it was terrific – lots of thrills and this house to give it all the glamour it needed. But, Michelle, let me show you the bathroom. I don't mind telling you, though, that right up until a few days ago I used to feel positively morning-sick every time I came up here – all this exotic red. Now, of course, I'm fine. The morning sickness just left me, like that.' She snapped her fingers and laughed.

'That's marvellous.' Michelle began to follow Laney through to the bathroom. 'I'm glad you're so much better, Laney.'

'So am I, believe me. I really needed you then, Michelle.'

'But not now?' Michelle asked, but she was smiling.

'Of course now, but in a different way. I don't have to lean on you now, and that's such a relief.'

'I was thinking,' Michelle took the opportunity of bring-

16

ing up the subject, 'perhaps I'll be able to find some sort of work while I'm here.'

Laney stopped and turned round. 'Not *while* you're here. We want you to stay for good. Have a little holiday first, though, before you even start to think about working.' She began to walk again and then she said, 'Now tell me, what do you think of this bathroom, Michelle? Isn't it just out of this world? Can you believe that such a bathroom exists?'

'Whew!' Michelle whistled softly. 'Well, honestly, as you say, this is just too much. Imagine Lyle Cunningham soaking himself in that sunken marble bath.'

'Imagine,' said Lyle Cunningham, directly behind her. 'I followed you,' he said, as Michelle swung round. She heard the small catch of her own breath.

Laney seemed quite unperturbed. 'Lyle, are those the red amaryllis lilies I gave you? In bloom already?'

'Yes.'

'You see, I told you they'd look marvellous blooming on that gold-veined marble ledge. Michelle, don't you think the ruby carpeting looks fantastic against the gold marble?'

'I do – yes.' Michelle smiled and then bit her lip, still feeling the embarrassment of having Lyle Cunningham find her up here and, what was more, talking about him.

'Lyle didn't want the lilies, but I insisted,' Laney went on.

'In fact, you've just about taken over up here.' Lyle sounded amused.

'He agreed to the hanging fern, though,' said Laney. 'It adds drama to the whole set-up. Look how it's reflected in the mirrors.'

'The fern was here, in the first place,' Lyle remarked.

'Yes, but you wanted to take it out,' Laney answered swiftly.

'What you can't seem to remember is the fact that I'm not a film star, Laney.' He gave Laney an engaging grin. 'You believe in these things, ferns reflecting in the mirrors and lilies blooming in the ledges. I don't.'

'It would be sacrilege to move anything in this house. The artist didn't – neither did that writer and his wife.'

Lyle's smile widened. 'No – they weren't here long

17

enough. I have hopes of being here a long time. It follows that certain changes must follow.'

'Just you leave those amaryllis lilies and that fern alone,' Laney mocked. 'Strict instructions!'

They left the bathroom with its wall of mirrors and went back into the bedroom, their footsteps making only brush-noises on the ruby-red carpeting.

'What else would you like to see?' Lyle asked casually, looking at Michelle.

'I don't know what there is,' she smiled, her eyelashes carefully down, still smarting over her remark about the bath. 'Besides, you'll be wanting to go back downstairs.'

'There's time to show you the guest bedroom,' he said, 'in case you ever stay here.'

'I can't see that happening,' she tried to keep her voice as mocking as his own. 'I mean, why should I? Laney and Peter's farm is virtually "just round the corner".'

'Just for the experience, maybe.' She could feel his amused glance playing over her.

In the guest-room, with its vibrant purple carpeting, Michelle said, 'It's very attractive.'

'The bathroom has the same carpeting,' Laney started in the direction of the door, '*and* an indoor garden. I've never seen so many indoor gardens.'

'They all added to the glamour,' said Lyle, 'in the film.'

'I suppose we'd better go back down,' Laney put in. 'You'll have to show Michelle around another time, Lyle. I'm sure she'd love to see the whole house.' When they were back downstairs she said, 'Look after Michelle, Lyle, while I go and see what Pete is gesticulating about.'

In desperation Michelle said, 'Well, thank you for allowing me to see over your magnificent house. It's been quite an experience.'

'Come over with Laney, one day, and have a proper look round.' He gave her an easy smile and then went on, 'By the way, the hair-stylist at the hotel is leaving to get married within a week – or two, at the most. She wants to leave as soon as possible to complete her shopping and so on. Would you like the position?'

'At the hotel?' She widened her blue eyes at him. So that

18

was it! That was why Liza Monatti had looked so put out.

'Yes. Believe it or not, she's kept busy most of the time. On the whole, though, she's her own boss.'

Michelle laughed lightly, feeling an excitement growing within her. 'I didn't think getting a job was going to be quite that easy. At least, not right here in the mountains, and certainly not so near to Peter and Laney's farm. It is still quite a walk, though. How would I get there? I mean, supposing it should be raining or storming? I wouldn't dream of asking to borrow Peter's car. That's the only snag.'

'No snag there. The hotel would provide the necessary transport. If you met someone and decided to accept another lift – well and good.'

'Met someone?'

'Yes, you might. It happens all the time, with our receptionists and hair-stylists. They come and go – all the time, as a matter of fact. But what I'm driving at is, the hotel would provide transport for you, picking you up in the morning and driving you back to the farm, after work. If you happen to organize a lift, at a later date, well, that will be all right. Just let us know.'

'Who could I possibly meet to lift me?' she laughed a little.

'Well, one of the drivers, maybe. One of them happens to stay not far from the farm.'

'Drivers?' She widened her eyes at him.

'The chaps who drive the Land-Rovers up the Sani Pass. All heroes in their particular kind of work.'

'Oh, yes. I see.' She told herself that she would have to make sure that she did not meet those hypnotic blue-green eyes. Not all the time, anyway.

Turning her head she said, in a light tone, 'I can see you have the wonderful knack of making a woman feel quite irresistible by suggesting that she just has to cast a look at one of the drivers and she'll have organized herself a lift.'

'I think you'd better resign yourself to the fact – you *are* quite irresistible. You're all these things one reads about,' he told her.

Turning to look at him, Michelle laughed lightly to hide her embarrassment. 'I wasn't hunting for compliments.

About this position as hair-stylist, though. Are you serious?'

'I'm perfectly serious. Receptionists, hair-stylists – they all come and go, and we need them all the time. So what do you say? Directly I heard you were a hairdresser I knew I'd have to act quickly.' He smiled at her and she met his eyes for a moment, then looked away.

Beyond the huge windows, the clouds were moon-shaped mountains, competing with the real thing. Hoping that there was nothing to show that she was having to do a lot of thinking before deciding, Michelle said, 'I'll take you up on that.' Her hair, shoulder-length and turned in at the neck, caught the lamp glow.

'Fine,' he said. 'And I'll take you up on that too, before you change your mind. It doesn't always pay to run away from the things that frighten you.'

She felt a tingue of colour come into her cheeks. 'Why should I be frightened?' she asked. 'I'm not a – a chancer. I meant it when I said I was a hair-stylist.'

He gave her an easy smile. 'That's not what I meant, actually.'

Lyle Cunningham was shrewd, she thought. He knew where to hit her with his light remarks because, she was honest enough with herself, she had fallen in love with him at first sight.

CHAPTER TWO

Two days later the telephone at the Abbotts' farm rang. It was Lyle Cunningham asking for Michelle.

'When can I pick you up?' he asked, and she could see him in her mind – fairly tall and well proportioned, his complexion clear and tanned.

The sound of his voice was doing something drastic to her breathing and she waited a moment before she answered. 'Pick me up?'

'Yes. I'd like to show you around the hotel. Introduce you to my father and to Sylvie, before she leaves.'

'Sylvie? Oh, you mean the girl from the salon?' She knew she was being stupid.

'Yes. You haven't changed your mind, have you?' He sounded faintly impatient and, deliberately matching her tone to his, she replied, 'No, of course not. I – I take it you haven't either?'

'Would I be calling you if I had?' His tone was mocking now.

'No, I don't suppose you would be. Well, I can be ready at any time.'

'In, say, half an hour?'

Michelle glanced down at the cinnamon-coloured slacks she was wearing with a golden-yellow top. 'In half an hour, if you like,' she replied.

It all sounded crazy and wonderfully incredible that here, at the foot of these mountains, she had practically landed herself a position without even trying. Her eyes went to the windows in the direction of the mountains which, close up, would be forbidding rather than beautiful. From here, however, they were beautiful and from Lyle Cunningham's film-set house they had been beautiful – all purple and browns, slashed with shadows, and in some of the remote crevices there was even snow, although the heat down here was stifling.

'That was Lyle Cunningham.' Michelle glanced over at

Laney, who was arranging flowers.

'So I gathered.' Laney's voice was amused. 'You sounded so breathless!'

'Oh, nonsense, Laney. He's coming to pick me up to take me to the hotel to meet his father and Sylvie, the girl who's leaving to get married.'

'So you've more or less decided to accept?' Laney stood back and squinted at the flowers.

'Yes, but I'd – I thought he'd forgotten.' Michelle made sure there was just enough carelessness in the tone of her voice to show Laney that she didn't care, one way or the other.

'Not Lyle. But, Michelle darling, we had hopes that you'd have a holiday with us first before you took off and landed yourself a job. When I say take a holiday with us first I mean that Pete was going to neglect things a little so that he could take us for drives and so on, just the three of us.' She laughed and patted the bulge. 'The four of us.'

'But don't you see, Laney? This is an offer too good to be true, an offer I'd be a fool to turn down. It means that I can work here, practically on the doorstep of the farm. I won't have to leave the Berg, as you call it.'

'I know.' Laney sighed. 'It is, as you say, a marvellous opportunity, and you *would* be a fool to turn it down, seeing that you've made up your mind to work. I see what you mean.' She shrugged. 'Well, perhaps later on in the year, after the baby is born and is big enough to take on jaunts. By then Pete might be in a better position to take a little holiday without really leaving the farm.'

'I keep thinking,' Michelle said. 'He – Lyle Cunningham – remarked that the receptionists and hair-stylists are always moving on. Why is this, do you suppose? Is he very hard to get on with?'

'No, it's not that. As a matter of fact, Lyle is very seldom at the hotel. The hotel is mostly his father's baby. As I explained to you before, Lyle has this tourist and garage concern in Thabana – you know, where we stopped for provisions on our way back from picking you up at the airport. It's only a short drive by car to Thabana. Once the glamour has faded – to get back to the receptionists and hair-stylists

—they leave to take up jobs in towns, or other holiday resorts. Sometimes they meet a man and fall in love with him and leave to get married. They come and go all the time. I suppose living at the same hotel can become monotonous to them.'

'So they live at the hotel?' Michelle was curious.

'Yes—unless they happen to be staying with parents in the Thabana area and travel to the hotel every day. Mostly they stay there, though. I'm hoping you won't, though, Michelle. Not unless you really want to, one day. You could get bored here at the farm. I mean, you're only young once.'

'He didn't mention anything about my staying at the hotel,' Michelle replied.

'I suppose he knew you wanted to be with us—and that we want you,' Laney answered. 'I mean, you've only just arrived. I'm not going to let him pinch you, Michelle.' She was laughing, but she sounded disappointed.

'I'd better do something to my hair and face,' said Michelle. 'These slacks and this top will be all right, won't they? To meet his father, I mean? I don't have to change?'

'You look stunning. You look elegantly casual, which is how everybody always appears at the hotel.'

Lyle Cunningham regarded Michelle appreciatively when he called for her. 'Obviously you're not like Laney,' he said, smiling, 'because Laney is always late.' Meeting his eyes, Michelle felt the usual shock at their uncanny magnetism.

'In this heat,' Michelle laughed, 'I wouldn't blame anyone for being late.' As she spoke she could feel the tiny dew drops of perspiration trickling down inside her blouse, and she wondered if it looked as damp and clinging as it felt.

Lyle's blue-green eyes went over her swiftly. 'The main thing is that it doesn't show.'

'Thank you.' She laughed again, but she was feeling a little embarrassed now. 'I—er—I like to be reassured on that point.'

They went outside and the heat seemed to be bouncing off his blue car. Inside, it would be trapped there, Michelle found herself thinking.

As Lyle opened the door for her she said, 'In England they're probably freezing right now, do you know that?'

'Roll on my next trip to England,' he replied lightly, and closed the door.

Sunlight showered Michelle's face as she waved good-bye to Laney.

'What makes you want to freeze?' she asked, as Lyle slipped into the driver's seat.

He laughed lightly and gave her an easy look. 'This heat makes me want to freeze.'

'You'd soon change your mind,' she told him, in a kind of despair, and wiping away a tiny moustache of glistening beads which had formed on her lip. 'The cold can be terrible, believe me. I think I prefer to be hot.'

'I was afraid you wouldn't,' he told her, and started the car. Before driving off, he gave her a direct look.

With the sun came a certain amount of shade, however, and she sat back and enjoyed the drive to the hotel. There was a reddish-gold dust being spurted up by the wheels of the car and the sound of the stones, making contact with metal as they flew up, created a feeling of contentment within her.

To make conversation she asked him to tell her a little about the Bushmen paintings which were found in the area. 'I'll take you to see them, one day,' he said, 'if you're prepared to walk the distance.'

'I am. I'm very interested. Besides, as I told you, I like walking.'

Lyle parked the car beneath one of the huge windows of the hotel where golden flowers with pollen-dusted petals were arranged on the wide window-ledge of the office behind it. A tall lean man with an excellent tan and silver hair looked up from his position behind the desk. Only Lyle Cunningham could come up with a father like this, Michelle found herself thinking, because right away she knew this was Cunningham senior.

'Your father?' she asked, turning her head. Lyle had switched off the engine and his fingers were loosely draped over the steering wheel.

'Yes.' He turned to look at her. 'Otherwise known as Cunningham Senior.'

She laughed. 'Behind his back?'

'Behind his back – but he knows about it,' he answered, smiling.

'It's strange, but when I saw him through the window,' she said, 'I thought of him as Cunningham Senior. I don't know why.' Her eyes went towards the window again. 'Why is it that women pay an absolute fortune on rinses and tints to get just that shade of silver and never quite succeed, while men like your father just go ahead and change salt-and-pepper to that fabulous colour almost overnight? I should know, being in the business.'

'You shouldn't admit to that,' he gave her an amused glance as he leaned across her to unfasten her door. 'You're supposed to keep those kind of secrets to yourself. You'll lose custom if you admit to such failures.'

Without turning her head, Michelle was conscious of his fingers resting lightly on the chrome catch while he looked at her with those blue-green eyes and, while their eyes locked for just a moment, she found herself thinking that this was no time for moonsick thoughts. She was here, after all, to be interviewed for the position of hair-stylist.

The office with the golden flowers on the wide window ledge was air-cooled and that sluggish feeling was stripped away immediately upon entering it. The foyer, too with its arrangement of flowers, indoor plants, original paintings of Basothos wearing colourful blankets and golden straw hats and of ranges of great rugged mountains beneath stormy-looking clouds, was air-conditioned.

Cunningham Senior stood up and the creases in the long trousers of his cane-coloured safari suit were immaculate. 'Well,' he held out a tanned hand, 'Miss Abbott?'

'Michelle Abott,' said Lyle. 'Ex-London. She used to do the Queen Mother's hair.'

'Oh,' Michelle laughed, a little breathlessly, 'I didn't say that!'

'How are you finding the heat, after England?' Lyle's father asked pleasantly. 'But I suppose everyone asks that. Do sit down.'

'Well, yes, they do.' Contrary to her inner feelings Michelle was thankful that she sounded very cool and assured as they sat talking.

After an interruption, when a man about Lyle's father's age came into the office, Michelle found that Cunningham Senior's name was Paul.

Finally Lyle took her along to the tiny salon, which was down the corridor on the opposite side of the foyer. There was a notice pinned on the door: Back in ten minutes.

Lyle pushed open the door and stood to one side for Michelle to enter. Her blue eyes flickered around the wall-papered room and, after all that sun and air outside, her nose felt suddenly clogged with the familiar smells of spray, lotion, shampoo and wet hair. She had almost forgotten these smells, she thought.

'As you probably assumed, by looking at the notice on the door,' Lyle was saying, 'you're very much your own boss here.' There was a pause and then he asked, 'Well, how do you feel about it?'

'It's perfect. I feel sure I'd love it here.'

He gave her an easy smile. 'Fine.'

When Sylvie arrived on the scene she said, 'Sorry, have you been waiting long? I've been upstairs to comb somebody's hair. She has a very fussy hair-style, which she simply can't manage herself. Personally, I just don't understand why she has it.'

Lyle introduced the two girls and then said, 'I'll leave you two to discuss things. I'll be in my father's office, Michelle, when you're ready.' Glancing at his watch, he looked up. 'Have lunch with me. I'll ring Laney for you and put her in the picture.'

'Thank you. You're very kind.'

'Not at all. It will be my pleasure,' he told her.

After he had gone Sylvie said, 'Well, here you have it. There's not much to discuss. You'll find working conditions attractive here. I'm very seldom rushed, as you can imagine. I often think I could help out at the desk, but,' she shrugged and laughed, 'I'm too lazy for that – and I mean, why should I? For one thing, I couldn't stand working with Liza Monatti. Anyway, let me show you where things are and put you wise as to what goes on around here.'

Later, Sylvie walked to the foyer with her. 'You remember where his father's office is, don't you? The first door to the right. I'll be seeing you before I leave, of course, but in any case, have fun!'

Lyle was in his father's office and looked up as Michelle walked into it. 'Well?' He gave her a smile. 'Finished with Sylvie?'

'Yes.'

'I should imagine everything is pretty plain sailing down that end, Miss Abbott,' Cunningham Senior said pleasantly. 'It's just a case of getting settled and arranging things to your own liking, I should imagine. Am I right?'

Michelle found herself enjoying the closeness of both father and son. 'That's so, Mr. Cunningham,' she replied.

'Well,' Lyle's father looked at his watch, 'I've promised to meet Sid Lupin on the terrace before lunch, so if you'll excuse me? I'm told – Lyle tells me – that you'll be having lunch with us.' He nodded his approval. 'That's fine. I'll see you later, in that case.' The blue-green gaze, so much like Lyle's, embraced them for a moment.

Down at the reception desk a telephone shrilled. There was the smell of expensive leather in Cunningham Senior's office. The golden-honey chairs looked new. A woman's laughter, followed by a man's, floated down the corridor. Lyle said, 'Well, how about something cool to drink before lunch?'

'A cool drink would be welcome,' Michelle murmured politely.

'I'd like you to meet Liza and Debbie, if they're still about.'

'Receptionists?' Michelle asked.

'Uh-huh.'

'But I've – I think I've met Liza, haven't I? I didn't see her at the desk when we came in, though.'

'She should be there now, if I'm not mistaken.' He looked puzzled. 'But where did you meet Liza?'

'I met her at the party. The party at your house, soon after I arrived.'

'Oh, of course. I'd forgotten – about Liza, I mean . . .

27

being there,' he replied, and Michelle felt a small glow of satisfaction.

With an almost imperceptible touch of his fingers on her arm he guided her towards the door. 'I can tell them, then? That you're going to be our new hair-stylist?'

'Yes.' She supplied the answer very casually, but she was aware of an excitement stirring in her.

At the reception desk Liza Monatti was there with a girl called Debbie. Liza's almost black eyes swept Michelle's face. 'So you've decided?' Her expression was almost hostile.

'Yes,' Michelle answered.

'But I thought the object of your visit was to be with your brother and his wife? Apparently you decide on something with considerable haste, don't you?' Her smile was a brief thing. 'Do you always do this?'

'No, not always.' Michelle tried to keep her smile bright. 'This time, however, it seemed to suit – all round. I'm very happy to accept.' She hoped the sudden dislike she felt for this girl had not shown.

'Will you be living in?' Liza asked.

'How do you mean?' Michelle was puzzled.

'I mean, will you be living here at the hotel? Or will you stay at the farm with your brother?'

'Oh . . .' Michelle's mind reeled, 'I'll be living with Peter and Laney, I guess.'

'I see.' Liza drew the words out. 'And travelling every day?' There was a kind of relief in her voice.

'We've come to a suitable arrangement,' Lyle cut in. 'I've arranged the necessary transport.'

'Oh, I see.' Liza's eyes flickered from Michelle to Lyle.

'We're going to lunch now,' he said. 'By the way, Liza, did those brochure people turn up?'

'The photographers, you mean?' Liza's voice was cold and measured. She glanced huffily away. 'No. They can't come, after all. Not today, anyway. They're going to ring us later on this week.'

On the way to the dining-room Lyle said, 'We're having a new brochure drawn up.'

'I see,' Michelle replied.

When they were seated, she said, 'It's a most attractive hotel in an equally attractive setting. Well,' she smiled, 'a magnificent setting, really.'

He gave her an easy smile. 'Well, we think so too. The hotel has a name for offering something for everybody.' He glanced towards the windows. 'Stimulating mountain air, peaceful or sophisticated relaxation, quiet or strenuous walks.' His eyes met hers. 'Then there are those daring climbs where people get lost and walks for the not-so-young, bowls, tennis, riding, sun-filled hours beside the pool . . . air flights over the Berg, Land-Rover trips up the Pass . . .'

'To live with all that beauty every day,' she said. Her eyes took in the view of the mountains. She sat back, listening to the pleasant murmur of voices above muted music and the faint clinking of glass and cutlery. There was a pungent smell of salads – a subtle pervasive quality which made her mouth water suddenly.

'I hope you're hungry,' Lyle said, and she laughed. 'I'm ravenous!' She found herself growing easier with him. 'Those salads,' she turned her head in the direction of the long, white-clothed table set against a far wall, 'smell marvellous. Do you grow your own vegetables here in the gardens?'

'Some of them.' She watched him as he lowered his head for a moment and then he looked up. 'Actually, we're hoping to buy more land in the near future for the purpose of growing fresh produce on a large scale. Deep-freezing, nowadays, encourages this. We aim at doing our own deep-freezing of vegetables.'

Michelle's eyes went in the direction of the windows. 'Where will you buy land? Near here?' She glanced back at him.

Lyle's manner changed at once. 'Adjacent,' he told her, 'but,' he shrugged, 'there's much more to it than that, I'm afraid.'

Why had his blue-green eyes changed so swiftly? she asked herself. And why was it that his voice had been almost casual, but not quite? She watched him over the rim of her glass and wondered about him and wondered what there was about growing vegetables to meet the hotel's requirements to

29

make him look like that, and felt a sense of bafflement.

While they were waiting for the next course, she allowed her eyes to drift around the tremendous dining-room with its massive stone fireplaces, pieces of copper and gorgeous flower arrangements. The guests were all elegantly casual, suitably dressed for lunch in a luxury mountain hotel. It was obvious, she thought, looking at some of the women, that the hotel hair-stylist was kept suitably busy.

When they were drinking their coffee Lyle said, 'I hope you enjoyed your lunch?'

'I did, very much, thank you. The drink, too, before lunch.'

'I'll take you back, then, when we've finished coffee.'

'Thank you.'

While he put through a telephone call she took the opportunity to visit the powder-room and she was waiting for him by the time he had finished.

Outside, the heat lay waiting for them. Several people were already in the foyer discussing a walk within scope of the afternoon, and, passing them, Michelle found herself wondering where they were going to get the energy from.

In Lyle's car she said, 'We didn't see your father again, and he didn't say when I should start work.'

'Any time,' Lyle told her, 'but in any case, if you came a couple of days before Sylvie is due to leave she'll be able to show you the ropes. Tomorrow, if you like,' he turned to smile suddenly at her, 'or the next day. It's entirely up to you.'

Although she was keen to be with Laney the urge to start work at the hotel took possession of her. 'Shall we make it the day after tomorrow, then? I'm sure Laney won't mind. My original plan was to be with Laney so that I could help her. I don't know if you're aware of the fact that she hasn't been at all well lately? However, she's over the worst now and says she's never felt better, which is wonderful, of course. As both she and Peter – I can see I'll have to get used to calling him Pete – are keen for me to settle in this country I think it would be a good idea if I *did* get settled right away, and this is the most wonderful opportunity. I haven't thanked you. I'm terribly grateful, believe me.'

'That cuts both ways. By the way,' his tone was explorative, 'if you feel, in time to come, that you'd like to live in at the hotel do discuss this with my father. You might eventually prefer to be on your own, with the comforting realization that Pete and Laney are right next door, so to speak. I didn't mention this earlier, owing to the fact that you've only just arrived and will no doubt enjoy being with them for a while. You see,' he gave her a sideways glance, 'I'm doing my best into talking you into settling here for good.'

'Oh, that wouldn't be hard, believe me,' she replied, laughing a little.

'That's all I want to know,' he answered.

The road was corrugated and dusty. Sunlight burst against the windows of the car. 'You'll get used to these roads, by the way,' Lyle turned to her again, grinning, 'although you possibly find that difficult to believe. Near Thabana, though, the road is tarred.'

For a while they drove in silence and then Michelle said, 'By the way, I'll bear in mind what you had to say about living in at the hotel. It might just be a good idea, at a later date, especially as there's going to be a baby. Laney will want to get the nursery in order and so on. At present I'm using it.'

'You sound almost definite,' he answered, 'about staying on.'

'Well,' she sounded cautious, 'I must admit, the moment you mentioned the position to me I could see all the advantages.'

'It came up just at the right time, in that case,' he answered.

After a moment she said, 'Oh, there's your house. It's very spectacular, even from here. More so, I expect, because it's set against such drama. I suppose that was the intention of the film people? What does the word Drakensberg mean, exactly? I've often wondered.'

'It means Dragon Mountains. How the name came to be given is not known. The Zulu name is Quathlamba, meaning a barrier of up-pointed spears.'

'How fascinating,' she replied, feeling the golden glow of sun on her face. She felt like laughing back at the sun. Suddenly she felt drowsy with dreams.

At the farm she said, 'Well, thank you so much for everything.' Her mind was busy with the problem as to whether she should invite Lyle Cunningham into the house or not. Then she decided to leave the matter in his hands because, after all, he apparently knew Laney and Pete well enough to make his own decisions on this point.

'Someone will pick you up here,' he was saying, 'the day after tomorrow. Eight-ish will be plenty of time. If you run into any tangles phone me.'

'Thank you.' She held her breath while he leaned over and opened the door for her.

Out in the sunshine she stooped and said, through the open window, 'Well, goodbye.'

'I'll be seeing you,' he smiled at her. 'Be good, Michelle.'

She lifted a hand. 'I will.'

Laney was working on accounts. 'It's enough to drive me up the wall,' she said, looking up as Michelle came into the room. 'This trying to make ends meet is too bad. Into the bargain, Pete and I acted like a couple of fools and borrowed quite a sum of money which we have to pay back. At the time, the offer was like a miracle, but now . . .' she shrugged and broke off, 'I find myself wondering. Some time before you came, we actually had the farm on the market and then it was such a suggestion of defeat that we withdrew it. Now we're battling again. I'm sorry we bought these curtains, which at the time seemed like a reasonable idea.' Laney glanced round the room. 'You see, the accounts have just come in.' She turned to Michelle and laughed lightly, but her eyes were serious.

Michelle gazed round the room. 'The curtains are beautiful, Laney. I'm sure that in the end you won't regret your decision – once they're paid off, I mean.' This was the one room in the house where considerable money had been spent and the curtains, which hung from rods with spear-heads at either end, were lined. They went well with the wooden ceiling, being oatmeal-coloured with large bronze and blue flowers. Money had also been spent on the off-white sofa and chairs.

'I had all sorts of schemes, when we bought this place,' Laney undid the slide in her blonde hair. 'Anyway,' she slid the clasp back into position and shook back her hair, 'let me stuff these accounts away. How did you get on with Cunningham Senior?'

'You know, Laney, it's strange that you should call him Cunningham Senior, because that's exactly how *I* found myself thinking of Lyle's father.'

'Lyle is very like him, don't you think?' Laney shoved a drawer into place.

'Yes,' Michelle began straightening the scatter cushions which were made of the same material as the curtains and highlighted with white fringing, 'I do, as a matter of fact. I got on very well with him, actually. I'm to start the day after tomorrow. What a cute little salon. Have you seen it, Laney?'

'Yes, I have. You'll be entirely your own boss there.'

Michelle felt a sudden surge of guilt. 'Laney, are you sure you feel better? My main reason, after all, was to be here to help you over this bad spell – quite apart from wanting to see you both.'

'I feel such a fraud for writing you all those complaining letters,' said Laney. 'I feel so well now. I can see, though, what you mean about availing yourself of the opportunity to work. It seems too good to be true.'

There was a small pause and then Michelle said, 'Lyle Cunningham mentioned that at a future date I might like to live in at the hotel.'

After a moment Laney agreed, 'That might be a good idea, later on. You'll at least enjoy some life there – night life, I mean. But it's entirely up to you, of course. We love having you here. Are they going to send a car over for you every day? I suppose when you can afford it you'll be thinking of a little car of your own?'

'He said that transport would be provided to and from the hotel. When I've saved up a bit, I might be able to afford a small second-hand car, reasonably priced, of course,' said Michelle.

Laney scanned the desk. 'Sometimes, Michelle, I think I'm a bad manager,' she said, in a small remote voice.

'Everything's put away now until tomorrow. But in any case,' she looked up, 'Pete isn't the best of farmers, if it comes to that.' The slump of her shoulders registered her fatigue.

'Well,' Michelle found that she did not know what to say, 'I mean, he knew nothing about farming . . .'

'No – and at the time of taking over this farm I'm afraid we never even questioned the wisdom of this. Mind you, when I'm in the mood, I find all this very funny,' Laney laughed cheerfully.

'You always manage, Laney, to make life seem great.'

'Well, isn't it?'

Thinking of being here with Pete and Laney, her new position at the hotel, the sun and the mountains – and Lyle Cunningham, Michelle said, with a sharp little intake of breath, 'Yes, I guess it is, Laney.'

CHAPTER THREE

IT bothered Michelle that she might be hurting Peter and Laney by accepting Lyle Cunningham's offer so soon that she should live in at the hotel, and yet on the other hand, she was afraid that by making her home with them she might be taxing their financial problems. When the question of paying board had cropped up both Peter and Laney had grown touchy and withdrawn. Finally, however, they had set a figure which, to Michelle's mind, would not go towards feeding a bird.

For two weeks Knowledge Mkize, one of the waiters who could drive, called at the farm for her in the morning and drove her back in the late afternoon. During this time Michelle saw nothing of Lyle Cunningham and was told one morning by Knowledge that Mr. Lyle Cunningham was away for a few days on a business trip.

By the time he returned Michelle was installed, with Peter and Laney's blessing, at the hotel. It had all happened at the suggestion of Cunningham Senior, who felt that the accommodation was there anyway, and that Michelle would have 'some sort of night life' instead of being tucked away at the farm.

Michelle was surprised how busy she was kept. While most of the young girls on holiday preferred to let their shoulder-length hair bounce about their shoulders the older and frankly mature women made a point of appearing elegant, even if casually so, and enjoyed immaculate hairstyles.

On the day Lyle Cunningham turned up Michelle was behind the reception desk, helping out during lunch. This was something she had offered to do during slack periods and she completely enjoyed herself.

'Since when have you become a receptionist?' she heard him say and, taking her eyes from the change she was counting, she said, 'Oh, hello ...' She broke off and smiled. Seeing him unexpectedly like this caused her to blink. 'I'm

35

just helping out,' she told him. 'Debbie isn't very well and Liza is at lunch.'

They studied each other for a moment and then he said, 'Well, don't let them take advantage of you.' She was aware of the gentle mockery in his voice.

'I don't mind in the least. In fact, I enjoy it.' She hoped there was nothing to show that she was excited at seeing him again.

'How's the climate been treating you?' he asked. 'I'm told it's been extremely hot while I've been away.'

'I've loved it. Wasn't it hot where you were?' she asked.

'Yes, it was hot, as a matter of fact, but then I'm used to it. I've got past the stage when I question it. How are you liking it here, by the way?'

'Very much. I'm – I'm staying at the hotel now,' she added uncertainly. 'I mean, I've left the farm, you know.'

'So my father tells me. Tell me, what did Pete and Laney have to say about it? It was the reason I didn't suggest it, in the first place, as a matter of fact. I thought I'd leave it for you to work out – for yourself.'

'After they'd thought it over they were pleased.' She hoped she sounded convincing. 'They seem to feel that it's another step in the direction of my settling in this country – that I'm taking this position seriously.'

'And aren't you?' His smile was mocking, and she felt herself blush.

'Well – yes, of course. Whatever I do, I take seriously.'

Suddenly he laughed. 'You have a habit of betraying your feelings with those eyes of yours. *You* are here to stay,' he added, his eyes rapidly losing their mocking expression.

Her shoulders moved in a small shrug as she smiled back at him. 'Can I help you?' she asked.

'I'm on the hunt for change.' She watched him as he placed a note on the desk. 'Can you change that for me?'

'Yes, of course.'

As she counted the money she could feel his blue-green eyes on her and, ruffled, she said, 'I'm trying to get used to this money business, but I'm learning. Will this do?' She looked up.

'Thank you. This will do very nicely.'

36

'There were several trips, up the Pass, while you were away,' she told him, as he slipped the money into his pocket. 'I happened to be helping out at Reception when the guests gathered here, waiting for the Land-Rover to pick them up. Frankly, I didn't know whether to envy them or to be sorry for them,' she laughed lightly.

'You'll be able to form your own opinion soon,' he smiled easily, 'when you go up.'

Liza Monatti chose that particular moment to come back from lunch. 'Hello,' she sounded excited, 'so you're back?'

'I'm trying to talk Michelle into going up the Pass,' Lyle explained, after he had greeted her.

For a deliberate moment, just long enough to create the effect she desired, Liza paused, then said, 'Oh? Well, I'd leave well alone, if I were you. She might just end up having hysterics on one of the famous hairpin bends, and I know that if there's anything you or the drivers can't stand, it's an hysterical female on your hands. By the way,' her black eyes went in Michelle's direction, 'were there any snags while I was at lunch?' Turning to Lyle, she said, 'Debbie is ill again, by the way.' She made it sound like a crime.

'So I've been told,' he answered. 'She's having a rough time.'

'There were no snags.' Michelle tried not to show that she was peeved.

'Good,' Liza replied with open rudeness. 'Well, don't let me keep you. I'll manage now.'

Obviously Liza expected Lyle Cunningham to remain, talking at the desk, and there was a little disconcerted silence when he said, 'Have you had lunch, Michelle?'

'No.' Stung by the way in which Liza had spoken to her, Michelle's voice was cool. 'I'll have to hurry. My next appointment happens to be at two.'

'Do you mind if I join you?' he asked.

Now that the moment was over she had herself in control again. 'No, not at all.'

Liza's dark eyes followed them as they went in the direction of the dining-room and Michelle could almost feel them boring into her back.

At the table, Lyle said, 'Apart from settling in here what

37

have you been doing since I last saw you?'

'Well . . .' she found herself groping for something to say, 'apart from settling in there – there just hasn't been much time.' There was a little pause. 'I'm thinking of getting a small car,' she told him, on an impulse. 'It would be wise, I think. If you happen to hear of a small second-hand one, would you let me know?'

'As it so happens, I could put you on to one right now.'

'You could?' She tried not to let her wild enthusiasm show.

'Yes. It's a Mini. I could take you to see it.'

'I'd like that, very much. Thank you.'

'We'll have to make a date, in that case. What about this afternoon?'

Laughing lightly, she said, 'This *afternoon*? You don't waste much time.'

'I'm a fast worker,' he gave her an easy smile. 'How busy are you going to be?'

She thought for a moment. 'Well, I have an appointment at two – just after two, actually, and there's a shampoo and set after that – no other advance appointments. People come into the salon on the spur of the moment, more often than not – after a walk or a swim.'

'I'll wait for you, then. It so happens that I have a few things to see to here before going back to Thabana.'

'Thank you.' She gave him a direct look. 'Just as long as the price is suitable. I haven't very much money left, I'm afraid.'

'We'll see what we can do for you,' Lyle answered.

As she put the last touches to her customer's hair Michelle found herself hoping that there would be time to go to her room and change out of the short dress she was wearing beneath her pale-yellow loose-fitting overall and was relieved to discover that Lyle Cunningham was not waiting for her at Reception.

By the time she had changed he was in the foyer waiting for her. 'I'm sorry,' she said, 'I hope I haven't held you up?'

He gave her a contagious smile. 'It's all part of the service – don't give it another thought.'

38

The light was shifting about on the leaves outside and it was not as hot as it had been earlier on.

In the car, Michelle said, 'Do tell me more about the car. I'm longing to know.'

His sideways glance was appraising. 'What would you like to know about it? The colour?'

Laughing a little she replied, 'Well, yes, the colour. You've already told me that it's a Mini. Mainly, of course, it's the price I'm concerned with.'

After he had named a figure there was a small silence and he said gently, 'Is that bad, Michelle?'

'Well, I was just trying to work it out, but – it is, rather.'

'In that case, I'll have to see what I can do for you. The colour, by the way, happens to be cinnamon brown, with a narrow cream band passing right round at door-handle level. The colour will complement that tawny hair of yours and the yellows and oatmeal shades you seem to enjoy wearing. What's more important, though, Michelle,' he became serious, 'it's most economical on petrol. I think that matters a lot, these days.'

'Well, of course, I quite agree with you.' After a moment she added, 'It seems a pity to drive a car over these corrugations, doesn't it?'

'On the whole,' he answered, 'this is not a bad surface. Don't forget, you're not in London now.' His voice was teasing.

'Oh, I hadn't forgotten, believe me,' she laughed. She allowed her eyes to rest on the scenery and then said, 'Is that another hotel, over there?'

'You're looking at the mountain holiday chalets which belong to Glen Hayes. You'll probably meet him one of these days.'

'Oh? Where?' She turned to look at him.

He shrugged. 'About.'

'I see. How are these chalets run?' she asked. 'I have in mind the problem of meals, of course.'

'Oh, you can dine in style in your own attractive chalet, for the very simple reason that there happens to be a modern supermarket which is there to satisfy the needs of people

39

enjoying that type of holiday. These chalets are very attractively furnished and equipped with small efficiently planned kitchens.'

She thought for a moment, then said, 'And so these chalets don't present a – a threat to your hotel?'

'I can see that you have a business head on your shoulders,' he laughed, looking at her.

'I'm sorry. I was being tactless,' she replied quickly.

'Not at all. I'm impressed, as it so happens.'

He parked the car outside Little Switzerland Motors, which was on the outskirts of Thabana. 'This is your business?' she asked. 'Your other business, I mean – apart from the hotel?'

'Yes, strictly mine. My father has nothing to do with it.'

'It's very attractive,' she told him, smiling shyly.

'Wait until you see the back!' He laughed lightly. 'It's a junkyard.'

There was a small showroom, Michelle noticed, but it was obvious that this was not the main interest of the business. There appeared to be three attractively furnished, air-conditioned offices, one of which belonged to Lyle Cunningham.

A girl was in charge of the tours section while a young man, who obviously managed the business and the control of the Land-Rovers, repairs and sales of spare parts and vehicles occupied the other office.

There was a hot wind blowing which scudded across Thabana, and it was a relief to enter the long, low building. Lyle led Michelle straight into the small showroom and she spotted the Mini immediately. 'Is that it?' She let out her breath softly.

'Yes,' he said.

'But it's beautiful,' she said in a low voice. 'It's almost new, isn't it?'

'It's been well looked after.' She watched him as he opened a door and then he stood to one side for her to look inside the car. 'That goes for the engine, as well. Hop in and I'll take you for a test run.'

She stood back and straightened up. Placing one thumbnail against her teeth, she said, 'I'll never be able to afford this. I can't see how the owner will reduce the price. Remember, you said you would try to come to an arrangement.'

He grinned down at her, his blue-green eyes slightly narrowed. 'How do you know?' he teased.

'Just by looking at it.' She laughed suddenly, caught up in the absurdity of the moment.

'Anyway, let's take it out on the road and then we can come back and talk. I have some news for you.'

Her mind blanked for a moment. She did not want to waste his time – and her own, for that matter. After all, she was working for a living now. Their eyes held for a moment and then she said, 'Well – all right.' However, she found herself regretting that she had taken him up on this matter.

They drove out of the showroom, back into the fusing of sun, wind and fine particles of dust which seemed to be flying about the streets of Thabana. In the distance, the deeply-etched chasms and gorges, the ageless peaks, looked very blue.

Michelle's mind was divided between looking at the small but busy country town and the feel and drone of the small car.

'Well,' Lyle asked eventually, 'what do you think of her?'

She gave a small sigh. 'It's super, absolutely super – and that's what worries me. I find myself in one of those very embarrassing situations, actually. I've gone and got you all involved, but I'm not going to be able to afford this car. I – I've been rash, I can see that now.' She was wide-eyed with concern and he laughed softly.

'I told you I had news for you. Well, the owner has agreed to drop the figure.' He named another figure and she sat, saying nothing, working out finance in her mind. Finally she said, 'I'm tempted, of course, but I know I shouldn't – not yet, anyway. Later on, of course, this car will have been sold and I'll have been too late in making up my mind. Who does it belong to, by the way?'

'It belongs to the wife of a doctor. She's decided on a new

car. Although she suggested a figure she asked me to "get what I can for it". Without being unfair to her, I approached her about dropping the original figure, which she agreed to do. She and the doctor are really in very good circumstances, although that's beside the point. I believe, however, that the figure I've named is a fair one. As I said, before we left the garage, it's been well cared for, but it's certainly far from new.'

'Could I think about it?' she asked. 'At least until tomorrow?'

'Certainly,' he answered, and she sensed the tension in him.

Lyle Cunningham, she found herself thinking, with a quickening of her pulses, wanted her to buy this car. By buying it, she would be one more step nearer to settling here. She felt herself beginning to breathe differently in the excitement she felt.

'When we get back to my office,' he was saying, 'I'll work things down to a fine detail for you, Michelle.'

'Thank you,' she murmured, and after she had said the words she settled back, enjoying the motion of the car, the views of the surrounding mountains, willows sighing in the hot wind, new houses with thatched roofs, old houses with rondavels in the gardens and – being close to Lyle Cunningham.

Back at Little Switzerland Motors, Lyle showed her into his office which came as a surprise. 'This is most attractive,' she said impulsively.

'Brown for basics,' he grinned, 'with yellow, beige and off-white to tone up the differences – or something like that. So I was told, anyway, when I got somebody to fit it out for me. Sit down, Michelle.'

Her eyes, as she took the chair opposite his desk, went to the traditional chess table in front of the sofas, off-white curtains with brown and yellow at the edges, the contemporary palm tree in a corner and the brass table lamp with a gold shade. There was a Persian rug in browns, cream and gold. 'What do you mean by differences?' she asked.

'The differences between modern, contemporary and traditional. The young lady who was responsible for the décor sounded all very clued up.'

He laughed lightly and Michelle's mind took a moment to adjust, then she said, 'Oh, I see. Well, I must say it's very attractive. I'm always attracted to the harmony of colour and bold designs of Persian rugs. They blend well with modern furnishings.' She longed to be able to ask him whether Liza Monatti had been responsible for the furnishing of his office. She watched him as he took the chair on the other side of the desk. 'When we're finished discussing figures,' he said, 'I'll show you round. I'm sure you'll be interested to see the Land-Rovers that labour up the Pass.'

She listened attentively as he talked about the Mini and once again asked him to give her the night in which to think things over.

Jean brought in coffee and, at Lyle's request, she and the young man, whose name was Vic, joined them. Good-naturedly, they answered Michelle's questions about such topics as Bushmen paintings and the great spectacle beyond the windows, which was the Drakensberg.

Afterwards, Lyle said, 'Come along, I'll show you all there is to be seen – not that there's much, but you seem fascinated by the Land-Rovers.'

'I am. I'm utterly fascinated to think that *any* vehicle can climb those mountains out there.'

There was a large piece of ground behind the building. Some of it was under good lawn, but most of the lawn was chewed up by the tyres of vehicles. Somewhere, a motor was running continuously – possibly, thought Michelle, re-charging a battery belonging to one of the Land-Rovers, several of which were parked to one side of the Sani Ski vehicle. Apart from the Land-Rovers, which all appeared to be in excellent shape, the yard seemed to be full of broken vehicles and empty drums. There were also several petrol pumps. An African was sitting on a drum and the sight of the blanket draped around him staggered Michelle because of the intense heat. 'How can he bear that blanket?' she asked, 'in this heat?' She glanced up at Lyle and the hot wind blew her hair about her face and she shook it back, laughing. Suddenly she could sense the hidden strength in

43

Lyle Cunningham and the thought of him driving one of these vehicles up the rugged Sani Pass had the power to thrill her. 'I suppose,' she struggled to keep her voice light, 'you keep all the old vehicles for any parts which might not be worn out and which can be used again as spares?' She looked up at him seriously. Her hair was blowing across her face and she swept it back with both hands. Before he had time to answer she asked, 'By the way, where are the drivers?'

'There are three,' he told her, 'all expert mechanics – and all out, apparently.'

On the way back to the hotel he said, without looking at her, 'Michelle, would you mind very much if I picked something up at the house?'

'No, of course not,' she answered, after a moment. 'I didn't have any afternoon appointments, as it so happens.' She tried to control the fluttery feeling she had in her chest.

To strangle this feeling she said, 'Thank you for your trouble today, by the way. It was very kind of you. I'm just sorry I've got to ask for time to think about the Mini. You see, I seem to have used up so much money lately, but I would like a small car. It would save a lot of bother, all round.'

The mountains were pulling the clouds in from the distant sea. Lyle parked the car in the spacious parking area. In the late afternoon light the exotic plants in the pottery urns, which flanked a blue-tiled archway, appeared even more exotic.

'Come in for a few moments,' he said, 'and I'll pour you a drink while I hunt out some papers which my father particularly asked me to bring back with me. They're all to do with the new brochure I was telling you about. As soon as I've found them, I'll join you.'

'Don't bother about pouring a drink,' she murmured demurely, as they walked along the pale beige ceramic pathway leading to the front door. 'I can wait.'

The ceramic flooring continued through the door and her footsteps made clinking noises. Glancing down, she noticed that Lyle was wearing suede shoes with a soft sole,

44

suited to the safari suit he was wearing.

With the grandeur of an Eastern palace, the silent entrance hall greeted them. However, somewhere there was the tick-ticking of a clock, slow and measured, and Michelle stood next to Lyle, undecided as to what she should do and feeling her nerves beginning to tighten up. As she met Lyle's blue-green eyes she knew suddenly that he was as much aware of her as she was of him, and filled with these conflicting thoughts she said, 'Where shall I wait?'

'Through here. You know your way about,' he answered. The carved sliding door with the heavy brass handle was partly open and she watched him as he opened the door completely. There before her was the breathtaking honey-shaded carpeting leading in the direction of the conversation pit so reminiscent of a sheikh's harem – the coloured cushions in shades of emerald, shocking pink, orange, turquoise and purple were almost jewel-like in the late afternoon sun. Apart from the fragile notes of the clock, striking now, there was the sound of cascading water which, she knew from having visited the house before, came from one of the many indoor gardens.

'It's so beautiful,' she let out a breath. 'Isn't it?'

'And yet for all that, it's really a white elephant,' he said. 'Walk around and amuse yourself. I'll get you something to drink.'

'Please – I'd rather wait,' she said.

'Just as you wish.' His eyes met hers and she felt the usual shock at their magnetism and so she began moving about the room.

'There are so many beautiful things,' Michelle did not turn her head, 'I don't know which to admire first. It's strange that the film people left everything here. One would have thought that all this,' her shoulders moved slightly, 'would have been taken away and sold and the house rented.'

'After the film – the shooting of the film, I should say – was over,' she heard him say, 'an artist decided to buy the house as it stood. He and his wife lived in it for the better part of a year before they realized that it was too far from everything – even for them. They'd had an option on the

45

place, you see, but when the lease was up they left. They were followed by an author and his wife and when the book he was writing was finished they went back to Johannesburg. After this couple left plans were, in fact, under way for everything to be removed and sold. The house would then be empty and sold or, failing that, rented once again. This is when I decided to step in, and arrangements were made to leave the house as it stands, and for me to rent it on a lease with the option of buying it when that lease expires.'

She turned. 'Oh, I hope you do. It's perfect – just the way it is. Besides,' she smiled, 'this is your "stamping ground", as they're so fond of saying, in this country. Your work is here – apart from the hotel.'

'It needs a wife in it,' his voice had an edge of ridicule to it, but his eyes were serious. There was a feeling of tension in the air. 'As you can imagine, it can be lonely.'

'Well . . .' her voice was deliberately light, 'you could always change that, I guess.'

'I intend to,' he answered mockingly. 'I've already put an advert in the papers – wanted, beautiful, intelligent and good-natured girl. Matrimony offered to right person.'

'You don't want much,' she laughed, and knew that she was shaking a little. For a wild moment she had thought of Liza.

'Well, browse around,' Lyle told her. 'I'll be with you in just a moment.'

While he was away, Michelle wandered about the fabulous room, overwhelmed at the immensity of her good fortune. Just to have had the opportunity of visiting this mansion was an experience of a lifetime, she thought, quite apart from the experience of working in a luxurious hotel situated in the mountains. Suddenly she thought of Peter and Laney and felt determined that, at all costs, they would keep their farm. Now she could see why they had chosen it. Nervous and angry at their inability to make it pay, she began to work out how she could help them.

Lyle Cunningham chose that moment to come back. 'You look very purposeful,' he told her.

'I was just trying to work things out,' she said.

'Think about it,' he told her, obviously with the Mini in

mind. 'You'll realize what a bargain it is.'

'I was thinking of Peter and Laney – and the farm, as it so happens. They're talking of selling, but I'm determined that they're going to keep it.'

'How do you profess to make it possible, Michelle?' He sounded puzzled and – a little annoyed. 'Let's face it, Pete and Laney are in debt. They're struggling . . . they have no money.'

'It makes me sick just to think about it!' Her voice was heated. She ran her fingers through her hair which was wind-blown and honey-coloured, almost the same exotic colour as the deep carpeting.

'Yes, I know that,' he turned impatiently, 'but the farm isn't paying – not the way it's being run at present. Therefore, it must follow that certain changes must be made – or, failing that . . .' he shrugged, 'it will have to go. There's no other way out.'

On the verge of sinking into depression, Michelle said swiftly, '*I* don't think so.' Her eyes followed him as he went in the direction of the panelled bar, in the entrance section of the room. He began to pour drinks. 'Why must it follow?'

When he had poured them he turned. 'And when did *you* become an expert on the subject?' He sounded more amused than annoyed now and she had the feeling that by pouring drinks he had himself in hand again.

Remembering who he was, she murmured, 'Well, I'm not an expert, of course.'

Lyle turned back to the drinks and dropped two ice cubes into the chunky glasses, then turned again. 'So?'

She moved her arm in a helpless little gesture. 'I don't know. All I know is that they mustn't be allowed to sell.'

He picked up the glasses and came over to where she was standing and gave her one. 'It's not strong,' he told her. 'See if you like it.'

'Thank you.' She dropped her lashes and took a sip. Then, drink in hand, she began wandering about the room again.

Now that she was here during the daytime she was able to see that the house was uniquely situated to capture vistas of

47

the stunning mountain formations. Changing the subject, she said, 'How wonderful to be away from city smog and traffic – just looking at all that, out there, makes one decide almost instantly that one doesn't need city life. The whole site must have been worked over by the architect. It's perfectly obvious that the exact spot for the house was very carefully researched. Don't you agree?'

'Yes.' His eyes were on her face. 'But don't change the subject, Michelle. You've already said enough today to destroy my peace of mind about Pete and Laney.'

Honestly puzzled, she said, 'Oh, I'm sorry. I guess I got carried away. I'm – I'm not given to wild outbursts as a rule.' She took a small sip from her glass, to hide her discomfort, and watched him over the rim. Her hair slipped forward and she shook it back.

'I think you'd better resign yourself to the fact, Michelle, that Pete and Laney have big problems.' There was more than a hint of impatience in his voice now.

'Well,' she shook back her hair again, 'that could be a challenge, couldn't it? I don't think they should just give up like that!' She lifted one slim hand.

'I'm in emphatic agreement, but why not talk it over with Laney, some time?' he asked.

'I have talked it over with her.'

'Has she told you the extent of their problems? Have you a complete picture of the set-up?' he asked.

'It depends what you call complete. I happen to know that they owe money – here and there, of course. I didn't ask where, of course. In any case, it would mean nothing to me. I don't know the people involved.' They studied each other and she dropped her eyes again.

Lyle moved away slightly. 'It's difficult to know how to help these two,' he swirled the liquid round in his glass. 'Two very nice people with very little idea of how to run a farm and a whole lot of stubborn pride into the bargain.' He glanced up. 'That's what happened here. *I* should know. But it's time they faced up to their problems.'

'They happen to be – to be sensitive about these things,' Michelle replied, with a faint trace of sarcasm. 'And I should know. I'm closest to them.' Wishing now that she hadn't let the sarcasm show, she went on hurriedly, 'I'll really have to be getting back to the hotel, you know.'

'Why?' There was anger behind his words.

'In case I'm needed at the salon. People turn up, looking for me, at the oddest times, without an appointment.'

'Relax. You mentioned that you had no advance bookings, so why worry? Besides, it's late now. Too late for setting hair.' Some of the anger had come back into his voice and she kept her head down as she tried to understand how he could have spoken to her like that. What was Lyle Cunningham really like? Suddenly the loneliness and isolation of the house made itself felt and she glanced around for a place to put her glass. Somewhere in the house a door thudded and she felt a stab of relief and was even able to smile at him, trying not to have those hypnotic blue-green eyes bullying hers into clinging to them.

'I'll give you another figure for the car in the morning,' he said, 'and I'm sure you'll have to agree with me that it will be a fair one. So think about it . . . take your time. You don't have to rush things.'

'I'll let you know – finally,' she replied.

'The female mind,' his voice was mocking now.

'No.' She tried to make her voice light. 'I'm afraid it's the female purse. This time, anyway.'

'In all honesty,' he said, 'could you stretch to the figure I've already mentioned?'

'Yes – only just.'

'I intend bringing that figure down.'

'Yes, I know.' Suddenly she felt impatient with him. 'It's so difficult. You see, if I do buy this car I'll feel trapped.'

'Trapped?' He gave her a sharp look, then lowered his head for a moment, while he waited for her to finish speaking, his arms folded across his chest. Then, without warning, he looked up and his blue-green eyes clashed with hers.

'I mean I'd feel that I'd have to remain here – if not for good, for a long, long while. You see, I'd have to save up again, and that takes time. Don't you see?' Her blue eyes widened.

He didn't move but stood stiffly looking at her, his very attitude matching his tone. 'What is there back in England for you now that Pete and Laney aren't there?'

Listening to him, Michelle felt tense and restless. 'This was only supposed to be a holiday,' she said, not telling him about her last-minute decision to pack and crate her belongings in case she decided to make her home in this country. Feeling utterly caught up, she said, 'Even if I wanted to stay, don't you see, Pete and Laney might well go back if this venture ends in disappointment for them and,' she lifted her shoulders, 'what point would there be in my staying here? I'd be completely alone in a strange country.'

'A fair question, Michelle.' He was giving his full attention to her hair, her eyes, her lips . . . Beneath her feet the honey-gold carpeting seemed to fall away. She was alert to danger. A sudden, overwhelming silence filled the room.

Beyond the windows the peaks of the mountains were becoming obscure as clouds drifted across them. It was cooler, but outside, the heat of the sun would be retained on the paving-stones.

Looking at Lyle Cunningham, Michelle was quite resigned to the fact that she was hopelessly in love with him.

'What is it?' His voice was soft.

'Nothing.' She bit her lip and then went on. 'Except that I'll have to be getting back.' She moved away slightly, deliberately not looking at him now. It had been a moment before she had trusted herself to speak.

'I hadn't forgotten,' he answered quietly.

CHAPTER FOUR

On the day Michelle was to take delivery of the Mini Lyle Cunningham drove her into Thabana. Looking at her tanned dreaming face, he said, 'Well? Are you excited?'

Michelle laughed, slanting her eyes at him. 'Yes, madly excited! I had a tiny car in London. Eventually, it broke down – it was a complete write-off and I had to take what I could get for it, which was next to nothing, as it so happens. It wasn't like this, though.' Her eyes scanned the mountains.

'Like what?' He sounded curious.

'One day I'll get into the Mini and drive and drive, with the sun splashing into the car and those magnificent peaks beckoning me on.'

He laughed. 'Are you, by any chance, contemplating driving up them?'

'No, of course not.' Although she was still shy of him she found herself relaxing with him. 'I'll take all the roads which appeal to me and drive until I know it's time to turn back. I'm terribly grateful to you for helping me to make up my mind and for helping me with the business side. So long as the insurance is in order that's the main thing.'

'You sound like a risky driver, Michelle.'

'No – not really.'

They passed a dam and the tall reed-like grass growing on the banks shivered its reflection in the water.

It was late afternoon and, very much her own boss, she had closed the little salon, but she found herself thinking of Liza's dark eyes as they had watched her leave the hotel with Lyle Cunningham. The memory of the expression on Liza's face disturbed her. Was there – or *had* there been something serious between Liza and Lyle? she wondered. She had grown to learn that Liza's sarcastic attitude was reserved for her when the three girls happened to be behind the desk together – for often, during the past few days, Michelle found herself helping out in small ways. In fact,

Cunningham Senior had noticed this help on her part and an arrangement and a slight increase in Michelle's salary had been worked out.

'What are you thinking about?' Lyle asked, breaking into her thoughts. 'If it happens to be about the drive back I'll follow you. There's no need to worry.'

'No, I'm not worried. I had a trial run, don't forget. I'm very pleased, really, all round.' She gave him a smile.

He had taken her into Thabana two days earlier so that she might complete the necessary negotiations and she had, at his suggestion, driven the Mini round the small town.

'You'll get used to the corrugations as time goes on,' he told her.

'I'll have to, won't I?' She sounded amused.

As they neared the outskirts of Thabana her nerves began to tighten up.

Lyle must have given orders for the Mini to be taken out of the showroom window and parked in the street, all ready for her to drive off.

As she stepped out of Lyle's car, she was aware of the heat which still clung to the town and of the harsh but stimulating climate. Thabana looked out on the distant great spectacle of the Berg and the lines of free-standing peaks were examples of weathering and erosion over the long years.

'Come into Vic's office,' Lyle touched her elbow and started to lead the way.

Vic looked up from his desk as they entered the office and then stood up. 'Feels like there's going to be a storm,' he grinned, 'it's hot enough. How are you standing up to it, Miss Abbott?'

'Oh,' Michelle smiled, 'I'm adoring it, to be perfectly honest. I'll admit, though, that sometimes it just about knocks me out. Do you get many storms?'

Vic whistled softly. 'Do we get many storms?' He laughed. 'I'll say we do!'

'The Drakensberg is the birthplace of storms, they say,' Lyle said. 'Remember that, Michelle, when you happen to be out walking or climbing. They batter the mighty crags out there.'

'I'll remember, don't worry,' she replied.

Vic gave Lyle the keys to the Mini and, in turn, Lyle tossed them lightly in Michelle's direction. She made an attempt to catch them, but afraid of breaking one of her cherished fingernails she allowed them to fall instead. Immediately Lyle was beside her. 'I'm sorry,' he said, 'I shouldn't have done that.'

'I was afraid of breaking a nail,' she answered, then watched him as he stooped to retrieve the keys from the floor. He gave them to her and she bit her lip and asked, 'So what's the position now?'

'The position is that you have tea with me and then we head back. How's that?'

'That's fine.'

'We'll have tea at the Mountains Hotel, just up the street.'

'Fine,' she said again.

They went outside just as a Land-Rover drew up. The driver, wearing a khaki safari suit, jumped out and began opening up so that his passengers, two girls and two men, might emerge. The girls were laughing and looked windblown and excited. 'Whew!' they both exclaimed together. 'What a trip!'

'It's good to know that we're back in one piece,' one of the men laughed.

Looking at Michelle, the dark girl asked, 'Have *you* been up the Pass?'

'No.' Michelle's eyes went in the direction of the vehicle, which was smothered in dust. A mirage seemed to be dancing on top of it and the heat of the engine could easily be felt. 'Not yet.' Her eyes came back to the girl. 'Is it exciting?'

'It's a *must*. You simply must go up. It's absolutely hairraising, of course, but you can laugh – afterwards.' The girl turned to the driver. 'Well, thanks,' she said, 'it's been wonderful. I wouldn't have missed the experience for anything.'

Eventually, after several moments of thanking the driver of the Land-Rover, the party drove off in a car which had been parked nearby.

'Meet Miss Michelle Abbott, our new hair-stylist,' Lyle was saying. 'Michelle – Jake Gobbi.'

After the introductions had been made Jake Gobbi said, 'By the way, that foursome came from the chalets. I'm told that Hayes is getting his own Land-Rovers soon. Two.'

'In that case he'll have his hands full,' Lyle replied, with some curtness. 'What kind of trip did you have?' He changed the subject. 'How was it up there?'

'Well, as hot as hell to begin with, but cold at the top. In fact, there's a howling gale blowing up there.'

'You wouldn't think so, would you?' said Michelle. 'I mean, it's hard to believe that it's so cold up there when it's so hot down here.'

'When are you going up?' Jake asked cheerfully.

'I've heard so many stories,' Michelle laughed, shrugging her shoulders, 'and then, to crown everything, there was a film at the hotel which put me off for life.'

Jake laughed. 'Have you heard the stories about the old-timers in the pubs?'

'No.' She gave a baffled little laugh.

'Well, the old-timers like to tell of the early days, before the track was improved, when even the horses had to bend themselves to get round the hairpin bends.'

Michelle's eyes widened. 'Then it's not quite so bad now? All the stories I hear about vehicles having to reverse backwards and forwards, in order to get round some of the bends, are not true, after all?'

Grinning back at her, Jake said, 'I didn't say that. They're true all right. Anyway, you must try it some time.' He winked at Lyle, who was a patient bystander. 'What do you say?'

'I quite agree. We'll see to it that she does go up. And now, how about that tea?' Lyle smiled at Michelle.

The Mountains Hotel had been orientated to the view and they sat on the veranda with its peacock chairs and sun-smelling fibre matting. Suddenly the heat seemed to go out of the day and Michelle shivered slightly; looking at her, Lyle said, 'When we get back I'll give you a drink – to calm your nerves.' He laughed a little. 'But not now – not with all those potholes and corrugations you have to drive over

54

presently.'

'That will be very nice, thank you,' she smiled back, forcing her mind to switch off to the fact that she was in love with him whereas he was just trying to be kind in getting her settled. 'I must admit I'm feeling a little on edge.'

'I tell you what,' he said, 'we'll go to the house and have one there. How's that?' The question was delivered smoothly and, brooding, she glanced away.

'Just as you like, although I should be getting back to the hotel.'

'Why should you be getting back?'

'Well, because I often help out at the desk.'

'Have you made plans to help out this evening?' His brusque superiority unnerved her.

'No, but the hotel is very booked – they'll be busy at Reception.'

'I don't remember Sylvie ever helping at the desk,' he said.

'I've come to an arrangement,' she murmured. 'With your father.'

'I see. Well, this evening is out.' He glanced at his watch. 'There won't be time. Now, what can you tell me? What have you been doing with yourself lately?'

There was a moment of silence, then she said, 'Well, nothing much, of course. I've spoken to Glen Hayes on the telephone.'

'Oh?' She was aware of his interest.

'Well, he often rings Liza – and . . .' she broke off, wondering whether she was doing the right thing, 'I often answer,' she finished lamely.

'No explanation is necessary,' he surveyed her coolly, 'Nevertheless, indirectly, we work along with him. Our Land-Rovers are at the disposal of people wishing to go up the Pass and so it follows therefore that people staying at the chalets get in touch with us. Although we have no arrangement, so to speak, with Glen Hayes, we work in with him. However, it would appear that he's going to operate his own vehicles in the near future.'

'Yes, I knew about it, actually.' She saw the flicker of hard interest in his eyes and realized, immediately, that he was of the opinion that she and Glen Hayes had become more than just a little friendly on the telephone. She was going to add that she had overheard Liza talking to Debbie about it, but decided that she had said enough. Feeling tense and uneasy, she sipped her tea.

Finally Lyle said, 'Well, shall we go? I'll drive ahead of you,' he told her when they had got back to Little Switzerland Motors. 'I'll keep you in my rear view mirror, don't worry. You won't get lost. If you went in front you'd probably miss the turn off to my house.'

So they were going? For a moment her mind argued with itself and then the argument as to whether she should go or not petered out.

'I'll be careful to follow, don't worry,' she answered lightly. 'I don't particularly want to get lost – the light will be fading soon.'

As she followed Lyle's car in her Mini Michelle gave her attention to driving. Once the Mini skidded across the corrugations and, bearing in mind what he had told her about corrugations, she let it ride until it sorted itself out.

The house looked pink in the light. The clouds on the distant horizons of Lesotho, which appeared as domes and prominent ridges, were tinged a pinky-grey. The storm which had been threatening seemed to be petering out – otherwise it had moved on, without breaking. That was something she still had to experience, she was thinking, the fury of a Berg storm, not to mention the snowfalls which she had been told could occur during every month of the year, although it was rare in summer. Often, however, the highest peaks did have snow on them, especially in the crags where the sun could not get at it.

Before the turn-off to Lyle's house there was a trading store with boards at the windows and a lean-to veranda where empty drums were stacked. The earth in front of the uneven steps had been brushed smooth by switches made of sticks and leaves and by the movement of feet and the scratching of fowls.

Lyle's house, in the distance, looked somehow out of place, and yet in a way it belonged here, in this beauty, more than it would have belonged in an exclusive suburb somewhere, Michelle thought.

She followed Lyle's car into the sweeping driveway and when she got out of the Mini he was already coming towards her. 'Well, how did it go?'

She ran her fingers through the tips of her hair. 'I got into a skid, once – but I did what you told me and . . .' she laughed, 'here I am!'

On the way into the house he said, 'It seems a pity not to have people to this house, to share its beauty.'

'Where are the dogs?' she asked. 'Listen to them barking. They must know it's you.'

'They're in the courtyard at the back. Usef watches over them like a hawk. Mostly they have the run of the place, however, unless Usef happens to be busy.'

When they were in the lounge Lyle said, going to the built-in stereo, 'Let's have some music on the subject, shall we? This can be a very silent house, as I've grown to learn.'

Michelle watched him as he put on a record and then she went to stand next to the windows. Beyond the trees in the garden the jagged peaks of the mountains rose up, piercing the clouds in some places. Behind her, Lyle was adjusting the volume and the music was soft. Impatient with herself, Michelle felt her breathing coming faster.

'I'll let the dogs in,' Lyle was saying, 'unless you're afraid?'

She turned. 'No, I love dogs. They sound huge. What kind are they?'

'Boxers – with funny faces.'

'Oh. They do have funny faces – I agree with you. Somehow I always expect a boxer to break into conversation.'

'Come with me, then I'll pour those drinks. Are you hungry, by the way?'

'No,' she answered. 'It's been too hot today to want to eat much.'

On the way to the courtyard he said, 'Would you like to see the kitchen? I think you'll like the highly glazed ceramic tiles.'

Designed for maximum workability, the kitchen caused her to take in a breath. 'It's perfect,' she said. 'I wonder if they ever used it in the film?'

'Yes, they did – but not for cooking . . .' his eyes mocked her, 'at least, not for the actual film. There was a love scene in it, actually.'

Recovering herself quickly, she said, 'Oh, was that all? It seems a pity, somehow. Still, I expect Usef makes up for it now.' Her eyes went to the floor to the ceiling window at the far end of the kitchen. 'Look at the view. Oh, how wonderful!'

'Wait here, and I'll let the dogs in,' said Lyle. 'They're very well behaved, as it so happens. They won't jump up.'

Michelle waited for him to come back and when he did he said, 'Meet my family, Michelle – Jason and Jacques. They were christened, by the way, before I bought them.'

She held out her fingertips and the dogs searched her face with their brooding eyes and came towards her. Michelle's expression became startled and a small shock went through her. No matter what she had to say about adoring dogs she was still nervous of them, until they got to know her. 'Hello,' she said, in a tiny voice.

'It's all right,' said Lyle. He took her fingers in his own and held them still. She had been about to snatch them away from the inquiring noses of the animals. Once again a small shock went through her, but this time it was because of the touch of his fingers on her own.

While Lyle patted the dogs with his free hand, she took her fingers away and stepped back, losing her balance, then she felt his hands on her shoulders holding her so that she would not fall. It could have been an embrace, she thought. 'Careful,' he said, releasing her.

The moment was over and she said, 'They must be wonderful company for you. Don't you feel terribly lonely at times?'

'It suits me very well here,' he replied. 'My father enjoys his life at the hotel – but I like to get away from it.'

'All those empty rooms,' she went on, 'especially at night.'

'Oh,' he shrugged, 'sometimes, to break the monotony, I throw a house-party. I have an assortment of friends in an assortment of places. They enjoy a break.'

Laughing, she said, 'But that's bad for business. What about the hotel? You should make them book in there.'

'I try to work when the hotel is completely booked up. It eases my conscience.'

'Is that important – your conscience, I mean?'

'Yes, it is important to me. I try to keep on the right side of it – usually, anyway.' He gave her an easy grin. 'Come and I'll get us something to drink.'

In the lounge he said, 'Sit where you can watch the sunset.'

Before he joined her he turned on the black-iron standard lamps with their crowns of yellow glass. From where she sat Michelle could see the mountains changing colour.

'Do you enjoy entertaining?' she asked, holding out her hand for the glass which he had brought for her. In it, tiny bubbles were surfacing to the top of the golden liquid. She knew she was asking a lot of questions, but she was afraid of the silence which made her heart beat too fast.

'I don't mind it, but I don't make a big thing of it. It has to be a special occasion. It's not as lonely here, as you think. I'm always busy. Tell me, what did you think of the Mini? How did she run?'

'Beautifully. I'm longing to show it to Laney and Pete. You see,' she laughed, 'I've got into the habit of saying Pete now, just like everybody else.'

'You'll always get your money back on the Mini,' Lyle said casually.

'You – you mean if I were to sell it?' she asked.

'Yes. If you decide to go back to England, that is.' She had the feeling he was testing her.

'I'm in no hurry.' She took a sip of her drink.

She refused a second drink and then they went outside and he showed her the garden. The air was like champagne now. It was amazing that such heat could have given way to this, she thought, shivering a little. Nearby, the dogs, Jason and Jacques, began romping dangerously near to one of the flower beds and Lyle spoke to them sharply and they stopped playing to look at him with their dark, moody eyes.

'You've made them miserable,' Michelle laughed.

'They'll make Usef more than miserable if they break those plants.'

'Tell me,' she said, 'do I have to cross that rickety little bridge to get back to the hotel, or can I by-pass it?'

'I'll take you back in your Mini and we'll by-pass the rickety bridge, then you'll know the way the next time.' His voice was mocking.

'And,' she sounded puzzled, 'how will you get back?'

'I'll make a plan. In any case, I'll probably walk back. I often do. It's good exercise, and besides, it's not far.'

Jason and Jacques were romping again, getting out of hand. They bumped against Michelle, sending her staggering, and once again she felt Lyle's fingers on her bare shoulders. 'Steady,' he said, 'I'll put them in the courtyard presently.' There was a frozen moment of waiting. For a moment she thought he was going to kiss her, then he said, 'You're very sweet, Michelle, do you know that? Somehow you're not my idea of swinging London – not my idea of swinging anywhere, for that matter.'

The dogs bumped them and the moment was over. Michelle moved away. 'That could be taken both ways,' she kept her voice very light, but she knew it was shaking a little. 'It could mean that – well,' she took a little breath and laughed, 'it could be a compliment or, on the other hand, it could be taken the other way.'

'There's a curious mixture of sophistication and little girl about you,' he said. 'It never ceases to amaze me, actually.'

'That gives me hope, anyway.'

'I'm not going to let you go back to England,' he told her.

'How do you aim to stop me?' she laughed again.

'Easy. I've already got you into financial difficulties, haven't I? I mean, you've already mentioned that you'll have to save up again in order to get back.'

That was true, she thought. She should have been frightened – but she wasn't.

'You should have known better, even if I didn't,' she told him. 'It was no good consulting Pete and Laney. They're just about as giddy about money as I am.' Sobering, she added, 'That's not true, of course. I'm just joking. They're not giddy, really. Just foolish, in some ways, perhaps.'

They went back into the silent house and she looked around for her bag and found it on a chair where she had dropped it. Lyle said, 'I want to tell Usef not to prepare a meal for me. I'll eat at the hotel. I won't be a moment. Usef was with us before my mother died, as a matter of fact. Then he came to the Berg with us and looks after me now. It all works very well. As a result of my mother's death my father likes company. I don't, particularly – not all the time, anyway.'

While he was away Michelle moved about the room, marvelling at the beauty of everything and then he came back and said lightly, 'Well, shall we go?'

Liza was at the desk when they got back. Looking up, she said, 'I was wondering when you'd get back.'

'I'll go straight up and change, Liza,' said Michelle, 'and then I'll come and take over here for you.'

'Is that all you have to say? Well,' Liza let out a long breath, 'that might not be such a bad idea, after all. I'm exhausted. I've been on my own all afternoon. Debbie had to go to the doctor again. She's slow in picking up, isn't she?' Liza looked at Lyle. She managed to sound patronizing.

Michelle turned to Lyle. 'Thank you once again, for everything. I think you've been very patient with me.'

'It's been a pleasure.' He smiled. 'I'm not in a position to do anything about the rickety bridge – I'm afraid it's there to stay – but . . .' his eyes met hers, 'you know the bypass.'

'Yes. I hope you don't have to walk back,' she said.

'Don't worry about it. I'm not.' He sounded business-like.

That was that, she thought. The mood had passed. Lyle Cunningham was just being kind as he tried to help her to settle down in a new country, she told herself, determined to dismiss him from her mind – if she could.

CHAPTER FIVE

DURING the following week Michelle was kept busy in the salon, but when time permitted she helped out at the desk. On her afternoon off she took Laney to Thabana to see her doctor.

'See what buying the Mini has done already?' she said to Laney. It's saved Pete a trip and it gives you and me a chance to go into town together.'

'You can't shop with a man around,' Laney answered. 'I've still got the nappies to get, plus a hundred and one other little items. Pete thinks he's helping, but honestly, he just succeeds in getting in the way.'

Turning her head, Michelle said, 'Look, there's Lyle Cunningham's marvellous house. Every time I go there I feel like a film star.'

The Mini rattled over the corrugations. 'Am I going too fast for you, Laney?'

'No. I'm used to this sort of thing,' Laney replied. She glanced at Michelle. 'But tell me – this sounds interesting. Have you been to Lyle's house again – apart from the night of the party?'

Michelle hesitated, then said, 'Now you've caught me out, haven't you?' She laughed lightly. 'But yes, I have. He took me there after we'd gone into Thabana to see the Mini and then again on the day I took delivery of it. The first time we went he wanted to collect something for his father and the second time he thought that there was going to be a spectacular sunset – which there was, as it so happens – and he wanted me to see it from the house.' She had tried to keep her voice casual.

'How times have changed,' Laney's voice was dry. 'Can you imagine our mothers – or our Aunt Vera, for instance – approving of this?'

'You're direct enough, I must say. Don't you approve, Laney?' Michelle gave a startled little laugh. 'But what about *you* – always going up to Lyle Cunningham's

62

bedroom?'

'Pete is always downstairs, talking to Lyle, and you know it,' Laney's voice was teasing. 'Anyway, I was just pulling your leg. I'll tell you something, though. I wouldn't visit Glen Hayes. A girl would have her hands full – I mean, if she has any reservations at all, that's all I can say. I've heard that he's quite a lad. I shouldn't listen to gossip, of course.'

'I haven't met Glen Hayes. We've spoken on the phone, of course. Liza Monatti is very friendly with him and he often phones for her. He also phones in connection with arranging for a Land-Rover to take people from his chalets up the Pass.'

'He's known around these parts as a bit of a shark,' Laney said.

'How do you mean, a bit of a shark?'

'Well, he has the reputation of being a bit of a twister, one way and another. He's put through some shady business transactions, from what I hear – but,' Laney shrugged and laughed, 'there I go again, gossiping! Look, there's going to be a storm. The clouds are gathering.'

Looking in the direction of the clouds, Michelle laughed. 'Do you know, Laney, that's all I seem to hear around here – there's going to be a storm, people say.'

'You'll laugh on the other side of your face when we *do* have one, I can tell you that much. Quite frankly, I'm terrified of them. I'll never get used to the storms.'

They had entered Thabana now and were passing Little Switzerland Motors. Michelle tried not to turn her head, but Laney said, 'By the way, what did you think of Lyle's flourishing little business?'

'The premises came as a surprise, I must say,' Michelle answered. 'Such décor, for such a little town.'

'Well, a lot of tourists go there,' Laney answered. 'Apart from that little showroom affair there's the tours side of things. His Land-Rovers don't just go up the Pass, by the way. There are other trips of interest to choose from.'

'He showed me the yard, as he called it,' Michelle told her. 'It told a different story. There were motors running and drums piled high and petrol pumps, not to mention spare parts lying about. I don't know why it is, Laney, but the sight of a Land-Rover baking in the sun always has the power to excite me.'

Laney laughed. 'You're easily excited, I must say. Are you sure it isn't Lyle who excites you – or one of the drivers, maybe? They're tough and very handsome.'

Michelle looked for a parking spot. 'There,' she said, 'how was that for parking? It's a super little car to handle, I must say. Now,' she turned to Laney, 'let's sort things out. Do I come with you? Or do we part company?'

They decided to part company while Laney visited her doctor and arranged to meet afterwards, when they would do a little shopping together and then have tea somewhere before going back to the farm.

'Where will I buy a pair of scissors?' Michelle asked. 'All I seem to see are farm maintenance businesses, hardware stores, a butcher and baker shop . . .'

'Over there,' Laney told her. 'They stock everything there.'

When Michelle knocked over a stack of small paint tins stacked to one side of the entrance to the shop which Laney had pointed out, she felt a surge of dismay followed by a sense of foolishness.

'Here, let me help you with that.'

Turning, she found herself looking into the almost tawny eyes of the speaker. The eyes were magnified by horn-rimmed glasses.

'I must have knocked one with my bag,' she murmured, 'and then when one fell the whole lot followed.'

Looking at her with something like disbelief, he said, 'No problem. I'll have them stacked in a minute.' He went on searching her face with his eyes, then said, 'Pardon me for staring, but when one sees a sight like you in Thabana one just keeps on gazing. I must be dreaming.' Michelle was aware of the hard interest in his eyes. He had the ability to make her feel beautiful and yet ruffled at the same time.

She gave him a direct look. 'Sight? I don't think I follow.'

'I've just become aware of a very beautiful girl,' he told her. 'By the way, I'm Glen Hayes – from the holiday

64

chalets.'

'In that case, I have spoken to you – on the telephone. I'm Michelle Abbott, from the hotel.'

'So?' Glen Hayes stood back and smiled at her and as she looked at him she was aware of an arrogance about him. 'Tell me, how did you get here?'

'I came by car.'

'Your car?'

'Yes. I've just bought a Mini,' she told him.

'Then,' he began stacking the tins, 'I can't drive you back?' He straightened up and gave her an easy grin.

'No – thank you, very much.'

'I can phone you, though, at the hotel?'

'We often do talk,' she said lightly.

'Yes, I know. As a matter of fact, I thought I knew the voice. Anyway, that was different. Tell me, where are you going when you leave this shop?'

'I'm going to meet my sister-in-law. We have some shopping to do before we go back.'

'Your sister-in-law?' He sounded interested.

'Yes. Laney Abbott. I believe you've met her – and my brother Peter. Everybody seems to know him as Pete.'

'Ah, yes, I remember now. Well, that didn't take long, did it?' Glen Hayes stood to one side and surveyed the tins. 'Let's get out of here before they fall down again.'

When they were out on the pavement Michelle said, 'Well, thank you so much for coming to the rescue. I felt such a fool. I'll have to be going, though. I promised Laney I'd meet her on the next corner.'

'I'll phone you,' he called after her. 'Now that I've found out who the voice belongs to I'm not going to let you go.'

Laney was already waiting. 'I'm sorry,' Michelle apologized. 'Have I kept you waiting long?'

'No. I've just arrived, actually. What did you do with yourself? I don't see any parcels.'

'First of all,' asked Michelle, 'what did the doctor have to say?'

'He's very pleased,' Laney answered. 'On my last visit I'd put on too much weight, but this time the weight gain is just right.'

'Well, I looked around,' Michelle went on, 'and then I went into this kind of hardware shop – the one you pointed out to me. There were a whole lot of little paint tins stacked near the door and my bag knocked against one of them, sending it flying, then a whole great number of them started collapsing and rolling all over the place. I felt such a fool – then guess who came to the rescue – Glen Hayes himself! He introduced himself.'

'Oh. What did you think of him?'

'A bit pushing, otherwise quite pleasant. Could be a shark, though.' Michelle laughed. 'I formed that opinion of him, as a matter of fact.'

They did a little shopping, then had tea at a small shop attached to a bakery. The sky, over the mountains, was black and threatening. There were fantastically formed pockets hanging to the clouds. The sun had disappeared and there was a chill in the air now.

'I've bought a newspaper,' Laney said. 'Listen to what it says in the Stop Press: Violent storm lashes Natal. A violent electric storm, with heavy rain, struck Pietermaritzburg this afternoon, causing a sharp drop in temperatures and flash floods.' Laney stopped reading and looked up. 'Obviously we haven't had it yet, but it's travelling around – one just has to look at that sky to confirm what I'm saying. So we'd better start moving.'

At the farm, Michelle said, 'Laney, I'm not coming in. I don't want to get caught in a storm. Give Pete my love – and look after yourself. Keep the weight under control!'

There was the usual activity in the foyer of the hotel. People were asking questions at the desk, or going along to the small shop which was next to the salon before it closed.

Eager for a bath before the storm broke, Michelle hurried up to her room. From her windows she was able to see the orange flashes of lightning hemstitching the clouds above the distant mountain peaks and could hear the low, threatening rumble of thunder. The light in her room was gloomy now, so she turned on the lights and left them burning while she had her bath in the adjoining bathroom.

In the bath, which was her usual place for dreaming, her

66

mind flounced away to Thabana where she had met Glen Hayes and she thought about his eyes and how they had flickered over her with a kind of amusement – as though she had turned up to amuse him just when the time was ripe.

Directly she stepped out of the bath she was aware that the air had chilled rapidly and a little shiver of excitement raced through her body. There was something wonderful about looking out warm clothing to snuggle into during a leisurely dinner, for she was free until the morning. It was difficult to believe that she was working at the hotel and not a guest, she thought, listening to the radio, which she had turned on.

From the windows she could look over the immediate mountains and, to one side, the jagged peaks which formed the most striking and distinctive geographical wall between the cold Lesotho plateau and the warm grasslands of Natal. The storm was drawing nearer and the sky was full of menace, and with a little shudder Michelle closed the windows and drew the curtains just as the first rain came pelting in from the mountains, splashing the paved terraces below until they glowed like black mirrors, reflecting the lights of the hotel. A sudden crash of thunder made her rush to the door and open it, then, trying to appear composed, she walked slowly in the direction of the staircase, above which was suspended an enormous crystal chandelier, and made her way down to the foyer.

In the foyer the sound of heavy rain was easily heard as it splashed down outside. Lightning forked in and out of the area and, behind the desk, Liza and Debbie remained completely unmoved as they went about their business.

By the time Michelle was eating her dinner at her table in the corner, right next to one of the tremendous windows, it was hailing.

Lyle Cunningham was in the foyer when she went through. 'Hello,' she said shyly. 'I'm beginning to see what people mean about the storms here. Isn't this vicious?' She put her teeth down on her lip.

She was aware of his eyes going over her before they came back to her eyes. 'The temperature has dropped sharply. In the morning you might well wake up to see those deep

67

gullies blotted out and slashed with snow – but then you're used to snow.'

'Yes.' She smiled back at him and there was a slight pause.

'Are you off duty?' he asked. 'When you were our hairstylist I was always sure, but now that you've combined this with helping out on the desk I never know.'

'I'm free until the morning,' she told him.

'Have coffee with me, in that case. I noticed that you walked right through, without stopping to have it in the lounge.'

'I was going back, later,' she told him. 'I just wanted to look through the glass doors to see whether it was still hailing.'

'Fortunately, it's stopped,' he said, 'but it's raining heavily, as you can hear. Come and have coffee with me.'

In the lounge the curtains had been drawn against the lightning and already fires had been lit in the stone fireplaces – one at either end of the room. Michelle found herself wondering why Lyle Cunningham was not at his house.

'What have you been doing with yourself today?' he asked, when they were seated.

'I took Laney into Thabana. She had an appointment with her doctor and then we did some shopping, had tea and drove back to the farm – just ahead of the storm, as a matter of fact. Laney bought a newspaper and there was a Stop Press concerning the weather. Apparently there was a heavy storm somewhere causing a sharp drop in temperatures and what they termed as flash floods.'

'You didn't get lost on the way?' His tone was friendly and his smile suggested a lot of things, and suddenly Michelle knew that his presence here was no accident through being held up by the storm and he was not merely being kind to her – he was more than just a little interested in her.

'It's difficult to believe that it can be so madly hot one moment and so cold the next,' she said, trying to control her thoughts.

Outside, it was obvious that the elements were going wild.

68

The lounge seemed full of thunder, wiping out the sound of conversation and the clinking of coffee cups and glasses.

'Would you like a liqueur with your coffee?' Lyle asked.

'If you choose one,' she replied.

After he had ordered the liqueurs he turned to her and said, 'So you shopped in Thabana?'

'Mostly things for Laney and the baby.' After a pause she said, 'I met Glen Hayes there – by chance, I mean.' She sensed Lyle's quick sideways glance.

'Oh? Did you?' He sounded interested.

'I knocked over some tins which were stacked next to the entrance of a shop and he came to the rescue and sorted them out for me. I felt such an idiot. We got talking . . .'

'I see. Well, as I once said, that had to happen. Glen Hayes is always about. It was just a matter of time.' His voice sounded easy, but Michelle sensed a change in him.

In the darkness outside the mountains surrendered themselves to the storm. On the terraces the colourful sun-umbrellas would have been folded and stacked away, leaving the terrazzo-topped tables and white cast-iron chairs to the mercy of the rain as it splashed down. In the morning the paving stones would be strewn with battered leaves and petals which had been blown off the plants by the wind.

Chilled by the sudden change in Lyle Cunningham, Michelle said, 'Thank you for the liqueur. I'll have to be going upstairs now.'

'Aren't you staying to play bingo?' he asked, giving her a trace of a smile.

'No. I thought of writing one or two letters back home,' she lied.

'We have a saying in this country, tomorrow is another day.'

She laughed. 'Tomorrow is out for letter writing, I'm afraid. I happen to be completely booked up in the morning. Later, when things quieten down in the salon I'll be helping at the desk.'

'I'm still puzzled as to how involved you've got yourself on the desk,' he said. 'Is it because of Glen Hayes?'

'I don't understand.' Her voice was stiff.

'Well, he's always phoning, isn't he?'

She turned away and watched the colours shifting about the grate as the logs burned brightly, leaping upwards through thin misty-grey veils of smoke. 'Glen Hayes comes through on the phone either to talk to Liza or to make arrangements for a Land-Rover,' she said, turning back to look at him.

'Yes, you did mention that you'd spoken to him on the phone.' He was smiling and his voice was mocking.

The storm did not appear to be lifting. There was a kind of tension in the lounge as the tables were being prepared for bingo.

'Will you be driving back to your house in this storm?' Michelle asked. 'That is, if it doesn't go away?'

'No. Actually, I have a room and bath here. Sometimes when I get sick of my own company I come over here. It suits me very well.' He grinned, easy with her again, and she saw that his mood had altered. Laughing a little, she thawed out again. 'Were you sick of your own company this evening – or were you afraid of the storm and needed company?' She made her face innocent.

'You work it out for yourself,' he told her, 'but it could be that I needed company. Look, let's get out of here and leave them to their bingo. We'll go and make ourselves comfortable in the Ladies' Bar where we can talk in peace.'

The bar was small and dark, with small amber lights, and there was the smell of mixed drinks – like chopped fruit, sprinkled with brandy. Apart from a girl and a man, four stools away, it was empty. There was a fire burning here, too, and the logs crackled and fell with a shower of red sparks. Beneath the storm-racked sky and within the circle of mountains the hotel could have been lonely and isolated. As it was, there was a warm atmosphere everywhere – the murmur of conversation, punctuated by laughter, soft music, piped everywhere, and the clinking of dishes, cutlery, glasses and bottles.

'Have you been to see the Bushmen paintings yet?' Lyle asked.

'No. There hasn't been all that much time. I hope to go soon, though. I understand there's a cave not far from the

70

hotel and then more paintings at the end of a long hike.'

'The paintings are being photographed this week, some time, for use in our new brochure,' he told her.

'They appear to photograph extremely well.' Michelle broke off as the barman placed drinks on the counter before them and while he and Lyle joked about the weather conditions.

Turning to her again, Lyle said, 'Yes, they do, as a matter of fact. It's amazing how the browns and red and white and blacks show up. These are the commonest colours, by the way. Green, blue, purple and pure yellow are practically never used. So I'm told, anyway.'

'It's amazing how they've lasted.' She reached for her glass, but did not lift it to her lips. Instead, she allowed her fingers to rest on the counter beside it. 'They seem so permanent, from what I've read.'

'Their permanence is phenomenal, actually. Practically no fading can be detected.' In the dim lighting Lyle's eyes met her own and she looked down at her glass.

There was a little silence, then she said, 'I wonder why the Bushmen painted?'

'Why does anyone paint?' he asked. 'To record events, I guess. Happenings. To illustrate folk tales or maybe just to denote ownership of a cave.'

In this semi-darkness so close to Lyle Cunningham Michelle felt shy – eager to make conversation and yet at a loss, somehow. It seemed best to go on about the Bushmen painting, so she said, 'Anyway, whatever the reason for painting, these small artists – for they were small people, weren't they? – left behind them a kind of monument.'

Four stools away the girl and the man went on talking earnestly. For a moment Michelle regarded them thoughtfully, then, turning to Lyle again, she said, 'One would wonder where these Stone Age artists got their colours from. There are some pictures in one of the magazine in the lounge, actually. I was looking at them yesterday and found myself wondering.'

A flash of lightning, which no amount of heavy curtaining could keep out, and a crash of thunder almost coincided. Her hand jumped wildly, just about knocking over her glass.

Laughing softly, Lyle moved the glass to one side. 'Steady on, there! What are you so nervous about?' he asked.

'It's just that it was so bright – and so loud,' she answered, in a frightened little voice. Looking across at the other girl, she felt better when she saw that the girl had her fingertips pressing to her temples.

Turning to Lyle Michelle said, 'Doesn't a storm like this ruffle you?'

'I never get ruffled,' he said, grinning, 'either by storms or by people or situations,' and then he said, 'No, I guess that's not true. Sometimes, I get very ruffled by people and situations – especially when I'm jealous.'

'You're making that up, aren't you?' she laughed. Then, changing the subject quickly she said, 'I keep thinking of my poor little Mini. I haven't been able to get a garage. They're all booked up.'

'No matter how many garages we have there are never enough,' he told her. 'However, just to console you, Michelle, my own car is out in this deluge as well.'

'Is it always like this in the Berg?' she asked.

'Not always, but often.' He sounded amused, tracing her lips with those blue-green eyes of his. 'When a storm comes along it usually likes to be the entire floor-show.'

'It's going to be awful if all storms are like this,' she said in a worried voice.

'I think you'd better resign yourself to the fact, Michelle.' His voice was half amused, half tender.

'Well,' she shrugged, 'it would appear so.'

'Anyway,' her senses jumped as he took her hand in his own, 'it seems to be dying away.'

'Yes, thank goodness.' She regarded their hands on the counter. Beside his tanned one her own looked very pale.

'Have another drink,' said Lyle.

'I still have some left,' she told him, her eyes going to her glass.

'A fresh one.' He signalled to the barman.

Later, he asked, 'What else did you do in London, Michelle?'

'How do you mean what else?' she asked. 'I was a hairstylist.'

'I mean, apart from hairdressing?'

'Oh . . .' she broke off, not knowing what to say, 'the usual things.'

The barman brought their drinks.

Lyle said, looking directly at Michelle, 'It's my intention to find out whether there was anyone in London. In other words – a man.'

'Well,' she allowed a little breath to escape, 'it would be absurd to say no, wouldn't it?'

'I don't know. Suppose you tell me.' Even in this light, she thought, his eyes were blue-green and direct.

'I have friends in London. What did you expect?'

'That's just what I expected, as a matter of fact. But anyone, in particular?'

'There *could* have been, but there isn't,' she told him, thinking about Ray Thatcher.

'How is that?' Lyle's voice was soft and curious.

'There were reasons – a whole stack of them.' Trying to sound casual she laughed lightly, 'You have a lot to learn. Usually, if nothing comes of it – there are reasons. This is what happened to me. There was somebody, or rather, there could have been somebody – but there were reasons, and so . . .' she shrugged and laughed again, 'there isn't, and that's all there is to it.' After a moment she said, 'Would you mind telling me why you're asking all this?'

She watched him begin to smile, then he said, 'If we examine the facts, Michelle, we'll discover that I happen to be interested and so,' it was his turn to shrug now, 'the rest must follow – the questions, the endeavour to trap you into saying something . . .'

'I see.' Her eyes flickered away from him and rested on the leaping fire, to one side of them. The flames were poinsettia-coloured, but changing to amethyst, indigo and rose. 'There isn't anyone in particular,' she said.

'Is it because, like most women, you're fickle?' His tone was mocking now.

'I don't think most woman are fickle at all,' she laughed. 'You just never give up, do you? I hate always having to be on the defensive with you.' She blinked. 'What were we talking about before? I seem to remember that we were

73

madly occupied in discussing the Bushmen paintings, weren't we?'

'Right now,' he said, 'you happen to be my major pre-occupation.'

At the far end of the bar the girl and the man slipped from their stools and went out, laughing and talking. The barman kept on polishing glasses.

'Anyway,' said Lyle, 'you must see the paintings for yourself – before you go back to England.'

Falling into his trap, she said quickly, 'I'm not going back.'

CHAPTER SIX

IN the morning there was snow in the deep gullies and mountain peaks and the intense heat of the past few days had, incredibly, given way to sharp, exhilarating conditions. On top of the mountains and on the slopes it would be freezing, even though the sun was shining.

Michelle was in the salon when Laney phoned. 'Well,' she said, 'we just got out of Thabana in time yesterday afternoon. Have you heard the news on the radio?'

'No,' Michelle answered. 'Hello there, Laney. What is the news? I had a quick glance at the morning paper. The papers had just arrived at the desk as I was passing through to open the salon.'

'A violent storm hit Thabana just after we left yesterday and fifty millimetres of rain were measured. Temperatures dropped rapidly – as you can feel for yourself. Actually, it's a treat, after all that heat.'

'I was thinking about you, as a matter of fact, during last night's storm,' Michelle answered. 'Did you suffer any damage?'

'Nothing really. The road is a mess, though. Whatever you do don't come and visit us until it dries up a bit. I adore this feeling of being cool for a change. You should see me, I'm wrapped in a great jersey with a high collar. I'm going to let everything slide in the house for today. This is a day for knitting. So I'll say good-bye now, Michelle. Be good!'

There had been several appointments in the book for hair-sets, but these appointments had been quickly cancelled owing to the fact that excited hotel guests were planning to walk out to the snow. Some of the nearer slopes were also covered, although not thickly.

Michelle was arranging sprays and shampoos on a shelf in the salon when her red telephone rang. It was Glen Hayes.

'Hello,' he said, 'Glen Hayes speaking.'

'Oh.' She blinked twice. 'Hello there.'

'I want to ask you a favour.'

'Oh?' she said again. 'Yes?'

'Are you terribly busy?'

'No, as a matter of fact. Everybody has gone out to see the snow on the mountains.' She wondered what was coming.

'Do you think you could leave the hotel?'

'Well,' she felt suddenly tense and uneasy, 'I'd have to – er – make a plan, you know. I often help out at the desk, so I couldn't just walk out, if you know what I mean. Why do you ask?'

'Did you know that the Utah Film Company is here, making a film?' he asked.

'No. What kind of film?' Her thoughts flew to Lyle Cunningham's film-set house. How many films did they shoot here in the Berg? she found herself wondering.

'It's an advert for the van Luit Wine people.' Glen Hayes spoke as if she should know who the van Luit Wine people and the Utah Film Company people were. 'Oh, on a grand scale, of course.'

'I see. Go on.' Michelle knew that she was curious.

'They are – the film people, I mean – staying here at the chalets. They want to shoot scenes in the snow – they were going to do it without snow, but,' he laughed softly, 'now that there's snow laid on, so much the better. They're planning an elaborate lunch to be served in the mountains and they're looking for a beautiful girl. Immediately I thought of you.'

'But,' Michelle felt flustered, 'there are masses of beautiful girls around, without having to turn to me.'

'I said – immediately I thought of *you*. Would you consent?'

After a moment she said, 'I haven't heard of the van Luit Wine people, by the way. For that matter,' she laughed lightly, 'I haven't heard of the Utah Film Company.' She broke off, wondering whether she should be offended or flattered by Glen Hayes' interest in her.

She heard his soft laughter. 'Ask anyone – and by the way, it wouldn't be for nothing. They will pay top model fees, so how about it?'

'Will there be other girls?' she asked, thinking about the money which would go into her savings account.

'Yes. Three or four – but one other in particular, with the kind of honey-toned skin you've got except that she has bright red hair. We want you both to pose in the snow in bikinis.' He laughed again and she could visualize him holding up a hand. 'Now, this shouldn't pose a problem, Michelle. After all, you're used to the cold, where you come from. Right?'

Michelle found herself beginning to get angry. 'Is this some kind of joke?' she asked stiffly.

'No joke, not in the least. I'm perfectly serious. It's all above board, believe me. There's to be a lunch set out on trestles in a glittering snow scene where champagne will flow like water. Should be a whole lot of fun, actually.'

'It sounds crazy,' she said. 'Are *you* going?'

'Yes, I am. Think about it. Find out whether you can make it and phone me right back. How's that?'

'Well, as you say, I'll have to think about it, of course. All right, I'll phone you later.'

'In about half an hour. Okay?'

'Yes.'

'Someone will pick you up at the hotel.'

'I could drive out, for that matter,' she said, wondering whether her Mini would start after being out in the cold.

'No need for that. You'd be collected at the door.'

'I'll let you know,' she said. 'Don't bank on it, though.'

As she replaced the receiver she realized that the whole set-up posed a problem for her. While one part of her wanted to go for the experience the other part, very reasonably, pointed out that it was nothing short of a nerve to ask for time off to model for a film company.

Glancing at her watch, Michelle left the salon and went along to the desk where Liza was busy working. Liza looked up and, as usual, her dark eyes remained cool. 'Did you want something?' she asked.

'Liza, what do you know about the Utah Film Company?' Michelle kept her voice easy.

'Why do you ask?'

'I'm anxious to find out whether there *is* such a film

77

company, as a matter of fact.' Michelle forced a smile. It was so difficult to smile in Liza's company, she thought with some resentment.

'The Utah Film Company happens to be right here, at the moment,' Liza replied. 'Is this what Glen Hayes wanted to talk to you about? I put him through to you a moment ago.'

'Yes. I happened to be shopping in Thabana the other day, with Laney, my sister-in-law, and Glen Hayes introduced himself. We had, of course, spoken on the phone here.'

'What did he want now?' Liza sounded impatient for a reply.

'He wanted to know whether I could get time off to go out with these film people and pose for them in some kind of advertisement feature. In a bikini, actually. That's what set me thinking.'

'Well, they're doing this thing for the van Luit Wine people,' Liza said. 'I know all about it, actually. I was at a party at the chalets the night before last. They asked me to go along and watch, as a matter of fact. Are you going to pose for them?'

'I don't know. In the first place, although there's nothing doing in the salon, because of the snow, I'd have to speak to Lyle's father about going off.'

'Lyle's father. So it's got down to Lyle now?'

'Not to his face,' Michelle tried to keep her temper. 'But in any case, we're not exactly living in the Victorian era.'

In a way, it had been Liza's sarcastic attitude that had influenced her to go to Cunningham Senior and speak to him about the matter.

'Go right ahead,' he told her. His eyes, so much like Lyle's, held her own. 'Who got in touch with you? The Utah crowd?'

'No. It was Glen Hayes – from the chalets.' All of a sudden she felt particularly edgy and felt her nails begin to dig into her palms.

'I see. Well, the film people are staying there, of course, and that will be for you to sort out, Michelle, but in any case, so far as we're concerned that will be quite in order. As

78

you say, it will be an experience for you to see them at work.'

'Yes,' she replied. She had not told him about having to pose in a bikini.

However, when she was back in the salon she stood for several moments trying to decide whether she *should* go, then the phone rang, shattering her confused thoughts. Reaching for it, she said in a flat little voice, 'Hello.'

'I couldn't wait for you, so I phoned instead. Well, what's the verdict?' Glen asked.

'Well, I have permission to leave here,' she told him dubiously.

'Why do you sound so uncertain?' She could sense his frown.

'Well, I am. I'm confused, actually. I don't know that I'd be doing the right thing. I mean, I haven't posed in front of big cameras before.'

'What makes you faintly – *just faintly* – interested in the first place?' he asked.

After a moment, she said, 'Well, the experience, mainly. After all, I'm new here, and when a chance like this crops up, I find myself tempted. I'd love to go up the mountains. They look beautiful with the snow on them.'

'Well, you've just made up your mind. We'll pick you up outside the foyer in . . .' she heard him shifting about, 'say, twenty minutes.'

'Did you honestly mean it about a bikini?' she asked quickly, before he rang off. 'I'm not used to this kind of thing. I wouldn't mind posing in slacks and a bright jersey. I'd certainly feel more relaxed and,' she laughed a little, 'it would certainly be a more appropriate way of dressing in this weather, wouldn't it?'

'Don't worry. You'll feel relaxed when you meet everybody. There's no need to worry. We'll be seeing you, then – and don't forget to wear the bikini *beneath* the slacks and colourful jersey.' He rang off before she could answer and Michelle stood looking at the receiver before putting it down. Somehow she had a feeling that Glen Hayes had scored a triumph over her – not only over her but over Lyle Cunningham – and the feeling held little warmth.

Suddenly she was sorry she had become involved and decided to dial the chalets and cancel the whole thing, when, afraid of appearing a fool, she closed the door to the salon and went to her room to change.

A Land-Rover was waiting on her when she got downstairs. 'So you're going?' Liza called out.

'Yes.' Michelle turned. 'I am, Liza.'

'To pose in the snow?'

'Yes.'

'In a bikini?'

'I don't really know yet.'

'But you've committed yourself, haven't you? Glen just told me. He was in here a moment ago.'

'Yes, I suppose I have committed myself.' Michelle found herself wishing that she could confide in the other girl that she was already regretting her impetuous decision.

She went out to the Land-Rover and Glen Hayes made the introductions. 'The others have gone on ahead,' he said, 'but meet Vanessa and Joe. Jump in, Michelle.'

Michelle got into the back of the vehicle and Glen joined her. 'I'll bet this is the first time you've been in a land-Rover,' he said, laughing at her.

'Yes. It was one of the things which prompted me to accept, actually.' She shivered a little in the cold.

'What were the other things?' he asked, regarding her with the assessing attitude with which she knew he must regard most girls.

'I was keen to see the film people at work and to go out to where the really big mountains start. I'm trying to get up enough courage to go up the Pass one day.'

'After today,' he mocked, 'you'll go up anything.'

'That sounds terrible,' she answered. The Land-Rover skidded in thick mud and she caught her breath.

'We're driving up to a very spectacular spot,' Glen told her, 'where we'll park the vehicles and walk – not a great distance, just enough to get this simply stupendous backdrop for the film. We're going to drink a whole lot of champagne – or anything else you like, actually, except for the film – and eat a super lunch. Everything is to be filmed.'

'Don't forget to tell her about the snowball fights,' Vanessa called out from the front of the Land-Rover and above the noise.

'All in good time!' Glen shouted back.

The journey out to the film set was an ever-changing combination of hanging over space and avoiding huge walls of boulders directly in front of the Land-Rover. The vehicle skidded sickeningly at times and Michelle found herself hanging on to her breath. Often she closed her eyes and when she opened them again she laughed breathlessly. Glen Hayes put an arm about her. 'Don't look,' he teased, 'if it scares you.'

The edge of the road, which appeared to be in a shocking condition, slid beneath the grey body of the Land-Rover. In front, Venessa with the flying bright red hair was doing a lot of laughing.

Three other Land-Rovers were already parked in a kind of parking area which had been hacked out on the side of a steep track. A colourful scene was created by bright jerseys and ski-hats and various forms of equipment.

Nobody took the slightest notice of names, and then, leaving the Land-Rovers parked in the area, they began the walk to the site which, as Glen Hayes had informed Michelle, was not a long one with very little climbing to do.

'I can see why they chose this particular site,' she said to him as they stood watching the unfolding and setting up of three long trestles which were then covered by heavy red linen cloths. Foliage-green place-mats went on top of the cloths and cut glasses glinted in the sun which had no strength in it but nevertheless had the power to sharpen the senses, not to mention the appetite. The sunlight defined everything it came in contact with – the rim of a glass, a strand of hair which had strayed from beneath a colourful ski-cap, the intricate patterns of Fair Isle jerseys, the green, round shape of wine bottles and tall champagne bottles, topped with white and silver foil. Vanessa, the girl with the bright red hair, had tied a long purple scarf about her head and the ends flapped against her cheeks.

The result was nothing short of spectacular.

Lunch, which was filmed, was a hilarious affair, with the cameraman sitting down later. Whoever had been responsible for the catering, Michelle thought, nibbling at a chicken bone, needed a medal.

'Who is responsible for the catering?' she asked Glen. 'The food is out of this world.'

'See that couple over there?' He placed a careless arm about her shoulder and rubbed his cheek against hers. 'That thick-set fellow and the plump woman with the red top-coat? Well, they're Italians. I'll tell you about them one day. In any case, you'll be hearing about them from other people, in the near future.'

The sun was beautifying and angling everything it touched now. The champagne was going to Michelle's head and she put it down to the thinness of the snow-laced mountain air.

A snowball fight was filmed after lunch with close-ups of people drinking more champagne and laughing a lot, then it was time for the bikini scene – which really should have been at the beginning, Michelle thought, shivering at the thought, when the sun might have been just that little bit stronger. The lighting, however, was superb for photography.

Vanessa frolicked in the snow first, the cold and the wind taking the breath from her. The purple scarf had been removed and her bright red hair cascaded about her shoulders, except when she turned into the wind and it was swept back from her beautiful face. 'I know you'd never think so,' she called out, laughing and shivering in her purple bikini, 'but I love clothes. I have so *many clothes* I could open a dress shop.'

'Okay,' one of the cameramen called out, 'pipe down, Vanessa. You're on set.'

Eventually it was time to focus the cameras on Michelle. Slim, and already bronzed by the South African sun, she made a stunning picture in her black bikini which she had decided to wear because she knew that, like the Bushmen paintings, it would stand out in sharp contrast to the snow.

Both girls had been clued up as to what would take place and Michelle knew that two handsome heroes were going to appear from nowhere bringing with them two fabulous fur coats. These coats would be draped about the slim, shivering shoulders of the girls, who would then be presented by the heroes with glasses of bubbling champagne in glittering goblets.

It was impossible to say just when Lyle Cunningham and Liza Monatti had come on the scene. Michelle knew that her breath had caught in the back of her throat as she spotted them at the very moment when the fur coat was being slipped over her shoulders by a strange and dashing young man. When the blur had passed she went on smiling in the direction of the cameras and wishing that the earth would open up and swallow her from sight.

'Okay, cut!'

Thankfully, she knew that shooting was over, then bit her lip as Glen Hayes came up to her. 'Here,' he was saying, 'put your arms into the sleeves of this thing and get warm.' Her teeth were chattering, possibly from nerves, she thought, and she slid her arms into the sleeves of the fur coat. 'I must go along to the tent and change,' she told him.

'Keep it on for a while.' Glen's face was close to her own. 'Let me pour you a brandy.'

'Oh, no!' Michelle laughed suddenly. 'Not a brandy. I feel quite lightheaded as it is. Didn't I hear someone mention coffee?'

'Coffee, then,' said Glen, 'laced with brandy – or rum, if you like.'

'Laced with milk,' she answered.

It was quite obvious, she was thinking even as she was talking to Glen, that Liza had asked Lyle Cunningham to drive her out to the film set, because, out of the corner of her eye, she had watched Liza introducing Lyle around.

On her way to the small tent which had been erected for the purpose of changing, Michelle caught Liza's dark eyes with her own. Liza's eyes were cool with amusement, icy with spite.

It was practically dark when Glen Hayes dropped Michelle off at the hotel in his car. 'You were super,' he said. 'Tell me, why wouldn't you stay at the chalets? There's going to be a whale of a party. Actually, we're all going out to the farm. That's where our Italian couple hang out, by the way.'

'I'm sorry,' she answered with an attempt at lightness, 'but it was impossible. Another time, perhaps.'

'When will I see you again?' he asked. She knew that he had been drinking steadily all afternoon and had been worried at the thought that he was to drive her back to the hotel.

'I just don't know, at this stage. Thank you for asking me today, though. I thoroughly enjoyed it. The lunch was superb.' Her voice was sedate, her day shattered. She had been perfectly aware of Lyle's eyes, summing her up as she shivered in her bikini beneath the fur coat.

As she changed for dinner Michelle felt utterly drained. What should have been a day of fun had turned into a disaster for her, more so as Lyle Cunningham, she discovered later, was apparently spending the night at the hotel.

As she came face to face with him in the lounge he said, 'I'm pleased to see you're not suffering from a chill after being out in the snow in your bikini.' His eyes went slowly over her. 'Anyway, you appear to be suitably clad this evening.' Michelle found herself shivering even though she was wearing an off-white, light wool floor-length gown with long sleeves. Shocked by his sarcastic tone, she nevertheless recovered quickly.

'I was asked by the Utah Film Company to take part in their film. I went for the experience, mainly, and because ...'

'I didn't know you knew any of the Utah people,' he cut in.

Meeting him head on she said, 'I didn't. Glen Hayes got in touch with me.'

'I see.' He shrugged. 'And I guess one thing led to another? Well, Glen Hayes always did have a mind for detail – and so you said yes?'

'Yes, I did. I spoke to your father about going, though.' She was eager to defend herself. 'Anyway, it was only for fun.'

'You must be quite ravenous, after all that – fun. Join me at my table. I see you're on your way into the dining-room. That is, unless you've arranged to meet someone?'

'I hadn't arranged to meet anyone,' she replied coolly,

84

stung by his remark. The thought of eating at his table did nothing to steady her.

'Well,' he took her arm, 'come along, then.'

Michelle walked ahead of him while a feeling of annoyed frustration surged over her. When they were seated at his table and had given their respective orders she said, 'I'd like to know – are you annoyed with me because I happen to have taken part in this kingsize film advertisement, or is it merely because Glen Hayes asked me to? Have I broken some kind of – of etiquette – some unwritten hotel rule that I know nothing about? I mean, I was paid for my services – for my part in the film.'

'You're free to please yourself what you do in your free time. I must admit, though, that I was more than just a little surprised to see you skylarking there in your bikini. Anyway, your ability to pose in the semi-nude will impress a lot of people, I'm sure.' She did not miss the sarcasm in his voice. 'You certainly looked tantalizingly beautiful.'

Why then did he condemn her with those cool blue-green eyes, she asked herself, when only the night before they had held a very different expression? 'It was obvious,' he was saying, 'that you were enjoying yourself.'

Giving him a level searching look, she said, 'Somehow I seem to be missing the point. What do you mean by that?'

His eyes flickered over her with a kind of contemptuous amusement, before going to the immense leather-bound wine list. 'What did you think I meant, Michelle?'

After a moment she said, 'Liza didn't mention that she wanted to go. If she had, I would have stayed behind and helped at the desk. Taking part in the film wasn't all *that* important to me.'

'Things were very quiet here,' he said. 'Liza asked me to drive her out to see the filming – or what was left of it. I was surprised to see you there and then, later, with Glen Hayes. I had no idea you'd become so friendly with him.'

'Hadn't you?' she found herself saying in a tight little voice. 'Well, now you know.' What she was feeling for Liza Monatti, right now, was something like a tumultuous and rebellious tide. Liza had done this on purpose.

Relaxing her grip on her napkin and placing it on the

table, she said, 'I find I'm not very hungry. Will you excuse me?'

Lyle stood up, smiling easily, but there was an angry look in his eyes. 'Well, you had a big lunch, after all, so it's not really surprising, is it?'

As she picked her way amongst the tables on her way to the foyer Michelle felt the urge to seek out Cunningham Senior and hand in her resignation there and then, but she knew that her position here was nothing short of a stroke of luck. Not only was she near to Laney and Pete, but she was earning good money and, quite apart from anything, she enjoyed her work and living in such spectacular beauty.

In her room she pulled the long zip and let her gown slip to the floor. Immediately she found herself shivering and went straight into her bathroom and turned on the taps. Instead of eating dinner she would have another bath, she thought bitterly.

The cold spell did not last and, within two days, the heat began building up, lying in wait for anyone who happened to leave the air-cooled hotel. Snow still glistened in high crevices, however. Michelle had learnt by now that at the altitude of the mountaineers' chalet, snow could fall in almost any month of the year and that frosts occurred, even in summer.

With the approaching week-end everyone wanted a set and she found herself completely occupied in her tiny salon.

Lyle Cunningham had driven up to the hotel in one of the Land-Rovers, one morning looking tanned in a safari suit. Breakfast was still being served and Michelle, whose first appointment was for nine o'clock, was standing outside on the steps leading to the foyer when he arrived. She had known that a Land-Rover was expected to take a party up the Pass, but was unprepared for the fact that Lyle would be driving the vehicle himself.

Too late to flee, she watched him get out of the Land-Rover and slam the door and then he came in the direction of the steps. 'Hello,' he said, joining her on the top one.

'Hello.' Her voice was abrupt.

'Enjoying the morning sunshine?' He permitted himself

86

the briefest of smiles.

'I'm due to do a light perm in a few minutes,' she told him.

'What have you been doing with yourself since I last saw you?' he asked her with a smile that was about as sarcastic as he could make it, she thought.

'I've been very busy,' she answered.

'Well, that makes two of us,' he replied, and went through into the foyer.

Long, hot days drifted by. Michelle was kept busy both at the salon and at the desk. The more she had to do the less time she had to brood on Lyle Cunningham, she told herself. She and Liza had little to say to one another. However, she was very friendly with Debbie, who confided that she, too, found Liza irritating and difficult to get along with. 'I don't trust Liza,' Debbie said one day. 'In my opinion, she keeps Glen Hayes informed as to what goes on here at the hotel. I actually heard her reading out the wording of our new brochure to him, the other day. I mean, what's it got to do with *him*?'

'Talking about the brochure,' Michelle said, 'have the photographers made a definite appointment with us? I'm thinking of the flower arrangements, as a matter of fact. Liza told me to see to them.'

'Yes, they have. They're coming on Thursday. They'll be here early in the morning and will leave again the following day.'

'I'll have to order the flowers, in that case,' said Michelle.

'I believe there's a new nursery about to open,' Debbie said, 'not so far from here. Have you heard?'

Michelle was feeling depressed. 'No, I haven't.'

'They'll be supplying flowers by air to florists all over. I suppose they'll be getting orders from us in the near future. It will save a lot of bother and fuss. I have known times when our flowers have failed to turn up because the plane couldn't land because of bad weather.'

'I'll order from our usual source,' Michelle replied, her mind on other matters. After a moment she asked, 'Why are we having a new brochure made?' She had been reading through an old one. 'These look okay to me.'

'But we've added on,' said Debbie, coming to stand next to her. 'Don't you see? Here's the new ladies' bar and here's the new sun-lounge.' Michelle watched Debbie's finger tracing where these additions had taken place. 'Apart from that there are a few alterations to make regarding the tariff and the excursions, by Land-Rover, up the Pass.'

The photographers duly arrived on the Thursday morning, along with an invitation to Michelle, Liza and Debbie to attend a party to be held at the luxurious film-set house rented by Lyle Cunningham.

CHAPTER SEVEN

THERE was an undertone of excitement in the hotel directly two photographers set up cameras and lighting in the foyer, and it was obvious even to the casual observer that several women were loitering there in the hopes of being photographed. As it so happened, however, lenses were aimed at a party who had just arrived with a whole lot of expensive tan leather luggage.

Throughout the morning, photography continued with a break on the main terrace for tea.

Michelle was kept busy in the salon and there was no time to help at the desk. Just before lunch, Cunningham Senior came along to the salon and, wondering what he wanted in this small woman's world, Michelle went over to where he stood in the doorway.

'Is there something you want?' she asked, pleasantly. 'Anything I can do for you, Mr. Cunningham?'

'I wondered if you would console the photographers with your company, after all that work, for a pre-lunch drink on the terrace? Liza will be there.' His eyes went to the two driers. 'How busy are you here, Michelle?'

'I'm just about finished here, before lunch.'

'You don't mind, then?'

'No, not at all.'

'It's just to put them at ease. They'll be going in to lunch soon after that and then finishing off with the photographs afterwards. As you know, they've been invited to spend the night here and are to attend the party at Lyle's house.'

'Well,' Michelle lifted one shoulder, 'I'm practically through now until after lunch, Mr. Cunningham. I'll be pleased to help out.'

'Good,' he smiled. How like Lyle he was, Michelle thought, meeting his eyes, or rather, how like his father Lyle was. 'That's fine,' he was saying. 'I'll be along myself for a moment or two, but if I know young fellows at all, they'll enjoy the company of a couple of attractive young ladies to themselves.'

Liza and Lyle's father were already on the terrace with the photographers by the time Michelle was able to get away from the salon. 'I'm sorry,' she looked at Cunningham Senior, 'but my customer's hair took so long to dry. I had to allow another ten minutes.' She smiled dutifully as the introductions were made.

A little later Lyle's father left them and there was the usual desultory conversation about the weather, holidaying in the Berg and the possibility of being confronted by a leopard while out climbing or walking.

Guests, lethargic after a morning of walking, climbing or swimming in the sparkling pool, lounged at nearby tables set about the terrace and conversation was punctuated by the clinking of glasses and occasional laughter.

Liza was called to the telephone and Michelle found herself alone with the two photographers. She was laughing at something one of them had said when Lyle Cunningham chose that moment to arrive on the scene. He would, Michelle thought with considerable resentment. She had been instantly aware of his blue-green eyes narrowing slightly directly he spotted her.

It took a lot of nerve on her part to remain there, casually sipping at her drink and trying to listen to the conversation about her with an attentive and interested air when all she longed to do was escape. It was a relief, therefore, to see Liza approaching the table.

'Well,' Liza looked directly at Lyle. 'May I join you?' The way in which she said this made it sound as if she had only just turned up, especially in view of the fact that her empty glass had already been removed by one of the stewards before Lyle arrived. Something in Liza's attitude caused Michelle to believe that the other girl had spoken this way on purpose in order to create the feeling that she had only just arrived on the scene.

At this stage Cunningham Senior joined them again and Michelle found herself trapped there until the party broke up for lunch.

'I'll be seeing you this evening,' Lyle looked at Liza. It was apparent that he was sharing a table at lunch with his father and the two photographers.

'Yes,' Liza answered, 'I'm looking forward to it.'

Michelle found herself tensing as Lyle turned to her. 'And you, of course. I'll be seeing you this evening, I take it?' He gave her a level, searching look. 'I take it you are coming?'

Because there was nothing else for it she murmured, 'Yes.'

'Michelle will be there. She *adores* cameramen, don't you Michelle?' said Liza, laughing lightly. Turning to the photographers, she said, 'By the way, you should have seen Michelle posing in her bikini in the snow recently. The Utah people were doing a short for the van Luit Wine people and they drove out into the thick of the snow – walked the last bit – carting along cameras, tripods, lunch trestles, food, wine – the lot! I wa's *longing* to go out and watch them shooting – I'd been invited, actually, but I was madly busy at the desk. However,' she smiled at Lyle, 'Lyle drove me out later on in the day, but by then, most of the fun had died down. Apparently there'd been a fabulous lunch and some kind of champagne orgy which was filmed. Anyway, there was Michelle – posing in a *bikini*, mind you, in all that snow . . .'

Michelle felt herself tensing, not knowing how to respond to Liza's spite, then she decided to play it cool. 'It would be absurd to say,' she broke off, laughing a little, 'that I wasn't cold.' She shivered prettily, 'I was, believe me. But it was worth it.'

'Yes – but then you had that gorgeous fur coat wrapped about you at the end, didn't you?' Liza gushed. 'What a pity you couldn't keep it, Michelle. I believe it was on loan from Dermot's?'

'I believe it – *they*, because there were two of them, Liza – I believe they were on loan. In any case, though, I wouldn't want to keep a fur coat.' Michelle tried to match Liza's tone. 'I happen to feel very strongly about animal fur.'

'Wouldn't you?' Liza shrugged. 'Well, that's a surprise.'

Trying to suppress the anger she was feeling, Michelle

said, 'Will you please excuse me?'

'Knowledge will bring the station-wagon to the front this evening,' said Lyle, 'and he'll collect the lot of you and drive you over to the house.' His smile was easy, but it was focused on Liza and the photographers. Then he turned to Cunningham Senior. 'And that goes for you too, Dad.'

From her room, Michelle was able to look down on the terrace. Liza was not there and the men had apparently decided on more drinks, before going through to the dining-room for lunch. Her mind became hostess to a seething mass of thoughts as she looked down on Lyle's dark head – and then she caught her breath as he looked up suddenly. The fact that he must have seen her at the window was humiliating and did nothing to soothe her feelings.

The afternoon was broken for her by the photographers invading her tiny salon. 'Where's your bikini?' she was teased. 'What about posing for us in your bikini?' The remarks were passed jokingly and meant nothing, but Michelle had to cling on to her temper.

'It doesn't necessarily mean that because I took part in a film wearing my bikini it must follow I do the same thing now,' she replied, somewhat snappily. 'I'll keep out of the way while you finish here – for I take it that you do want to photograph the salon?'

By the time she reached the desk she was seething with rage. Liza, who was alone, glanced up. 'Yes? Is there anything you want?' she asked.

'Yes, Liza, there is something. Would you mind dropping the subject about my little effort in the film? I find myself resenting your remarks, for the simple reason that they make me appear quite ridiculous.'

'What are you moaning for?' Liza's voice was hard, to match her eyes. 'You proved yourself a born performer.'

'I just don't happen to like being the victim of these silly little dining-out stories of yours, Liza. I'd rather you dropped the subject.'

'Certainly I'll drop the subject, but it still doesn't alter the basic facts, does it?' Liza stared coolly into Michelle's furious eyes.

'I have no regrets about posing, if that's what you mean,

I'm not ashamed of what I did, Liza. It was done for the experience and was a lot of harmless fun into the bargain. However, you're turning it, or are intent on turning it, into something nasty.'

'What gave you that impression?' Liza drawled.

'It was a smart decision on your part, wasn't it, to get Lyle Cunningham to drive you out to the film set? Just what were you hoping to achieve, Liza?'

'What I do and who I do it with has nothing whatsoever to do with you, Michelle,' Liza snapped.

'And that fits *two* ways, Liza. Please remember that.'

As she dressed for Lyle Cunningham's party Michelle was tense. There seemed little sense in throwing up her position here at the hotel just because of what had happened, but on the other hand, the entire set-up had changed. She no longer felt happy and, so far as Lyle Cunningham was concerned, she felt that she had never been subjected to a sharper appraisal.

Acting on an impulse, she decided to wear a beautiful gold silk caftan which she had bought in London just before leaving for South Africa. She had done this with golden sunlight in mind.

The silky folds, falling to the carpet, emphasized her slimness more than they disguised it. Her hair, almost the same colour as the material, cascaded to her shoulders.

Lyle Cunningham showed no evidence of pleasure at seeing her as she was shown, with the rest of the party, into the magnificent lounge. One of the photographers gave a low whistle. 'Too much,' he said, 'but this house is too much!'

As in the case of the party in Michelle's honour, there was a fair smattering of people present and the murmur of voices stopped only for a few seconds as new arrivals were being shown in by Usef.

Pete and Laney were already there and Michelle spotted them almost immediately. Before she could join them, however, Lyle was saying, 'Where's Dad?'

Surprised that he had asked her, and not Liza or Debbie, she said, 'He was detained at the last moment. He was waiting for a trunk call coming through. He said he would drive

93

himself over – later.'

'I see.' His eyes went over her.

Only a short while ago, she thought bitterly, she would have been flattered and pleased that he had referred to his father as 'Dad' to her. Now it meant nothing. So far as Lyle was concerned, just a slip of the tongue.

A buffet supper had been laid out in the dining-room which was divided from the conversation pit by means of an ornate wicker screen. The pink, gold and orange curtaining had been drawn to one side of wide windows to reveal a small but exciting white-walled garden where the exotic shrub leaves glinted in the lighting, which was concealed.

Guests mixed with the ease of the sophisticated.

'You're looking fabulous,' Laney whispered, as she and Michelle helped themselves to food, later on in the evening.

'Thank you, Laney. Do you like it?' Michelle inclined her head. 'I bought it in London just before I left. It seemed perfect for this kind of climate. In my wildest dreams, though, I didn't anticipate wearing it quite so soon and in such a fantastic house. I feel like a film star in it. It was worth all the money I paid for it, although I felt guilty at the time.'

There was a little silence before Laney said, 'Michelle, have you and Lyle Cunningham had a tiff?'

'A tiff?' Michelle tried her best to sound vague.

'Yes – you know, have you had words, a difference of opinion, an argument of some sort?'

'Of course not.' Michelle went on helping herself.

'He seems to be avoiding you and yet constantly aware of you, if you know what I mean,' Laney went on. 'And the same goes for you. You seem to be avoiding him and yet constantly aware of *him*.'

'You seem to forget that Lyle Cunningham is in a sense my boss, Laney.'

As though Laney had anticipated this answer and was ready for it she said, 'It's not that. I've been watching you both all evening – and into the bargain, Liza Monatti seems to be watching both of you. Now come on, what's it all in aid of?'

Michelle stopped serving herself so that she could look at Laney. 'I've heard that some women crave for all sorts of things to eat, Laney, when they're expecting an infant.' She laughed lightly. 'I can't help wondering whether you're developing an obsession for asking silly questions. Any more questions, Laney?'

'No, not any more.'

'Why not?'

'Because you've just answered *all* my questions, a moment ago,' Laney replied dryly. 'With your eyes.'

'Oh,' Michelle shook her head slowly and laughed, 'come off it, Laney! Look, I've been very busy at the hotel – busy in the salon and busy helping at the desk. I don't see all that much of Lyle Cunningham and we certainly haven't quarrelled.'

In the background, the murmur of voices and clinking of crockery and cutlery and glassware was like something on a soundtrack. 'It must have been very much like this when they were filming here,' Michelle tried to change the subject, 'don't you think, Laney?'

'Yes, it must have been, and in that fabulous caftan you're wearing you could be the main star. I'm going over to join Pete. Come along when you're finished here, Michelle.'

'All right. I won't be a moment.' Michelle went on helping herself, her face closed now and somehow immune to everything which was going on around her.

When Lyle Cunningham came to stand next to her she felt herself tensing. The crowd milling around the table had thinned. Michelle lifted her eyes, searching the room for Laney and Pete. 'That curry,' Lyle was saying, quite pleasantly, 'happens to be very hot. I hope you don't regret your choice of food.'

'I won't,' she turned to look at him. 'Besides, I'm always prepared to take a chance.' She spoke without thinking and flinched when he said, 'Yes, so I've noticed. That's something I've noticed about you, as a matter of fact.'

Preparing to move away from him, she said, 'Well, please don't worry yourself. I'm not.' She felt fury welling up inside her. Was he never going to give up over the bikini affair?

'By the way,' he began to follow her, 'you're looking very stunning. You could have been made for these rooms.'

'Thank you.'

'You appear to be looking for someone,' he went on, 'but if it happens to be Glen Hayes he hasn't arrived yet.'

'I'm not looking for Glen Hayes.'

'Oh, aren't you? I understood otherwise.'

Turning her head, she said, 'Is there any foundation for your belief that I might be looking for him?'

His mouth turned up faintly at one side. 'I'll be honest with you, Michelle. I only invited him because you were going to be here.'

Curiosity, rather than retaliation, was her motive now and she asked, 'Did you make it obvious to him that you were inviting him on these grounds?'

'Of course not. I never give a reason at the back of an invitation. However, I do give a lot of thought as to who I should ask – and why.'

'Well, perhaps, in this case, you've started something you can't finish. As you say,' her blue eyes swept the room and then, furious, they came back to his face, 'Glen Hayes hasn't turned up.'

'Don't settle on that.'

'And that's all that matters to you, isn't it?' she asked. 'That he *should* turn up and give you the satisfaction of watching to see what we get up to next.'

'That's where you're so wrong,' he told her. 'It's not the sort of game I play. I invited Glen Hayes here because you and he happen to be very friendly at the moment.' There was impatience in his voice.

'I see.' Michelle stared back at him. 'Well, I don't know what gave you that idea, but if this is what you choose to believe, well and good. In any case, Mr. Cunningham, we'll take it from there – the way *you* want it!'

She spotted Glen Hayes as she stood talking to several people she had been introduced to at the party which had been in her honour.

Glen had a glass in one hand and a plate with cold cuts and salads in the other. 'I think I know everybody here,' he said as he joined them. 'How's it, Bob? How's the farm?

Norma . . . hello there.' Eventually his tawny eyes came to rest on Michelle's face. 'And hello to *you*.' Behind the horn-rimmed glasses he wore his eyes moved over her with a kind of bored speculation. He went on chewing, where he had left off.

'Hello,' answered Michelle.

He came over to her. 'I just couldn't get here earlier,' he said, 'and that's a fact.' He looked around for a place to put his glass, then gave up. 'I can't help but wonder to what I owe the honour. I haven't been invited to the Cunningham mansion for some considerable time.'

'Presumably he has a reason,' Michelle's voice was tight. 'He usually has – or so he says.'

Glen laughed lightly. 'Well, actually, that fits two ways. I had my own reasons for accepting.' His eyes went over her. 'I might tell you, you were one of them. I'm also interested in some land *he* wants to buy – the more land I can buy up, the better. But,' he took a sip of his drink, 'why play around? It happens to be the farm belonging to your brother.'

Michelle felt herself go pale. 'My brother?'

'Yes. Didn't you know? Lyle Cunningham is trying to buy them out! Actually, there's been so much dilly-dallying going on that we – my partners and I – have bought another farm. I might go so far as to say a much better farm in that the house is beautiful and the grounds well established.' He pronounced it beaud-i-ful, drawing the word out. 'However, we're always interested in land, for the very simple reason that we have a lot of schemes up our sleeves. The Berg is opening up all the time. But don't tell me you didn't know?'

'I knew they were struggling,' she answered, 'and that there was a possible buyer at the back of things, but I didn't know that Lyle Cunningham was trying to buy them out.' She thought for a moment. 'Lyle had mentioned some land – adjacent to the hotel land, of course.'

'So?' Glen's voice was soft. 'The boundary of the hotel divides them.'

She drew in a long breath and kept it there for a long moment before releasing it. 'I'm a bit dazed, actually. He's supposed to be *such* a good friend of theirs.' Her voice was bitter. 'Laney said somebody was interested but that they'd decided *not* to sell.'

'Well, it couldn't have been me, at that stage. They don't know anything about my interest.'

'Who keeps you so well informed?' Michelle asked bluntly.

'Aha!' Glen grinned at her, his eyes mocking her from behind the lenses. He was, she thought, the kind of person who looked as though he wore glasses as a gimmick. 'That would be telling, wouldn't it?' He laughed softly, and something told her that he had been drinking before he turned up at the house. She watched him thoughtfully as he began searching for a place to put something and then, giving up, he lifted his glass to his lips while the plate of food, in his other hand, tilted dangerously.

'Take it easy,' he said, 'and relax. Why do you look so worried, Michelle, as you stand there wrapped in your silken folds?'

'It's the way I feel,' she replied curtly. As she turned away from him she saw that from across the room Lyle Cunningham was watching them.

'What have I done now?' Glen asked, laughing. He had put his glass on the floor at his feet and was busy eating from his plate, stopping to feel his teeth with his tongue every so often. 'Tell me, Michelle, what have I done, now, to make you cross?'

Because Lyle was watching them she laughed lightly. 'Nothing,' she told him. 'In fact, Glen, you've just put something *right* for me.' How could she have imagined herself in love with Lyle Cunningham? she asked herself bitterly. Suddenly she knew she didn't have to care any more about him.

'As soon as I've finished eating,' Glen was saying, his speech very slightly slurred, 'I'm going to dance with you, Michelle.'

Prolonging the next smile until she knew Lyle was looking, she said, 'Well, I hope you realize what you're in for.'

'That's what I mean.' He laughed softly. 'I *know* what I'm in for.'

'Let me take your plate for you,' she said. 'You're going to have an accident presently. Don't forget your glass, at your feet.'

'I won't,' he answered, bending down to pick it up. 'Next to women, Michelle, this is my other weakness.' He followed her to the table and when she had saved his plate from possible disaster said, 'Come on, let's go and dance.'

'I'm interested.' She kept her voice easy. 'Tell me, what had you planned to do with my brother's farm?'

'I'll show you one day. It's too late for that now. But if I do buy it I'll convert it into a luxury inn. What else?' He looked serious.

'But you have all those chalets. It doesn't make sense. Then there are one or two hotels in the vicinity at the moment – not to mention a couple of hotels at Thabana, if my memory serves me correct. Where do you expect to find people to occupy all these places – enough people, I mean?'

'Don't worry. Just *you* try getting in at the Berg during the school holidays and public holidays. It's virtually an impossibility. We could do with a whole lot more places, believe me. I aim to attract people.' He was still searching around in his mouth, his tongue busy amongst his teeth. With him, there was something sensual in the way he did this.

'At the moment I'm launching my own Land-Rover service.'

'So I understand,' she replied drily.

'At special tariffs – cut-throat prices.'

'What's all this about cut-throat prices?' Liza's voice cut in, and a shiver of shock passed through Michelle when she saw that Liza was with Lyle Cunningham. 'What are you and Michelle discussing special tariffs for?'

'We're sure to tell you,' Glen replied easily. 'This happens to be our secret.' He glanced at Lyle. 'I was just saying a moment ago that it's some time since I paid you a visit.'

'I'm pleased you could come,' Lyle answered.

'I wouldn't have missed it for anything – even if I *was* late,' Glen laughed. 'I've just asked Michelle to dance with me.'

'Well, don't let us keep you,' Liza said sweetly.

Michelle allowed Glen to lead her in the direction of the patio and on to the ceramic-tiled floor. The swimming-pool glinted not far from it. 'Good,' Glen whispered against Michelle's hair, 'the blues, played by Duke Ellington and Johnny Hodges. So romantic!'

They danced in silence for a while and then he said, 'I've been out with the bowlers all day.'

Suddenly she laughed. 'Don't tell me you play bowls!'

'Why not?'

'You just don't look the type.'

'I'll tell you something – I'm not, but I've been drinking with them, most of the afternoon. Those are the kind of duties a chalet owner has to perform from time to time. In other words, I have to mix.'

A warm bronze moon was rising above the trees. There was a splash as someone dived into the pool – followed by another splash.

Some time later Michelle got separated from Glen Hayes and found herself involved with other people. Pete and Laney had gone home because Laney was feeling tired, she said.

Directly Cunningham Senior turned up at the party he asked Michelle to dance and when they were on the patio he smiled down at her. 'I wasn't being fair in asking you to dance with me, Michelle, but I knew you'd be patient with me. I'm not very good at this sort of thing – not any more. I always feel I must show up at some of Lyle's parties, though, mostly given in the interest of the business.'

'I'm glad you did ask me,' she smiled back. Lyle's father was still an extremely good-looking man – tall and lean, with a good tan, clean-shaven face and that fabulous silver hair. Any girl would be proud to be seen with him. Michelle was honest enough to admit to herself that she was not sure whether she was pleased that he had asked her to dance with him merely to show that he had turned up at the party. She told him this, laughing a little, and he took it in good part, laughing down into her face. As he did so, she was reminded of her feelings towards his son.

By the time the music ended they discovered that they

were the only two on the floor and somebody was clapping. 'Nice work,' Lyle was saying, coming towards them and still clapping. 'I can see you also have Dad under your spell.'

Michelle felt suddenly hot and exhausted. 'You finally made it, then?' Lyle was looking at his father. 'Better late than never, I suppose. What do you say, Michelle?'

'I agree with you,' she answered in a polite little voice.

'What held you up?' Lyle turned to his father again.

'I was expecting a trunk call and then I got involved — you know the way it is. Anyway, I'd like to get back, if you don't mind.'

'Mr. Cunningham,' Michelle said quickly, 'could I go back with you? I don't think I'll stay on, if you don't mind.' She turned to look at Lyle. 'I'm feeling rather exhausted.'

'I do mind, very much.' He bullied her with those blue-green eyes of his. 'Stay a little while longer, then I'll take you back myself.'

'That's more like it,' Cunningham Senior said, smiling. 'After all, you're only young once, Michelle. I've just found that out.' He smiled, puffing elaborately.

Michelle made a gesture which showed her reaction after Lyle's father had gone. 'I wanted to go,' she said, 'but short of — of causing embarrassment all round, there was nothing I could do about it.'

'I'll tell you something — you don't look exhausted.' His smile was without amusement.

'Well, I am,' she answered in a furious little voice. 'It's a state of mind that goes with the stupid situation I happen to find myself in right now.' She had the frustrated feeling that she might as well be talking to herself.

Ignoring her remark, Lyle said, 'You will have a Martini with me and then I'll drive you back to the hotel. All right?'

'All right,' she replied, 'but it doesn't mean I'm going to be pleasant about it.'

'I doubt if you *could* be pleasant lately, Michelle.'

Most of the guests were in the pool and Lyle led the way to the conversation pit, which was empty, except for a couple who were standing talking near the indoor fountain.

Michelle watched him as he went to pour their drinks and when he came back he said, 'Sit down, Michelle.'

'Is this an order?' she asked.

'What are you talking about?' he snapped. 'Do *you* know what you're talking about?'

'You're running true to type,' she told him, but she sat down and nestled against some of the brilliantly hued cushions.

He passed her the Martini, then lowered himself beside her.

Outside, the sound of people diving into the pool made a peculiar hollow and pounding noise as the water broke apart and closed again. There was the thump, thump of feet chopping the water.

Michelle waited for him to say something. Their eyes met: 'Where did Hayes get to?' he asked.

'I don't know,' she answered. There were a lot of empty glasses and small plates with scraps of savouries on them and Lyle began to move them to one side, and she was surprised to see that his hand was shaking slightly.

Her eyes brooded on him, then she said, 'If you're embarrassed on my account, because he's apparently left, please don't be. Until you spoke I hadn't even missed him.' There was an undertone of irritation in her voice. The feelings she had for this man she hardly knew did not make sense. Right from the beginning, he had had the power to excite her. Now, however, she was disappointed in him. All that was over. After what Glen Hayes had told her tonight, she felt she despised Lyle Cunningham.

'I find our attitude lately rather disconcerting,' Lyle was saying. 'I'd like to get to the bottom of it. I'm quite aware of the fact that I was rude to you over the film, but I thought things might be running their course by now.'

'Oh, they are. Believe me, they are.' Her voice was bitter.

'Just what do you mean by that?' he asked.

'If it really bothers you, why don't you just sit back and think about it?' She turned her head away so that he would not see the tears which threatened to well up in her eyes.

'That doesn't answer my question, Michelle.'

'It does answer your question, if you think about it.' She knew she should stop talking before she lost her temper completely and said things which would cost her her job, and she didn't want to lose that – not right now, anyway. Not when the farm (who were Pete and Laney to pit their feeble financial strength against the great Cunninghams?) and her own affairs were at the lowest ebb, so far as money was concerned. She needed her salary and she also needed to be near to Laney who was expecting her first child and needed her. It was as simple as that.

'I'd like to ask you a question,' Lyle broke into her thoughts.

'Go ahead.'

'You may not like this.'

'Ask it anyway.'

'What is Glen Hayes to you?'

'I'm not going to answer that,' she told him.

'Why not, Michelle?'

'For the very simple reason that it would get me into the kind of talk you want us to get into. But you could say that Glen Hayes is the same as Liza is to you – if you wanted to. It makes no difference to me.'

'Right away, we have a disagreement on our hands,' he said.

'Stop trying to trap me!' She met his glance full on for a moment, then glanced away. 'May we go now?' she asked, her face still turned from him. 'I'm not in a very good mood right now.'

'Well, I'm open to suggestion. Perhaps we can rectify that – put matters right between us?' He took an impatient breath. 'How long are we going to keep this up, Michelle?'

She remained silent, then he said, 'All I ask is that you meet me half-way.' He sounded exasperated.

There were still splashing noises coming from the pool and although there was music, nobody was dancing on the patio.

Suddenly Michelle stood up. 'I'd like to leave now,' she said. 'I shouldn't have stayed in the first place.'

'Don't push me too far, Michelle.'

'What do you mean by that?' she asked angrily. 'Haven't I a perfect right to say when I've had enough? I want to go back to the hotel. If you aren't going to take me there, I'll walk.'

'What's happened to make you like this – quite apart from the filming episode?' He sounded puzzled and annoyed. 'I refuse to accept that there's nothing more to it than that.'

'If it bothers you so much,' she said, 'why don't you take time off, some time, to sit down and think about it?'

'I find you totally baffling,' he told her.

'I think I could say the same of you. But I can't think why you should find me baffling. *I* have no secrets.'

'What do you mean by that?' he asked.

'Just work it out.'

After a moment Lyle said quietly, 'I'll take you back now, Michelle.'

'Thank you,' she replied in a small voice. She knew that when she got back to her room at the hotel she was going to cry.

CHAPTER EIGHT

MICHELLE's way of defending herself against Lyle Cunningham was to carry on with her position at the hotel as though nothing had happened and to work things so that, whenever he happened to be around, he found her flirting with any man who happened to be present on the other side of the reception desk.

Several of these meaningless flirtations also took part on the telephone should she be talking to one of the drivers from Little Switzerland Motors about booking a Land-Rover to take guests up the Pass.

The expression on Lyle's face, whenever he happened to see the intricate smiles and blinking of lashes on her part, was enough to reward her. If he chose to misunderstand her she would give him something to misunderstand her about! Lyle Cunningham had made up his mind about her when he saw her posing in the snow in a bikini and, so far as he was concerned, that was that. No matter what he had said about 'finding her attitude rather disconcerting' and admitting that he was rude to her over the film, but was now of the opinion that 'things might be running their course', the fact was he had insulted her whenever the opportunity presented itself. In the first place, he had tried to trap her, with his questions and sly remarks, about Glen Hayes, not to mention his sarcasm when he had discovered her dancing with his father. 'I can see you also have Dad under your spell,' he had said, coming towards them, clapping his hands. Michelle found herself seething every time she thought about it.

Looking at Lyle Cunningham sometimes, she was staggered at his treachery and wondered what Pete and Laney would think about their very good friend if someone had to tell them that he was trying to buy them out. In view of the fact that they had decided not to sell the farm – not yet, anyway – she had decided to keep this information to herself. It was no good stirring up trouble at this time when a baby was on its way.

The days were long and hot and guests arrived back from walks exhausted and red-faced and more than ready for a bath or a shower and drinks, on the terrace, before lunch or dinner.

There had been several Land-Rover trips up the Pass, and once the passengers had been guests from the chalets; it was Glen Hayes who had made the arrangements, speaking to Michelle because she happened to be at the desk at the time. He had asked when he was to see her again and she had replied that she was very busy and was seeing a lot of her brother and sister-in-law in her spare time.

On one occasion Lyle Cunningham had driven a party up the Pass himself, and as she watched the Land-Rover leave the hotel Michelle had found herself more than just a little envious. Lyle had looked handsome and there was the kind of tanned strength about him which made her know, instinctively, that he would be a superb driver. He certainly did not look the cad she knew him to be.

A few days later she happened to be helping at the desk when Jake Gobbi phoned about a trip the following day. While Michelle was discussing the matter with him she glanced up to see Lyle Cunningham walk into the foyer where he stood talking to Cunningham Senior.

On the phone Jake was saying, 'What's this I hear about your salon being closed?'

'Only for two days,' she told him, smiling elaborately – for Lyle's benefit. 'There's a wallpaper man coming from Durban.'

'Well, what are *you* doing, then?'

'I'm helping out here, as you can hear.' She kept her lashes and her voice down in an effort to make the call appear to be very confidential, but she was, nevertheless, aware that Lyle's eyes were resting on her face as he continued his discussion with his father.

'Why not get permission to come up with us, in the morning?' Jake asked cheerfully, oblivious of the fact that Michelle's smiling voice was solely for the benefit of Lyle Cunningham.

'I'll have to see.' She lifted her lashes. Cunningham

Senior had left the foyer, but Lyle was still there, reading a letter.

'Surely you're not all that scared?' Jakes voice teasing. Michelle felt ashamed, suddenly. Although Jake meant nothing to her, she had often used him when Lyle was around, smiling into the mouthpiece and laughing softly at everything Jake had to say.

'Of course not. Everybody seems to get back safely – even with you driving,' she teased back.

'Well, let's make it tomorrow.' He was silent for a moment. 'There's a place for you in the Land-Rover.'

'Yes, I know there's room for me.' Her eyes scanned the names on the list before her.

'Are their papers in order?' Jake asked. 'I don't want to get half-way and find that somebody is without. What about vaccination certificates?'

'I've checked, Jake.' Out of the corner of her eye she could see Lyle Cunningham speaking to Liza now and Liza had begun searching around in the drawers of one of the filing cabinets. 'Everything is in order.'

'Well,' Jake went on, 'you've been vaccinated, and I don't know what, inoculations against this and inoculations against that. Right?'

'Right.'

'Well, shall we take that as settled, then?' Jake coughed and then came back on the line. 'Sorry. Anyway, I'm sure you'll be able to get away. After all, they're doing out your salon, aren't they?'

'Yes. I'll put my name down, on the off-chance. There, it's down, Jake. Are you satisfied?' she laughed lightly.

'I don't want you backing out at the last moment,' Jake said.

'I won't back out. All right, then. I'll see you tomorrow, Jake. Good-bye for now.'

As she replaced the receiver Lyle Cunningham looked up and greeted her stiffly and she noticed the flicker of interest in his eyes before she began checking figures again.

She had known perfectly well that she was in a position to accept Jake's challenge because, in any case, had the trip up the Pass not cropped up she had intended driving into Thabana in the morning and she was not expected to help at reception in the afternoon.

'Michelle,' Liza said in a loud voice, 'I wish you'd warned me that you and Jake Gobbi were finally drawing your long, intimate chat to an end. I wanted to speak to him about those spare parts for the station-wagon.'

Michelle took a breath while she calmed herself. 'I'm sorry,' she said, 'I didn't know you wanted to speak to him.'

'That's ridiculous – of course I mentioned it. Anyway, let's not waste any more time. Are those figures ready for the adding machine?'

'Yes, they are.' Michelle's voice was very quiet. How baffling Liza Monatti was! There always seemed to be a lot of hostility behind her words and the expression of those dark eyes – especially if Lyle Cunningham happened to be within earshot.

Coming over to the desk, Lyle asked, 'What parts are those, Liza?'

It was a moment before Michelle could trust herself to continue working, although she made a pretence of writing something down on a small jotter. Had she been imagining it? Had she detected Lyle's annoyance and, if so, was he annoyed with her – or with Liza's abrupt manner?

Glancing in Michelle's direction, Lyle said, 'Was Jake talking about tomorrow's trip up the Pass?' There was challenge in the question.

'Yes,' she replied. She hoped her face showed nothing. 'He was just checking.'

'I see.'

As she waited on the arrival of the Land-Rover the next morning she felt tense and apprehensive. She had heard so many stories about this trip up the Pass that her heartbeats quickened when she saw the rest of the party – two girls and two men. They were obviously a foursome who were out for kicks. To Michelle they looked the type, especially the girls, who would cheer Jake Gobbi on if he did decide to show off a little. They would dare him on with their laughter and their brashness.

The Land-Rover drew up at the foot of the shallow steps

leading to the foyer and Michelle went outside to greet Jake, and caught her breath sharply as Lyle Cunningham jumped down from the vehicle and took the steps two at a time. His eyes swept over Michelle and then, beyond her, to the foyer where the rest of the party was waiting. Stunned that he was going to drive the Land-Rover himself, she stared at him in disbelief before she pulled herself together.

'Well,' he said, 'I take it we're all set to go? Come through to the foyer, Michelle, while I check for necessary documents.'

She found herself doing as he said and then stood watching as Lyle examined the travel documents, which included passports. When he came to her he said, 'May I see your vaccination certificate?' His eyes dropped to her bag which she had not opened.

'I'm not sure about going up,' she told him in a voice that was not quite steady. 'I really haven't made up my mind.'

'No?' There was scorn in his voice. 'But you arranged with Jake, didn't you?'

'Yes, but . . .'

'And you've paid, haven't you?'

'Yes, I have. But I'm not sure I want to go. As I've just told you, I haven't really made up my mind about going up.'

Lyle's face altered, but he merely said, 'I see.' There was a slight pause, then he went on, 'In that case, allow me to make it up for you. You're booked to go on this trip and so you'll go.'

'I was expecting Jake.'

'That means – what?'

She met his hostility with silence and then he said, 'Jake had to go off somewhere else – at the last moment. I'm standing in for him. This is a kind of routine with us.' His eyes swept over her. 'Satisfied, Michelle?'

Without a word she opened her bag and took out the necessary papers and handed them to him, then watched while he went to the counter and looked through them, along with the others which had been handed to him at the last moment.

Moodily, Michelle's eyes followed two members of the

kitchen staff carrying out the food hampers which were to travel in the Land-Rover up to the Mountaineers' Chalet situated just inside the Lesotho border – the highest licensed hotel in Africa. The hampers would be handed in at the kitchen at the Chalet where they would be opened up and the food prepared for lunch by the staff there.

After handing back all the other documents Lyle came back to her and held out her papers which she put into her bag. As their eyes met she felt herself flooded with longing for him and she immediately loathed herself. 'Have you brought something warm to wear?' he asked, his eyes going over her. 'You'll need something warmer than that by the time you get up top.'

'I have something in here,' she told him, holding out her spacious bag. She stared back at him from beneath the brim of her black linen sun hat.

'Good. It can be bitter up there.'

'So I'm told.'

'Your mood can be seen in those blue eyes,' he said. 'Sometimes you're so transparent.'

'Really? And yet you find me totally baffling.'

'Too bad Jake Gobbi couldn't make it,' he laughed lightly, 'but it happens sometimes.'

Michelle had herself under control now. 'Especially if *you* have anything to do with it?'

At that moment one of the girls of the party came up to them. 'What kind of driver are you?' she giggled. 'Good, I hope?'

'Terrible.' Lyle's voice was mocking, then he laughed dutifully as the girl shrieked, 'Oh – noooo!'

'But I've learned not to show it,' he added, for her benefit.

'Tell me,' the other girl sauntered up, 'how are the brakes? The reports I've heard about this trip are enough to make my hair stand on end.'

Playing up to them, Lyle smiled, 'Don't you worry about it. Leave the worrying to me.'

From behind the desk, Liza Monatti gave Michelle a hard look.

The seating arrangement sorted itself out the moment

they went out to the Land-Rover. Immediately the party of four climbed into the back and Michelle found herself having to occupy the front seat with Lyle, even though there was room for her at the back. She was quick to notice the flicker of amusement in Lyle's glance as he opened the door for her.

The Sani Pass, she discovered, appeared to have been hacked out of the terrifying mountains, leaving a roughly scarred wound, and right from the start, the noise was deafening as the Land-Rover rattled and shook itself over corrugations and boulders, but the going was easy and the thick tyres ate up the road.

So far, Michelle thought, beginning to relax, it was nothing like the film which she had seen at the hotel. In fact, it was fun.

Over and above the engine and rattling noises the girls in the back shrieked and giggled and there were hoots of laughter from the men. However, they remained quiet and interested every time Lyle explained points of interest. 'Let me know,' he had to shout to make himself heard, 'if you want to take photographs and I'll stop and you can get out.'

Loose sand was licked up by the tyres, and left a plume of dust behind and almost obliterated everything from sight. A lot of it found its way along with the stifling heat, into the Land-Rover. The vibration inside the vehicle increased, if that was possible.

They were climbing steadily and there was a lot of gear work. In the distance, the mountain peaks were blue and slashed with snow in those places which never saw the sun. The bends in the dusty track were becoming more frequent now and, often, Lyle hooted as he approached them.

Sitting beside him and trying to hear what he was saying, as he kept up a kind of commentary for the benefit of his passengers about the history of the Pass, Michelle looked at his vibrating tanned hands and accepted that the physical attraction she felt towards Lyle Cunningham was overwhelming. Her thoughts went to the time he had helped her to buy her Mini – everything had seemed so right then. Her mind came back with a jolt as the Land-Rover skidded and the girls in the back shrieked and laughed loudly, clinging to their boy-friends. Michelle looked over her shoulder and laughed too, but Lyle, his eye wonderfully blue-green and alive, scanned the track for more potholes, although he seemed utterly relaxed behind the wheel.

'I'm immensely thrilled,' one of the girls was shouting. 'I love this senseless speed – so reckless over this crazy track. I'm so glad we came. I wouldn't have missed this for anything!'

'The chances that we reach the top are improving all the time,' Lyle called back, and then suddenly Michelle knew the journey was just beginning.

The rock faces were ominously near. She was alert to danger. It all seemed so carefree and yet she knew that the possibility of skidding and going over the side of the track – rolling down, down, down, was highly possible. Lyle's tanned hands on the wheel were strong and capable and it was amazing to see that his fingers rested only lightly there. One would have expected them to be tightly clenched so that the knuckles showed up whitely.

For all that, however, she had to struggle to convince herself that the speed Lyle was travelling was not outrageous.

A trickle of fear went down her spine as she saw the cab of a truck in the distance, where it had rolled down. Turning briefly to look at her, Lyle said, 'That was caused by a rockfall only seven and a half months ago. The truck was hit by a boulder. There's the other part of it, down there.'

'It's getting steadily worse,' she said. 'I'm scared to look out – the wheels actually seem to be hanging over space.'

'They are.' His smile was mocking.

The Land-Rover skidded again and she watched him fight for control, wrenching the wheel, and when the moment was over, he turned to grin at her. They appeared to be hanging in the air one moment, Michelle thought, or making for the side of a mountain the next. The huge tyres bit into the boulders on the track jolting the passengers in the Land-Rover unmercifully.

Proteas, clinging to the mountainsides, flashed past. Wild flowers, scarlet beneath the sun and undefeated by the dust, blazed back their colour.

Lyle was giving his full attention to the hair-raising bends, almost jockeying the Land-Rover as he raised himself slightly from the seat.

Suddenly he braked sharply and brought the Land-Rover to a halt, then opening the door on his side, he jumped out on to the track.

'Ooh, look! He has a snake,' one of the girls screamed.

In a moment they had all joined Lyle and stood looking at the snake which he had caught and dropped into one of his socks. 'You must have got that sock off pretty quick, man!' Everybody laughed as the young man made this statement. 'What do you intend doing with it?'

'They make very good pets,' Lyle answered. His mocking blue-green eyes went to Michelle. 'It's a skaapsteker.'

He went to the door on the driver's side which was hanging open, and put the sock with the snake in it in the flap on the inside.

'Don't tell me we're going to travel with a snake in the Land-Rover?' one of the girls said loudly.

'He's quite safe there. Besides, if he escapes he'll bite me first,' Lyle answered, still in the same mocking tone.

'Why do you want it?' the girl persisted and, irritated, Michelle found herself asking the same question. Was Lyle doing this on purpose? she wondered. Was he trying to make her nervous as she sat there in front with him, so near to the snake?

'I don't want it. I want it for someone else who has a private snake park. I often catch them.' Immediately he seemed to forget about the snake. 'Here's a chance to take some more photographs. You're lucky, those packhorses are approaching just at a convenient moment.'

Now that they had stopped it seemed very quiet, apart from the laughter and conversation of the girls and their escorts, who had started to take photographs.

Lyle went to lean against the Land-Rover, crossed his ankles, crossed his arms and said softly, 'So? Have you nothing to say to me, Michelle?'

There were cooling down noises, now, coming from beneath the bonnet of the Land-Rover.

'Aren't you asking for trouble?' she asked. 'I can't say I relish the idea of travelling with that snake in the front of the Land-Rover.'

'It's quite safe there,' he told her, smiling. 'It's not the first time I've had a snake as a passenger.'

Michelle's eyes dropped to his feet. 'One sock on and one sock off. I'm surprised you don't carry a – a little bag or something with you for this sort of thing.'

'That's an idea.' His smile was mocking.

She started to take off her jersey. There was the hot smell of oil and simmering metal as the Land-Rover baked in the hot sun. 'You'll begin to need that jersey when we get going again,' Lyle said.

'I'm boiling hot. It doesn't seem possible that I'll need it.'

They fell silent and Michelle watched a lizard dancing on a rock. Thinking about the snake, she began to feel irritated. 'Don't you catch lizards, too?' she asked, with sarcasm in her voice. 'You could put it on *my* side of the Land-Rover, just to make things really zing for me. Why only *partly* destroy my peace of mind?'

He gave her an easy look. 'Why all this falling apart?' he asked. 'Are you really so nervous of a snake? You didn't particularly strike me as nervous the day I saw you frolicking in the snow with a sheer drop to the valley below – only metres away.' His voice had an edge of ridicule to it.

'I don't want to hear a remark like that again.' She spoke with frustrated annoyance. 'I already know your opinion of my character, so you don't have to go into detail. All I've said is that I happen to be nervous just knowing that there's a snake in the front seat – I mean in the front of the Land-Rover – with me.'

'It's on my side,' he mocked her.

'Well, see that you keep it there.'

'If that's the way you feel about it.'

'It is.'

The others came back and they climbed into the Land-Rover and got going again.

Nothing was too small for Lyle to point out – a brilliant bird on a rock, a sparkling waterfall and, later, a frozen waterfall in a dark crevice. He also kept up a kind of good-natured running commentary with information regarding the Sani Pass. Even from her position in the front of the Land-Rover Michelle found it difficult to hear him over the noise of rattling, flying stones and groaning engine noises.

The huge spare tyre on the bonnet steadily collected more and more dust. Colossal boulders loomed up as the Land-Rover approached the hairpin bends. Being in the front seat Michelle was able to notice all these things more and she also nursed her fear of the snake, glancing in the direction of the flap on the inside of the door on Lyle's side.

Once again Lyle stopped so that the party in the back could get out and take more photographs. 'Would you like to get out?' he asked her.

Outside, there was a strong wind now, laced with cold, and reaching for her bag Michelle said, 'You were right, I'll need a jersey.'

'I'm usually right,' he replied easily.

'I couldn't help but notice,' she said, 'you didn't put your hand-brake on.'

'It isn't working,' he told her, and she studied his eyes for mockery. Was it that he wanted to see her nervous and unhappy today just because he was at the wheel and not Jake Gobbi? 'But in any case,' Lyle went on, 'it does happen to be in gear.'

'Thank you for that,' she answered sarcastically. After a moment she said, 'All the same, it could run back, couldn't it? I mean, it is so steep.'

'I think that's unlikely – but,' he shrugged, 'it's a possibility.' He reached over and opened the door on her side and Michelle got out and immediately began to shrug herself into her jersey. Then she walked round the Land-Rover and went to the edge of the track on the other side where she tucked her hands, thumbs out, in the pockets of the white denim jeans she was wearing and surveyed the Pass. The wind caught at her linen hat and sent it flying and she ran to retrieve it, the wind blowing her hair about her face.

The Pass writhed its way up to where they had stopped and then continued up and up, to where they still had to go. The mountains over and around it ruled it, ever threatening it with their landfalls and the unpredictable weather conditions which they constantly drew towards them.

It took cool courage, she thought, to be a driver of one of these vehicles and courage – or plain pig-headedness – to be a passenger in one when there was really no need. She was acutely aware of the possibility of an accident and her face was serious as, moodily, her eyes rested on the two girls who were spending more time giggling and getting in the way than posing for photographs.

There was the sound of an engine some time before another Land-Rover, labouring and protesting and packed full of Basotho men, came into sight. Behind it there was the inevitable plume of dust. No wonder they had called the film *A Plume of Dust*!

High up the peaks stood remote from them, like a maze of minarets and towers – aloof, unsmiling, ageless, lonely, isolated and waiting for them with their wind and their cold and the snow in the crevices where the sun couldn't reach. She felt another sudden surge of fear.

Lyle came to stand beside her and she did not turn. 'What did you expect when you so flippantly made your arrangements with Jake Gobbi?' he asked softly.

Shaking back her hair, she said, 'This is exactly what I expected, as a matter of fact.'

They both eased over and turned to look at the Land-Rover, carrying the Basotho men, as it approached and then groaned past the stationary Land-Rover, which Lyle had pulled right on to the side, with absolutely no room to spare. The groaning vehicle was boiling, the squat bonnet half hidden beneath a cloud of white vapour.

'Well then,' said Lyle, 'what's the problem, Michelle?'

'I have no problem.' She turned to look at him and gestured and the gesture took in the whole scene. 'My so-called flippant arrangements were no more flippantly made than those of the two girls – over there. But in any case, if there's one thing I don't need right now, it's a whole lot of sarcasm.' The fact that he was in a sense her boss did not bother her now.

'Are you as nervous as all that?'

'I'm not particularly nervous. It's a fantastic experience

and I'm not oblivious to the fact that it has its dangers. It's not that – I happen to resent a few things, that's all.'

'For instance?'

The other Land-Rover had stopped further up and a man was pouring water over the steaming bonnet, presumably to cool it down, Michelle thought. She noticed that Lyle's blue-green eyes were watching him moodily and then they came back to her face. 'For instance?' he said again.

'Well – that snake, for instance.' She took a deep, almost shuddering breath. 'Then there are the barbed remarks you keep aiming at me and the reckless speed you're keeping up.'

At that he laughed outright. 'Speed? What speed? You want to wait until we're on the way down before you talk about speed!'

'I meant further back – before we actually started on this tortuous climb. Apart from that, there's all this – this – playing up, on your part.'

'Playing up? Does that mean what I think it does?'

'Yes. You once mentioned that the storms here enjoy being the whole floor show – something like that, anyway. Well, I hate to see and hear somebody trying to be the whole floor show when it happens to be at someone else's expense. I feel you're doing your best to create nervousness on the part of your passengers – or rather on my part.'

'Has it ever struck you that I might just happen to know what I'm doing?' His tone was angry.

'Oh . . .' she sighed impatiently, 'is it so important?'

'Yes, I think it is.' His blue-green eyes were angry.

The wind whined and whistled across the mountains. Shivering a little, she said, 'By the time we get back, *if* we get back, I wouldn't want to live through this trip again.'

'I see,' he said, and that was all.

The photographers and their girls were making their way back to the Land-Rover the wind whipping their hair. 'I was beginning to think there were no challenges left in life,' one of the girls was saying, breathlessly. 'Honestly, this is a super, super trip. The only thing I've got to moan about is,' she laughed and slanted her eyes at Lyle, 'that you're not going fast enough, man!' She was stylishly off-beat.

Michelle had heard the others calling her Marie.

'Before you form an opinion,' Lyle answered with a meaningful smile, 'wait until the down trip. We're climbing now, or have you overlooked the fact?'

'I haven't overlooked anything,' Marie grinned back cheekily. 'I'll keep you to your word – coming down, don't worry.'

'You won't have to.' Michelle thought she could detect annoyance in his voice, controlled though it was. 'However, I'd better just put you wise – it's never been easy to make me do anything I didn't want to do. Okay?' His voice was pleasant again. His eyes mocked the situation. 'All set? Jump in, then.'

Higher up the Pass, the Land-Rover had cooled off a little and the radiator had been topped with water. In their colourful blankets and mealie-straw hats, looped at the top, the Basotho men were climbing back in. Lyle gave the signal to the driver that he would follow him.

Immediately Michelle felt her nerves begin to tighten. Would the vehicle in front of them stall and run backwards, crashing into them before anyone knew what was happening? Tense and apprehensive, she wished Lyle would not keep as close to it as he did. Their own Land-Rover seemed to be groaning in agony, a noise which was transmitted directly to Michelle's shrieking, protesting nerves. Why couldn't she relax and enjoy herself, she thought bitterly, like the others?

At last they reached the security base where there was a notice reading, NO VEHICLE WHICH IS NOT EQUIPPED WITH FOUR-WHEEL DRIVE MAY PROCEED BEYOND THIS POINT WITHOUT THE PRIOR APPROVAL OF THE ADMINISTRATOR OF NATAL.

There was a general disembarking and a showing of papers and they were away again, the Land-Rover bearing the straw-hatted Basothos following this time. The Land-Rover bounced, rattled and shook over a causeway of boulders and past a cave which seemed to be jutting out in their path – until you got there and saw that the track swerved abruptly past it.

Once again Lyle stopped to point out a waterfall, although they did not get out of the Land-Rover.

There was a new roughness to the mountains now and the air was rare. The girls in the back were quieter as the vehicle moved forward and began to climb, roaring and protesting its way through watery, boulder-filled beds only to wrench itself around hairpin bends. The ground on the one side began to fall away and the speed of the Land-Rover slackened off alarmingly. Michelle was terrified that they were going to slip back and gather speed as the vehicle hurtled backwards, completely out of control.

Three mountain rhebok bounded across the road in front of them, with rocking-horse action, showing the white undersides of their tails, and were soon lost from sight as they disappeared into the bush. The thick woolly coats of the animals blended beautifully with their environment and Lyle stopped the Land-Rover for a moment or two, and the sharp, coughing sound of the rhebok could easily be heard. And then once again they were able to see the animals as they fled up the mountain, their fluffy tails held erect.

Although it was hot in the Land-Rover there was every evidence that it was cold outside and growing colder by the minute as they advanced up the Pass.

At times, Lyle's entire body seemed to gather itself together as he basically stood up to reverse backwards and then forwards again to take the hairpin bends, the steering wheel seemingly to spin beneath his fingers as he manipulated this feat.

There were more things of interest to see – some huts, half buried beneath an avalanche, a water tank washed down by floods. 'This is known by the Basothos,' Lyle had almost to shout above the noise, 'as the place that eats people.'

The snow in the crevices of the mountains appeared to be thick. Far down in the valley there were the carcases of vehicles that had not been able to make the grade and had gone plunging downwards.

In the back of the Land-Rover the girls were going wild again as Lyle gave all his attention to getting round a bend which seemed to be hanging against the mountainside.

'Whew! We made it!' they screamed, laughing.

'That's Gray's Corner,' Lyle told them, 'known by the local Basothos as Grace Corner, and when asked why, they explain that it's "only by the Grace of God that you get round it". I think that about sums it up.'

Gears screaming now, they were on the last lap. The Land-Rover battled up and up. Far below, down in the valley, the wrecks could still be seen if you dared to look back. The air became even thinner and more bracing. Behind was the vast panorama of the plains of Natal, opening out in a vista of limitless mountains and valleys. At last they levelled out. They were at the top. A notice board loomed up . . . 9,400 ft. Alt. SANI PASS, and Michelle felt her stomach muscles release their hold on the walls of her stomach. A long sigh escaped her lips. Lyle turned his head and gave her an easy smile. 'Thank goodness!' she said.

At the gates a blanketed man with a wooden peg-leg offered to sell them a straw hat.

After the necessary papers had been presented to the authorities they drove to the mountain chalet where they were welcomed by two exuberant cross St. Bernard dogs who quite obviously knew Lyle. The wind was nothing short of freezing and everybody had added yet another jersey. 'You'll find the pub open,' Lyle told them. 'Do feel free to go along while I attend to one or two things. I'm sure a drink will be more than welcome.'

Immediately he had given this right-away the foursome went into the chalet, taking their noisy laughter and chatter with them. Uncertain and tense, Michelle remained standing, holding out her fingers to the large dogs.

'Go and order yourself a drink, Michelle. Don't stay out here in the cold.'

'I'll go in presently.' She did not look at him.

'Go in now.' His voice was curt, and she looked up at him.

'Why?'

'Because I'm ordering you to, and as I've told you, I'll be with you all in a few moments.'

Michelle caught her lower lip between her teeth. She felt provoked, for some unknown reason, into telling him not to think he could shuffle her about as he was trying to do to Pete and Laney but, in view of the fact that he was only thinking of her welfare, she thought better of it and, turning, went to join the others in the small pub.

CHAPTER NINE

As it whined and licked around the corners of the building the wind could be heard inside the chalet.

Michelle went in the direction of the voices. Managing a casual smile, she said, 'All roads lead to the pub, I see. Who would have said it was going to be as cold as this up top?' She shook back her hair, which felt damp and tangled.

The foursome turned to look at her and the young men stood up. 'All this way up and we haven't yet exchanged names,' one of them said, smiling.

'In any case,' said Michelle, 'conversation in the Land-Rover was virtually impossible – whew, all that shaking and groaning! I don't know how you people feel, but I feel all shaken up.'

'Where's our good driver?'

Michelle shrugged. 'He was last seen going in the direction of the kitchen ... something to do with the food hampers.' Suddenly she felt reckless. 'I suppose he had a few more orders to hand out. He said he'd join us in a few minutes.'

'Anyway, I'm Carl – this is Heidi, Pieter and Marie. We two are from Germany – these are our friends, kindly showing us around.'

'Well,' Michelle's blue eyes went from face to face, 'I'm Michelle, and I'm very pleased to have met you. I'm from England. Right now, I'm very glad to be alive and in one piece.'

'It was some trip – but very enjoyable,' said Carl. 'What can I get you to drink?'

'What about a rum and Coke?' Marie cut in. 'Good for the cold.'

'That sounds like an invitation to a party,' Michelle laughed lightly. 'Right, a rum and Coke it will be. Thank you.' She slipped on to a stool in the primitive little bar where a great Basotho man acted as barman.

'We must write our names on the wall,' Marie was saying.

'Look, every person who visits here does it, apparently.'

In fact, the walls of the chalet were decorated not only with the names of many visitors, but also with local information and maps. It formed part of the rugged décor.

Michelle turned her head to look at a gaily coloured blanket which was suspended from a hook on one side of the bottle-laden shelves. 'Oh, I'd love that,' she said. 'Is it for sale?' she asked the barman.

'It is for sale, yes. But there are others in that little room at the end there. Perhaps one of them – different colour?'

'May I go through?' she asked.

'Certainly.'

She left her drink to go and look at the other blankets and items made from straw and sheepskin. Somehow she knew that the burnt orange, dark brown, tan, white-and-black blanket in the pub would also serve to remind her of her trip up the Pass, so when she came out of the small cement-floored shop, she said, 'I'd like to buy that one. Am I being very difficult? Will it be a lot of trouble getting it down?'

'No trouble at all,' the barman replied, then there was a lot of laughter as he took it down and began to demonstrate how it should be folded, Basotho style. 'Basotho ride horses, hey?' He looked seriously at them.

'Yes, that's so,' Pieter replied.

Some of the tension went out of Michelle's slim shoulders as she listened and sipped her rum and Coke.

'Well, this is how Basotho folds blanket for saddle.' They watched him as he folded the blanket and then tried to master the art themselves.

Michelle paid for the blanket and sighed loudly. 'After a very bad start, this has just made my day,' she said.

Behind her, somebody coughed, then Lyle Cunningham slipped on to the stool next to her. 'Yes,' he said, and his faint smile was unamused, 'so I notice.'

'Tell me, man, where did you learn to drive?' Marie asked. 'You were fantastic!'

Laughing, Lyle said, 'I'm glad you thought so. Thank you.'

'But if you do this sort of thing very often surely it must be bad for you – bad for the health?' Carl was saying, twirling his glass round and round on the counter.

'Well, I recognize the insidious damage driving a Land-Rover up this Pass, day in and day out, could do to a man's health,' Lyle answered, 'but as a matter of fact, we don't do it every day – or rather, I don't.'

Marie was listening to him with hushed fascination. Then she said, 'You have more than one driver, then, in your business?'

'Yes. I help out, when necessary, and today was – necessary.' His voice held a hint of amusement. He had the manner of the confident – the arrogant, Michelle thought resentfully. Confident that he would get his own way in everything. Confident that he could buy Pete and Laney out.

'Tell me, are there any other concerns, running these Land-Rovers up and down the Pass?' Piet wanted to know. 'You know, other Land-Rovers quite apart from your own?'

'There are, yes. There are more Land-Rovers coming into operation soon, I believe. Another concern in the making – but ask Michelle. She knows more about it than I do. I've heard about it, but haven't found out whether it's true – no way of knowing, actually. Although I should have been informed, being indirectly involved, I haven't been notified. However, I don't intend to get uptight about it.'

All eyes were on Michelle, the girls leaning over on their stools so that they could see her, pushing their curtains of windblown hair back from their attractive faces, the men pretending by their smiles that they had not noticed the sudden chill in the atmosphere.

Michelle managed a half-hearted smile. 'I'm from England, don't forget. I'm not up to your local gossip – which incidentally appears to be the chief occupation in these parts.' She made sure there was just enough sarcasm in her voice to make Lyle lift his dark brows. 'However,' she went on, 'I'm aware that a certain party is going into operation soon.'

Lyle compelled her to look at him. 'Into operation – or opposition?' His eyes held hers.

'That I have no idea, but you could always make it your

business to find out,' she told him before giving him the benefit of her shoulder as she turned away from him.

The chalet seemed to ring with the sound of the wind. Beyond the windows of the little bar it looked bleak, barren and rocky outside. Inside, it was snug. It was difficult to believe that when they went back down the winding Pass they would probably find themselves taking off their jerseys.

Michelle's pulse quickened as, by accident, her hand brushed against Lyle's and she could sense the tension in him.

'How long before lunch?' Carl asked suddenly, looking at Lyle. 'I'll tell you why – is there time for some walking? Just a little way, to see the view. Not far.'

Lyle seemed to be considering the question, then he said, 'Yes, but don't get lost. Don't let the girls fall over.' His eyes went to Marie and Heidi, who giggled.

'We might push them over,' Pieter joked. 'They make far too much noise, what do you say?'

'You are coming?' Carl looked at Michelle.

Not wanting to be in the way, she said, 'I'll stay here. I'd like to look around and have another peep at those sheepskin slippers back there in the shop.'

Except for the wind, it was very quiet when they had gone. Michelle sipped her rum and Coke, enjoying the spice of it and listening idly to the conversation between the Basotho barman and Lyle. A delicious warmth was creeping over her and she felt almost completely relaxed, so it was easy for her to fall into the trap of overlooking the fact that Lyle Cunningham was busy trying to make certain negotiations to buy her brother's farm. If it were not for the Cunninghams Pete might well, given time, make good.

With these thoughts in mind she slipped from her stool and, drink in hand, began an inspection of the small pub and the adjacent shop where there were also a number of Basotho straw hats and quaint little donkeys made from straw.

When she came back into the pub she said, 'May I look round the chalet?'

Lyle stood up and pushed back his glass. 'Of course.'

She went into the passage, glancing into the kitchen as she passed it. Black girls were busy opening tins of food and preparing to heat it and cutting bread and cheese. There was a rattling of crockery and cutlery.

At the end of the corridor there was a dining-room which she imagined could seat about twelve people or more.

'There are five bedrooms, each with bunk type beds, mattresses, bed linen and blankets,' Lyle said behind her. Michelle blinked but did not turn. 'Twenty-six people can be accommodated at one time, in case you're wondering. Believe it or not, rooms have central heating. Meals are catered for and a cook is on hand for those who bring their own food.'

'Like today?' she asked, still not turning.

'Today you'll be eating mostly out of tins,' he told her, and she knew he was smiling.

'Well, it's very quaint,' she murmured. 'Rough and ready – a proper mountain chalet, but attractive.' She turned to look at him. She wanted desperately to believe in him, she thought. But how could she?

'Do people come up here to rest?' she asked. 'What I mean is, it is right at the top, so they can't come here to climb – you know what I mean . . .' she broke off, laughing a little.

'Snow can fall in almost any month of the year here, although more likely during the months of June, July and August. Skis, sticks and boots are hired out and there's a ski-lift in operation. Skating in winter on a lake, nearby, is becoming more and more popular. Excursions from here are arranged. It's a favourite resort all round.'

'And yet nobody, apart from us, today?' she said again.

'It goes like that.'

'I suppose it storms up here? It must be terrible.' Because she was so aware of him she kept her voice carefully expressionless.

'They occur roughly every two days out of three during midsummer.'

After an uncomfortable silence she said, 'The others are taking a long time, aren't they?'

Glancing at his watch, Lyle said, 'There's about ten

minutes to go before lunch and I can't see them missing that.'

'No, I suppose not, but I was thinking about falls ...'

'They'll be all right. They've just gone up there to get a better view. Apparently they're keen photographers.'

'Is there a better view?' she asked incredulously.

'Come through here,' he said, beginning to lead the way towards a large room with window-seats, a table and cane chairs. There was a hurricane lamp on the fireplace.

The wind was more noticeable here, licking around the corners of the building. A glass door opened to what surely, Michelle found herself thinking, must be the Roof of Africa. This was Africa's Switzerland, she mused, where the people were black-skinned and blanketed to cope with the cold.

'Is it really always as cold as this?' she asked Lyle who was sitting at the table now, writing.

'It's usually cold up here, make no mistake about that.' He met her eyes for a moment, then he began writing again.

Her eyes rested on him for a moment, then she went to the glass door, opened it and stepped out into the wind and cold. The wind sucked the door closed with a shattering bang and, catching her breath, Michelle swung round, expecting to see the glass falling out of the white frame, and was relieved when it didn't.

The mountains appeared to be carved out by wind and far below them there were the beautiful if barren valleys.

The cross St. Bernards came round the side of the building to greet her, pushing and nudging themselves into her legs. She was suddenly nervous as the male took the sleeve of her jersey between his teeth and began tugging at it.

'Down, boy,' she tried to keep her voice calm. 'Down!'

The door opened and Lyle came out. 'They won't bother you,' he said, 'but let's put an end to this game, shall we?' He coaxed the animals into leaving her alone.

'I hope the others don't get blown over,' she said. 'This wind is terribly strong and all round there are these fantastic drops.' Her eyes took in the hairpinned, indistinguishable track that lost itself amongst the mountains. 'Is *that* where we came from?' Her eyes were wide and there was wonder in his voice.

'Yes – and where we still have to go,' he answered.

'I don't know how you can bear to drive people up here. Don't you think about it?' her voice carefully controlling the concern she felt for him.

'Yes, I do think about it. It would be foolish to insist that there was no danger. There is an element of risk and uncertainty, certainly. Disaster could follow neglect of reasonable precautions.'

'And yet,' she felt provoked into saying, 'often you were quite reckless. Was that to scare me?'

'I don't think you quite know what you're talking about, Michelle.' His voice was abrupt. 'Whatever I did to control the bumps and the skids would appear reckless to you.'

Suddenly, her excited eyes took in a number of Basotho riders, wrapped in colourful blankets, riding like the wind on sturdy mountain ponies which nevertheless looked a size too small for them. Her mind memorized the red-and-indigo, sky-blue-and-yellow, brown-and-cerise colours of the blankets which were in such contrast to the brown, boulder-strewn track on which they were travelling.

'Come in, out of the wind.' Lyle took her arm and she put her teeth down on her lip and allowed him to guide her to the door.

When they were back in the chalet she sat on a window-seat, which she surmised could double up as a bed, and gazed out of the huge pane of glass, curtained in green and gold sun-filter, which was all that separated her from the cold of the buffeting wind. Everything was so bleak and windswept, she thought. She could see the dogs with their thick coats blowing in the wind. Poor animals, she thought. There's nothing for them, except each other and waiting for the people they know bringing tourists to the chalet.

Her eyes strayed in the direction of the table where Lyle still appeared to be writing and she was acutely aware of him – and something told her that he was aware of her.

For a crazy moment she wanted to tackle him about the farm, her eyes brooding on his tanned, handsome face. She wanted to clear everything up, once and for all. How could he do this to Pete and Laney, while pretending to be their very good friend? Surely there was other land on which to grow vegetables for their deep-freezing?

Suddenly Lyle looked up and, because it was too late to drop her lashes, Michelle met his blue-green eyes. She realized that by doing so she was skating on thin ice and that, razor-thin, it could crack at the slightest movement on her part. For a long moment they studied each other, then she felt a wild impulse to shock him. 'To think,' she said, with an attempt at flippancy, 'I should have been sitting here with Jake Gobbi. It just goes to show,' she shrugged elaborately, 'that you can't plan ahead, doesn't it?' She stood up and went to the glass door where she remained looking out, then she caught her breath and a small shock went through her when Lyle came to stand next to her.

'I've never been able to make out what all this is about,' he said, his tone angry. 'Why bring Jake Gobbi's name up right now? I thought we were beginning to cope rather well, considering. Suppose you forget about the snow episode and stop punishing me for it? After all, you're entitled to do as you like.'

The wind was rattling the glass door and she watched him as he went to turn the key. The rattling stopped and he came back to her.

'You're giving me a hard time, Michelle.' There was accusation in his voice. 'However, I can sympathize with your feelings about Jake.' He placed his hands on her arms and drew her towards him. 'And the planning ahead, Michelle. This time, though, we're not going to concern ourselves with planning ahead.'

She had not been prepared for this turn of events, she thought, as his lips came down upon her own – and yet hadn't she been aware of the tension in him – in both of them?

In the kitchen at the end of the corridor, there were noises of talking, a faint giggle, pots being scraped across the big range, crockery rattling and, sharply and disturbingly, the falling of cutlery and more giggling.

Lyle Cunningham's kiss was a calculated insult – and she knew this. Yet she found herself unable to take her lips away. Vaguely, she was aware of resentment that her lips were letting her down by responding, leaving her drained.

When he released her she still had her eyes closed while she waited for everything to stop spinning and when she opened them again the dizziness had stopped and he was saying, his voice hard, 'I doubt if even Glen Hayes, let alone Jake Gobbi, could have done better than that!'

While her rapid heartbeats relayed their frantic message to her she did her best to appear taunting. 'That's a matter of opinion, surely? But, to put you in the picture, I have to inform you that your remark was based on an unfortunate calculation on your part.'

'Why unfortunate?'

'Unfortunate,' she got herself under control with some effort, 'because you're so self-centred that it must come as a terrific blow to you to discover that you're quite mistaken.'

'Frankly,' his eyes went over her face, 'it's no longer important.'

There was the sound of the dogs barking in an excited manner, followed by laughter, talking and the stamping of feet. The foursome had returned and had entered the chalet by means of the main entrance.

When packing the food hampers the hotel had decided upon curry, tiny seed potatoes, green beans and carrots, to be followed by peaches and cream – all out of tins, except for the bread, biscuits and cheese and fresh fruit. Although she had been feeling hungry before Lyle had kissed her, Michelle found that she did not feel like eating now that lunch was finally served. Immediately she had eaten she experienced the discomfort of acute indigestion, which was all the more unpleasant because she was not used to it.

Over coffee Marie said, 'See how you can send it going down. Give us a few more thrills to remember.'

'You should know better than to talk like this,' Lyle answered. 'Don't dare me – I might just do that.' He laughed. 'All within reason, of course.'

'You said you'd take us down that part that was washed away. You know, the part that some guy had cemented to form two strips, at one time or another. Remember, you said although we couldn't go up it – we could ride down it, although I can't help wondering how on earth we can when the cement was suspended over a deep donga. Do we just collapse down over it?' Marie went into giggles.

Smiling easily, Lyle said, 'Okay, Marie, I'll see what I can do to scare the daylights out of you.' There seemed to be a shell of indifference about him now.

Michelle sat and fumed as she listened to them, her indigestion like a rock on her chest.

As they made preparations to get back into the Land-Rover she said, 'Would anybody else like the front seat going down? You'll see more, I'm sure. What about you, Marie? You're the daredevil of the party.'

'Let's stay the way we were,' Marie answered quickly, and this was followed by the approval of the others, so once again Michelle found herself sitting next to Lyle.

The blanketed man with the straw hat and the peg-leg tried once again to sell them a mealie-straw hat, looped at the top, but far too small to wear.

When official routine matters had been adhered to they drove across the border and Lyle stopped the Land-Rover again so that Carl could take a photograph of the party standing next to the vehicle. With the wind tearing at their hair and cutting right through them they formed a group and laughed obligingly, Michelle clutching at her blanket to give colour to the slide when it was projected on the screen.

As they pulled off again, amidst shivering noises and rubbing of hands on the part of the young people in the back, Lyle turned to glance at Michelle. 'I got carried away back there,' he said softly. 'I promise to be more careful in the future, but in any case, what would you have done in my position?'

'You've proved yourself to be the cad you are,' she answered. 'I wasn't surprised, actually.'

There was a brief silence, then he said, 'And you certainly weren't immune. I know I wasn't, at the time. You know it too, but you're not honest enough to admit it.'

'Talking about honesty,' she answered in angry despair, 'that's a subject best left alone. I should have thought you would have known that.'

'What exactly are you driving at?' He turned his head quickly to look at her, then gave his attention to the road. 'I've a feeling that it's something to do with me.'

They were in the thick of the hairpin bends, now, and he was giving his full attention to them and she thought it better not to go on talking.

The vehicle tilted forward and Michelle found herself holding her breath. The girls in the back screamed with a mixture of fear and sheer delight.

'I promised you wouldn't be disappointed,' Lyle tried to make himself heard over the rattling of the Land-Rover and protesting compression noises.

'Let us know when we reach that bit with the cement strips dangling in mid-air,' Marie yelled back. 'I don't want to miss it.'

'I won't have to let you know,' Lyle called back. 'You'll know well enough!'

Once again the journey was an ever-changing combination of hanging over sheer space on the one side and avoiding huge walls of boulders on the other which seemed to hang in the path of the Pass. It was worse, Michelle thought, than going up. This time she felt as though they were being pitched forward and at any moment the Land-Rover would tilt forward on its bonnet and turn over, crushing them beneath it before rolling down into the valley, smashing it to pieces.

At one time, as Lyle made the short detour to drive over the cement strips which had been laid as an experiment and which had been partly washed away and the experiment abandoned, she quite resigned herself to this fate. Usually tough and able to cope, she began to feel ill and the tinned curry lay heavily on her chest. She found herself wondering whether she would have enjoyed the trip better had Jake Gobbi been at the wheel, instead of Lyle Cunningham, and she had not been subjected to the tension of Lyle's presence and remarks.

Once the Land-Rover seemed unlikely to make one of the hairpin bends and she caught her breath sharply as Lyle tamed it in an instant, bringing it round, missing the insecure wall built up of boulders and stones which was all that stood between them and an awesome drop. When she slanted a look in Lyle's direction she was almost disappointed to find him smiling mockingly at her.

'I can't see us getting down in one piece,' she said hotly. 'The way you're driving, we could go over the side at any moment!'

'On no account must this possibility be overlooked.' There was nothing in his voice.

The bends were coming quickly and at times Lyle appeared to be fighting for control as he wrenched the wheel round. Michelle found herself wondering whether he was playing up the danger for her benefit. Whatever it was, though, it was a magnificent display of skill on his part.

'Don't you find yourself beginning to panic sometimes?' Marie called out, from the back. 'I know I would.'

'Let's be honest,' he laughed back, 'panic is no stranger, but I've learned to extinguish it quickly.' Although Lyle answered questions and joked with the passengers in the back of the Land-Rover the task of keeping the vehicle in control demanded all the alertness and skill he had to give. That was obvious.

Michelle was becoming uneasy now, about her indigestion. Feeling close to panic, she tried to concentrate on the scenery. The worst bends seemed to be over now and the jumble of menacing rocks did not appear so menacing.

Suddenly Lyle stopped the Land-Rover and switched off. She watched his tanned hand go to the brake. 'Would you like to get out and look for stones?' he asked, turning in his seat.

'What kind of stones?' Carl wanted to know.

'Agate, chalcedony, malachite, amethyst, quartzite – all to be found here, near Twin Streams. You might find it interesting. When I saw the men digging and widening the road I thought they might have unearthed something – no harm in looking.'

Michelle joined in with the others, searching for stones. She was desperately aware of the fact that she wanted to be sick and stopped scratching around in the sand which had been excavated to listen to Lyle, who was talking to a fascinated Marie. 'Pebbles of agate,' he was saying, 'are formed in an interesting way. As volcanic material solidifies, gas bubbles are trapped in it. Mineral-rich liquids percolate through the rock and get into these holes to form concentric layers of beautifully coloured agates, quartz and chalcedony.'

'Fascinating,' Marie exclaimed. 'Utterly fascinating!' She turned to look back at the mountains. 'Looking at all this, I ask myself how it all started, you know?' Then she went on, 'I know a farmer who keeps great shallow baskets in all sorts of show places in his home. His wife has created a lovely sun-room with thick, nobbly yellow sun-filter curtains, cane furniture, books, African masks and beadwork, copper and baskets of the most fascinating stones you ever saw. The result is superb.'

Watching her, Michelle found herself thinking that Marie was giving her a bad time. She longed to get back into the Land-Rover and to get back to the hotel where she could take something for the indigestion and nausea which was plaguing her. The strong taste of curry kept entering her mouth. If only she had some antacid-alkalizer mints with her for the relief of indigestion, she thought, how much better she would feel – but then she did not, as a rule, suffer from this complaint.

'Would you like to visit a trading store before I take you back?' Lyle asked, making things worse for her.

'That sounds great,' Carl called out as he stood turning some stones over in his hand.

'I'll laugh if Michelle sees a blanket there at half the price she paid for it,' Marie giggled. 'Michelle?'

'It wouldn't matter,' Michelle tried to smile brightly, 'I particularly wanted this one, to remind me of today, right up there. So far away now. It seems incredible that we've been right to the top.'

For a few moments they all turned to look up at the great spectacle of the Pass – the lines of free-standing peaks, examples of weathering and erosion between fracture planes, boulders scrubbed by flood waters, rounded summit domes and broken kranses, the result of weathering. Beyond it was Lesotho, cold, sometimes bleak, often snow-covered and, judging from the views from the mountain chalet, thought Michelle, apparently lifeless. Normally this would have been a wonderful experience for her, but Lyle Cunningham had made sure that he had ruined it for her. And yet no matter what happened, she would always remember this day – the feel of his arms about her, his mouth on her own . . .

Before going back to the hotel they visited one of the trading stores in the area. On the veranda there was an assortment of ploughs, sacks of flour and cooking pots while inside the shelves were piled high with vividly coloured blankets, rolls of cloth, boots, tobacco, combs, and vaseline.

Michelle's troubled eyes searched for one item – fruit salts – then she went to the man behind the counter. 'Excuse me,' she said, 'have you any fruit salts?'

He did not seem to understand, and then, from behind, Lyle made the request in the man's own language while to Michelle he said, 'What's the problem? Why are you asking for fruit salts?'

'I can't define my problem, but I think I have acute indigestion.' She knew that she sounded as she felt – vaguely distracted.

Giving her an amused glance, he said, 'A young girl like you?'

'Yes. I don't think it's uncommon.' Moodily, she watched the man as he went in the direction of a small cardboard box which stood on one of the shelves. No wonder she had not been able to find the stuff, she thought.

Marie and Heidi were busy choosing dark blue and white printed cotton while Carl and Pieter stood beside them, looking amused.

Lyle said, 'He says he has only two packets left.'

'No bottles?' she asked.

'No bottles.' His eyes searched her face. 'Why don't you wait until you get back to the hotel, Michelle? You'll get what you want there. These packets looked rather ancient.'

'I'll take these,' she said, preparing to pay for them. The moment Lyle left her she intended asking the owner for a glass, cup, enamel mug – anything – of water.

'I'd think twice before taking that,' Lyle's eyes went to the packets. 'The packets are yellow with age, Michelle. He probably doesn't have much demand for stuff like this.'

Feeling impatient with herself – and him, now – she turned away, dropping the packets into her bag as she did so. She would have to wait, she thought. It wouldn't be long now. 'I'll decide presently,' she said.

'You're entitled to do that, I guess.' Behind her, she knew Lyle had shrugged impatiently. 'But my advice is – lay off, until you get back and are able to get something else.'

The others were leaving the store and there was nothing for it but to follow them out to the Land-Rover which was cooling down in the dust-laden air.

Lyle dropped them all off outside the hotel and waited until the food hampers were off-loaded. After he had parked the Land-Rover he joined then in the foyer. 'We're back in time for tea,' he said.

Brushing dust from her slacks, Marie said, 'That will be followed by a nice hot bath.'

'Followed by a nice cold beer,' grinned Carl.

'Followed by a nice tasty dinner,' Heidi giggled. 'Thank you for a super day. It's been fantastic.'

'That goes for everybody,' Carl and Pieter were saying together, while Michelle kept on smiling, nursing her discomfort and longing to go to her room.

'It's been a pleasure,' Lyle replied. 'I've enjoyed it. Thank *you*.' His eyes flickered to Michelle. 'Take it easy,' he said. 'Relax. You'll find what you want at the shop. Take my advice and toss what you have in the waste-paper basket. I think it's been standing on that shelf back there since the beginning of time. In fact, the salts appeared lumpy to me.'

'I'll be all right,' she answered. She felt a huge sense of let-down. 'It's not really important.'

The others were going towards the staircase, laughing and joking and filling the foyer with their noise. Michelle turned to leave, then stopped as Lyle said, 'I think, Michelle, we should have a talk, in the very near future.'

'I don't see what about,' she said, her voice cool, 'unless it happens to be about my work?'

136

'This cat and mouse game is beginning to wear me down. Your work has nothing to do with it.' His voice was quiet.

'No?'

'No.'

'Well, in that case, I don't think we need to have a talk. Thank you for the trip.'

His eyes held hers for a moment before he said, 'Don't thank me. It's all part of the service.' She watched him turn and make his way outside to the dust-covered Land-Rover.

As soon as she reached her room she opened her bag and removed the two little packets containing the fruit salts. Indeed, they did look yellow with age, she thought, unless they had been in a part of the shop where the rain leaked through a hole in the roof and the water had dripped on to the cardboard box, moistening the contents of the packets and yellowing as they dried again. She pressed one packet in an endeavour to break down the salts which had become lumpy, then, going through to her bathroom, she filled a tumbler with water, added the salts and gulped the fizzing liquid down.

After a hot bath she felt much better and the indigestion had left her, but she experienced a bloated sensation in the region of her stomach.

Although she was not hungry she went down to dinner, but found that she could not eat much. It was during the late hours of the night that she woke up, violently ill, and was left feeling spent and wretched. There were severe pains in her stomach. By two o'clock in the morning she was desperate, and when at last the sky suddenly became tinged with the colours of dawn, she was utterly thankful. Directly she was able to use the phone she rang Laney.

'Laney,' she said, 'I'm terribly ill. Please get Pete to come and get me.'

Laney did not waste time asking questions and within a short time Pete knocked at her door and she let him in. 'What's happened?' he asked, his eyes going quickly over Michelle.

'Oh,' she moaned, '*you* tell *me!*'

'Laney's preparing your bed,' he told her. 'She'll look

after you. We'll get the doctor.'

'Oh, gosh!' Michelle sat on the side of her bed. 'I'm so ill, Pete. I've been through a hideous night. I'll have to notify them downstairs, of course. I can't just go off without putting them wise.'

'I've already done that.' Peter sounded worried. 'What can I do for you?'

'Just sling these in that case for me.' Michelle doubled over and groaned.

At the farm, Laney helped her into bed in the small guest room with its thick white walls and grass watusi bedroom suite. At the far end of the room there was a white cot, waiting. This was to be the nursery. Already Laney had been to work here and, ill as she was feeling, Michelle knew rage and despair to think that Lyle Cunningham was trying to buy the farm which had become home to Pete and Laney. Gradually they were putting all they had into it. Was it all going to be for nothing?

'Pete is phoning our doctor,' Laney was saying comfortingly. 'You must be suffering from food poisoning, Michelle. Do you realize that? And yet Pete phoned the hotel to find out whether the others were affected by the food sent up in the Land-Rover and was told that not only are the four people who did the trip up the Pass okay, but the entire hotel. So we just can't understand what it's all about. Anyway, we'll see what doctor says.'

The doctor, when informed about the fruit salts, wanted to see the remaining packet which, fortunately, was still in Michelle's handbag. 'I'll look into this,' he said, pocketing it. 'It could have been standing next to something on the shelf – or it could be that it had been inadvertently sprayed with insecticide.'

'Oh, no!' Laney exclaimed, shocked. 'Don't say that!'

'At any rate, it should be investigated by the health people,' he replied. 'The packet is certainly discoloured and it's been moist.' He took it from his pocket and examined it again. 'Anyway, she's over the worst now, and that,' he glanced in the direction of the prescription which he had placed on one of the grass watusi bedside tables, 'should fix her up in no time.'

'Let us know about the fruit salts, will you, Doctor?' Laney asked.

'I'll do that. It should be looked into.'

Michelle was dozing after such a hideous night when Lyle Cunningham arrived and Laney was shaking her shoulder lightly.

'Wakey–wakey,' she said, 'somebody to see you.'

'Don't wake her,' Lyle was saying as she opened her eyes. 'Perhaps she should sleep.'

'No. She'll be thrilled to see you, Lyle. She'd be terribly disappointed if I told her you'd been and I hadn't called her.'

Michelle looked up. 'Hello.' Lyle's voice was soft.

'I'll go and put the kettle on,' said Laney, leaving them alone, and a huge silence settled on the room.

Eventually Lyle said, 'How do you feel now? I understand you had a very rough night, Michelle?'

She followed him with her eyes, her lashes heavy, as he sat down on the side of the bed, although there happened to be a very comfortable chair nearby.

'Have you lost your tongue, Michelle?' His blue-green eyes went over her face.

In despair, she turned her head away from him. She was in love with him and he was the man who was doing his best to smash Pete and Laney, quite apart from the fact that he had done nothing but humiliate her ever since he had seen her posing in the snow bikini.

'Something went wrong along the line somewhere,' she murmured. 'For some unknown reason that tinned curry didn't agree with me and I got the most awful attack of indigestion, and then, as Laney has probably told you, the fruit salts could have been tainted. Anyway,' she added in a voice that was not quite steady. 'I don't feel like talking about it. Everything seems so pointless.'

'What seems so pointless?' he asked.

After a while she said, 'Everything.'

'Well, I'm open to suggestions, Michelle.' He took her hand in his own and she put her teeth down on her lips and held her breath.

'I'd rather you didn't touch me,' she said, trying to free

her hand.

'I lost my head yesterday. I'm sorry, Michelle.' His voice was gentle.

Looking at him through a sheen of tears, she said, 'Is there a difference? You only lost your head because you happen to think I'm – I'm – to use an old corny word, even in these permissive times – *cheap*. Isn't that so?'

'No, that isn't so.' He sounded angry now.

However, she went on, 'But even cheap girls like to choose the men they want to have an affair with.'

Where, she asked herself, was the girl who used to swing around London as though it belonged to her? Who, in her place, was this wretched girl with the stomach pains and the feelings of a moon-sick schoolgirl?

At that moment Laney came in, carrying a tray. Michelle took her hand away from Lyle's. 'Laney,' she said, 'I hate to do this to you, but could you have it in the living-room? I'm not feeling all that much like company. I'm sorry.'

'Fine, Michelle. Don't worry about it.'

Lyle stood up. 'Let me carry the tray for you, Laney.'

As he followed Laney from the room Michelle's eyes filled with tears. 'Traitor,' she whispered. 'Traitor! Why can't Pete and Laney see through your little game?'

CHAPTER TEN

THE fruit salts had been contaminated by insecticide spray and the trading store owner duly advised of the outcome of tests and cautioned. 'A lot of these sprays should be struck off the market,' the doctor had said, 'although I understand that a lot already have been – and with more to come, I hope.'

Laney drove Michelle back to the hotel after she had spent a day and a night at the farm. 'Be careful, Michelle, where and what you buy in future.' Laney's smile was not without worry.

Michelle felt drained and calm. 'I'll be careful, Laney, don't worry. Honestly, while the attack lasted, I thought I was going to die. It was awful!'

Soon after she was back at the hotel she met Lyle Cunningham in the foyer. 'So you're back?' He smiled briefly, but his face recovered its cold aloofness almost immediately. 'Have you quite got over your ordeal?'

'Yes, thank you,' she answered, wondering at the sudden pleasure the sight of him gave her. She forced the feeling aside.

'I had a feeling about those salts,' he told her. 'I wish I'd been firm about it. I didn't want you to buy it.'

She made no reply at first and then, after a pause, she murmured, 'Yes. I know, it was entirely my own fault. I should have taken your advice and gone along to the shop at the hotel and bought a bottle. I guess I was feeling desperate.' She shrugged slightly and even managed a casual smile.

'Anyway, you've recovered, that's the main thing.'

Michelle sensed the tension in him. Their eyes held. Cunningham Senior was coming into the foyer and Lyle turned. 'I have a customer under the drier,' she said. 'Please excuse me.'

As she passed the desk on her way to her small salon, Michelle was aware of Liza's dark eyes following her. She stifled the temptation to ask Liza, with sarcasm in her voice, whether there was anything she wanted.

Long, sunny days slipped by and, although Glen Hayes had a talent for irritating her, Michelle had found herself accepting invitations to go out with him whenever she was free. It was about time, she thought, that she started finding interests outside the hotel – time she stopped brooding and thinking about Lyle Cunningham.

Glen had phoned her one day, soon after she had been up the Sani Pass with Lyle Cunningham. 'I haven't seen you around,' he said. 'What have you been doing with yourself?'

'I've been busy,' she murmured.

'How are you?' he asked.

'Oh . . .' she tried to think of something flippant to say, 'I – er – stagger along, I guess.'

'Let's not waste any more time,' Glen had said. 'What about having dinner with me tonight?'

Well, she had found herself thinking, why not? She was free to do as she wished when she was not working, and so for the past two months she had avoided Lyle Cunningham and gone out with Glen Hayes.

Glen was always up to form, making passes at her with a subtle sense of timing – passes which she always rejected. It was amazing how he kept on phoning her, she thought, and sometimes she felt mean as she went on seeing him when all the time there was this faint, involuntary contempt which she felt towards him.

One day Liza said, 'Aren't you seeing rather a lot of Glen Hayes these days?'

Keeping her anger under tight control, Michelle replied, 'And aren't you seeing rather a lot of Lyle Cunningham these days? It's the same thing, really, isn't it?'

The fact that Lyle often called for Liza and took her out in his car had not escaped Michelle's notice, and she knew she was jealous.

'I was going out with Lyle Cunningham long before you came on the scene, as a matter of fact,' Liza replied hotly. 'And by the way, that goes for Glen Hayes, as well.'

'Oh?' Liza's constant sarcasm was beginning to get on

Michelle's nerves. 'I hope I haven't destroyed your peace of mind?' she said.

'Not at all.' Liza's voice was cutting. 'I'd like you to feel absolutely reassured on that point.'

Glen Hayes had taken delivery of his Land-Rovers, although there had been no organized trips up the Pass. It was not like Glen Hayes to delay anything and Michelle found herself wondering why the vehicles were not in operation.

She was having dinner with him one evening at a farm on the outskirts of Thabana, when he said, 'I intend to go one better than the Cunninghams. Our excursions up the Pass will be cheaper. In fact, whatever they do, I intend to go one better.' He gave her a meaningful smile.

'Is that what you have in mind?' Her voice was sharp.

'That's what I have in mind.' His eyes were lazy behind the horn-rimmed glasses, tawny and deceptively lazy.

'What have you got against the Cunninghams?' Michelle watched his eyes close – a habit when he was preparing to answer a question.

When he opened them he said, 'I'll tell you.' He put one elbow on the table and rested his cheek on his hand. 'When the hotel came on the market I was interested. I didn't act quickly enough, though. I could kick myself now. I've had my eye on these parts for some time, now – along with my partners, that is. So I – *we* – did the next best thing. We built the chalets. We intended including an à la carte restaurant, but we scrapped that. The chalets, as you know, are equipped with super little kitchens, pots and pans, electric stoves, refrigerators – in fact, the lot ... There's a small supermarket to cater for the average holidaymaker and – well, there you have it. Do you get me?'

'I'm beginning to understand, I think.' Michelle watched him roll his tongue around his teeth and take it away with a little smacking sound. Glen always created the impression that he was just in the act of finishing off some tasty morsel. In any other person this could have been nothing short of a disgusting little habit, but there was something aggravatingly fascinating about the way in which he performed this small ritual, while in the midst of conversing.

'But,' he went on, 'we had this idea about a farm.' Michelle's nerves tightened suddenly as she listened to him. 'We've been keeping a close watch on the market. In other words, when your brother's farm came up for sale, we were all there, believe me.'

'I see,' she said softly.

'As you probably know, your brother and his wife found themselves in such a financial mess that they put the farm on the market. That was before you arrived here, of course. Then they withdrew it. However, Lyle Cunningham is still doing his best to get them to sell. In fact, he loaned them money, I understand, which he knew damned well they'd never in a hundred years be able to pay back. It could be that he's using this as a lever to get his own way with them. I don't say it is – but it could be.'

'That's generous of you.' Michelle's voice was bitter.

'Don't get uptight with me, Michelle. I'm just trying to put you in the picture.'

'Thanks!'

'He had some big scheme up his sleeve, but,' he took his arm off the table and sat back, 'it's too late. So far as his little scheme is concerned, it's too late now.'

'I'm not sure I understand all this. What is it you're trying to say?' She regarded him with troubled eyes.

'Do you know why I wanted that farm, Michelle?'

'No.'

'Well, do you know why *he* wanted it?'

'Yes, I do, as a matter of fact.'

'Why? Why did he want it? Tell me.'

'I'm not prepared to tell you. I'm sorry,' she answered, thinking about the deep-freezing project and remembering how reluctant Lyle had been to discuss it.

'Well, you don't have to tell me, as it so happens. I know about it.' He lowered his voice confidentially. 'He wanted to do very much what we've done here.' Glen's gesture took in the entire room.

Across the small table Michelle blinked in puzzlement. She had visited this farm before – several times, in fact, with Glen – for dinner. She had understood that it belonged to the people who were managing it – the middle-aged Italian couple Glen had pointed out to her on the day of the filming for the wine people. Glen had told her that the farm had only recently changed hands and that the home had been opened to the public as an exclusive restaurant.

A corrugated road led to the farmhouse which, with its stark white walls and tall chimneys, looked like a picture postcard of a scene in the English countryside, not a restaurant in the Drakensberg Mountains.

Glen had even gone so far as to inform her that the farm was fast earning a reputation as 'fabulous and unique.' It was only three hours by car from Durban, via Pietermaritzburg, and with people as they were, thinking nothing of spending a week-end at the Berg, either at the chalets or caravan sites, there would be no need to wonder whether the project would pay. In fact, it was going to pay – all the signs were there, after only two months.

The farm, Michelle knew, welcomed visitors of discerning taste. It was not advertised, and yet already the visitors' book read like the latest Who's Who. The Italian couple prepared all the food themselves and their international menu, with an unmistakable Italian touch, was well on the way to becoming known by connoisseurs throughout the country.

She was aware, too, of the fact that vegetables were being grown. In fact, Glen had taken her on a tour of the extensive gardens and nursery. Long continental loaves of bread were being baked daily. She had surmised that it was because of a close friendship with the Italians that Glen had felt free to show her over the huge kitchen, whereas, in fact, the entire project belonged to him – or rather to him and his partners, whoever they were. Chickens laid eggs and there was a supply of fresh cream and milk from the dairy. He had shown her that too. In fact, it had all been fun and she had enjoyed it tremendously. There was a comprehensive wine cellar, with row upon row of the finest South African and European wines and, air-conditioned and built of insulated concrete, the cellar kept them all at the correct temperature.

'What are you trying to say?' she shook her head in wonder. 'Are you telling me that – this place is – yours?'

'Mine – and two other chaps'.'

Suddenly she felt uneasy. 'I see. I didn't know, of course.'

'Well, you know now.' From behind the lenses his tawny eyes mocked her. He irritated her with his habit of rolling his tongue around the inside of his mouth, feeling for good in his teeth.

'It's all so simple,' he was saying. 'After a trip up the Pass in one of my Land-Rovers, my customers will be brought back here in the evening – at a price, of course, if they're willing to pay, and *I* think they will be. For those who aren't willing to pay,' he shrugged easily, 'well, they'll be taken back to their chalets with the natty little kitchens where they can provide their own meal.'

'I had no idea,' she said again. 'You've certainly been very busy.' Her blue eyes roved about the intimate dining-room which was furnished with Italian furniture and set with fine linen, silver and crystal.

In the beautifully beamed lounge beyond, where guests could relax and have a drink, there were antiques and Persian rugs. During the day, or before sunset, there were splendid views of the mountains and, by night, a floodlit garden. There was also a swimming-pool.

'So this is what Lyle Cunningham had in mind,' said Glen, 'so far as your brother's farm was concerned. Anyway, I'm not worried about missing out on your brother's farm. This one cropped up instead, and, if you won't take it amiss, it is a *far* better one.'

Suddenly Michelle felt involved – as if she had been working hand in glove with Glen Hayes these last two months just by keeping company with him.

'There seems to be dirty work going on all round, in all directions, doesn't there?' Her voice was hard. She went on, 'It's rather tragic, really, in this wonderful setting where everything else is so pure.'

'Don't get uptight, Michelle. I'm only telling you how it is. Take for instance this nursery business. I happen to know that Lyle Cunningham and Cunningham Senior had this same thing in mind. They were going to hire the assistance of a nursery manager. They were going to build greenhouses, with motor-driven fans to keep them cool and thermostats to keep the temperature constant. Sorters were to do the picking and the sorting . . .'

'What were they going to grow in the greenhouses?' she asked, thinking of Pete's farm as it could have been and as it was – nothing short of a failure.

Glen laughed softly. 'Flowers, of course. What else? For dispatch to the florists in Pietermaritzburg, Durban – all over, in fact. But I think we've outsmarted the Cunninghams. Work has already started here.' He moved his head in the direction of the huge glass windows. There was a gloating expression on his face.

'Well,' Michelle shrugged, 'you're sharp, all right.' Her eyes rested on his handsome face. Then she turned for her mohair stole which was draped across the back of her chair. Glen came round and placed it about her shoulders.

'Does Liza know about all this?' She tilted her head to look up at him.

'Aha . . . Liza. Now there's a thing. Well, yes, Liza knows quite a bit about what goes on in these parts, as a matter of fact.'

'Good for Liza!'

Ignoring the sarcasm in her voice, Glen put his tongue in his cheek. He began to follow her from the dining-room. 'Anyway,' he said, 'you're still driving up the Pass with me, aren't you? It's time I christened one of the Land-Rovers. I tell you what, we'll smash a bottle of champagne over the bonnet. How's that?'

'I don't know,' she answered shortly. 'Somehow I find all this disconcerting.'

'All what – disconcerting?' he asked, and then, before she had time to reply to his question, they stopped to say good night to a bowing Gino and his wife Alida.

When they were outside, next to his car, Glen asked, 'What is all this about finding things disconcerting?' As usual, he had been drinking too much.

'Oh . . .' her voice was bitter, 'the story of the farms. After all, my brother happens to be involved, to an extent. He's practically finished, from what I've heard, and the vultures are sitting on the fence, waiting. Window-shopping, if you like.' Her voice broke a little. The man she was in love with was also sitting on that fence.

'My war is with the Cunninghams,' said Glen. 'I hardly know your brother and his wife.'

'Why are you at war with the Cunninghams? Just because they happened to get in first and buy the hotel from under your nose?'

'You're missing the point,' Glen sounded aggressive now. 'I'm a businessman.'

Starlight gilded Michelle's face. 'Hasn't it struck you, Glen, that you might have bitten off more than you can chew?' she asked.

'I don't think along those lines.'

'When I think of what's been going on behind my brother's back I could be sick,' she murmured, getting into the car.

Glen got in on the other side and slammed the door closed. 'Let's not get touchy,' he said carelessly. 'I've only done what Lyle Cunningham had in mind. My partners and I happened to be in luck. When this place,' he waved a hand, 'came on the market it was already built up – just had to be taken over and utilized. Not like your brother's farm – a white elephant which had to be changed into something worth while. Even if the Cunninghams had bought it they would virtually have had to start from scratch to get anywhere.'

'You must feel pretty good, Glen.' Michelle's voice was deceptively soft.

'Yeah, I do, as a matter of fact – but then I always do. Besides, who doesn't like money? And in order to have money you've got to make money. It's as simple as that. And in order to make money, you've got to be on the ball. Money doesn't just fall into your lap. You've got to work . . . and I'm prepared to work – *a point.*' He laughed lightly.

'I haven't seen you work very hard – not like Pete, my brother. You should see his hands – and Laney's, for that matter.' Michelle's voice was bitter. 'Even the Cunninghams. They've worked to get where they are. Lyle . . . apart from the hotel there's Little Switzerland Motors, and often he drives people up the Pass himself . . .'

They drove in silence until the lights of the hotel began to

148

show. Glen drove through the entrance and brought the car to a halt at the steps. He leaned over to open the door on Michelle's side. 'I'll phone you,' he said, 'about going up the Pass.'

'I'll have to think about it,' she told him. 'After all, it does happen to be a nerve-racking experience, and I've already been up.'

'You promised.' His voice was mocking and accusing at the same time.

'Yes, I know.'

'Well? So – I'll phone you, Michelle.'

The hotel was completely booked up and Michelle was busy in the days to come, with little time to spare for helping out at the desk. Twice, however, she drove to the farm to have dinner with Pete and Laney and she told them about Glen's farm which was, in fact, a restaurant, and about the nursery.

There was a strange silence, then Pete said, 'We've heard something about it, as a matter of fact. It's not advertised, of course, and yet it's drawing tourists. Actually,' he cleared his throat, 'there was interest shown in this place, for the very same reason – or rather, from the nursery point of view, not the restaurant.'

'Was the interest shown by Glen Hayes?' Michelle felt mean for trying to draw Pete and Laney out to talk about their problems, but she wanted to get to the bottom of everything.

'No, not Hayes. I mean the interest shown to us personally was not by Hayes. I learned afterwards from the agents that he was also interested in buying the farm. There was someone else . . .' He broke off. 'Anyway, we took it off the market and tried to make another go of it. We borrowed some money . . . the next best thing.'

'I sometimes think we made a mistake,' said Laney. 'We should have sold and given up the responsibility, when we had the opportunity.'

'I didn't come out here to buy a farm to work for a boss,' Pete cut in. 'I bought a farm to make a go of it and to be my own boss. I don't mean to accept defeat.'

149

'Now you're twisting things,' Laney sounded faintly annoyed. 'It wouldn't have been accepting defeat.'

'To me it would have,' Pete ran bronzed fingers through his fair hair, 'at the time. Now that you're pregnant I guess it's different. I might have considered it. I can't expect you to go on putting up with all this worry.'

'If only you'd told me before, in your letters,' Michelle said, 'instead of after. I'd have let you have what money I could, instead of spending it to come here. It would have saved you from borrowing the money from him ...' she checked herself quickly. 'I mean borrowing it from the person who ...'

'It needn't go on being a secret,' Laney cut in. 'It was Lyle Cunningham, Michelle.'

Michelle felt suddenly sick. 'Had I known,' she said, 'I'd never have bought the Mini. I'd have let you have what I could towards paying him back.' He made sure he had us all tied up, she was thinking bitterly. Pete, Laney and me.

'All that's being taken care of,' said Pete, 'and we're paying it back – slowly, but we're paying it back. We shouldn't have borrowed money in the first place.'

Laney was looking upset now. 'Pete, you shouldn't say that. The money was a godsend at the time, and you know it.' Turning to Michelle, she said, 'He didn't want it back – Lyle Cunningham, I mean. He's been marvellous, actually.'

No, thought Michelle. Lyle Cunningham hasn't been marvellous. He wanted it over you.

'Well,' Pete shrugged, 'we missed the boat and we'd better just make the best of it. It'll take time, but we'll manage. I didn't want to involve Michelle in all this.' He looked at Laney and his voice was accusing and, anxious to get off the subject, Michelle said, 'Your dessert was super, Laney. That cream ... umm!'

After a couple of weeks the hotel started emptying. It went like that – depending on the weather, the school holidays ... Michelle had time on her hands to help at the desk, although there was no urgency.

It was true, she found herself thinking, about what Laney had said. It was difficult to make permanent friends when you lived and worked at a hotel. People came and people went. Friendships were formed and friendships fizzled out. After all, one couldn't keep up letter-writing with nothing much in common except a brief acquaintanceship at the hotel, indefinitely. Something had to give and so letters and letter-writing slackened away eventually to stop.

So it was that she found it difficult to keep on refusing Glen's invitations to dine or to go for a drive or to see a film at the chalets. He seemed quite unperturbed by Michelle's aloofness, so far as his advances were concerned.

Although Glen's Land-Rovers were now in operation up the Pass she had not driven up with him. It was common knowledge at this stage that his brochures were carefully worded so that the reader could be misled into believing that his vehicles were the only ones available to tourists.

Michelle was having dinner with Debbie one evening, when Alex Winters, who was responsible for the entertainment side of things in the hotel, came up to them. 'Hello there. We're having trouble getting people together for tonight's Check Your Mate programme. How about taking part?'

'This is a fine time to tell us,' Debbie joked. 'We both had a date.'

'You both have one now. I want to see you both in the main lounge around eight. Right, Michelle?'

'All right. It looks as if we don't have much choice, doesn't it? But what are we supposed to do, Alex? This is a game for married or engaged couples.'

'We'll find you both a mate, don't worry.' Alex lifted a hand and left them.

The hotel was blessed with a small crowd; most of the guests lethargic after a day of lounging in the sun on the terraces, their conversation punctuated by the clatter of teacups or the clinking of glasses and, so far as Alex Winters was concerned, the going was heavy as he tried to organize amusement.

Michelle was completely unprepared for the fact that she had been paired off with Lyle Cunningham, who apparently was spending the evening at the hotel. Up to now she had avoided him successfully, although she was always aware of him, always thinking about him and, like a fool, loving him.

When he saw her he gave her a mocking glance. 'So Alex has paired us off? He's having a thin time, apparently. They don't even pretend to laugh at his jokes. He's roped me in this evening into helping out.' His blue-green eyes met hers.

'I wouldn't like his job,' Michelle answered with a feeling of helplessness. 'It must be difficult to arrange entertainment, unless there happens to be a film show, or dancing, and that takes care of things.'

'All right, then,' Alex was saying, embracing everyone in the lounge with his smile, 'so we're going to play Check your Mate and we are going to ask for volunteers ... We already have four, as a matter of fact. Michelle Abbott here and – er – Lyle, who's visiting us this evening. This is Debbie, as you all know, and Jake Gobbi. He drives people up the Pass when he's not making passes at the girls.' There was a small polite round of laughter. 'I'm going to start with this four-some first,' Alex continued, 'but before we get going and to set the ball rolling I'd like all those volunteers to come up to the table here and sit down – ladies on this side, gentlemen on this. Right?'

With a feeling of helplessness Michelle listened to Alex as he tried to get things going, and it was with some relief that she heard him call upon Debbie and Jake first. This gave her the time she needed to calm herself in preparation for her part in the lounge game which, under different circumstances, could have been amusing.

Eventually Alex called upon her to answer the questions he had before him. 'Michelle,' his eyes were mocking, 'it's a fair assumption, I think, to say that you know Lyle rather well, although you're not married to the guy, or engaged, for that matter. Right?'

She was standing next to Alex now. 'Right.' She hoped her voice sounded normal and smiled obligingly at the small crowd sitting at tables in the lounge. The waiters were hurrying about with trays, bearing glasses and drinks. Laughter was becoming a little more spontaneous. Lyle had been locked safely away behind the heavy doors which led to

152

the foyer leading to the dining-room. He was well protected from eavesdropping.

'No, Michelle,' Alex laughed, 'don't try to run away. You met Lyle some time ago, at a house party, I believe?'

'Yes.' Her smile was tense.

'Can you remember the very first words he spoke to you?'

'I can't remember,' she said.

'Just take it easy. Relax. Of course you can, Michelle. Don't let me down. What did Lyle have to say when you first met?'

'I – I can't,' she murmured.

'Well, what do you remember about him?' Alex coughed. 'Take your time. We all know you're nervous.' He grinned at the crowd, playing for time.

'I remember his eyes,' she said.

Alex looked relieved. 'His eyes? Why, Michelle?'

'Because they happen to be rather startling eyes – blue-green and very direct. I – I felt a shock at their – er – uncanny magnetism, actually.'

There was a murmur of approval from the audience. 'His eyes,' Alex was saying, 'caused a shock to run down the length of your spine. They were all you could think about. It's not surprising you can't remember what he said to you. I mean, let's assume that you were introduced to him in a crowd – as it was a house-party. Right?'

'That's correct.'

'But when you were alone? Can you remember what he said, Michelle?'

Laughing a little, Michelle said, 'I can't think what I've done to deserve this, but anyway, he said, you're a long way from home. I'm trying to get to the bottom of this – are you here to settle? Something to this effect, anyway.' She laughed again, to hide her embarrassment.

'I see . . .' Alex drawled. 'Well now, we're getting some place.' He grinned at Michelle. 'Okay, Michelle, now you stand right there and we'll have Lyle in.' He opened the heavy door and went through the foyer seperating the lounge from the dining-room. 'Lyle,' Alex's voice was loud, 'you can come out of the dining-room now.'

A wave of embarrassment gripped Michelle as Alex said, 'Now Lyle, you and Michelle met at a house-party, I believe. We've already asked Michelle what your first words to her were – after you and she found yourselves alone, that is, and she has told us. What we want to know from you, therefore, is what *your* first words to her were?'

Lyle regarded Alex with some amusement and then those blue-green eyes swung across to Michelle and one dark brow went up. 'Can you remember?' Alex asked.

'Yes,' Lyle's eyes continued to hold Michelle's, 'I can remember, as a matter of fact. I said, and I quote, you're a long way from home.'

'What else?' Alex asked, over and above the clapping from the audience.

Looking at Lyle, Michelle found herself thinking wildly that she had placed herself right into his hands.

Lyle paused for a moment, and then he said, 'I think these were my exact words – I'm trying to get to the bottom of this – are you here to settle?'

There was more applause and laughter from the audience, louder this time.

'You see,' Alex was saying, pleased that things were going his way at last, 'when two people meet they either click or they don't. Obviously, Michelle Abbott and Lyle Cunningham clicked first go. Now, Lyle, I want you to go back in there and – believe me, ladies and gentlemen, it's perfectly sound-proof – and wait until we call you again.'

This time Michelle was asked, 'Michelle, can you remember what you were wearing on the night you met Lyle for the first time?'

Michelle realized suddenly that her shoulders and neck were aching with tension.

'Yes,' there was more than a hint of impatience in her voice, 'I can remember what I was wearing.'

'Will you tell the audience, Michelle?'

She did her best to suppress her impatience. 'I was wearing a floor-length gown – white and very plain.'

There was a burst of applause. People were beginning to loosen up. Alex was grinning, showing the gap between his front two teeth, the tension easing its way out of him now.

'And now we'll have Lyle back in here and see what he has to say.'

Once again Lyle was called into the lounge and Michelle found herself catching her left wrist in her right hand, to stop it from shaking. How did I get involved in this? she thought angrily as she listened to Alex.

'Lyle,' he was saying, 'can you remember what Michelle was wearing on that unforgettable night?'

'Yes. Michelle was wearing white – something very plain, I remember.'

'A short white dress?' Alex asked. 'Was she wearing a short white dress?'

'It was floor-length,' said Lyle.

'But this is fantastic,' Alex almost shouted. 'And I can assure you, ladies and gentlemen, that it's absolutely sound-proof behind those doors.'

There were five more questions put to her and each one trivial but enough to give her away. Michelle was thankful when the ordeal came to an end.

When the game was over she left the lounge and went to stand on the terrace. She felt drained and empty. The silly little game had got out of hand, she thought. She had given so much away when all she should have done was to have treated the questions put to her by Alex lightly and with amused contempt.

'Admiring the stars?' She turned sharply as Lyle Cunningham joined her.

'Yes. I was just leaving, though.'

'I think we did rather well, don't you?' he asked. There was a certain enjoyment in his voice, she thought bitterly.

'I played to help Alex out,' she replied, after a moment. 'It meant absolutely nothing.'

'But you must admit the result was immediate and dramatic.' His voice was cool now.

'I wouldn't say that. Frankly, it's all rather stupid. For my own part, I merely joined in to help Alex out, as I've already explained. I guess somebody had to try and provide the laughs. Alex has been battling with this crowd for nights on end. They just wouldn't loosen up. On the night of the dance most of them didn't even dance. This seems to be one time when quite apart from the hotel not being fully booked, a crowd of people with no zest for anything except drinking, eating and sitting around has managed to get under the same roof at the same time – with devastating results.'

Now that the moment of discovering him beside her was over she felt comparatively in control of the situation.

'Talking about eating,' he said, 'what's the food like at the Sabaudia Restaurant?'

The question caught her off balance. 'The Sabaudia Restaurant?' she asked.

'Yes. You should know – it's practically your second home, isn't it? I'm referring to Glen Hayes' new project – the farm.'

After a moment she said, 'Sarcasm comes so easily to you, doesn't it? But, to put your mind at rest, the food is out of this world – especially their desserts. I'll be getting madly fat. You see, there's always a wide choice – from an exciting concoction of golden sponge, cream and almond liqueur topped with tiny, tiny eclairs to freshly picked giant strawberries and wonderfully thick cream.'

'All grown on the farm, naturally?'

'Yes, naturally. *You'd* be interested in that, of course. I mean, that is what you wanted my brother's farm for, wasn't it? So that you could grow things to deep-freeze and to set up a nursery where you'd grow flowers to send off to florists all over the place?' She took a shuddering little breath. 'What a pity Glen Hayes and his partners got in first!'

'You're so right,' he answered. 'It is a pity. The position might well have been so much easier for your brother had there not been so much pride in the way. After Pete and Laney made the mistake of going back on their decision to sell Glen Hayes was being kept supplied with all the information he needed to set his mind working.'

Michelle did a rough calculation in her mind. 'You speak as if you think *I* was the one to pass on that information. I've been here long enough, as it so happens, to do that, but I have never discussed these matters with Glen Hayes. I mean,' she broke off and shrugged agitatedly, 'why *should* I? I mean – my own brother's affairs! How ridiculous can you get?'

'Perhaps you were not aware that the information I'm referring to concerned your brother,' he said quietly, and she swung round to face him.

'What are you trying to say?' Her voice rose a little. 'I knew Pete and Laney had put the farm up for sale and then withdrew it from the market. They accepted a loan, instead – to try and get them back on their feet. A loan which was to bind them – because they'll either have to scrape the money together in order to repay it or they will have to sell the farm in the long run, won't they?' Her voice was accusing.

'You tell me,' he answered, and his voice was hard. 'You seem to know all about it, Michelle?'

'Oh, no. That's where you're so wrong,' she told him. 'I do know where the loan came from, but there's so much I don't know, believe me.'

'Suppose you ask Pete and Laney about it?'

'And suppose,' she went on, 'you ask Liza Monatti how certain information could have got into Glen's hands?'

There was the faintest hesitation, then he said, 'Perhaps now is the time, Michelle, to let you know that Liza has mentioned that you've been in the habit of discussing hotel affairs on the phone with Glen Hayes. Not that this matters very much. He probably would have found things out for himself, had you not been willing to supply him with the necessary facts.'

She was stunned. 'It's not true – and you should know it. How can you begin to think these things of me?'

'Why not? You seem to have *me* pretty well weighed up. *You've* never stopped to think, have you?' She knew his blue-green eyes were angry.

'I could ask you the same question. Have you stopped to think about me?' She felt herself begin to shake.

'More than you'd believe,' he told her, 'but there's a limit to how far you can go.'

'Well, that could be a good thing.' Michelle wished she could stop shaking. 'Perhaps now you'll leave me to get on with my own affairs?'

'I think we can arrange that, Michelle. In any case, I'm not in a position to stop you from seeing Glen Hayes – but maybe, just maybe, you'll come to see things as they really are one of these days.'

'I already know how things are – and you're right about Glen Hayes. I'm seeing him tomorrow, as it so happens. I'm going up the Pass with him – and I intend to go on seeing him.'

It was a moment before he answered. 'Feel perfectly free. That doesn't concern me – not any more.'

Michelle watched him as he turned and left her, then her eyes changed swiftly as she put her teeth down on her lip and began to cry softly.

CHAPTER ELEVEN

'I'VE brought the food,' said Glen the next day, glancing over his shoulder into the back of the Land-Rover, 'and the drink.'

Michelle felt as though she had fallen head-first into a trap. 'You aren't going to drink, are you? Not on this kind of trip?'

'We're both going to celebrate,' Glen replied.

'It would be madness!' Michelle took a breath. 'Perhaps you can see some humour in turning a dangerous trip up the Pass into a drinking session, Glen, but I'm afraid I can't.'

They were hitting the corrugations now, and the dust was flying in all directions. Glen was engaged in busy and constant gear work. In the distance, the mountains were blue with patches of snow in the cold, dark crevices. It was not as hot as it had been during the past two weeks and at ten o'clock in the morning the air was balmy.

'I've brought something to drink for on the way up,' Glen was almost shouting to make himself heard. 'So what's wrong in that?'

Although the Land-Rover was comparatively new it had been driven up the Pass a number of times and already there were rattles. Glen appeared to be handling the vehicle badly, Michelle thought.

'I see,' she answered and, incredibly detached now, she *did* see. She was suddenly detached because she was here and Glen was going to drink; she was going to be nervous, but there was nothing she could do about it now that they were on their way. Knowing Glen as she did, she knew that he could turn nasty over the least thing and if she said anything more he would only end up drinking more than he had originally intended.

Had she forgotten this awful – and yet incredibly wonderful – drive she asked herself. Had she forgotten how nervous she had been with an expert like Lyle Cunningham behind the wheel? Something told her that there was no expert skill in the manner in which Glen was handling his Land-Rover. He might be able to handle a low-slung sports car, she thought, but this was not the same thing. Into the bargain, he intended drinking. What a fool she had been!

From the beginning, right before starting on the laborious climb, the bends were hairpin and hair-raising. How could I have forgotten? she asked herself.

The Land-Rover broadsided around them, sending up stones and dust.

'Glen,' she said, above the noise, 'why don't you hoot at the bends?'

Glancing carelessly in her direction, he said, 'Why? Why hoot, Michelle? This isn't exactly a freeway, you know.'

'No, but had you thought – there could be a vehicle coming down? Don't you see? And you wouldn't know until it was too late. If you hooted first an oncoming vehicle could move over or stop or hoot back – or something – *anything*, and you could pass without danger.'

Laughing, he said, 'Let him do the hooting, then. You're in a disgusting mood, Michelle, do you know that?'

'I'm not in a disgusting mood, but I'll tell you something, Glen, I'm getting there.'

'Forget it,' he told her. Turning away from him, she tried to concentrate on the sight of proteas clinging to the mountain sides, the rock-fall which Lyle had pointed out . . . The sight of the cab of the truck which had been flattened in its path filled her with fresh fear.

Scarlet flowers raced past, the dust obscuring them. They had caught up to another vehicle and Glen braked suddenly and then accelerated again. The Land-Rover in front of them was packed with Basotho men, wearing blankets and mealie-straw hats, looped at the top.

The dust from the vehicle was smothering and Glen pulled into the side of the road and switched off the engine. 'Let them get on ahead,' he said, 'before we suffocate in their dust.'

Another vehicle was groaning and protesting as it approached, from behind, and then, with nothing to spare, passed them. 'They're taking beans up,' said Glen. 'Provisions.'

'I see.' Michelle sat back, but there was no relaxation in the movement. The groaning of the vehicles as they climbed on ahead could still be heard although they had disappeared from sight, obscured by the winding Pass.

With a sudden movement Glen slipped across the wide seat and Michelle caught her breath as his arms closed about her. 'Glen,' she said quickly, 'please don't.'

'Why?' His mouth was close to her own. 'Tell me why I shouldn't, Michelle. Just give me one good reason why I shouldn't.'

'You know the reason,' she said. 'I'm not in love with you. I've told you that before today.'

'I don't believe you. You wouldn't go on seeing me if you weren't.'

His was a handsome and yet a weak face, Michelle thought, and the thick, rimmed glasses did nothing to strengthen it.

'Do people have to be in love before they can spend time together?' she asked, while a kind of panic gripped her.

'I think so,' he answered. 'At any rate, there has to be some attraction. In any case, I'm in no hurry, Michelle.'

She cleared her throat and moved restlessly in the circle of his arms. 'I think we should turn back,' she said. 'It would be better all round if we turned back now. Don't you agree with me?'

Suddenly he released her. 'No, I don't agree, and we aren't going to turn back. You're giving me a hard time, but in any case, forget it. There, that ought to make your day.' His laugh was sarcastic.

'I was thinking,' she tried to keep her voice reasonable, 'it's getting awfully cloudy up there.' Her eyes went in the direction of the beautiful if barren valleys, the distant horizons of Lesotho. 'And you know what they say, Glen . . .'

'No. What do they say?' He opened the door and got out and stood looking up at her. Before she was able to reply he went to the back of the Land-Rover and opened the doors and took out a hamper. 'I think a drink is called for,' he called out cheerfully. 'Might as well let those vehicles get well ahead. We don't want to swallow their dust all the way. I mean, that should make sense.'

Turning in her seat in order to see him, Michelle said, 'They say thunderstorms occur roughly every two days out of three.' Moodily she watched him as he put the hamper back on the floor of the Land-Rover, then he climbed in and sat on one of the side seats at the back. He bent over, unfastening the clasp of the picnic hamper, and took out a bottle and two mineral bottles. Then he reached for a vacuum which was packed with ice. 'The weather is super,' he said, 'now let's stop worrying, shall we?' He gave her a mocking glance.

'Just pour me a mineral.' She sat quietly in her little pool of resentment and looked at him. 'I don't care for anything stronger. At any rate, not so early in the morning.' She forced herself to smile.

'Well,' he shrugged elaborately, 'have it your own sweet way, but I'm out to enjoy myself and I'm having something just a little bit stronger than mineral water, let me make that perfectly clear.' He regarded her with half-closed eyes and an amused smile. A moment later he handed her a glass, sparkling with ginger-ale. 'Cheers,' he said.

She reached over and took the glass from him. 'Thank you.'

There were cooling-off noises coming from the Land-Rover. 'Do you want anything to eat?' Glen said.

'No, thank you.' She tried to sound pleasant. Perhaps it would be all right, she thought. Perhaps she was worrying for nothing. So far as his advances were concerned, it had always been all right up to now. She had always managed him. But, a little voice whispered, there could be a turning point.

Glen finished his drink and, much to her relief, did not pour another. 'Okay.' He smacked his lips and grinned at her. 'Let's move, baby.' Michelle passed him her glass and watched him as he packed it away giving careful attention to the container holding the ice. 'We'll need this. I don't want it to melt. Nothing worse than a warm drink.'

His smile was beginning to get on her nerves. 'I'm surprised you haven't a portable fridge and bar in here,' she said somewhat cuttingly.

'Don't worry,' he told her, 'that will come in the very near

162

future.' He jumped down on to the dusty track and slammed the doors, then came round to the driver's side and got in. Before he started the engine he gave her a lazy grin. 'Minnie Moaner,' he said, 'you surprise me. I thought you had more go in you than this.'

They reached the security base and after showing their identity papers got back into the Land-Rover and drove on.

Michelle tried concentrating on the scenery – boulders galore, a cave, a waterfall emptying itself over more boulders. Her eyes strayed to Glen's hands on the vibrating wheel. Fairly tanned hands with tawny hairs on the fingers, just beneath the knuckles. His wrists were surprisingly thick, which came as a surprise, for he was slightly under medium height and not thick-set, by any means. She found herself comparing his hands to Lyle Cunningham's, which were strong and tanned.

Suddenly Glen braked. 'Look,' he said, 'a bearded vulture. See that?'

Michelle followed the flight of the great bird with her eyes. 'It has a terrific wing-span,' said Glen. Lyle Cunningham, she thought, would have known exactly how wide.

'That, I think, calls for another drink.' Glen got out and stood in the sun, stretching. 'It's not every day you see a bearded vulture,' he called out, grinning.

To some people this could have been a whole lot of fun, Michelle found herself thinking. To Glen's type of girl and to people like Marie – the girl who had gone up on the day she had driven up the Pass with Lyle – Marie, goading Lyle on and on, for kicks. To a person of sane reasoning, however, it was proving to be nothing short of a nightmare, and she only had herself to blame.

'Come on,' Glen was calling, 'get out into the sun and stretch those lovely legs and look about you. That's what we're here for, isn't it? There's no time limit.'

Michelle shrugged helplessly and opened the heavy door and jumped out. There was a raging, raw wind blowing and she shivered, pulling her jersey down over her slacks. Her hair was blowing about her face, strands of it sticking to her lips.

Glen poured more drinks and she watched him moodily. Mockingly serene, he watched her back. High up, the mountains jutted arrogantly in the clouds, alone and free. It seemed madness that she should be here, with possible death lurking at every hairpin bend, and she was provoked by a sudden anger to say, 'I've taken enough. I wish you'd stop drinking, Glen. I'm nervous enough as it is.' She sighed with the uselessness of it all. 'It's a good thing *you* don't drive your guests up here. At least you had sense enough to employ a couple of drivers.'

Glen looked pensive and sad, an affectation with him. Slowly he shook his head. 'I can't understand you, Michelle, honestly I can't.' His voice was gently accusing. 'You're letting me down. I feel utterly relaxed. Why can't you be? To get away from it all – wonderful! The rat race forgotten for a little while.'

'The only rat race is the one you've started yourself,' she told him with considerable heat.

The peaks of the mountains were becoming obscure as clouds were trailed across them. Down where they were, however, there were little explosions of sunlight on Glen's lenses.

'Look,' he sounded impatient with her now, 'I happen to like it that way, but I also like to get away from it once in a while. I mean, who doesn't? So relax, will you?'

Michelle pulled the collar of the jacket she had slipped on over her jersey around her chin. 'It's freezing,' she shuddered. 'This wind is freezing. The weather is changing all the time.'

'Well, let it change.' Glen stopped speaking as a group of blanketed men on horses which seemed a size too small for them came around a bend, on their way down the Pass. Perhaps they were ponies, Michelle thought, watching the colourful scene, black-skinned and blanketed to cope with the cold the men on their sturdy little animals passed beneath a mass of rock that overhung the road and which looked as though it might thunder down at any moment.

Glen packed the glasses into the hamper and they got back into the Land-Rover. This was going to be the hardest part now, Michelle remembered, with a feeling of fright.

Was Glen going to manage it?

The wheels spun as he fought for control. Down in the valley were several carcasses of fallen vehicles – vehicles that had not made the grade through, no doubt, carelessness on the part of the drivers. Eventually, however, they reached the top. They crossed the border into Lesotho and then drove the short way to the mountain chalet. The blanketed man with the peg-leg had greeted them as he held out a straw hat which Michelle bought, although it was far too small to wear. At the chalet the cross St. Bernards wagged their tails and the freezing wind ruffled their coats.

As Michelle climbed down from the Land-Rover she re-alized that her legs were ready to cave in.

'There you are, we made it. How do you feel?' Glen asked, grinning.

'Frankly, that my days are numbered, after that ordeal. This is positively the last time I come up the Pass.' Her eyes took in the fact that there were no other vehicles parked outside the chalet and she knew despair as the hope that she might have been able to cadge a lift back down the Pass faded. The return trip would have to be made with Glen Hayes, and her eyes were troubled as she stood looking down at the wriggling snake which was the Pass, twisting and fading from sight.

'I'll take the hamper to the kitchen,' Glen was saying cheerfully. For a moment Michelle watched him moodily, then, with her shoulders hunched, she followed him inside and went through to the big main room where she stood looking out of the big windows – remembering . . .

When Glen came into the room she did not move. 'There's time for a couple of drinks before lunch,' she heard him say, and because she knew that words wouldn't stop him from having them, she turned and followed him through to the small bar and this time she joined him in having a drink, feeling an almost urgent need of something to warm and settle her clamouring nerves.

'Good for you,' Glen laughed softly and appreciatively, 'I knew you'd thaw out.'

'There's going to be a storm,' she said, 'you know that, of course?' She kept her voice carefully expressionless so that she would not irritate him.

Through the window to one side of the bottle-laden shelves they could see the wind tearing at the plateau.

Glen swore. 'Forget the storm. Relax.'

'I can't,' Michelle said.

'Try to. Just try to.' He took a swallow of his drink. 'You know, it takes peak physical fitness to drive up here,' he said.

Yes, she thought rebelliously, and *you* haven't got it.

'One false move and a driver could foul the attempt and ruin a Land-Rover.'

'And kill his passengers into the bargain,' she replied, and saw from his face that he did not like the remark.

'The last thing I want to do is to kill my passenger or passengers. Talk sense!'

'I am talking sense. Drinking and driving do not go together. I'm only trying to be practical, Glen.' She tried to smile in an attempt to get through to him.

Outside, the wind rumbled and howled around the chalet. Michelle glanced at the barman. 'No visitors today?' she asked.

'No, not today.' She could see he remembered her. 'No blanket for you today?'

Shaking back her damp hair, she laughed. 'No, not today, thank you, although I might *have* to buy one yet.' She shivered. 'The weather is changing all the time.'

'You can't stop it,' he laughed throatily. 'You'll feel better after nice hot dinner. You didn't eat chicken à la Lesotho yet?'

'No.' She was immediately interested, while Glen looked on, amused. 'Tell me.' Out of the corner of her eye she saw Glen get up and go behind the counter where he helped himself to another drink. He put the money down on the counter with a defiant little slap.

'We cook in traditional iron pot – that give a good flavour. That is right, flavour?' the barman asked.

'Yes, that's quite right.'

'With this you drink our beer – but with special taste, to suit the Western palate.'

'I'd like to try that,' said Michelle. There was a whisper

166

of fear in her voice, for she was not giving her full attention to the man behind the counter. Instead, she was thinking about Glen. Glen, she realized, was drunk – not mildly drunk, but quite frighteningly so. Why do girls get themselves into these impossible situations? she asked herself bitterly. Don't we ever stop to think? Her eyes strayed to the window. The sky threatened rain from heavy clouds full of menace.

Glen had arranged a cold lunch. He would. Michelle's thoughts were full of resentment. Inside the hamper there had been cold cuts and salads and chilled wine which he said he couldn't buy up at the chalet.

They ate in the dining-room and there was a constant murmuring of voices coming from the direction of the kitchen, which comforted Michelle somewhat.

'I think we should leave as soon as we've eaten our lunch,' she kept her voice pleasant, 'don't you?'

'Look,' Glen's usually soft voice was even softer, 'there's going to be a storm. You said so yourself, and there's nothing you can do about it. There's nothing I can do about it. So? What's the answer? We've got to wait for it to pass. That's the most reasonable thing to do.'

'But it could go on for days,' she answered, with impatience now. 'Up here the conditions could remain terrible for days. Even *I'm* beginning to know the Drakensberg by this time.'

'That'll be the day,' Glen laughed mockingly. 'But look, like I said, Michelle, forget it.'

There was a crack-of-a-whip flash of lightning only a split second before an explosion of thunder and then, apart from the howling of the wind, complete, terrifying silence. Michelle found herself waiting for another flash, her nerves tensed beyond words. Outside, the wind tore at mountain crags and slammed itself against the precipices.

Glen was helping himself to biscuits and cheese. His movements were slow and precise. He shuffled fragments of food about in his mouth with his tongue and, looking at him, Michelle felt contempt towards him.

'Glen,' she said, 'hurry, please! Why are you doing this to me?'

'After I've had some coffee.'

'Here, let me pour it for you.' She went in the direction of the table against the wall at the far end of the room, where the maid had placed the coffee things. After she had poured the coffee, which was very strong, she brought a cup back to him. 'Drink it before it gets cold, then we can leave.'

Looking at her, Glen said, 'I don't like being cheated, Michelle, and you're trying to cheat me.'

'Nonsense. You don't come into it. I'm merely trying to cheat the storm.'

'Have some coffee,' he said.

'I have some. Look.' She went to her cup and saucer.

'When am I going to see you again?' he asked.

'You are seeing me. Let's have our coffee.'

When they had finished they went out to the Land-Rover and the wind forced Michelle to take two steps backwards. The clouds were low and the air moist, but it had not started to rain and there had been no more lightning.

Glen started the engine and hooted at the dogs to move out of the way. Michelle noticed the way in which the wind was parting the thick hair on their backs – and yet the animals seemed unperturbed by the cold.

It seemed absolutely incredible, but far, far down in the distance there was sunshine.

'Well,' Glen was saying, over the noise, 'we're on our way. It won't be long now.' However, Michelle knew almost at once that her trials were only just beginning. Glen's movements were fumbling. He took the first hairpin bend too fast. Soon after leaving the border and after having driven along a flat strip, the track seemed to come to a halt and a kind of wall, from piled up boulders, had been built across it. Beyond the wall, there was a drop which went on and on into the valleys below. Michelle's frantic eyes questioned Glen's fingers which clutched the wheel. This, then, must surely be the end – and then, incredibly, there was the track again and they had made it round the bend. For a brief moment she turned to look at the silent peaks behind them, jutting through the low clouds. The peaks were cold, bleak and lifeless. The Land-Rover was groaning against compression as it began the descent. Glen swore softly and his hand moved towards the brake. He brought the vehicle to a skidding, shuddering halt, then inched it forward again. 'So? What's the next step?' he asked. 'I'm stoned.'

Michelle's nerves began screaming as he took another bend, dangerously near another wall of boulders which was really not a wall at all. There was no cement to tie the boulders together – nothing to stop them scattering. They were merely piled here, as a guide – as a grim reminder to what lay behind. A Land-Rover could go right through them and over and over again – down, down.

'Why did you do this?' she shouted. 'Why, Glen? Answer me!'

'You want the truth? The real truth? Well, the reason is simple – I'm worried.' He turned to look at her.

'Keep your eyes on the track!' she told him, practically screaming. Then she plunged her teeth into her lips as the Land-Rover tilted forward. Surely if the back came up much higher the Land-Rover would do a somersault? The wheels did not appear to be turning but skidding, locked in the grip of the brakes.

'I've spent a lot of money,' Glen tried to make himself heard over the engine and rattle noises. 'Most of it wasn't mine. I borrowed it. And you know what? I'm not going to be able to pay it back. But don't let me bore you with the facts.'

'Forget about that now,' Michelle told him. 'Concentrate on driving, Glen. Nothing else matters at the moment. The rest can wait. I'm sure you'll be able to sort it out.'

'That's what you think. Being wonderfully honest is all very well, but being wonderfully honest doesn't get you anywhere, so you've got to work round it somehow. Make it seem honest.'

'Concentrate on your driving, Glen, please!'

'And,' he went on, lifting his voice, 'being dishonest, even a little dishonest, makes enemies, let's face it – and right now I have a whole lot of enemies waiting for me down there.'

The drop to one side of the passenger seat made Michelle gasp with fright. 'Oh, look out!' she yelled.

'This is a hell of a way to handle a Land-Rover,' he

turned to grin at her. 'Can you drive?'

Michelle stared at him in disbelief and said nothing.

'Can you?' he repeated. 'You've got a car.'

'That's different.'

'Is there a difference?'

'Of course.' She could hardly control the shaking in her legs. Should she ask him to stop and let her out? She could walk. They could both walk.

'Glen,' she begged, 'stop the Land-Rover and let's walk down. Leave the Land-Rover here. Ease it over so that another vehicle might pass, if need be.'

'Uh-huh.' Glen shook his head. 'I'm not walking. *Walk?*' He turned to her and laughed outright. 'What do you take me for?'

'*I'd* like to walk.' She had her hand on the door handle.

'You'll do no such thing. I'm sure to let you walk. My favourite chick.' Suddenly the Land-Rover was slipping forward again. It gained speed and Michelle heard herself cry out.

In a flash she saw the drop on her side and knew they were going over, and then, without realizing that she was doing it, she put out her hand and wrenched the wheel so that the Land-Rover swerved over and hit the side of the mountain on Glen's side with a dull thud before the engine coughed and died with a great shudder.

She found she couldn't stop shaking – then she was gasping – crying, really, without tears. The tears were blocked behind a great barrage of shock.

Glen seemed stunned. He sat there saying nothing and, when she was calm enough, Michelle said, 'Put the handbrake on, dammit!'

Suddenly he was sober. 'It's in gear, and anyway, jammed against the mountain.' However, he reached for the brake. 'I'm sorry.'

In a small, exhausted voice she said, 'Yes. I'm sorry too.'

It had started to rain now and soon the sullen Sani Pass would be a slithery mess. Michelle felt the sudden chill of isolation.

'So? What's the answer?' Glen asked, and when she made

no response, he said, 'As soon as I've got myself in hand I'll see what I can do, Michelle.'

They sat in silence, then he said, 'I know this sounds ironical, but do you want a drink? To steady your nerves?'

She shook her head. 'No.'

He did not suggest one for himself. 'I'll have to open the door on your side,' he told her. 'I can't get out here. I want to see how we can get moving again.'

Not wanting to be left alone in the Land-Rover in case, by some trick of fate, it became dislodged from its resting place and started to move forward, Michelle got out first. Then she stood in the wind and the rain, watching helplessly, as Glen walked around the back of the Land-Rover.

Above the sound of the wind, she heard it – the drone of another vehicle as it laboured up towards them, still out of sight, but close. Glen had heard it too and came to stand beside her – and then they saw it: a Land-Rover. It stopped and the door opened and, unmistakably, Lyle Cunningham walked towards them, covering the ground in great strides.

His glance took in the Land-Rover jammed against the side of the mountain, its wheels turned sharply at an angle. The turning of those wheels had saved Glen Hayes' Land-Rover from going over the side of the Pass.

'And who was the brains behind this?' Lyle's eyes swept over Glen before he turned to Michelle.

'There was nearly an accident,' she said. 'He turned the steering wheel to stop it from going over.'

'*Michelle* turned the wheel,' Glen's voice was quiet, 'to stop us from going over. I was incapable. There, that should make your day.'

'Get into the Land-Rover back there.' Lyle's voice, as he looked at Michelle, was vibrant with authority. 'Out of the rain and the cold.'

'No, I'll stand here.' She wished she could stop shaking. 'I'm afraid it might start moving.'

'You're not dealing with a fool now. It won't run backwards. Get out of this cold rain.'

'Why did you come?' she found herself asking.

'To find you. Why else would I come?'

For a moment her blue eyes questioned him, then she turned and walked slowly in the direction of his Land-Rover, the soles of her shoes causing the small stones to roll beneath them. The rain was coming down harder. Far below, there was no sign of the sunlight which had been breaking through the clouds earlier on.

From this distance, Michelle could not hear what Lyle and Glen were saying, but obviously they were quarrelling. The smell of liquor on Glen's breath alone would have been enough to start Lyle off.

Miserably, her teeth chattering, she watched Lyle as he got into the crippled Land-Rover, then she heard the engine revving. The huge tyres slipped as they were worked loose from their jammed position. Finally the vehicle was free. Through a curtain of rain Michelle saw some small boulders which had been dislodged begin to roll down the side of the mountain and scatter into the road. Some of them went over the side, plunging out of sight.

Lyle stopped the Land-Rover and got out and Glen climbed in and started to move forward slowly. He pulled up next to Lyle's Land-Rover and called out, 'I'm going on down alone. I'm okay now. You'll feel better with him, okay?'

'Okay.' She mouthed the word back to him and lifted a hand.

When Lyle came back and opened the door on the driver's side the wind hurled itself inside, carrying rain with it. 'Well,' he turned to look at her, 'that was a magnificent display of skill – ramming the Land-Rover into the side, like that – if nothing else.'

'I can't take any more,' she told him in a small voice.

'You won't have to. I'll have to go up a bit further to do a turn.'

He had turned the wipers on and they moved the rain to one side, clearing the big windscreen for a moment and then going to work again. Lyle was completely absorbed in his task of driving to a point where, incredibly, he managed to turn after manoeuvring the Land-Rover backwards and forwards several times. The engine roared.

Some time later he said, 'What shall we talk about, Michelle? Your trip up? It must have been some trip if what happened on the way down is any indication.' His voice was hard.

Michelle flinched at the sound of it. 'If we must talk about it, let's just say that coming on the trip was a dumb decision on my part, and be finished with it.' Her voice shook slightly. 'But it seemed almost like a good idea at the time.'

Lyle glanced at his watch. His temper had cooled. 'I began to worry. You should have been back at three-thirty, or thereabouts. I know about his drinking problem.'

Michelle had lost track of the time. She wondered what the time was. After a moment she said, 'Thank you. I'm grateful.'

The rain had turned the trunks and the branches of the trees in the valleys black. The wheels were slipping. In the distance they could suddenly see Glen's Land-Rover as it crawled like an ant, partly obscured by the rain and the mist. Behind, way above, the peaks were out of sight, thrust into the black clouds.

Gradually the shock was wearing off and Michelle felt calmer, but she had nothing to say. She felt all used up. This was a situation she felt ill equipped to meet. After a while she said, 'I'm sorry. It was good of you to come.'

For the moment Lyle was too preoccupied with driving matters to answer her, then he said abruptly, 'Are you in love with him?'

She turned her head. 'Would I be here with you if I was?'

'Well, let's not waste any more time.' She watched him take a sharp breath. 'I called in at the farm, before I left – to see if you were there. Before that, you see, I'd rung Hayes' chalets to see if you'd gone back there with him. Laney gave me some clothes for you – they're in the back there. She said you always left some of your things in a cupboard. We thought you might be wet and cold. It was obvious what was happening up there.' He glanced over his shoulder, in the direction of the mountain chalet.

'I'm not very wet.' She had to lift her voice above the noise of the Land-Rover and all she felt like doing was to whisper. 'Just a little damp.'

After a moment he said, 'I'm taking you to my place.'

The Pass was straightening out now. There was no sign of Glen's Land-Rover.

'I've told you – I'm not wet,' said Michelle, her tension climbing again, 'so I fail to see the connection.'

'The connection is very simple. You're going to change out of your wet things and get into the things Laney sent along. And then I'm going to give you a drink, followed by dinner.'

'But why?' she heard herself ask, in a small voice. 'I could do that at the hotel – or at Laney's, if you'd take me there.' She felt herself beginning to panic at the thought of going to his house again.

'Because it seems to be the reasonable thing to do,' he told her, as the Land-Rover rattled over the small bridge which led to it.

CHAPTER TWELVE

WARM and inviting, the house awaited them. Lyle turned the Land-Rover into the sweeping brick-paved driveway, past the twin obelisks which were vaguely white in the shrouding, pelting rain. The lanterns on top of them were lit, spilling their light on to the wet driveway. The leaves of the exotic plants in pottery urns flanking the blue-tiled archway glinted with water and the wrought-iron gates were open to the tropical oasis of palms, ferns and pond.

Bringing the Land-Rover to a halt, Lyle switched off the ignition and, pocketing the keys, turned to look at Michelle. 'And that's the position.' There was the fine edge of mockery to his voice.

'What is?' Michelle could not resist meeting his eyes.

The light was poor now. Lyle's lips quirked as he studied her. 'You're going to change – but have a bath first. And then you're going to let me mix you a drink and you'll have it in front of the fire. Afterwards, Usef will serve dinner.'

Tired, furious and rebellious, she made a small clearing-of-the-throat noise. 'I don't seem to have much choice, do I?'

'No, you don't. I've made the choice for you, which will save a whole lot of trouble.'

'It would be interesting to know what kind of trouble.' Instantly she regretted her brittle, flippant remark and saw his shoulders move impatiently. 'Well, it won't take all day for you to decide whether you're going to accept or not,' he said.

'I'd rather have gone back to the hotel,' her voice was choked and furious. Afraid of her feelings for him, she said, 'Have you brought me here to gloat over me?'

'On the contrary,' he replied, opening the door and getting out.

He came round to her side and for a moment she refused his outstretched hand before she placed her fingers in his and he almost lifted her from the Land-Rover. He held her against him and the physical impact caused a shuddering

175

emotion to pass over her. 'You're so damp, Michelle,' he said, releasing her. 'Come on.'

She had made her protest, but he had not been prepared to listen to it, so she found herself following him, past the white pillars which supported the wood-panelled canopy sheltering the short pathway leading to the front door.

Usef, in a white linen suit, let them in. 'Good evening, Usef,' said Michelle. 'It – it's very wet, isn't it?' She hoped her voice sounded normal.

'Hold it,' Lyle was saying, 'I forgot your things in the Land-Rover. I'll go back and get them.'

Moodily, she watched him leave the high-ceilinged entrance hall and then, feeling uncertain and unhappy, went in the direction of the lounge where the twin lamps on either side of the five-seater couch burned invitingly. Above the couch a long, exquisite artwork in brass, copper and enamel reflected back jewel-like colours. Michelle's eyes dropped to the brass standard telephone which stood on the coffee table to one side of the gold Turkish coffee set. Was the telephone just for show? she wondered. Or did it work? Could she phone Laney from here? All of a sudden her eyes were moist. More than anything, she wanted to talk to Laney – then she started as Lyle came into the room. He held out a small tartan case which had a zip fastener. 'From Laney,' he said. 'Your clothes.'

She met his eyes and felt the usual shock at their blue-green magnetism, but shock was giving way to anger. 'Thank you.' She took it from him, but remained standing. There was so much she wanted to say. In the first place, she wanted to inform him furiously that she did not intend to stay here, to bath here, change here and to eat here. The whole set-up was ridiculous. Her nerves were shattered enough without all this. A log shifted in the fire which was burning in the unusual fireplace set in a large recess backed by a wall of glass.

'You know where to go, Michelle.' Lyle's voice was soft. 'To the main bedroom or the guest-room. Take your choice and take your time.'

'I feel tired and – and – fed-up,' she told him, on a tiny breath, 'and I'm not overstating the facts.'

'Yes, I know. That's why you're here. I intend to change all that.'

With a small helpless shrug she turned and left him, then stood in the hall for a few moments, her mind suddenly a blank, before she went towards the burnt-orange carpeted stairway which swept past an indoor garden to the bedrooms up above.

There were lights burning in the master suite which cast a sherry glow over everything. Michelle caught a glimpse of the huge double bed covered in the shaggy goat-hair bedspread, on either side of which burned the bedside lights exotically suspended from the ceiling to hang over low kists on either side of the bed. Memories of the party in her honour moved in her mind.

In the guest-room, with its vibrant purple carpeting, she opened the tartan case. The zip made a tiny innocent, whirring noise as she moved it along. Outside, the wind could be heard buffeting the house with its arched grilles, through which a view of the flower-beds, during the day-time, could be seen. Michelle crossed over to the huge windows and looked out. The sky was dark now. What a time she and Glen had been away, wasting time up there when the weather was changing every minute. There were, she saw, flashes of lightning in the high mountains, but not down here, although it was raining steadily.

With her head bent forward, her tawny hair curtaining her cheeks, she began to sob quietly, lifting a hand to push her hair to one side now and then, but continuing to sob because the man she loved was a traitor – a traitor to the two people she loved most in the world. A man who had suggested that she had been responsible for carrying tales to Glen Hayes.

When she had calmed herself sufficiently she went back to the bed and opened the case. Laney, she saw, had packed a trouser suit of the finest honey-coloured wool. There was amber beadwork at the high neckline and she had left it at the farm because it was an outfit she wore only on special occasions. No doubt Laney had packed it because it was warm. The bra was her own, but the briefs were Laney's – new and still in their sealed packet.

Somewhere in the house a door thudded. The doors in this house were too heavy just to bang. They were outsize and larger than life, like the house itself, and the exotic furnishings which went along with it. Like the film, no doubt, which had been filmed here. Suddenly Michelle shivered and went through to the adjoining bathroom. Her eyes went longingly towards the bath and, before she could change her mind, she crossed the vibrant purple carpeting and turned on both taps. The water gushed, steaming, into the bath. The steam began to gather and clung to the leaves of the plants in yet another indoor garden of this fantastic film-set house. Moisture clung to the mirrors.

After her bath she felt better and, as she slipped into the trouser suit, the fine wool felt snug against her skin and immediately warm, without being overpowering and heavy to the touch. Using the cosmetics she carried in a little vanity bag in her handbag, she made up her face, then combed out her tangled hair. Shoes? Her startled eyes went to the case. Laney had forgotten to pack shoes. Well, there hadn't been any to pack, obviously, and besides, she had been wearing shoes, discarded now and damp and muddy. Wildly her eyes scanned the beautiful carpeting for mud-marks, but there were none.

She decided to go barefoot, no real hardship in these luxurious carpeted rooms, and leaving her case where it was, she went downstairs.

Lyle turned as she entered the lounge. He had changed, she noticed at once, into white levis and a black turtle-necked sweater. Very dramatic. To go with the house, she thought bitterly. His blue-green eyes went over her and came to rest on her mouth. 'I like what I see,' he said, 'but where are your shoes?'

'Laney didn't send any. I suppose there weren't any at the farm. I forget, right now. The others are wet and muddy, so I thought it best to leave them off.'

He had put on a record at a volume turned on just audibly. A girl was singing, 'You might as well surrender, surrender.' The piano notes were indolent, keeping just behind her. A burning log shifted in the fire. Michelle was aware of the wind outside, the rain, the mountains, the luxury of this magnificent house, of the feel of the finest wool against her skin, but most of all, she was aware of Lyle Cunningham. There was a long moment of what seemed like recognition for the first time between them, then he said, 'Your feet will be cold.' His eyes did not leave her face.

'No – all this carpeting.' She looked down. 'My feet sink into it. Then the fire.' She wondered whether he could see that she had been crying, then remembered that she had cried without tears, long shuddering sobs, coming from way inside her – too deep for tears.

'Sit near the fire,' he told her, 'while I pour you a drink.'

Michelle crossed over to the fire, keeping her eyes away from him, her feet, rosy from her bath, lost in the thick pile of the honey carpeting. One level down was the sheikh's harem, as she had come to think of the conversation area, with all its cushions and the black iron standard lamps which were topped with crowns of the palest amber glass. She tried not to be aware of it – of the waiting, vibrantly coloured cushions of shocking-pink, turquoise, orange and purple – tried not to see herself in Lyle's arms there.

He brought the drink to her and she remained standing. As she took the glass from him she tried to avoid touching his fingers – but failed. There was a tiny caught breath on her part, while their eyes met slowly, locking, then the telephone shrilled in the hall.

'I'd better answer it,' said Lyle, and she watched him as he went in the direction of the carved sliding doors, her heart thudding heavily.

While he was gone Michelle took a sip of her drink. There was an open magazine on a table and she glanced at the headlines. THE MIGHTY SANI PASS TO BOW TO THE FAMILY CAR. Sani Pass, she read, interested, the tortuous boulder-strewn road link between Natal and Lesotho, which rises nearly 1,200 metres in seven kilometres and has gradients of 1:3, is being rebuilt to enable family cars to get up it. The Pass, still officially described as a bridle path, was first opened to vehicles in 1949 but did not come into regular use until 1955. Since then, this ruggedly exciting route to the top of the Drakensberg escarpment, at a height of 2,850m, has been traversed by many tourists in four-wheel-drive vehicles, the only vehicles allowed up. Michelle's eyes hurriedly scanned the article. There was to be a new route, apparently.

The article came to an end, reading: Most tourists will, however, still prefer to travel in four-wheel Land-Rovers, in view of the fact that they prefer to travel the route with experienced and skilled drivers.

Lyle Cunningham was one of those drivers, she thought. Glen Hayes was not, and never would be.

Lyle came back and she turned. 'I've been chatting to Laney,' he told her. 'She's worried about you and wants to talk to you. My mind was on other things. I should have thought to phone her.'

His eyes went to the magazine.

'I saw the headlines and couldn't stop reading,' she said.

'It will be an important trade route and a potential wilderness region for tourists. The new road will still remain very steep, I gather, particularly the final stage, but the maximum gradient will change, making the journey possible in an average car. It will remain untarred, otherwise it would prove dangerous in slippery conditions – I'm referring to a hard surface now.'

She thought for a moment. 'Yes, I can see that.'

'Laney is holding on,' he reminded her.

'Of course.' Her eyes widened. 'I'm not functioning properly.' She glanced hurriedly around for some place to put her glass, then, barefooted and slender, she walked across the carpet.

In the hall she said, 'Laney?'

'Are you really all right?' Laney sounded frightened. 'Lyle tells me you are, but why didn't he bring you here – or take you back to the hotel? I've been practically out of my mind. So has Pete. What happened exactly?'

'It was a disaster, Laney. Glen started drinking soon after we left. Apart from that he was – well, he's just not the Land-Rover type. So it was a nightmare. When we got to the top there was more drinking in the little pub. He'd also brought wine along to have with our lunch. The weather was changing all the time and he made absolutely no move to get going. I should have phoned you, but I've been rather upset.'

'I don't know him very well, but I've never liked him – or trusted him, for that matter,' said Laney. 'Neither has Pete. We've heard rumours about some of his so-called successful business transactions. Anyway, he proved himself with the nursery business. The restaurant, of course, was his own idea. We hadn't even thought along those lines.'

'We?' Michelle's mouth had gone suddenly dry. 'I don't know about the nursery business, Laney.'

'It was Lyle's idea. He wanted to help Pete by buying this place and turning it into a nursery with Pete as nursery manager. This meant we could have gone on living here without any of the financial worries to go along with it. In time to come, when the concern started paying off, we would have had an option on buying it back. But,' Michelle could almost see Laney shrug, 'Pete's pride got in the way and he decided to take the farm off the market and try again – his way. That was when Lyle loaned us the money, to help out. Actually, he didn't want it back, but we are paying it back, gradually.'

'Talking about money,' said Michelle, 'this call is costing you money. But I didn't know.'

'I haven't wanted to say too much. You see, I thought you might be in love with Glen Hayes. You've been seeing so much of him lately, haven't you?'

'Yes,' Michelle murmured, in a wan voice. 'I guess I've been lonely.'

'Before you go,' Laney said quickly, 'Debbie came to see me this afternoon. She was here when Lyle came to look for you. She'd had a row with Liza Monatti and, in the mood she was in, she told Lyle that Liza's chief pastime in the office was passing on news which might be of interest to Glen Hayes. She was doing this and suggesting, very subtly, of course, that it was you . . . But anyway, I'll talk to you when I see you. Are you perfectly sure you're all right?'

'Positive. Good-bye, Laney. Thank you for ringing – and oh, for sending the clothes along.'

'It was all I could find.'

Lyle was putting on a record when Michelle went back

into the lounge and she sensed his sidelong glance, but did not look at him. She looked around for her glass, realized that she had put it on a small table near the fireplace and went to pick it up. As she took a sip of her drink she heard the sound of glass against teeth and realized she was shivering again.

Lyle straightened up and turned. 'Well?' A slight quirk came on his mouth. 'Did you put Laney's mind at rest?'

'Yes, at least, I hope so. Naturally she was worried. She doesn't like Glen Hayes, she doesn't trust him and she knows he drinks rather a lot. She hasn't mentioned much of this to me because she thought I was in love with Glen.'

'Are you?' he asked.

'If you ask me that again – I'll – I'll take off!' she told him in a small, high voice. 'I'm not in love with him and I never have been in love with him.'

'Sit down and get warm,' he said. 'You don't look relaxed standing there.'

'Well, I'm not relaxed, as it so happens.'

'Why not?' Their eyes met again.

'I don't know the answer.'

'Well, you could say it's mutual. I'm not relaxed either, but I *know* the answer.'

The music was doing nothing to steady her, she thought, but perhaps Lyle had meant it that way. She listened to the words, 'I wish you shelter from the storm, A cosy fire to keep you warm, But most of all, when snowflakes' (raindrops? Michelle's eyes went to the windows) 'fall, I wish you love . . .' A girl with a catch in her voice, singing about love. At the back of everything, Michelle thought, there is always love. Sometimes we don't – or can't – admit to it.

Her eyes went back to Lyle's handsome face. He was swirling his drink round and round in the glass and then, without warning, he lifted his eyes and they met hers, and there was nothing casual about the suddenly lifted lashes. His eyes did not leave her face and then she demanded, 'Why didn't you tell me? About the nursery scheme, with Pete as nursery manager?'

He was silent for a long moment. 'I didn't tell you for the simple reason that Pete wasn't interested in the scheme and that it fizzled out.'

'Nevertheless, you could have told me,' her voice was accusing. 'You went as far as to mention that you wanted to buy land, that you intended growing vegetables to meet the hotel's requirements. You wanted to deep-freeze them, you said. You didn't say it was Pete's land you wanted. Was the deep-freezing story just a blind?'

'No, it wasn't just a blind. I meant what I said. I was mainly concerned with flowers, however, and to supply as many florists as possible, delivery to take place by light aircraft.'

'You could have told me,' she said again. 'I've – I've been resenting you ever since I found out it was Pete's farm you were interested in. I'd heard you were trying to buy Pete and Laney out. I didn't know these things. I had to guess.'

'And guessing can be a dangerous thing.' He gave her a level look. 'I've found that out for myself.'

'Laney has just told me on the phone. I knew you'd lent them money and it all seemed to work in, somehow.'

He looked puzzled. 'How do you mean – work in?'

'It seemed to work in with your plan in trying to get them even more deeply involved financially, so that in the end they would owe so much money to so many people, including you, they wouldn't know which way to turn and would have to sell. Anyway,' her voice was stilted, 'I misjudged you. I'm sorry.'

Reflections from the dancing fire dappled her honey-bronzed skin and turned the amber beads on her trouser-suit crimson.

'Is that important?' he asked.

'Yes. It is to me, anyway.'

Over their glasses their eyes met and held.

Then he said, 'You misjudged me. I misjudged you. What are we going to do about it? Kiss and make up?' He appeared mockingly serene, but Michelle could sense the tension in him.

'You make it sound like a joke,' she said.

'Well, isn't it?'

In despair she turned away from him. 'No, it isn't. This whole thing has gone beyond a joke. There's much more to it than that.'

'I'd like to take you up on that, Michelle.' He spoke softly. 'It's my intention to try and clear things up between us, actually. In the first place, I owe you an apology. I found myself listening to rumours which seemed to fall into pattern. I'm sorry.'

'In other words, you listened to what Liza had to say about me?'

'Yes.'

'That's understandable, I suppose.'

'Why is it understandable?'

'Well, you're in love with her. However, none of her stories were true. I've never discussed the private matters of the hotel, or your intention of buying land to deep-freeze, with Glen Hayes. He was just somebody to go out with, when I found myself brooding.'

'What do you brood about?'

'That happens to be my own business.'

'Michelle,' she heard him take a deep breath, 'let me put you in the picture about Liza. You know that old tune, "Just someone to dance with because I'm a little on the lonely side." Something like that?'

'No, I don't.'

'Well, I'm telling you about it. Apart from the fact that Liza works at the hotel, that's all it ever amounted to. She's always known this and there've never been any tangled emotions, not so far as I was concerned, anyway. Any interest on Liza's part didn't fall into the category of love. I continued to ask Liza to go out with me and I'm afraid I've never stopped to question the wisdom of this. To convince you of my feelings towards Liza is important to me – just as it was important for me to learn of your feelings towards Glen Hayes.'

Unable to bear the tension a minute longer, Michelle demanded, 'Why? You – you don't have to say these things. After all, it's none of my business. The only thing which does concern me is the fact that she spread false rumours about me. I also happen to be sorry I misjudged your friendship, so far as Pete and Laney are concerned. I can see now that you're a very real friend to them. It nearly drove me mad, though, to think you were,' she corrected herself, 'might have been scheming against them. I longed to tell them what I believed to be true. I longed to be able to smash the so-called friendship between you. I didn't realize that you were in fact trying to help them. Very generously so, too, I can see that. Anyway, I'm going back to England soon,' she added on the spur of the moment, 'so I'm glad to have cleared up this humiliating situation.'

The girl on the record was singing. Her words filled the room, which was very still. 'I'll set you free . . .'

Somewhere in the house the fragile chimes of a clock broke the stillness.

'Going back?' Lyle's voice showed surprise.

'Yes.' Now that she had said it she felt calm.

'When did you make up your mind?'

There was no retreat. 'Now.'

'Hold it – let's get this straight. Now, Michelle?'

'Yes.' She tried to make her voice sound careless.

Why does there have to be heartbreaking music playing at a time like this? she thought. Those indolent piano notes, the girl, with a catch in her voice, singing, the music turned on, just audible over the wild beating of her heart.

'You said, at the beginning,' said Lyle, above the music, 'that it depended on whether you liked South Africa and – other reasons.'

'I believe I might have said something like this.' Michelle began to walk about the room, her bare feet sinking into the thick carpet.

'You did say it. You don't like South Africa?' His eyes challenged her to agree with him.

On the turntable the record was going round and round, 'For all we know, we may never meet again.' Michelle could visualize the girl singing, blonde, husky-voiced, exciting . . .

'I like it well enough, but I – let's just say I have reservations. Anyway, it's ridiculous to talk like this. I've seen nothing of South Africa. I've seen the Pass, of course.' Her voice was bitter. 'Twice, actually, and I guess that's something. The first trip, with you, was also a disaster, but at least *you* were one of those experienced drivers I have just

185

read about. I can see that now. I'd like you to know that I think your driving was superb. Glen Hayes will never make one of those drivers.' She took an impatient breath and shook back her hair. 'Besides, that isn't the point.'

'What is the point?'

'I *like* the country,' she said, in a flat voice. 'What I've seen of it. I like the people – most of them, anyway.'

Lyle came and took her glass and she watched him fixing new drinks, then he came back to her. 'It's not strong,' he told her when she shook her head.

'I don't care,' she said, in a small voice. 'I don't want it.'

Without saying anything he took their glasses down to the conversation pit and placed them on the table. He looked up at her. 'Come and sit here. Curl up amongst the cushions and get warm. They might have been put there as ornaments for the film, but so far as I'm concerned, they're there to be used.'

'No!' Her voice was sharp. 'I don't want to sit there, thank you.' Her eyes went to the cushions which at night looked like little gems of emerald, shocking pink, turquoise, orange and purple.

What was she like, the girl who was singing with the emotionally husky voice? 'We come and go like a ripple on a stream, So love me tonight, tomorrow was made for some, tomorrow may never come – for all we know . . .'

Lyle turned. 'Why? It's very comfortable down here. You can feel the warmth of the fire. Are you afraid, Michelle?'

'Yes, I am.'

'Why?'

'Because it's like a – a harem down there with all those cushions, those big green leaves.' Her eyes went to the indoor garden. 'I don't want any part of it.'

A slight quirk came on his mouth, but his voice was abrupt, 'I didn't plan it this way. It just happened. I've never bothered to have it changed. Besides, I'm only renting it – until I get married, that is. Maybe I'll buy it then. If she likes it.' He gave her a long, direct look.

Michelle felt as though she had fallen headfirst through a trapdoor. Suddenly she was aware of the dangerous balance between them. Part of her refused to accept what was happening. There was a tiny gasp on her part, then their eyes were meeting slowly, locking. 'Why go on like this, Michelle?' Lyle's voice was impatient. 'This is foolishness. I love you – surely you know that? Why do you think I brought you here? We've wasted enough time, and you know it.'

The record on the turntable was coming to an end.

'And so the story ends,
Why not call it a day
and end it the sensible way . . .'

Michelle felt a great surge of wild happiness as she watched him leave the conversation area, then he came towards her and placed his hands lightly on her shoulders. For a moment his eyes searched hers and his fingers tightened before he drew her to him.

When he stopped kissing her he said, 'You've never even used my name, do you know that?'

'I . . .' she broke off, 'I tried . . . You didn't seem to,' she shrugged and smiled, 'you know – *need* that.'

'What I need, Michelle, is you. I love you.'

Because she was shy, she kept him waiting, then she said, 'I love you too, Lyle. Did you play that record on purpose, by the way?'

He smiled suddenly, devastatingly. 'Yes, I think you could say that.'

The rain, driven by the wind, pelted the window panes. On top of the Pass it would be lashing the mountains. The wind would be blowing coldly across the slopes and trying to get to the peaks beneath the clouds.

Remembering, Michelle shivered against Lyle. Behind them the logs crackled and fell with a shower of poinsettia-red sparks.

A Publishing Event of special interest.

The autobiography of a warm and charming woman who has become one of the most famous authors of romantic fiction in the world

The Essie Summers Story

SEE OVERLEAF FOR DETAILS AND ORDER COUPON

The Essie Summers Story

One of the world's most popular and admired authors of romantic fiction, and a special favourite of all Harlequins readers, tells her story.

Essie Summers, the author of such best selling books as "Bride in Flight", "Postscript to Yesterday", "Meet on my Ground" and "The Master of Tawhai" to name just a few, has spent two years bringing the manuscript of her autobiography to its present stage of perfection.

The wit, warmth and wisdom of this fine lady shine, through every page. Her love of family and friends, of New Zealand and Britain, and of life itself is an inspiration throughout the book. Essie Summers captures the essence of a life well lived, and lived to the fullest, in the style of narrative for which she is justly famous.

"The Essie Summers Story", published in paperback, is available at .95 a copy through Harlequin Reader Service, now!

Why the smile?

... because she has just received her **Free Harlequin Romance Catalogue!**

... and now she has a complete listing of the many, many Harlequin Romances still available.

... and now she can pick out titles by her favorite authors or fill in missing numbers for her library.

You too may have a **Free Harlequin Romance Catalogue** (and a smile!), simply by mailing in the coupon below.

Catalogue of available titles is revised every three months!

Have You Missed Any of These
Harlequin Romances?

xx

Have You Missed Any of These
Harlequin Romances?

PLEASE NOTE: All Harlequin Romances from #1857 onwards are 75c. Books below that number, **where available** are priced at 60c through Harlequin Reader Service until December 31st, 1975.

Books By Emma Lathen

Published by POCKET BOOKS

EMMA LATHEN

SOMETHING IN THE AIR

POCKET BOOKS

New York   London   Toronto   Sydney   Tokyo

POCKET BOOKS, a division of Simon & Schuster Inc.
1230 Avenue of the Americas, New York, NY 10020

Copyright © 1988 by Emma Lathen
Cover art copyright © 1989 Don Brautigan

Library of Congress Catalog Card Number: 88-4491

ISBN: 0-671-68356-X

First Pocket Books printing September 1989

10 9 8 7 6 5 4 3 2 1

POCKET and colophon are trademarks of
Simon & Schuster Inc.

Printed in the U.S.A.

Contents

❧ 1 ❧

Often Soars Very High

On Wall Street, immortality belongs to the institutions. Individuals only attain fleeting fame—usually for the wrong reasons. Sooner or later, all the Jay Goulds lay down their proxies; holding companies can last forever.

Bank holding companies always do.

The Sloan Guaranty Trust has not only survived, it has flourished. The third-largest bank in the world, it now dwarfs the thousands of men and women who hurry past its portals or work within them.

John Putnam Thatcher, executive vice-president, was technically answerable to the Board of Directors for staff performance at the Sloan. In reality, there was a frightening amount of signing power in hands other than his. So, outside his own power base on the sixth floor where he commanded the Trust and Investment Divisions, he braced himself for the worst whenever he saw another Sloan bigwig beckoning. Even if it was simply a chance encounter in the down elevator with Kyle Yetter.

"John, just the man!" Yetter exclaimed, beaming. "Here's somebody I'd like you to meet."

Only a customer brought out the sunshine in Kyle Yetter, one of the pillars of Commercial Credit, where a million dollars was small change. Naturally, Thatcher inspected Yetter's companion with interest.

The youthful, solidly built man with brilliant blue eyes and a mat of thick brown hair was, it developed, more than a would-be borrower. He was a celebrity.

"Mitchell Scovil, president of Sparrow Flyways up in Boston. That's the commuter line that's one of the few remaining successes of deregulation, you recall," Yetter was saying when the doors opened on the executive lobby.

Thatcher always appreciated helpful introductions, although no reader of the daily paper, let alone the financial press, could have missed Sparrow Flyways. A dollar for every time it was described as no-frills would mop up the national debt.

Scovil barely let Yetter finish.

"Sparrow's commuter days are about to become a thing of the past," he said confidently. "Once we line up the right backing, we're busting out of the northeast corridor and offering coast-to-coast service. We'll be the high-tech link between Route 128 and Silicon Valley."

Thatcher recognized a born salesman when he heard one. He could only hope that Kyle Yetter did too.

Meanwhile Scovil was forging ahead. "Kyle and I are just going out to lunch. Why don't you come along, too? Then I could tell you all about Sparrow, and what we're planning."

His persuasiveness, reputed to perform miracles at Sparrow, was misplaced. At the Sloan, trying to go over Yetter's head could lead the enterprising Mr. Scovil out the door.

"Yes, John, join us if you're free," Yetter said, signaling his lack of objection.

"I'm afraid I have another engagement," said Thatcher. Then, incautiously, he added that it, too, was Boston-based.

"Does that mean you'll be coming up to Boston?" Scovil asked alertly. "Why don't you come and look Sparrow over? A picture's worth a thousand words, and ten minutes watching us run the shop will explain how Sparrow beat the competition."

Thatcher reminded himself that Commercial Credit paid Kyle Yetter a substantial salary. Let him earn it!

"I'm sure it would, but I see I'm running late. It was a pleasure meeting you, Scovil. I know Yetter here will take good care of the best interests of Sparrow—and the Sloan."

By the time Thatcher was on the sidewalk, Scovil and Sparrow were fast slipping from his mind. If he could remember them long enough to quiz Kyle Yetter, he would be doing well.

Since his fool's paradise included a chill November drizzle, he turned up his collar and headed north to other, more demanding, matters.

Kyle Yetter was not the only authority on Mitchell Scovil. What the other experts had to say depended on where they sat.

"He was a goddam nuisance from the beginning."

"And now he's a menace."

The site was St. Louis, Missouri, a few miles west of Lambert Airport where Atlantic & Pacific Airlines (known familiarly as A&P) maintained corporate headquarters. The voices raised in anger belonged to vice-presidents who had been abusing Scovil since the Airline Deregulation Act of 1978. Sparrow had started with twenty-five employees and three secondhand planes. Now this Mickey Mouse operation had thousands on the payroll, served the whole East Coast, and was rumored to be eyeing California.

"That cheap SOB's got a nerve," said Wilfred Merrick, longtime president of A&P. Savaging his Jamaican cigar, he rumbled: "He made a quick killing because he wasn't saddled with unions. Now he thinks he's ready for the big time."

The big time, it went without saying, belonged exclusively to Atlantic & Pacific Airlines and its few peers. After all, A&P had roots stretching back to the dawn of commercial aviation. Photographs on the boardroom walls celebrated early fragile biplanes, historic deliveries of the U.S. Mail, and rugged pioneers in leather helmets.

A&P had still been pointing to this illustrious past when it was sandbagged by deregulation, oil crises, and competition. Costs ballooned, revenues plummeted, and yesterday's muscle became today's flab.

The inevitable call for new blood had produced Fritz Diehl, the youngest vice-president at the table and the last to speak.

"There's no future for the commuters. Either they expand, or they go under," he said dispassionately. "Sooner or later one of them is bound to go coast-to-coast against us. But my guess is that they'll do it by acquisition—buying somebody else out. Whether or not it will be Sparrow —that's another proposition altogether."

"You should know," Merrick told him sourly.

The credentials that had brought Diehl to A&P included a stint at Sparrow Flyways. In fact, like Mitchell Scovil, he was one of its founders. This meant guilt by association to A&P's old guard. Everybody else envied him his profits.

Ignoring the crosscurrents, Diehl said: "Sparrow's innovations were perfect for the time . . ."

"Grr!" Merrick growled reflexively.

". . . but trying to expand them to California now would be damned near impossible. They're already having trouble keeping their profit margins up. Any more pressure and the whole system will crumble."

"What about Toronto?" challenged a rival. "Scovil's showing a profit after just three months, isn't he?"

"Toronto is the past," said Fritz Diehl coolly. "I'm talking about the future."

If Norman Pitts had anything to say about it, the future was pure gold. In East Boston, Massachusetts, home of Logan Airport and Sparrow Flyways, young Pitts was ready to do or die for Sparrow.

He had been on the payroll for exactly one week. And crowning the orientation course, here was Mitchell ("Call me Mitch!") Scovil himself.

"At Sparrow we're proud of our record, and we owe it to

the very programs that people told us would never work know you've had it drilled into you all week, but if you've got any questions—I'm here to answer them."

Scovil's sessions with the new recruits were always informal, but he did not take them lightly. To meet this batch, he had rushed up from New York as soon as he left Kyle Yetter.

"Nothing bugging you?" he asked, when silence continued. "You're not shrinking violets, are you? If so, Sparrow's no place for you."

Laughter broke the ice for one bespectacled young woman. "Mitch," she said, taking a deep breath. "I know about the team system, but will you explain why that means that Sparrow doesn't need a union."

Norman Pitts shuddered, afraid that the love feast was going to end. But Scovil was glad she had asked.

"Sure," he said. "The team system—and I'll bet you're tired of hearing us say so—is the real heart of Sparrow. When we have a problem like opening up a new facility, we pull a group, form them into a team, and let them handle the whole thing. The people we sent to Toronto set up banking facilities, hired a starter set of local people, and arranged everything from customs inspections to supplies. And all the team members got whopping stock bonuses. That's why we don't have unions. All of us are management."

His audience was starry-eyed.

"Is that why you make us all buy ten shares?" asked one of them admiringly.

Scovil scrubbed the heel of his hand across his hair, searching for the right words. "You see, we're trying to blast you into a new way of thinking. Sparrow is your company as much as it is mine. But unless you put out a hundred and ten percent, you won't cut it here. Lie down on the job and you're out. We don't carry deadweight, and we don't want it in our profit-sharing scheme. So if you're the kind who's happy going through the motions, look for another job."

He paused for effect.

"Now don't worry about not fitting in," Scovil resumed.

shows don't get as far as you have. If you hit
adjusting, it probably means you're in the
. Just talk to Eleanor Gough—and she'll fix you
, when you find the right niche, go to work. We
your brains and your energy and your creativity. As
as Sparrow's concerned, the sky's the limit. Welcome
.ooard—and God bless!"

With a wave of his tanned arm, he left the room. Before
he was out the door, Eleanor Gough was on her feet.

"Now, I just want to explain how the profit-sharing system works. . . ."

Norman Pitts, still dazzled, could barely listen.

There, he would have gladly told John Thatcher, is a
man in a million.

A&P and Norman Pitts covered the extremes. The truth
about Mitchell Scovil lay somewhere in between, as his
closer associates agreed.

Eleanor Gough and Clay Batchelder had been watching
their partner perform for five years. When Fritz Diehl
walked out of Sparrow, they had remained to form two
parts of the management triumvirate. Scovil was the front
man, occupying any and all spotlights, while the other two
ran the store.

Batchelder, only a few years older than Scovil, was big
and stolid, with the weathered skin of an outdoorsman. His
background included buying planes and leasing equipment,
and, at Sparrow, he functioned as chief of operations. He
and Scovil complemented each other neatly.

Mrs. Gough, however, was another proposition altogether. From the beginning, she had been Sparrow's all-
purpose troubleshooter, dealing with everything from FAA
compliance to employee relations. She was competent, attractive, and unmistakably older than either of her companions. With two adult children, she qualified as a
grandmother in the Sparrow youth culture. Just now, she
sounded like one.

"Clay, when will you talk sense to Mitch about Pittsburgh?" she said as they trailed out of the conference
room. "Conditions there are deteriorating every day."

Batchelder straight-armed a swinging door, waiting for her to precede him.

"Mitch doesn't like talking about failures," he said, as if she needed reminding. "The trouble is that Pittsburgh's not top priority."

"Well, it should be," she said tartly as they reached the so-called executive suite.

In keeping with Sparrow's stripped-down image, this consisted of a few cubbyholes opening off the larger space used to accommodate group efforts. Scovil stood at his desk, examining the mail.

"How do you think the talk went?" he said, looking up expectantly.

"The way it always does," said Batchelder, poker-faced. "After all, it's the same speech."

"Hey!" Scovil protested. "I cover the same topics, but I do it off the cuff."

With some impatience, Mrs. Gough ended the banter. "How did things go in New York?"

"It couldn't have been better," Scovil said, launching on an exuberant recital.

Both Batchelder and Mrs. Gough listened intently.

"And the Sloan isn't surprised that Sparrow wants to go transcontinental?" Mrs. Gough asked, when Scovil finally finished.

"How could they be surprised, Eleanor?" Batchelder asked reasonably. "Mitch has been leaking hints for months. He likes letting the competition know that we're nipping at their heels."

Scovil grinned, but Eleanor Gough remained thoughtful. "Scaring A&P is one thing, scaring our own people is another. Do you two realize that half the employees are on the verge of mutiny?"

"Don't exaggerate," said Scovil. "This is our biggest leap forward, so there's the most static. But once I explain—"

"Sure," said Batchelder, seizing his moment. "All you have to do is explain it to the employees' committee. I've set up a meeting with them next Thursday."

"Employees' committee?" Scovil said blankly. "Don't

tell me, let me guess. It has to be Phoebe Fournier, stirring things up. That kid is something else!"

"Which is why we chose her to run the Toronto team," Eleanor pointed out. "Besides, lots of people are nervous. That's why so many of them have been signing petitions."

But Scovil had moved on to the next stage of his thinking. "Tell you what—let's not make a federal case out of this. I'll calm Phoebe down tonight. She's coming to the party."

Sparrow, only five years old, was already encrusted with traditions. One was a lavish party at Mitch Scovil's waterfront condominium to reward successful team efforts.

"It won't be as easy as you think," said Mrs. Gough. "It's not just the expansion that's worrying people, it's Pittsburgh. We're losing money on every plane we fly there. That's a drain on the profit-sharing fund, and that gets everybody upset. Don't you realize how closely they follow our financial reports? For heaven's sake, Mitch, you just told them they're all stockholders."

His determined good humor faltered. "Lighten up," he said sharply. Then, with an effort: "I'll tell you what, you get on the phone to Pittsburgh. Tell Reardon we want results, or else. And, in the meantime, I'll fill Clay in about New York."

Eleanor Gough studied her two partners. Then, with a slight shrug, she turned, going off to do what had to be done.

✌ 2 ⤸

Young Birds in Transition

At six twenty-seven that evening, personable young women all over the United States were smiling into television cameras. In Boston, one of them was saying: ". . . so be sure to join us tomorrow night when we visit Plymouth Plantation, where Thanksgiving all began."

Then, leaving exactly two minutes for commercials, Kate McDermott unclipped her microphone.

"Want to come along for a quick one, Katie?" a colleague asked.

"Thanks, but I've got to get home," she replied, moving off the set. "You haven't forgotten the party tonight, have you, Dave?"

Dave had not, and neither had any other staffer on Channel Three's award-winning news team.

"I wouldn't miss it for the world."

"Good," she said, disappearing into a minimal makeup room. There she made a dive for the phone. "Mitch? I'm on my way."

"Who cares?" her husband replied affectionately. "I'm here—and so are the caterers. That's all that matters."

15

"Is that your way of telling me that things went well in New York?" she replied.

"Better than you'd believe," Scovil said. "I think I may have the Sloan hooked."

Even allowing for his inveterate optimism, this sounded promising and Kate said so. But, at the moment, other details took precedence. "Tell the caterers to make sure there's some place for all those toothpicks, will you?"

Everything else was being taken care of, if the caterers knew what was good for them. The setting was already perfect. The Scovil duplex on India Wharf combined expensive space with casual comfort. At the right time of year, their rooftop terrace overlooking Boston Harbor was a showplace. The other requisite for successful entertaining was no problem. The Sparrow side of the guest list was always ready to party. And, for her part, Kate provided touches of glamour in the form of the touring personalities like rock superstars, best-selling doctors, and presidential candidates, who paraded endlessly through Channel Three.

Her catch tonight was Number One on the charts.

"Straight home this time, Phil," she told her regular cabbie. "Mitch and I have people coming in."

"Just like you or me," Phil later told his long-suffering wife. "I mean not jittery or uptight or anything."

Phil's wife was a fan of Kate McDermott's, but she was not a doormat. "Give me the kind of money they have, and I wouldn't worry either."

If the hostess was carefree, the same could not be said of all her guests.

"Maybe I should have gone home to change," said the young lawyer, still dressed for success.

"Oh, for heaven's sake," laughed Phoebe Fournier, although she had done just that.

The home they shared was an apartment in nearby Brookline and it had taken Phoebe less than an hour to shed her Sparrow uniform and hurry downtown to join Bryan Kiley for dinner.

"But should it have been a tux—or my leather jacket?"

he mused. "You never can tell who you'll meet at the Scovils'. Judge Grayson was there last time."

"Oh, just relax," she said, reminding them both that she was the real authority on the subject. Phoebe Fournier had been to so many Scovil celebrations that she had lost count. A small, dark-haired bundle of energy, she was also Sparrow's role model par excellence. Starting out as a raw recruit the day Sparrow opened its doors, she had soared. Today, aged twenty-eight, she was an expert on airline finance, and the owner of ten thousand shares of Sparrow common.

". . . which has been losing ground for months," she said a few minutes later. "If Mitch seriously pushes California, the bottom could drop out. As if Pittsburgh isn't bad enough."

Bryan winced. "I hope you're not planning to bring that up tonight?"

"Who me?" she replied, confirming his worst fears.

Alan Whetmore *was* wearing his leather jacket. Like Phoebe Fournier, he worked at Sparrow, but there the resemblance ended. Whetmore was advertising's Older Man, complete with deep tan and full head of hair. Even so, he was a Sparrow newcomer, one of the many pilots who had been laid off elsewhere. Far from being a jubilant team member, he was attending Scovil's party as the escort of one of Kate's Channel Three colleagues. Nevertheless, he whistled happily as he set forth to collect Mary Lou. Tonight, he felt sure, was going to be wonderful. His tomorrows looked damned good too.

At ten-thirty, Kate knew she had another winner. Bar and buffet were doing land-office business. In the greenhouse, people sat cross-legged, singing country music with the star attraction, while everybody else ate, drank, laughed, and talked.

"Who could ask for anything more?" she hummed to herself. Then she came face to face with her husband and had no trouble deciphering his expression.

"Why so hot and bothered? You were the life and soul of the party ten minutes ago."

With a broad smile for public consumption, Scovil muttered under his breath: "I've just come off a tough round with Phoebe."

"Oh dear," said Kate, glancing toward the animated group in the corner. "But she looks as if she's having fun."

"You can say that again," replied Scovil bitterly.

Phoebe Fournier gave group fun five more minutes, then detached a lanky young black man and took him aside.

"Joe, I've got to talk to you. Mitch is losing his mind."

Joe Cleveland was a mechanic, not a lawyer, but he shared some of the instincts of Phoebe's Bryan. "You shouldn't tackle Mitch at his own party."

"I didn't tackle him," she retorted. "He tackled me. Mitch seems to think I'm the only one who's worried about Sparrow."

"How can he?" Cleveland objected. "Clay has already agreed to a meeting because we represent a majority of the employees."

"According to Mitch, I'm stirring everybody up," she responded. "Otherwise people would be happy as clams."

After some thought, Cleveland said, "I guess we've got to set him straight, only I don't see how. Mitch is a great guy, but he can be stubborn as a mule."

"Don't I know it!" she said. "But I've had a brilliant idea. If I do all the talking, Mitch will know that he was right. So, we should get someone else to speak for the committee."

"Don't look at me," said Cleveland hastily. "I understand the numbers when you lay them out, but if I tried explaining them, I'd just mess up."

Phoebe already knew he was not her man. "What about Alan Whetmore?" she suggested.

Joe gaped. "Whetmore? But, Phoebe, he's a pilot."

It was a legitimate objection. As a group, pilots were the least enthusiastic converts to the Sparrow system. Like Whetmore, most of them came from elsewhere, and Sparrow meant smaller paychecks and one week each month doing lowly ground work.

"Besides," Cleveland continued, "Whetmore's never even signed any of our petitions."

"That's what makes it so neat," she argued. "This committee would be the first time Alan moved his butt. When Mitch sees that, he'll realize everybody is up in arms."

Cleveland still had reservations. "Maybe," he said reluctantly. "I suppose it's worth a try. But you and I have to be there, to sit on Whetmore if we have to. He's got a pretty good opinion of himself."

"He's a loudmouth," she agreed. "Just what Mitch deserves. C'mon."

Before Joe knew it, they had Whetmore cornered.

Looking bored, he let Phoebe rattle through the preliminaries. "Yes, I heard that some of you are going to meet with Clay and Mitch," he said. "Frankly, I doubt—"

"We were wondering if you'd act as our spokesman," Phoebe broke in.

There was a pause, then Whetmore brightened. "That never occurred to me. But, you know, you may be right. I have had twenty years' experience, and I've handled executives before."

Cleveland had to swallow hard as Alan Whetmore rolled on: "In fact, the more I think about it, the better I like it. And you know what? I might draw up a written list of demands. That way we could take care of everything at once."

"I suppose that would be all right," said Phoebe hesitantly. Then, warming to his proposal, she went on: "You could use the background material I've already developed. And, while you're working on that, I'll check the stockholder list again. We might do something with that, too."

Whetmore was judicious. "I'll have to decide what kind of approach to take."

Before Phoebe could reply, Mary Lou emerged, demanding attention. She did not remove Alan Whetmore one minute too soon.

"How you can stand that conceited jerk, beats me!"

Cleveland exploded. "Did you hear him? *He's* going to have to decide!"

"Alan's doing what we want, isn't he?" Phoebe replied.

"He's planning to give us the benefit of his guidance," Cleveland said. "Christ, he's so dumb it's unbelievable."

"Well, thank God for that," she said. "If Alan wasn't so dumb, he'd realize that all we want is a figurehead."

Her plot was beginning to confuse Cleveland. "What was that about the stockholder list that you just happened to slip in?" he demanded. "You've got something up your sleeve, don't you, Phoebe?"

"Boy, do I!" she said, pleased with herself. "This morning I did a computer printout of employee stockholdings. Guess what I found?"

Furrowing his brow, he said, "Well, I suppose we control a fair amount, between stock bonuses and the payroll plan. Even those initial purchases have to add up."

"To thirty percent of Sparrow," she said. But her triumph was yet to come. "Then I asked who owned the rest. And guess what?"

"You're losing me," Cleveland confessed. "Mitch and Clay and Eleanor each own ten percent. The rest must be spread around."

"Wrong!" Phoebe crowed. "The biggest stockholder of all is some bank in New York. And they own a big, fat twenty percent."

When Cleveland did not break into cheers, she prompted him.

"Thirty plus twenty equals fifty, Joe."

As he had said earlier, if somebody laid the numbers out, he understood their significance. "But, Phoebe, that means you're talking about control of Sparrow!"

His awe made her laugh aloud. "And just wait until we slide that one past Mitch!"

❧ 3 ☙

Sporadic Wanderer

"Mr. Thatcher," said his incomparable secretary early the following week, "is out of town."

Miss Corsa's formula was not good enough for some of Thatcher's senior staff. Charles F. Trinkam, fearlessly risking a snub, elicited more detail.

"Boston, eh?" said Walter Bowman, chief of research. He considered every Sloan client north of the Bronx, then said: "There's that Cetonix secondary."

Charlie inclined toward software. "John wouldn't bother about them. I bet he's huddling with Crocus."

Their colleague, Everett Gabler, was too conservative to evince any enthusiasm for biomedicine or computers.

Miss Corsa ended the suspense by announcing: "Mr. Thatcher is meeting with Rupert Vernon—from Edinburgh."

On the whole, Gabler would have preferred the frontiers of science. Rupert Vernon headed the Scotch real estate developers who operated shopping centers in the Midlands, industrial parks in Kuwait, and resort hotels on islands previously unlisted in any atlas.

"And what," Everett demanded with patriotic indignation, "is Vernon doing in Boston, of all places?"

He was, at that very moment, massing an all-out assault. On a windy downtown corner within sight of the Public Garden, he stood gesturing broadly. "They've barely scratched the surface here," he announced with a drumroll of R's. Around him, young people ducked into boutiques, fur-coated matrons swept out of Elizabeth Arden, and business groups descended on upscale restaurants. "Just look!"

"Yes, Rupert," said Thatcher. "I can see this is Gold Coast territory, but how much of it is available?"

Too much, it developed, as Vernon's tour was designed to illustrate. Taking Thatcher in tow, he plunged up Commonwealth Avenue, along Clarendon Street, down Marlborough Street, pausing only to draw attention to clusters of old-fashioned town houses. His grand finale was a group of larger buildings occupying a complete city block.

"And all this belongs to some college I've never heard of?" Thatcher asked when they finished their trek.

"Correct!" said Vernon. "They're cash poor and land rich, so the intention is for Gauthier College to move to the suburbs. It's a wise solution for them."

"And a windfall for you," Thatcher observed.

Vernon certainly hoped so. "Of course, I'll be doing this again tomorrow when my chaps arrive, but I particularly wanted to show it to you today."

Thatcher, who had done business with Rupert Vernon before, recognized the technique. He was being primed so that when the investors from the UK disembarked, they would wade straight into a sea of euphoria.

"But why bother, Rupert?" he asked frankly. "This Gauthier property speaks for itself."

"I want all the support I can get," Vernon confided. "You see, on Thursday afternoon, I am taking this proposal to His Honor the mayor."

He was considerably understating his need for allies, as Thatcher discovered that evening upon studying the proposal's fine print. Apparently Vernon intended to treat the Back Bay like some squalid corner of the Third World, bulldozing everything in sight. Omitted from consideration were the protesting hordes of community activists, environmentalists, and local politicians. But Thatcher could see them, in their serried ranks, and he had no doubt that His Honor would be able to do so as well.

This presentiment was so vivid that when the hotel phone rang, Thatcher thought it might be Rupert Vernon raising the clans. But the voice belonged to someone much younger.

"Thatcher? This is Mitch Scovil, from Sparrow. We met last week when I was down talking to Kyle Yetter. I called him today and he mentioned that you're in town."

Thatcher could scarcely deny it.

"You remember we said it would be a good idea for you to look at Sparrow?" Scovil continued. "I was wondering if you could make it tomorrow."

Thatcher recalled that the idea had been exclusively Scovil's. Then an incautious movement tumbled Rupert Vernon's folio from the desk, and produced an inspiration.

"I'm busy tomorrow, but I could be free on Thursday," he said, seizing the lesser of two evils.

"That's okay with me, except that I've got a noon meeting," Scovil said. "How about two o'clock?"

"Fine," said Thatcher.

Sparrow Flyways could not be worse than round one at City Hall.

Mitchell Scovil and Rupert Vernon were not the only ones revving up for Thursday.

Alan Whetmore, clipboard in hand, arrived at Clay Batchelder's office the following morning ready to roll. "If you and I can get the ground rules straight, the meeting will go that much better," he announced.

"I'll never understand why they picked you for the job," Batchelder replied.

"Experience," Whetmore said, busying himself with a file folder. "I knew about labor negotiations before they were born."

"Labor negotiations? Is that what you're calling this?" Batchelder said sourly. He knew for a fact that Whetmore's participation in the Pilots' Association had been limited to paying his dues and doing what he was told.

"Sparrow's employees do have legitimate demands," Whetmore replied complacently.

"Okay, shoot," said Batchelder, rumpling his hair with an oil-stained hand.

Whetmore, just off a flight from Chicago, was the neater of the two, as well as the more articulate.

"Now, Clay, you admit everybody on the payroll wants changes made," he began. "Mitch has got to give somewhere. These suggestions should help both of us—and that's what we all want, right?"

Without comment, Batchelder took the folder and began reading. After some minutes, he looked up: "You've gone way too far," he said flatly.

Whetmore shrugged. "Try thinking of it as a starting point for discussion," he advised.

Batchelder scowled in thought. "Have you shown this to Phoebe Fournier, or Cleveland? Or anybody else, for that matter?" he finally demanded.

"Hell no!" said Whetmore, shaking his head. "I'm not letting anybody screw this one up. We've got to keep our eye on the big picture."

Ironically, Batchelder riffled the closely typed pages. "The big picture?" he said. "It seems to have picked up a lot of detail."

Whetmore's demands included employee power at every level. He had outlined so many committees, subcommittees, reviews, and votes that they almost obscured his purpose.

"Mitch will blow a gasket when he sees this," Batchelder warned.

"Oh, come on," said Whetmore with assurance. "You give a little to get a little. Sure, we'll yield on some things, then you'll yield on other things." He paused for effect. "The trick, Clay, is for us to pick the right things."

Batchelder remained impassive. "Well, I hope you're ready for a rough ride. You're going to have them all climbing the wall."

"They chose me," said Whetmore, "they can live with me."

He watched Batchelder drum his fingers and, when the silence protracted itself, added: "I don't see why you're making such a big deal out of this, Clay. There was going to be a fight anyway. I've just changed its direction a little."

"Sure," said Batchelder, barely able to say even that. "We'll just have to wait and see how the meeting tomorrow goes."

Whetmore was willing to call it a day. "Exactly," he said. "But I wanted to give you and Mitch the broad outlines. That way we avoid shocks and surprises. In the end, you'll find that we can all work together real smoothly. We'll manage a few big changes, and that will take care of the little problems. That's how I see it."

Torn between contempt and apprehension, Batchelder watched him withdraw.

"Phoebe, baby," he said to himself. "You picked a real winner."

By that afternoon, she was beginning to think so too. All her plans to coach Alan Whetmore had foundered.

"You're never here," she said, when she finally ran him to earth. Beside her, Joe Cleveland scowled supportively.

"They pay me to go places," said Whetmore, without breaking stride.

Phoebe knew he had been avoiding her, but she stuck to the main issue. "We've got to sit down together," she said, trotting to keep pace with him. "I've got a lot of material that you aren't familiar with."

"Not now," he said dismissively. "I'm in a hurry."

"Look, we're meeting with Mitch and Clay tomorrow," she snapped.

Finally, he halted. "The meeting's at noon, isn't it? Okay, I'll give you an hour before that. If you have anything useful, I can incorporate it in my presentation."

Then, turning smartly, he marched off.

Dumbfounded, Phoebe stared after him. "Who the hell does he think he is?"

Joe tactfully raised another problem. "What do you suppose he means when he talks about his presentation?"

"God knows," she said tartly. "But whatever it is, we'll have to let him get it out of his system before we can show Mitch and Clay the really important figures."

Cheering up, Cleveland said: "Important is right—if you're talking about the petition. Almost everybody signed."

Although she appreciated the effort, she had to set him straight. "Actually those weren't the figures I meant, Joe. I'm talking about Sparrow's debt burden for Mitch's new toys."

"Peace," he said, begging for mercy. "Stuff like that makes my head spin. Do you honestly think you could make Whetmore understand it?"

"I could," she said balefully, "if he'd give me the chance!"

But Alan Whetmore really was in a hurry. When he left Phoebe, he trotted to the bulletin board outside the cafeteria. After five minutes' scrutiny, he grunted with satisfaction and went to the nearest in-house phone.

"Mavis, this is Alan Whetmore. You say you need a pilot for Flight 723 tomorrow morning. I'll take it."

"*You'll* take it? This is really Alan Whetmore volunteering?" Mavis asked sarcastically.

"Himself."

"Why break with history now?"

His patience wore thin. "Will you can the funny talk and just put me down? But one thing first. That flight gets me back here at eleven fifty-five, right?"

"Right."

Whetmore was smiling as he cradled the phone.

At six o'clock, when Joe Cleveland thought the end of the workday was in sight, a harried young man came bursting into the service bay.

"Can you lend me a wrench? My car's just died on me!"

Cleveland had a good memory for faces. "I've seen you in the locker room, haven't I? You're new."

Norman Pitts blushed with pleasure, introduced himself, then said: "And I've got the date of a lifetime tonight."

Joe sprang to his feet. Here was a brand-new employee —and one who could have been overlooked. "Why don't I just come along and see what the trouble is?" he suggested.

On the way to the parking lot, Norman learned a great deal about employee activism at Sparrow. His car required less of Joe's attention. Within ten minutes, there was a sustained healthy throbbing.

"That should do it," Cleveland announced, tossing the wrench to Pitts. "Just put the filter back on, and tighten the nut. I have to split now. I want to get out of here myself."

"Thanks a lot, and I'm sorry I held you up," Pitts said gratefully. "Do you have a date, too?"

Joe, a much married man for six months, flashed white teeth. "You could call it that," he said, strolling off.

A good deed should be its own reward, but in one of his pockets there was a copy of Phoebe's petition, duly signed by Norman Pitts.

❧ 4 ❧

Croaking Noises

John Thatcher set forth for Logan Airport on Thursday at a psychologically satisfying moment. Rupert Vernon and associates had just departed, en masse, for their gunfight with the city fathers.

Even Thatcher's cabby was a happy omen. He not only spoke English, he had something pertinent to contribute. As they sped through the Callahan Tunnel to East Boston, he congratulated his fare on the unparalleled smoothness of their trip. Delays, bottlenecks and, too often, claustrophobic passengers were nearer the norm.

"Then how do people ever catch planes?" Thatcher inquired.

"The smart ones take the MBTA," the cabby retorted, with fine disregard of his own interests.

These were not idle words, Thatcher soon realized. They crept past the main terminal and proceeded to a recycled freight facility some distance from its glossier brethren. The buses that collected passengers from the subway stop were unloading beneath the Sparrow sign. Across the road, similar buses were waiting to ferry arriving passengers back to public transport.

Could this be the secret of Mitch Scovil's success? Sparrow's pitch was aimed at the subway crowd. If they were the only ones who could get to the airport, Scovil had a real edge over the competition.

Inside the Spartan terminal, Thatcher encountered the famous no-frills efficiency. Two-way traffic was kept moving briskly by cheerful personnel wearing the mouse-brown jackets that echoed Sparrow's brown-and-gray color scheme. Behind the scenes, however, management did not measure up. Following directions, Thatcher rounded a corner to come upon Mitchell Scovil at odds with his partners.

"Dammit, Eleanor, it's not my fault that Whetmore's been held up in Buffalo. And you know that the Sloan is a helluva lot more important than this garbage."

Mrs. Gough stood her ground. "Don't talk that way," she said uncompromisingly. "You promised to attend, and now you have to show up."

"But the only reason I have to be there is to explain the situation," Scovil argued back. "You can do that better than I can. Anyway, Eleanor—oh, hello, Thatcher. I didn't see you."

Thatcher had drawn the obvious conclusion. "I gather your meeting is late."

"It hasn't even started," said Scovil with a grimace, going on to introduce his partners.

Mrs. Gough was courteous but adamant. "Late or not, I'm afraid that Mitch absolutely has to sit in," she told Thatcher.

"Now wait a—" Scovil began, only to be overridden by Clay Batchelder.

"Eleanor's right, Mitch," he said heavily.

Thatcher's appointment at Sparrow had paid its way as soon as Rupert Vernon's crowded taxi left without him. Now he was more than willing to retire gracefully. When he said as much, Mrs. Gough and Batchelder indicated gratitude. Scovil, however, was still reluctant.

"God knows how long we'll have to wait," he began. "I suppose I could give—"

Just then a door opened, and a small whirlwind burst into the corridor.

"Our wandering boy is finally back," she announced unceremoniously. "Let's get this show on the road, Mitch."

Scovil had to capitulate. "All right, Phoebe. I'll be along in a minute." Then he had a happier thought. "Thatcher, let me introduce Phoebe Fournier. She's what Sparrow is all about. Phoebe's been with us from day one and you wouldn't believe all the things she's done. Right now, she's heading the employee group that wants me to explain why Sparrow has to expand."

Her correction was perfectly friendly. "We're going to do more than listen, Mitch. We've got some facts of our own to present."

"Since when has anyone been able to shut you up, Phoebe?" he rejoined. "By the way, this is John Thatcher, from the Sloan."

She was thrilled. "The Sloan Guaranty Trust? Is that the one in New York?" Without waiting for confirmation, she continued in a rush: "Then your timing couldn't be better. You'll want to hear this, too. After all, the Sloan owns twenty percent of Sparrow. If we're worried about our thirty percent, then you—"

"I beg your pardon?" Thatcher broke in.

Phoebe heard his doubt and produced the clincher. "I just checked it out on the computer."

Thatcher had heard that one before. "Perhaps," he said noncommittally.

Phoebe was not letting him off that easily. "It belonged to Jim Vandervoort," she persisted.

Good God! The Vandervoort Trust was the repository of one of America's great dynastic fortunes. In those vast holdings, there could be almost anything.

"It must have been part of his estate," Thatcher muttered to himself.

The distinction was lost on her. "Whatever!" she said robustly.

Just moments earlier, Thatcher had felt superior about

the confusion prevailing at Sparrow. Now the shoe was on the other foot. It seemed all too possible that Kyle Yetter, on the third floor of the Sloan, was making decisions in total ignorance of what the sixth floor was doing.

Normally Thatcher did not rage against the Sloan's labyrinthine complexity, for the excellent reason that he was in charge of it. But he was human, too. Clamping down hard, he said: "Perhaps I should join this meeting of yours, Scovil. That is, unless you have any objection?"

Mitchell Scovil was somewhat rueful. "None at all," he said. "It's not what I had in mind when I offered you an inside view. On the whole, we like to introduce people gradually to our way of doing things. But if you're strong enough to take the plunge—it's fine by me."

Opening the door, he waved a spacious invitation. But as they trailed into the conference room, it was Clay Batchelder who, under the bustle of providing extra seating, introduced Joe Cleveland and Alan Whetmore.

". . . and this is John Thatcher from the Sloan. He came up here a couple of days ago—and we're giving him a chance to see how things really work around here."

Alan Whetmore did not echo management geniality, perhaps because the names meant nothing to him. Thatcher decided this must be the case when the pilot said waspishly:

"I don't think we want just anybody watching us while we try to negotiate."

Far from being offended, Thatcher was amused. But Mrs. Gough, he saw, had been embarrassed.

"The Sloan may be paying for our new air fleet, Alan," she said snubbingly. "We're all very happy to show Mr. Thatcher anything he wants to see."

Instead of replying, Whetmore shrugged the rebuke aside. "All right, then let's get started," he said.

He rose, and produced a sheaf of papers. "Now Clay and Mitch have already read this, but the rest of you will need copies to follow along while we discuss the points I've drawn up."

Scovil glanced across the table, then turned to Batchelder. As papers were shuffled around, Thatcher heard him whisper.

"What's all this, Clay? I thought they were going to parade their numbers about California, then I was going to straighten them out."

"For God's sake, Mitch," Batchelder hissed back. "I told you to look at the damned thing, didn't I?"

"Keep your shirt on. I'll read it now."

Meanwhile Whetmore was already in full flight. ". . . the work force is tired of this breakdown in communication. To keep it from happening again, I've tackled the root problem. You'll find that . . ."

Thatcher, who never listened to introductory remarks, was skimming the first page. It prepared him for Scovil's initial reaction.

"This must be some kind of joke."

Whetmore was reproachful. "No it isn't, Mitch. As I explained to Clay, it may seem radical at first, but it sets us on the right path for the future. Just look at the organization table on page five—"

But that was not really necessary. Beneath the verbiage, Whetmore's aim was unmistakable—at least to Thatcher. This plan called for the total reorganization of Sparrow Flyways. With some curiosity, he flicked forward to see what further atrocities lurked.

Mitch Scovil, on the other hand, had already seen enough. "I came here to tell you why Sparrow is taking on California," he said evenly. "If any of you would like to hear—I'm willing to go on."

"That's only one part of the problem," Whetmore told him. "We've got to restructure the whole Sparrow philosophy—"

"This damn thing proves you don't know the first thing about Sparrow," said Scovil, flinging Whetmore's production across the table. "Somebody should have told you that I wouldn't come here to give away management control."

"We're not talking about control, Mitch," Whetmore said earnestly. "We're talking about employee feed-in."

"With veto power over capital expenditures? Who are you trying to kid?"

Thanks to the usual breakdown in distribution, Eleanor Gough was only now receiving her copy. Without glancing at it, she said: "You must be out of your mind, Alan. Everybody knows you can fly a plane, but that's it. You can't even read our annual report."

Thatcher was growing more and more puzzled by Alan Whetmore, who had already demonstrated abysmal ignorance of banks and bankers. If Mrs. Gough was right, the man was also a business primitive. Why, then, was this uniformed nonentity so much more prominent than the much-touted Miss Fournier?

Whatever the reason, Whetmore occupied center stage. His brow furrowed with effort, he was still concentrating on Scovil.

"Look, this is a first approach. If there's anything you want to modify, we'll be reasonable. And we'll understand if you want to offer counterproposals."

"There's only one thing I'm going to do with this bunch of crap," said Scovil dismissively.

Whetmore's face set in mulish lines. "Why are you being so damned stubborn," he complained, "when I'm willing to compromise?"

"What you mean," Scovil translated, "is that, instead of stealing the whole store, you'll settle for three-quarters. You're crazy."

Clay Batchelder, sitting next to Thatcher, semaphored an appeal for intervention to Mrs. Gough.

Lifting her eyes momentarily, she said halfheartedly: "We don't want Mr. Thatcher to get the wrong idea. Sparrow will always listen to reasonable proposals."

If nothing else, she reminded Scovil that he had partners. "Jesus, Clay," he demanded, "why didn't you warn me we had a nutboy on our hands? I've got better ways to pass the time than listening to this kind of bullshit."

Scovil's casual contempt made Alan Whetmore forget his lines. "You'll have to listen," he almost stuttered. "I represent ninety percent of the employees, and you can't run Sparrow without us."

"I ran Sparrow before you came along, sonny boy," said Scovil, losing his control, too. "I can go on doing it."

Throughout the hostilities, Phoebe Fournier had been reading steadily. When she finished the final page, she was white-faced.

"How come there were advance copies for Mitch and Clay?" she said quietly. "While Joe and I walk into this mine field without warning?"

Her unnatural calm misled Mrs. Gough. "What difference does that make?"

"It makes plenty of difference," said Phoebe stonily. "It looks to me as if this is some kind of end play. Now Mitch thinks he can go roaring ahead—without even hearing the real employee objections."

"If anybody put Alan up to something, it wasn't us," Mrs. Gough shot back. "You're the ones who named him to the committee. We didn't."

Thatcher saw that additional skirmishes were the last thing Batchelder wanted.

"Would both of you just calm down?" Batchelder pleaded almost desperately. "This mess isn't your fault. And getting mad at each other isn't going to help."

Mrs. Gough turned on him. "What do you mean, it's not her fault? Alan Whetmore didn't just turn up here by accident. They must have had something in mind."

Bristling, Phoebe defended herself. "How could we know he'd try to pull something like this? But you know damn well, Eleanor, if you'd shown me that list yesterday, he wouldn't be here today."

"How could I show you something I'd never seen?" Eleanor replied nastily.

Phoebe's disbelief was obvious, but before she could put it into words, Batchelder tried once again.

"That's my fault," he said hurriedly. "You weren't there when I gave the damn thing to Mitch."

While Thatcher's attention had been diverted to their sideshow, the main event had been going strong. By now Scovil was on his feet, his body canted over the table.

". . . your career as troublemaker is about to end."

"If you think this is trouble," Whetmore lashed back, "you haven't seen anything yet."

The threat was still hanging in the air when a new voice sounded.

"We're making this too complicated," said Joe Cleveland. "This stuff about committees is a lot of smoke. All Alan wants is the part about an employee rep who gets to be vice-president with a seat on the board. And that shows you how dumb he is. Because, even if we really wanted that, it would be Phoebe—not him."

His taunt made Whetmore swivel. "What are you talking about? I'm the employees' official spokesman."

With a menacing smile, Cleveland said: "Not anymore. You've just been canned."

Whetmore was already swinging back to Scovil. "Forget these two," he directed. "You're talking to a grown-up now. And I'm the one who gets the seat on the board."

"How dare you!" Eleanor Gough exploded.

"Damn the seat on the board!" Phoebe Fournier yelled. "We want to talk about California."

Scovil's contribution was even noisier. "Nobody's going to be a director!" he thundered. "Nobody gets a damn thing. This meeting is over, finito! And, Whetmore, if you ever try this again, I personally will wring your neck!"

Slamming the door to underline his threat, he stormed out of the room.

This abrupt departure confounded Alan Whetmore.

"He can't just walk out like that," he sputtered foolishly.

Batchelder was unhappy too. "Dammit, why didn't Mitch just read the stuff when I told him to?" he lamented. "We could have avoided all this."

Unbelievably, Whetmore took this for encouragement.

"You're right," he said quickly. "And once Mitch gets over the first reaction, he'll be willing to take a different tack."

With a glint in her eye, Eleanor Gough said: "Don't bet on it."

But Clay Batchelder was belatedly recalling that they were not alone. "We're forgetting Thatcher came here to take a look at Sparrow. Why don't you give him the grand tour, Eleanor? That way you can prove that we really know how to run an airline. We don't spend all our time at each other's throats."

Mrs. Gough saw the wisdom of this. She was rising, when Phoebe Fournier interjected herself: "Oh no you don't. That way, Mr. Thatcher will never hear our views at all. Why don't I just come along with you?"

Thatcher could see the abyss yawning before him. "I appreciate your offers," he said with great presence of mind. "Unfortunately I have to get back downtown."

Then, allowing no argument, he held the door for both ladies. As they preceded him, he observed Alan Whetmore and Joe Cleveland, still seated, glaring at each other.

Batchelder did not like the combination either.

"Okay, Joe, fun's over," he said. "We've gotten this far without trading punches. Let's call it quits and go back to work."

Thatcher honored the effort, heavy-handed as it was. From what he had seen, Sparrow Flyways needed all the peacemakers it could find.

5

Labored Flapping

As Mitch Scovil stalked past, the executive receptionist flagged him down.

"Mr. Islington's here," she announced, conscientiously adding: "He's down at the water cooler. And people could hear you shouting the length of the corridor."

"Oh hell," he groaned, abruptly deflated. He could walk out on Alan Whetmore, but not the problem.

Five short minutes at the water cooler constituted a crash course in Sparrow gossip. With Don Islington, this could spell disaster. He was selling the aircraft that Scovil was determined to buy. What Islington learned about Sparrow had to be rigorously sanitized.

As a result, Scovil was radiating self-confidence by the time Sally ushered in Islington.

"Great to see you, Don," he said. "Hey, Sally, how about getting us some coffee? To tell you the truth, Don, if it wasn't for the house rules, I'd order something stronger. We've just had a meeting that had to be seen to be believed."

Islington's long, narrow face was pendulous with

chronic disappointment. "I heard," he said briefly. "Does that mean it's no-go for California?"

"Are you kidding?" Scovil replied with a laugh. "I run Sparrow—not some bunch of kooks."

Islington wanted to believe him. As a customer, Sparrow Flyways might not rank with the Department of Defense or United Airlines, but global budget-cutting made any sale look good.

"They said your people are ready to fight any expansion," he pointed out.

"Window dressing!" Scovil snorted. "Highway robbery is what this bunch was after. Here, take a look at this if you want a good laugh."

He tossed Whetmore's manifesto across the desk. "This is the brainchild of one of our pilots. Have you ever seen anything like it?"

He waited until Islington was obediently reading, then threw in a casual afterthought. "And to make matters worse, we had the Sloan right there, drinking it all in."

"The Sloan?" Islington said eagerly. "I know you've been talking to Yetter in New York. You mean you've gotten far enough for him to come up?"

Financing was always the sound barrier in deals like this.

"Oh, we've moved past Yetter," said Scovil airily. "These days we're talking with John Thatcher."

Islington began to hope. "Then you'll want to show him these payback plans we've come up with. We're extending the time period by a generous margin. But before we get to that, what about this pilot? Is he serious about pulling the rug out? And if he is, what are you going to do?"

"I've been thinking about that," Scovil acknowledged. "And you know what? I know exactly how to handle Alan Whetmore."

Phoebe Fournier's well-developed instinct for smelling a rat led her to Mavis Tassone in scheduling before the hour was out.

"That bastard," she spat, when she heard the details. "He set me up from the beginning."

"I thought it was fishy," said Mavis sympathetically. "Whetmore volunteering is Whetmore up to something."

"Then why didn't you warn me?" said Phoebe, itching for a whipping boy. "Don't you realize how much Alan has cost us?"

But Mavis was not a born cheek-turner. "Don't blame me. I thought he was trading shifts for his latest girlfriend. If you feel like criticizing, look at what you've done. It was your bright idea to put him on the committee."

"Oh, don't," moaned Phoebe, who already felt like kicking herself. "There are thousands of us. And our stock and our jobs could both go down the drain because of Alan Whetmore. With him around, nobody's going to listen to us—not Mitch and not the Sloan. Oh, damn, damn, damn!"

She was arching her fingers back, then curling them forward, like a cat flexing and retracting its claws.

"I've never seen you like this before," said Mavis uneasily.

"I'll kill him," said Phoebe, still talking to herself. "So help me God, when I find him, I'll kill him!"

Joe Cleveland was getting even less sympathy. Sparrow's senior mechanic listened to the obscenity-laden description of Alan Whetmore's behavior, then produced his one all-purpose response:

"What do you expect when you get mixed up with pilots?"

Cleveland wanted a spark, any spark, to burn off his anger.

". . . and Clay didn't help, either. Telling me to butt out—as if taking care of Whetmore wouldn't be a public service."

His chief, mounting a ladder, did not bother to look down. "What do you expect when you tangle with the brass?"

Eleanor Gough, putting her accumulated spleen to good use, went straight to the water cooler.

"Well, I hope you're satisfied," she said to the gathering.

39

"I work like a dog to set up this meeting, and what do you do?"

Her audience was not visibly cowed. "We've got a right to make Mitch listen to us," said one of them spiritedly.

"He goes along with that," she said. "That's why Mitch was there. But, instead of a reasonable discussion, we got Alan Whetmore demanding to be vice-president of Sparrow."

As she had gambled, this was news to them.

"Alan?" gasped a programmer. "That's plain silly. The one you should talk to is Phoebe—"

"Phoebe's the one who dragged in Alan—and that little list of his," Eleanor cut in. "And I've got to tell you, I don't think there's going to be much listening around here for a long time. Mitch is boiling mad. And for that matter, so am I!"

By outstaying Joe Cleveland in the conference room, Clay Batchelder lost his chance to rehash the situation with Scovil.

"Mitch has got Mr. Islington with him," said Sally a little avidly. "Do you want to join them?"

She was reaching for the intercom, but Batchelder shook his head. "Skip it," he said, disappointingly normal. "I'm not in the mood. I'll catch him later."

Whatever his feelings, Batchelder always found work the best form of release. He spent the next hour and a half revising all the equipment procedures he could find. When he returned, Scovil's empty cubbyhole told its own story. The coat was gone, the desk was bare. Sally, reappearing a few minutes later, confirmed the obvious.

"Mitch decided to call it quits after Mr. Islington left. Naturally, everybody has been looking for him ever since."

"I'm glad he got away early," said Batchelder. "It's been a long day, and the sooner it's over, the better."

But Sally had some good news for him. "Mitch's day isn't over, Clay. He went home, but he's having dinner tonight with Mr. Thatcher."

"Well, I'll be damned," Batchelder exclaimed, pleased

and surprised. "That old son-of-a-gun pulled it off despite everything!"

The old son-of-a-gun had not pulled it off. It was John Thatcher himself who had taken the initiative. This was the direct consequence of the telephone call he made as soon as he cleared Logan.

"Yes, Mr. Thatcher," said Miss Corsa, sounding poised for action despite the miles between them.

In his haste, Thatcher began barking commands. He came to his senses soon enough.

"You're not the one I should be shouting at," he said, making amends. He then glossed this apology with an appeal to her loyalty. "But I don't like having the Sloan's affairs explained to me by a girl who isn't old enough to be my daughter."

Miss Corsa liked it even less.

"I'll have our Sparrow holdings checked immediately," she assured him.

"Of course, she could be making a mistake," Thatcher interjected hopefully.

Miss Corsa was ready for all contingencies. "If she is, I'll call back to tell you. But if this Miss Fournier is correct, I'll ask Mr. Nielsen to talk to you."

Half an hour later Homer Nielsen's cranky accents greeted Thatcher. "John? Miss Corsa seems to think there's some problem with our Sparrow stock."

"There certainly is," said Thatcher. "Can you explain how twenty percent of a company like that got into the Vandervoort Trust—and why we've let it stay there?"

"Because there's not a damned thing we can do about it," Nielsen said thumpingly. "This isn't part of the general trust. It's one of those rinky-dink deals to celebrate paternity. You know what they're like."

Thatcher did indeed. In spite of the family's boundless wealth, all male Vandervoorts insisted on creating nest eggs for children who were millionaires at birth. It was a gesture they enjoyed mightily.

"And a damned nuisance for us," said Thatcher, completing his thought aloud.

Nielsen produced the honk which served him for laughter. "And this one's worse than usual. We have no power to dispose of the stock. All we can do is invest the dividends."

"I suppose that was only to be expected," said Thatcher, who knew that Nielsen had a taste for horrors.

"You see, Jimmy originally owned ten percent of Sparrow," Nielsen said merrily. "That only cost him three dollars a share. But two weeks before his death, he picked up another ten percent—just when the stock was hitting its all-time high. That cost him an arm and a leg. But no matter how much Sparrow falls, we're stuck with it. We've got eighteen years to go until Jimmy's son comes of age."

Thatcher contemplated a time dimension that would appall any prudent man. "Obviously, we're going to have to make our presence felt up here before that."

After Nielsen hung up, Thatcher continued to ponder the situation. Miss Fournier had been quite right about the Sloan's twenty percent of Sparrow's stock. Could she have been just as accurate in her fleeting reference to *our* thirty percent? If so, Sparrow was a disaster in the making. The Sloan could not sit idly on the sidelines—not for eighteen long years.

So, for openers, Thatcher decided to invite Mitch Scovil to dinner.

🗦 6 🗧

Chiefly Nocturnal

Rupert Vernon, either with his shield or on it, was due back at the hotel at any minute. Bearing this in mind, Thatcher set off to meet Mitchell Scovil with far too much time to spare. He stilled the pangs of conscience with a lesson culled from experience. Going directly from one demon entrepreneur to another was counterproductive. By inserting space between Scovil and Vernon, he was exercising banking acumen. Today this involved wandering through Historic Boston, instead of redesigning it.

Fortunately, the New England Aquarium crossed his path. Thatcher seized the opportunity to enjoy a brief and refreshing interlude. When closing time came, he proceeded through light rain to Quincy Market, drawing invidious comparisons between man and fish as he went. It was after seven o'clock before he returned to duty.

He was already ensconced in the bar when Mitch Scovil rushed in a few minutes later, appearing at the head of a short flight of stairs. After a worried look around, the younger man located Thatcher. Smiling broadly he shrugged off his raincoat, stopped for a word with the hostess, then hurried down the stairs.

"Our table's ready," he announced when he reached Thatcher. "Why don't you bring your drink along?"

Scovil began by playing the host, with suggestions from the menu and consultations about the wine list. But, as soon as the waiter departed, he confronted Thatcher squarely. "Well, I asked you out to Sparrow, and you got a real eyeful, didn't you!"

Thatcher could see that he had been cast as audience, with Scovil choosing the subject matter. To set things straight, he said: "And an earful, too. I find that Miss Fournier was absolutely correct. The Sloan does have control of a full twenty percent of Sparrow's stock. Tell me how Jim Vandervoort became so deeply involved in the company."

If Scovil was taken aback, he managed to hide it. "Oh, Jim was one of our miracles," he said. "When deregulation came along, a bunch of us working at Bayou Airline could see it was the chance of a lifetime. The trouble was, we had to come up with five hundred thousand dollars as seed money—and that was a bare minimum."

"Not much," said Thatcher, playing his part. "I mean, in view of the size of the undertaking you had in mind."

"That's what all the bankers said," Scovil replied. "It may not have seemed like much to them, but it was damned near impossible for us. But then things began to happen. Fritz Diehl's father died and left him something. Then he ran into his old college roommate, who just happened to be Jim Vandervoort. And Jim—God bless him!—said that, if we could each ante up one hundred thousand, he would too. Naturally, Clay was raring to go, but I was still the problem child. Then guess what? The next week I bought a winning ticket in the lottery. How's that for timing!"

"Excellent, if somewhat unorthodox," said Thatcher, considerably entertained. "However, that still adds up to four hundred thousand dollars, doesn't it?"

His simple arithmetic came as a surprise to Scovil.

"Oh, and Eleanor, too," Scovil said, as if everybody

knew. "But Jim's real contribution came when we went grubbing for venture capital. He and Fritz would waltz in together. Between the Ivy League touch, and the Vandervoort name, lenders started falling all over themselves. In those days, Clay and I stayed in the background."

His voice was tinged with indulgence—or was it derision? Either way, the romantic touch was a mistake. Thatcher always grew suspicious when a simple question flushed Technicolor answers.

"Remarkable," he said politely. "Now that explains the ten percent Vandervoort acquired at three dollars. What about the second ten percent—which is what makes the Sloan your largest stockholder?"

Scovil was leaning back casually, one arm draped over the adjacent chair. "That belonged to Fritz Diehl." Unconsciously he clenched his fist. "Fritz decided he could do better for himself."

"It often happens," said Thatcher blandly. Young men who can work together building the ship and launching it, often part company afterward.

"I suppose so," said Scovil, reaching for a bread roll. Breaking it into pieces seemed to occupy his attention as he continued. "Anyway, Fritz decided to sell out. And that put us in a ticklish situation. We didn't want him to dump his shares on the market—even if we were doing pretty well. Sparrow's never had a really big following. Selling ten percent—all at once—could spell trouble. But that's when Jim saved our bacon. He had done so well with his original Sparrow that he was willing to buy Fritz's. And, of course, he could afford to. But it didn't make any difference. Jim never took an active part in management."

"Did Fritz Diehl?" Thatcher asked bluntly.

After some hesitation, Scovil said tonelessly: "Sure."

Thatcher noted the constraint, but delivered his own message anyway. "The end result, of course, is that the shares of both men have ended up at the Sloan," he said. "As you must realize, this materially changes the circumstances surrounding your application for financing. Kyle Yetter will no longer make his decision as a simple lender. Since we are substantial owners, we are interested in Sparrow's long-term vitality—quite beyond the firm's capacity to repay any debt due to us."

Scovil quirked his eyebrows. "And you didn't like what you saw this afternoon," he said. "There's no excuse for what happened. Believe me, it honestly was a glitch. Whetmore should never have been there, and I shouldn't have lost my temper. God, I just got suckered into going after a curve ball."

"I'll accept that," said Thatcher, holding up a hand. "But it was my impression that Miss Fournier is strongly opposed to the expansion plan which is central to your current thinking about Sparrow. And she represents not only the majority of your employees, but thirty percent of your stock as well. Surely that's more than a glitch or a curve ball."

"You're dead right. But that's because I never got the chance to explain," said Scovil, who had come to give precisely this speech. "Phoebe and her people don't understand that if it's risky for Sparrow to expand, it'll be riskier for us to stand still. We've had a long run of good luck under optimum conditions. In the current environment, if Sparrow doesn't grow, it'll be out of business in two years. Every day some airline folds, and the shakeout will go on until there are only a few lines left. It's the only way to go—the economics, the demographics prove it."

"Have you considered the alternative?" Thatcher asked him. "I mean acquiring other regional carriers?"

Already shaking his head, Scovil said: "Not on your life! You can't mix the Sparrow system with a regular union shop. Look what happened to People Express. They went that route, and now they're dead. It could happen to us, too."

The last remark was so unexpected that Thatcher wondered if it were a cue. "So you're worried about being targeted for a takeover. Are there any raiders in sight?"

"Not yet," said Scovil, choosing his words with care. "But I know damn well they'll be nosing around if the stock sinks another ten points. That's why—"

"Any candidates?" Thatcher interrupted.

Scovil shrugged. "I suppose any one of the takeover artists is possible, but my best bet would be a major carrier. And that's why Sparrow has to become too big to swallow."

"You think your only protection is to become a major carrier yourself," Thatcher suggested.

"Exactly!" said Scovil. "And I can persuade the employees too. If not—well, they'll just have to lump it."

"And what about Sparrow's famous participatory management?" Thatcher inquired.

"Look, I'm not knocking it," said Scovil, leaning forward earnestly. "The system was a winner in the past—and not just because it kept the unions out. But I've never made it into a religion, the way some people have. That's because I always knew it could only work for so long. When things get tough, the decisions get tough too—and someone has to make them. You can't take a round-table vote. Sooner or later, the system has to go. Right now, Sparrow is facing its first real turning point. Let me explain. . . ."

By the time they were waiting for the check, Thatcher found himself considering the things that had not been said. For all Scovil's talk about a first turning point, he was ignoring an earlier one. Before Fritz Diehl's departure, everything had worked like a charm. Afterward, the erosion began. Even allowing for changing market forces, that could have been more than sheer coincidence.

This was suggestive enough to shed new light on Sparrow's current difficulties. If Scovil's sense of authority was already strained, any threat could be serious.

With his imagination outstripping the facts at hand, Thatcher made his farewells. Scovil's reply included a final assurance.

"I'm as confident as I've ever been."

"Yes," said Thatcher, keeping his thoughts to himself. "I can see that you are."

"And I've got damned good reasons, too," said Mitchell Scovil.

The rain that had spangled coats early in the evening had turned into a penetrating clammy drizzle. Along the shoreline, where Logan Airport thrust into the sea, the fog was settling in.

At eleven o'clock, when most passenger flights were over, the murk blanketed runways and parking lots. By midnight, the terminal was a tomb with shuttered coffee shops and gated newsstands. Outside, visibility was measured in yards. Sound was muffled and distorted while, above the harbor, the foghorns bayed mournfully.

Two security guards, driving the outer perimeter of the field, picked their way cautiously along the line of reflecting posts. A turn taken too sharply skewed their headlight beams across the fringe of scummy water.

"What's that?"

The driver, a veteran of many years, backed the jeep carefully and looked again toward the shapeless heap.

"A present from up the coast," he predicted, clambering out and wading toward a human body face down in the rushes.

His companion was a rookie. Wordlessly, he followed, then picked up the legs and helped haul the corpse from the water. Swallowing hard, he stared at the invisible sea.

"Damned tide," he muttered. "Carries everything in here and dumps it."

The driver was bent over, studying the sodden uniform.

"Not this one. He's a pilot from Sparrow," he announced, straightening up. "And the back of his head has been bashed in."

⚡ 7 ⚡

Difficult to Flush

At seven o'clock the next morning a hand-picked officer from the Massachusetts State Police was midway through the Callahan Tunnel, waiting for a breakdown to be cleared away. He had been summoned from the other side of the state and, until ten minutes ago, had been making good time.

Now, instead of chafing, Captain Gregory Lemoine was studying a large-scale map of the area. Logan Airport was a virtual island, approximately one and a half by three miles. To the south, directly across from downtown Boston, lay the shipping lanes to the city's piers, a channel to the locks on the Charles River and, underneath all that water, one subway and two automobile tunnels.

Captain Lemoine did not worry about other exits. Indeed, from the eastern end, one could look out over Boston Harbor, Massachusetts Bay, and ultimately the Atlantic Ocean. The first solid object, apart from a remote island housing a correctional facility, would be Spain.

When Lemoine finally left the tunnel, he drove directly to the spot where Alan Whetmore's body had been found.

The area had been roped off and several troopers were squelching through the mud, while a biting east wind flattened the beach scrub. The tide had retreated and a noisome aroma was rising from the flats to greet a few gulls squawking desolately overhead.

"Christ!" said Lemoine, a landsman to the core.

He did not leave his car for two reasons. Protocol required that he meet with the head of the permanent force at the airport, fortunately an old acquaintance. More important, there was no visibility. An unenthusiastic sunrise had begun just before he entered the tunnel, but it would be hours before the fog burned off.

Five minutes later he walked into a small out-of-the-way office to find Lieutenant Crawley hard at work. The whine of jets speeding early morning commuters down the Eastern Corridor was clearly audible.

"You're not going to like this one," Crawley warned him.

"I already don't," Lemoine grunted. "Ed, suppose you start by telling me the real reason they yanked me out of bed and took me off a case?"

"There's some kind of labor trouble at Sparrow. Everybody is afraid it may be a company murder."

Lemoine groaned. Politicians always take a fatherly interest in major employers.

"What makes them so edgy? On the way in, I drove past the scene. It's not exactly company headquarters. Maybe the guy was fooling around with someone's wife."

Ed shook his head sadly. "We found the weapon in the mud. It's a wrench marked: PROPERTY OF SPARROW FLYWAYS."

"So? Maybe hubby works for Sparrow, too."

"Nobody thinks so. They had a meeting yesterday where the president threatened to break Whetmore's neck. Then, some lady vice-president came out telling the world that Whetmore was ruining everything. And—wait until you get this one—some girl from the labor side said they had to get rid of him before he did any more damage."

Lemoine bowed to reality. The victim's co-workers would know exactly what waves he had been making.

"Whetmore sounds like everybody's favorite. What have we got on the killing itself?"

Ed rummaged through the papers before him. "Just a minute, the autopsy report is here somewhere."

"Already?"

This was unprecedented speed in Lemoine's experience.

"I warned you there was a lot of pressure on this one, Greg. Here it is. Whetmore's skull was fractured by one blow from the wrench, delivered from behind, and he crumpled over the guardrail there. It's only two and a half feet high, and we found shreds from his uniform in the cable. After that, it's anybody's guess. Whetmore could have slid into the water on his own, or the killer dumped him in."

"Or even a combination," Lemoine suggested. "He slid in, and the murderer rolled him over face down. I suppose we're not going to get any footprints on that surface."

Crawley shook his head. "Not a chance. However it was done, Whetmore's death is technically due to drowning although he would have died anyway. Did I mention that the wrench was clean?"

"You didn't have to," Lemoine said equably. "Okay, do we know anything about Whetmore, yet?"

"Aged fifty-two, unmarried, a commercial pilot for over twenty years. So far, that's it. The people at Sparrow are stonewalling, claiming they don't know much about him— or anything."

Lemoine looked up. "If the help isn't talking, how come you know so much about the meeting?"

"They're not talking to us. But, boy, are they talking to each other." Ed beamed. "The first shift comes on at five o'clock and they want coffee. I've had a man sitting in their cafeteria since it opened. A lot of them were blabbing about the meeting even before they heard of the murder."

"Okay. Now what about Whetmore's movements? Do we know why he was down by that godforsaken bog?"

Ed had no idea. "The early shift wouldn't know," he explained. "The people who might won't show up for hours."

"Well, we've got a hell of a lot to do. We'd better start by getting organized."

The result of their efforts was a list of assignments, divided between the two forces. The Logan regulars would circulate throughout the airport searching for witnesses who had seen Whetmore, with or without companions. The homicide specialists would devote themselves to the coroner's report, the laboratory examination of the wrench, and Whetmore's apartment. Captain Lemoine reserved for himself interviews with the principals.

In short order, he discovered two things about Sparrow. The staff arrived early and unanimously regarded his investigation as an intrusion.

At eight o'clock, Eleanor Gough was the first to sound a note which he would hear again. "I don't have much time. Can we do this quickly?" she said, pausing in mid-stride.

"This is a murder case," he retorted.

Her impatient grimace said it all. The murder of Alan Whetmore was a tragic crime of violence, but it had nothing to do with Sparrow Flyways.

"Then you shouldn't mind talking to me about that meeting of yours," said Lemoine ironically.

To his surprise, she did not. Where he saw motive, she saw unlucky coincidence.

". . . and," she concluded a few minutes later, "all this is going to make a bad situation worse. I do wish Mitch hadn't flown off the handle yesterday."

"You said some pretty strong things yourself."

"I was furious," she agreed absently. "First with Phoebe, then with Alan. The whole meeting was so stupid. This is a critical time for Sparrow and the last thing Mitch needs is to be distracted."

Even a request for her movements did not puncture her absorption. "Let's see. Oh yes, I was in my office until about four-thirty, then I went over to accounting and I stopped by procurement. Then about six, Clay was ready to leave and we went out to dinner together."

She refused to take yesterday's fireworks seriously, she denied having seen Whetmore after the meeting, and she wanted Lemoine to finish so that she could find a replacement pilot.

Clay Batchelder was just as bad.

"I've got to hand it to Whetmore," he said. "Getting himself murdered was probably the only way he could cause even more trouble."

Asked about his movements, Clay was willing but vague.

"I was all over the lot. Oh yes, I wanted to catch Mitch after he was through with Don Islington, but I let it go too late. When I asked Sally—she's our receptionist—she said he'd already gone home. So I must have been with her around five. And I remember I went out to the maintenance manager after that. I caught Eleanor for dinner about six or six-fifteen. Somewhere around then, anyway. Are you through with me? I've got a hell of a lot to do."

Insofar as possible, Sally confirmed these statements. "Everybody was in and out all the time," she said cheerfully. "That's the way it always is."

"Doesn't anybody tell you where they're going to be?" Lemoine demanded.

"Not unless they're taking off downtown or something. They usually check back with me about messages and things every now and then."

It sounded like a criminal's paradise to a policeman.

"And Scovil had left by the time Batchelder was looking for him at five?"

"Oh yes. Mitch must have been gone for a quarter of an hour by then. I remember Mr. Diehl was looking for him around ten minutes earlier."

Other than that, Sally could only say that both Batchelder and Eleanor Gough had been out of the office for some time before making their dinner plans.

Labor matched management in insouciance.

"Oh, I could have strangled Alan," Phoebe Fournier admitted freely.

"I thought it was Mrs. Gough you tangled with," Lemoine reminded her.

"Only because I was surprised. But Eleanor's too smart to pull something that raw. Alan was the dumb one, and it

53

had to be his own clever idea. That includes lying to me about his morning schedule so I couldn't squash him before the meeting."

After Phoebe, came Mavis Tassone.

"Yes, Alan Whetmore piloted the morning flight from Buffalo, but he wasn't on duty for it," she reported. "He called me and volunteered to cover for that specific flight. I knew there was something funny about it. Alan never put in an extra hour in his life."

Joe Cleveland, tracked down in the cafeteria, even admitted to a threat that had not yet made its way to the police.

"Sure I was burned up after the meeting. I said I'd deck Whetmore if I ran into him, but I didn't. He thought he was going to use the rest of us, and it was time somebody straightened him out."

"Or got rid of him?" Lemoine suggested.

Joe never batted an eye. "All we had to do was bounce him."

By nine-thirty Captain Lemoine had a mass of unhelpful detail and one missing person.

"Isn't Scovil in yet?" he asked.

"No, but we know where he is," Ed Crawley reported. "He called to say he was having a late breakfast at the Marriott. They expect him here at eleven."

Lemoine frowned at this first break in the pattern. "You know, all these people are pretending this meeting yesterday was just your usual office row, but one thing they couldn't hide," he said slowly. "There was an outsider there, some banker called Thatcher. You want to bet that he's being primed, right now? Maybe I should join this breakfast."

But when Lemoine was ushered to Mitch Scovil's table at the Marriott, the man with the receding hairline was introduced as Fritz Diehl.

"Fritz is a vice-president at A&P these days, but he used to be with Sparrow," Scovil explained.

"Sorry to interrupt your breakfast, Mr. Scovil, but I expected you to come to the office when you heard about Whetmore."

Scovil's answer was pat. On a normal morning he would have been at his desk by nine, but today he had gone to the Boston Athletic Club for a workout. When he encountered Diehl in the weight room, they had decided to breakfast together. News of Whetmore's death reached him only when he called his office. From that brief account he assumed the pilot was another mugging victim.

Lemoine ignored this justification. "You go to this club regularly, Mr. Scovil?"

"Not as regularly as I should, but I manage to get in once a week or so."

Fritz Diehl seemed amused. "I've been telling Mitch for years that you've got to do it every day, but he's too lazy."

"And the two of you met by accident?"

They both nodded.

On the face of it, their account was plausible. These days executives did meet at the Nautilus.

Lemoine tried another tack. "You see, we're trying to get a fix on Whetmore's movements," he said. "We know he was at your meeting after he came in from Buffalo but, after that, it seems to be a blank."

Scovil now exhibited the curiosity that should have surfaced earlier.

"Didn't Sally tell me the murder was around midnight? Whetmore could have been doing anything by then."

"The body was discovered at midnight. But he was killed a lot earlier. Probably between four and seven."

Scovil pursed his lips in a silent whistle. "That makes a big difference," he conceded. "Someone should have seen him around. But I'm no help to you. I went home early."

"And when would that have been?"

If Scovil noticed that the subject had shifted from Whetmore's movements to his own, he gave no indication.

"It must have been a little before five."

"You say that's early," Lemoine pressed. "Any particular reason?"

Scovil smiled. "There sure was. I was having dinner with my banker and I wanted to review my facts in peace and quiet. When the Sloan is financing a multimillion-dollar expansion, they're happier if you know what you're talking about. Wouldn't you agree, Fritz?"

"I sure would," Diehl said urbanely.

During this exchange Lemoine finally identified the tickle that had been bothering him.

"I understand you were out at Sparrow yesterday yourself, Mr. Diehl?"

"That's right. When I visit A&P's regional office here, I have dinner with Eleanor Gough if there's time. I tried to catch her, but she wasn't in her office. Then I asked for Mitch, but he wasn't around either." Diehl paused before adding softly: "Mitch is always my second choice."

Scovil chuckled. "Fritz and Eleanor are friends from way back."

Lemoine's gaze remained fixed on Diehl. "Then you didn't actually see Mr. Scovil?"

"Nope. Didn't get Eleanor either. I ended up eating alone."

"It's a shame we didn't make contact, Fritz," Scovil commented. "You could have had dinner with Thatcher and me."

Diehl's glance slid sideways. "That would have been a real pleasure, Mitch," he murmured.

Lemoine's professional instincts were flashing a warning. These two men were sparring with each other, and that meant he should separate them.

Without undue concern for etiquette he announced his decision.

"I've got some more questions, Mr. Scovil. But as they're about internal affairs at Sparrow, we'd better be private."

Fritz Diehl remained relaxed to the end.

"That suits me," he declared. "See you around, Mitch."

"Sure thing, Fritz."

Within two minutes Lemoine was congratulating himself. At least he was getting his witness's undivided attention.

"I'm not denying I got hot under the collar yesterday,"

Scovil said almost boastfully. "I've got a pretty short fuse and Whetmore was completely unreasonable."

"You sure you want to go on record that way, Mr. Scovil?"

"You mean because he was murdered?" Scovil was no more impressed by this fact than anybody else at Sparrow. "You're not listening to me, Captain. When I say unreasonable, I mean off-the-wall . . . flaky . . . out of sight. Nobody was going to take that stuff seriously."

"Apparently Whetmore did."

Scovil snorted. "We don't know what he was really aiming at, but it wasn't what he put down on paper, believe me."

Lemoine was at his most phlegmatic. "I don't know much about this sort of thing."

"You don't have to. Just read that list."

"So what are you saying? That Whetmore was around the bend?"

"No." The flat negative was bitten off as if there was more to follow. Scovil's gaze flickered over the captain, then away. It took a moment for him to recapture his fluency. "I'm just saying that list wasn't a threat, that's all. If you don't believe me, then ask anyone. Ask Clay, ask Eleanor, for God's sake, ask Phoebe."

Lemoine had a better idea.

"No, I think I'll ask John Thatcher instead."

❧ 8 ❧

Languid Warbling

Within forty-five minutes, Thatcher found himself assisting the Massachusetts State Police in their inquiries. Not that he had any choice in the matter. Captain Gregory Lemoine had appeared out of the blue and extorted an hour from Thatcher's already tight schedule. Then, treating the hotel like his squad room, he invited Thatcher to begin at the beginning.

"Well, I met Scovil for the first time last week in New York," Thatcher said. With more care than usual, he outlined Scovil's overtures to the Sloan Guaranty Trust.

Lemoine patiently encouraged him to get to the point. "I see. And that's how you happened to be sitting in on this Sparrow meeting yesterday afternoon?"

"I'm afraid so," said Thatcher with real regret.

Discussing the financial intricacies unfolding at Sparrow was at least congenial. Unfortunately, Lemoine was more interested in raised voices, slammed doors, and threats of personal violence. Thatcher did his best, but he was happy to have his recital end.

". . . and that is the full extent of my recollection," he

said, finally. "I may have missed some of the minor exchanges, but I think I've told you everything of substance."

Lemoine was quicker than he looked. "Well, I'm grateful for all the facts I can get," he said ambiguously. "But I'm looking for someone who cracked Alan Whetmore's skull. So the important thing is how mad these people really were."

Thatcher did not hesitate to rebuff this none-too-subtle invitation to editorialize.

"I am the last man who can tell you that," he said, stating a policy position. "Remember, these people are almost strangers to me. For all I know, Scovil may lose his temper every other day, then forget about it instantly. I could tell you that neither Mrs. Gough nor Miss Fournier struck me as capable of homicidal mania—but I do not know either of them. Batchelder and young Cleveland are unknown quantities—and so, for that matter, was Whetmore himself."

"Okay, you don't know these particular people," said Lemoine, still angling. "But you do admit that all this fighting is way out of the ordinary, don't you?"

Thatcher had to agree that it was somewhat unusual.

"How unusual?" said Lemoine, pushing his advantage. "Is it the kind of thing that would happen at your bank, just to take an example?"

"I certainly hope not," said Thatcher, tempted to claim that the Sloan operated on unadulterated sweetness and light.

But since they were talking about murder, he was more realistic. "What struck me at Sparrow was not the dissension. That can, and does, occur anywhere. It was the fact that everybody was caught by surprise, and by an unpleasant surprise at that. Nobody came prepared for what took place—and that, to put it charitably, shows extremely poor organization on both sides of the dispute."

Driving the point home, he managed to get in a few good words for his own team. "Yes, we at the Sloan can have meetings where people pound the table. But at least those people have done their homework."

"Even when you're negotiating with the union?" Lemoine interjected quickly.

"Especially when we're negotiating with the union," said Thatcher emphatically. "They present written proposals, we present written proposals. Then everybody goes away and vents emotions in private. The negotiations themselves are dull as dishwater, and that is the way we intend to keep them."

Lemoine grinned. "I'll remember that when I talk to the boys down at the PBA," he said. "Now, after the meeting, what did you do, Mr. Thatcher?"

For several intoxicating moments Thatcher wondered if he figured on the suspect list. Then common sense and Lemoine brought him back to earth.

"You say you had to wait for Scovil at the restaurant?" the captain said, ignoring the aquarium altogether.

"Perhaps five minutes," Thatcher replied. Simple humanity, as well as other considerations, made him hope that he was not tightening a noose.

Lemoine pondered, then veered unexpectedly.

"It must have been raining by the time you got there."

Thatcher agreed that it had been drizzling and tried to guess what Lemoine was after.

"How wet was Scovil when he came in?"

Dutifully Thatcher flipped through his mental photographs. "His coat may have been damp, but it was not sodden. That is all that I can remember."

"No umbrella?"

"Not that I saw," said Thatcher.

Lemoine retreated into private cogitation. When he emerged, it was to make preparations for departure.

"Thanks again for helping out, Mr. Thatcher," he said, lumbering to his feet. "I've got a feeling you may have pointed us in the right direction."

From Thatcher's point of view, Captain Lemoine's departure came moments too late. Rupert Vernon was just bustling in, a new roll of blueprints under his arm.

"For the benefit of the Back Bay Association," he began without preamble. "They have some bee in their bonnet about sidewalk usage, so I've given them enough umbrella tables for the South of France. I can't imagine what they think will happen from November to May. You do have snow here, don't you?"

"Frequently," Thatcher agreed.

"So I thought. Have you ever noticed how adamantly summer-minded all these civic bodies are? They want bright airy clothes, people strolling of an evening, children with ice-cream cones. If I had lambs roasting on spits in the forecourt, they'd rally to my support without question."

Thatcher proffered what comfort he could. "Most community groups are only advisory, Rupert," he said. "And this is not an election year. You should get your permits and clearances before any candidate starts campaigning against you."

"The financing comes first," Vernon remarked, his eyes gleaming.

"I see no insuperable difficulty."

"Aha!" Reassured, Vernon now turned his attention elsewhere. "I could not help noticing that chap who just left. Not the customary uniform, was it?"

Briefly Thatcher explained the Boston Metropolitan Police, the Massachusetts State Police, and the tangled jurisdiction at Logan Airport. He was resigned to explaining more than that. After all, he had canceled out with the British contingent, and they all knew why.

"I met the murder victim yesterday afternoon," he concluded his short tale, "and the police had a few questions."

Artlessly, Vernon recounted the latest television bulletins. "They claim there was bad feeling between the victim and the company president. Now that's the fellow you dashed off to meet yesterday evening, isn't it?"

"The police had a few questions about my dinner as well," Thatcher admitted.

Vernon was smug. "Let this be a lesson to you, John," he said. "I don't claim that Wilson and poor MacTavish are the most scintillating companions I could provide, but at least my dinners do not attract police visitations."

* * *

Yesterday Thatcher had reminded Mitch Scovil of the Sloan's double-edged interest in Sparrow. But what if Scovil himself was about to be plucked from the scene? Rumors alone were enough to galvanize the market.

Without delay, Thatcher dialed the Sloan and asked for Everett Gabler.

"Everett," he said, "what's happening to Sparrow?"

"Down over two points."

Of course Gabler knew. Many complained of his rigidity; nobody ever denied his capacity for detail.

Briskly Thatcher described the situation at Sparrow. A pending loan, a tricky expansion, employee disaffection, and now a possible murder charge against the president—together they created a picture that almost outstripped Gabler's capacity for prophesying disaster.

But not quite.

"There is one further element that you may not be aware of, John," he said, characteristically complicating an already complex situation.

"Yes?"

"Walter Bowman has just been in," Gabler said. "There's talk on the Street that, when the stock hits twenty-five, there will be a takeover move."

After Scovil's analysis last night, Thatcher took that talk seriously.

"We're going to have to send somebody in to look at the books," he decided. "Scovil is synonymous with Sparrow. If he goes to jail, God knows what we'll have to do."

There was no more militant defender of the Sloan's privileges than Everett Gabler, but the habit of playing devil's advocate was too strong to be suppressed.

"I don't know, John," he said dubiously. "There is, after all, no question of reorganization. And the market may rebound if nothing happens to Scovil. They could object."

"If they want our cooperation, they're going to have to give us theirs. Who can you spare for the job, Everett?"

For once Gabler was not ready with an instant response. There was silence for several seconds, then: "If I can have a day or two to put things in order, I could be available."

"Nothing better," said Thatcher sincerely. Everett's skills

in ferreting out falsehood were unparalleled. No paperwork of any sort could defeat him. But there were other considerations. "If you are willing to undertake what may be a demanding chore. Sparrow isn't run like IBM, you know. They believe in the casual approach."

But lack of a recognizable hierarchy, like accounting chicanery and deliberate obscurantism, was grist to Gabler's mill.

"So I gather," he said with muted relish.

"Fine," said Thatcher, eager to close with the offer. "Then I'll start twisting a few arms at Sparrow."

⚹ 9 ⚹

Ranges South

By the time John Thatcher had mobilized his troops, Captain Lemoine was closeted with the next witness.

"Yes, I saw Mitch yesterday afternoon," said Don Islington. "I had to wait for him to finish his meeting."

"Did you know what it was about?"

Islington pursed his lips. "There was a lot of excitement around the water cooler. But I only paid attention to the parts about the California expansion. After all, I'm selling Sparrow the planes."

"What were they saying about Whetmore then?"

Thanks to Crawley's man in the cafeteria, Lemoine knew how they felt now. He wanted to learn if there had been any significant change.

"I never heard him mentioned. They were all gabbing about some girl named Phoebe."

Despite the universal tendency to dismiss Alan Whetmore, Lemoine had proof positive that somebody had taken him seriously enough to murder him.

Lemoine was still pondering this anomaly when Islington added: "Mitch was the one who told me about Whetmore."

"What did he say?" Lemoine pounced.

"Oh, he was caught off base by that list, and I could understand why. But it was no threat to California, so that was okay."

"About Whetmore," Lemoine prodded.

"What's to say? We both agreed that he was poison, but Mitch said he knew how to handle him."

When these unfortunate words evoked an appreciative silence, Islington tried to explain them away.

"Come on, Captain. Mitch had calmed down by then. He just meant there was nothing for me to worry about."

"Sure," said Lemoine flatly.

The material awaiting Captain Lemoine when he returned to Logan increased his general dissatisfaction. First came the report on traffic conditions in the tunnel.

"It was a bad one last night," Lieutenant Crawley summarized. "Stop and go, mostly stop, from four thirty-five until six o'clock, with cars backed up to Airport Road."

"Scovil's playing games," Lemoine rumbled. "According to him, he whipped through the tunnel and went straight home. Later on, he walked five blocks to the restaurant. The whole story stinks. Nobody was whipping through that tunnel last night and Scovil should have been soaked when he showed up to meet Thatcher."

Ed Crawley was systematically checking off points. "His condo won't do us much good. The tenants have plastic keys for the underground garage and there's always a mob at that hour."

"You can bet that's what Scovil was relying on."

"So you think he's lying."

"He was doing something else from five to seven all right." Lemoine took a deep breath and said prosaically, "I just hope he wasn't killing Whetmore."

Ed, thinking of all those politicians at the State House, agreed. "Are you going to lean on him?"

"Not until I have to. Anything come up on Whetmore's movements, yet?"

"Yeah. It may not mean much, but it does narrow the murder time," said Ed. "Whetmore went from the meeting to the scheduling office and arranged his next shift. Then he must have picked up his car, because he showed up at a little Italian place a couple of miles away. At four forty-five he had a couple of beers and some cannelloni. Then he looked at his watch and made noises about wanting his tab in a hurry."

"The time?"

Crawley shook his head sadly. "The waitress didn't notice. Somewhere between five-thirty and six is as close as she'd come. The only other thing I've got for you is Whetmore's car. It was spotted at the far end of the lot at Whalen's Freight. They're a quarter of a mile from the murder spot."

"Let me guess," Lemoine said resignedly. "Nobody noticed him parking."

"Have a heart, Greg. It was misting and foggy. Besides, it was after regular hours so there was only one line of cars at the building. They couldn't have seen Whetmore if they'd looked straight at him."

Lemoine's next words were a half apology. "I think what burns me up is this business-as-usual attitude at Sparrow. They're too damned cheerful."

"Then I've got just the witness for you."

"I should have taken the wrench back, first thing," Norman Pitts said miserably.

By now the murder weapon had been traced from Joe Cleveland's tool box to Norman Pitts's car.

"Well, what did you do with it?" Lemoine asked again.

"The thing is, I was late to work yesterday morning." For some unaccountable reason, Pitts reddened. "And the other guys notice that kind of thing here. So I rushed into the locker room to put on my jacket and decided to leave the wrench until the coffee break. I was going down to the hangar then."

Lemoine had already figured out what was coming.

"And where was the wrench in the meantime?"

"I just dumped it on the bench there. When it was gone at ten, I figured somebody had taken it back for me."

The next piece of information that Lemoine elicited was even less helpful.

"They're so damn democratic here, they don't have a separate place for the executives," he complained to Ed. "Everybody uses the locker room."

"Not everybody. Mrs. Gough and Phoebe Fournier are in the other one," Ed pointed out. "And by the way, they're still buzzing in the cafeteria. . . ."

After Crawley's briefing, Lemoine decided to pay Mrs. Gough a second visit.

"Would you like to revise what you told me about the meeting yesterday?" he began.

"Not at all. This was just a bad time—"

"Baloney!" Lemoine said deliberately. "I've had a man in your cafeteria all day. Half your work force wants to walk out because Scovil knocked off their boy. The other half thinks the same way, but they want to give him a medal."

Mrs. Gough bristled. "They're young and they're dramatizing the situation. But remember, Captain, I was at that meeting, and they were not."

He had her where he wanted her.

"Exactly," he shot back. "But what set them off? You rushed out and told them Scovil was boiling mad. Or weren't the kids there for that one either?"

Eleanor Gough was openly dismayed. "Yes, I did say that, but you have to realize I had a reason," she explained. "They all heard Mitch slam out of the meeting. I didn't want them thinking he'd refused to listen. Whetmore's list could have been designed to produce that very impression, and I'm still not sure it wasn't. I had to get management's side out right away, and make it clear that Alan had pulled a fast one on us. That's why I exaggerated how angry we all were."

Now that he had her in the palm of his hand, Lemoine hoped to get more from Mrs. Gough. "I've read your personnel file on Whetmore," he said, indicating a manila folder. "But I'm looking for something more personal. Who were his friends at work? Who did he socialize with?"

"I don't think there is anybody." She leaned forward earnestly. "Most of our pilots have been laid off by other airlines. And when companies cut back, it's usually the younger pilots. Alan was almost twenty years older than the others. They just didn't have much in common."

This was the first insight that had been offered to the police about the victim.

"So he was a kind of odd man out?" he said encouragingly.

"Yes, and it's one of the reasons Alan exasperated me. At his age, he wasn't finding it easy to get jobs, and he should have been grateful to Sparrow instead of causing trouble."

Lemoine tapped the folder. "He sure bounced around a lot. I suppose that's why he never got seniority anywhere."

"Yes, he's worked for five different companies just since Bayou Air. And there was nothing wrong with his technical ability. He simply didn't get along with people. That's why he was always having a fight and flouncing off."

Lemoine thought he had missed something. "What's special about Bayou Air?"

She was surprised he had to ask. "That's where we all worked before we started Sparrow. The story's been written up dozens of times."

"I don't get a chance to read that sort of thing. Suppose you tell me about it," Lemoine directed.

"Mitch will have to get another PR man," she said, before complying. "Fritz Diehl and Mitch and I were all working at Bayou. When deregulation looked as if it was going to be a golden opportunity, they started scratching for money and a lot of other things. Clay was just a consultant at Bayou, but he knew all about the secondhand market, so they roped him in. They needed me because I could deal with the FAA. I sold my house to join them, and that's all there is to tell."

Lemoine stared at her in disbelief.

"Then you all knew Whetmore before and you've been hiding it," he charged.

"Don't be absurd!" It was the original Eleanor Gough. "For heaven's sake, we barely saw him at Bayou. He was only there a couple of months before we left. By that time, Bayou was really seedy. Every now and then a pilot would get picked up for running drugs and a new one would be hired. They were always coming and going."

One word more than any other rivets police attention.

"Drugs?" Lemoine repeated, with a sudden new perspective on the desolate meeting place where Alan Whetmore had been murdered. "You think that's what he was into?"

She was aghast. "Not in a million years! He never would have been hired if there'd been the slightest suggestion of that. We're careful at Sparrow."

"I'll bet you are."

"You can be damn sure of it," she replied angrily. "Check with his other employers if you don't believe me."

Lemoine had every intention of doing so. Before he could reply, a uniformed officer put his head in the door.

"Listen, Cap, they're calling you from the office. Something new has come up."

While Captain Lemoine was interviewing Eleanor Gough, the magic hour struck when many shifts at Logan Airport changed. The troopers who had been questioning personnel at foreign exchange booths, at magazine stands, at coffee shops, squared their shoulders and began anew with the replacements.

In the main terminal one trooper plodded down an endless corridor to a small bar overlooking several departure gates.

"We're trying to trace the movements of this man yesterday afternoon," he said, flourishing a photograph of Alan Whetmore. "Did you see him?"

The new bartender, busy polishing a glass, cast a lackluster glance at the exhibit. "Nope."

"He looks a lot different without the cap. You want to take a gander at this one?"

The studio portrait showed Whetmore in full uniform. The snapshot caught him on the dance floor.

"It's not that different," the barman corrected. "And the answer's the same. Never saw him before."

"Are you sure?"

"Of course I'm sure. That's a Sparrow uniform, and their terminal is half a mile from here. When they show up, we notice them."

The trooper was already turning away when the barman was inspired to produce additional evidence.

"Hell, when Mitch Scovil walked in here, I told myself I hadn't seen anybody from his outfit for at least six months."

Taking a deep breath to steady himself, the trooper said: "Are we still talking about yesterday?"

"Sure. Must have been a little bit after five."

It sounded too good to be true.

"If you almost never see anybody from Sparrow, are you sure you can recognize Scovil?"

"Are you kidding? He's Kate McDermott's husband."

The trooper had detected the note of a genuine enthusiast.

"You mean you watch her?"

"Every day," the bartender said proudly. "That Scovil is one lucky guy."

Personally the trooper preferred homebodies. But this was no time to alienate his witness.

"He sure is," he agreed sycophantically. "But she's the one on the screen. How come you know what he looks like?"

"They're big news. They get their pictures taken all the time. Wait a minute, I'll show you."

It soon became apparent how the bartender passed his spare time. From a shelf beneath the counter he produced a sheaf of reading material. There were tabloids and local magazines and national magazines.

"See, *People* did an article on Sparrow, and there's a picture of them coming back from their honeymoon. And look, here in *Boston*, you can see them at a fundraiser last month. And, I remember, there was one someplace else. . . ."

While the bartender was rummaging, the trooper organized his questions. One stood out as all-important.

"Was Scovil alone yesterday, or with someone?"

"He was alone, but I think he was expecting someone. He kept looking at the door and checking his watch. And every time a batch of people came in, he gave them the once-over."

"Are you sure he didn't meet anyone, even for a minute? If people kept coming in, you must have been busy."

The barman shook his head stubbornly. "I kept an eye on him. You see, I thought maybe he was waiting for Kate and I'd get her autograph. But whoever it was, he got stood up. Because he was still alone when he took off."

"And when was that?"

This required tremendous concentration and an audible rundown of departing flights, before the triumphant conclusion. "Must have been a couple of minutes after six. The gang for the Denver flight had to rush."

Lemoine congratulated himself.

"I knew he was covering something. It can't be an accident, Scovil sitting in Logan and checking his watch until he gets up to leave, and Whetmore doing the same thing a couple of miles away." Then, with a sudden attack of anxiety: "He's sure about the identification, this barkeep of yours?"

The trooper was confident. "One of those pictures was a big, slick job, clear as a bell. And, if you ask me, that guy moons over those pictures a lot. He's got a real case on Kate McDermott."

"Scovil will have to come clean now," Crawley predicted. "Of course you can read this bar business either way, even if he did have a meeting with Whetmore up his sleeve."

"Oh sure," Lemoine agreed readily. "Whetmore was supposed to show up at the bar. Maybe he didn't make it because he was being murdered by someone else. On the other hand, maybe Scovil got tired of waiting and went looking."

"If I were Scovil, I'd pick the first reading."

Mitch Scovil picked neither.

"So I had a drink before going home. Big deal!"

"Were you waiting for Whetmore?"

"No way. I was through talking with him."

71

"Then who were you waiting for?"

Scovil set his jaw. "Nobody. I was having a drink, that's all."

"The barman says you kept looking at the door and checking your watch."

"I was waiting for the tunnel to clear. It's usually better after six."

Lemoine was openly sarcastic. "And that's why you kept an eye on the door?"

"What else is there to look at in that bar?"

They had reached a new plateau. Scovil was lying and he knew that the police knew he was lying.

"Mr. Scovil, I want you to think about your situation. We've placed you at Logan at the time of the murder. You left that bar at six and you joined Thatcher at seven-thirty. You don't have any alibi. Isn't it time you came clean?"

"I wasn't killing Alan Whetmore, and that's all that concerns you."

For the next ten minutes Scovil defended this position stubbornly enough to convince Lemoine that they were at a temporary standstill.

A story could be shaken; an unyielding silence presented no obvious point of attack. Lemoine had no choice but to withdraw, knowing he needed more ammunition.

Surprisingly, when it came, it had nothing to do with alibis.

"This is Jason Tiedeman. He was doing steward duty on the Washington run today," Ed Crawley explained. "That's why we didn't get to him before."

Jason had been in the locker room at nine-thirty the previous morning. He had seen the wrench on entering.

"People always leave company property lying around that way," he said priggishly. "I was going to take it back."

On the whole Captain Lemoine decided he preferred Norman Pitts.

"And why didn't you?"

With no diminution of righteousness, Jason explained that he had visited the men's room first. There he had greeted Mitch Scovil who was washing his hands. When Jason reemerged, both the wrench and Scovil were gone.

"Let's get this straight. Was anybody else around there?"

"Not at the time."

"And when you exit from the men's room you have to go through the locker room?"

"That's right. So I assumed Mitch had taken the wrench. But of course anybody could have ducked into the locker room. I was gone about three or four minutes."

Lemoine smiled. "I guess that means another little interview with Mr. Scovil."

Inevitably the pressures on Mitch Scovil were beginning to take their toll.

"No!" he snarled, shouldering his way past Phoebe. "I've got too much on my plate to waste time now."

"You're just trying to stall us until it's too late," she retorted.

"Look, Phoebe, in case you haven't noticed, we're in the middle of a murder investigation. And thanks to that little meeting you rigged up, I'm a number one suspect."

She snorted. "You mean thanks to keeping us in the dark about Alan Whetmore's fun and games."

"Call it what you want! The most important thing for Sparrow right now is keeping me out of jail."

"Don't give me that. They're asking everybody questions. And I say the most important thing is keeping Sparrow from losing a bundle."

The last shreds of employee democracy wilted.

"Then say it someplace else," Scovil ordered. "I don't want to hear it."

ぇ 10 ৵

Flocking Together

John Thatcher was not forced to use strong-arm tactics with Sparrow.

"Sure, send your man along whenever he gets here," said Mitchell Scovil when he finally returned the call. "I probably won't be around to talk to him. If I'm not wasting my time with the cops, I'm tied up with my lawyers, and they're nearly as bad."

"How true," said Thatcher encouragingly. When this did not flush more confidences, he added: "But Gabler will really want to see your accounting people."

"Okay," said Scovil indifferently. "I'll alert somebody to give him whatever he wants."

Somebody was willing to do more than that. When Everett Gabler, loose ends tidily wound up, finally arrived at Sparrow, the welcoming committee consisted of Miss Phoebe Fournier.

"Morning, Mr. Thatcher," she said brightly. "I volunteered to show Mr. Gabler the ropes."

"Very nice of you," he replied, straight-faced.

But Phoebe was not sailing under false colors. "I wanted

another chance to talk to you," she admitted. "Come along and I'll show you the work station I've set up."

When she was not facing the public, Phoebe exchanged her uniform jacket for a Sparrow sweatshirt. Everett Gabler, assimilating the jogging shoes, inhaled sharply.

"Perhaps I should inform Mr. Scovil of my arrival," he said, hoping for better things.

"Not a chance," she said over her shoulder. "Good old Mitch has gone into hiding. He's trying to duck all the problems here. You'd think he's the only one who's had to talk to the police."

Everett's initial reaction to the Sparrow style was not favorable, but he held his tongue.

"I put you next to one of the girls at the computer," said Phoebe. "That way, your data's right there. And here are the extension numbers of almost anybody you might need —although you can always stick your head out and yell."

Shuddering, Gabler honored the efforts in his behalf. "I'm sure it will do very well," he said nobly.

When he busied himself at the desk, Phoebe turned her attention to Thatcher. "Now let me tell you the real facts about California," she said.

First, Scovil had tried to go over Kyle Yetter's head. Now, here was Phoebe playing the same game with Gabler.

"Fine," said Thatcher, standing fast. "We'll both be happy to listen."

She not only accepted his ruling, but improved on it. "Actually I should wait until Mr. Gabler finishes. Then he'd be on our side."

Gabler preferred to have his support solicited, not assumed.

"Before I hazard any judgment, I shall have to study Sparrow's assets and liabilities, your relative costs—"

Excitedly she broke in: "You can forget about that. We taught the industry about cost-cutting and, believe me, they learned. Nowadays, the only advantages we have left are our debt ratio and our image."

Everett had always been death on intangibles.

"Image?" he repeated sternly.

"You bet," Phoebe insisted. "Sparrow offers good service at a fair price, but what we really market is the package—plain New England frugality and hard work. We're like those stores that sell salvage goods in old warehouses —that is, if you know the ones I mean."

Thatcher realized that Miss Fournier, like so many people, wondered if Wall Street bankers knew the facts of consumer life. Fortunately, Everett Gabler was here to set her straight.

"I have read about them," he said austerely.

"Well, some of the people you see there are real comparison shoppers," Phoebe said. "But most of them just assume the stuff is cheap."

Thatcher thought she deserved some support, so he weighed in. "Wallenstein, Ev, Wallenstein."

For her benefit he went on to describe one of the Sloan's larger customers, who had made his pile by hanging garments on rusty pipes and selling them at list.

"You see?" she said gratefully. "As soon as Sparrow builds flashy passenger lounges, we lose our appeal. Unless we scrap this pie-in-the-sky California scheme, every one of us is going to see our money go down the drain!"

Gabler had not taken her full measure. "Ah yes," he said with misplaced kindliness. "Sparrow has a stock-purchase program, doesn't it? That means that you all have something at stake."

"Ten thousand shares," she said promptly. "That's what I've got at stake."

Then she spelled it all out. "Eighteen months ago, it was worth four hundred and twenty thousand. Last week, it was three hundred and fifty. Today? Well, maybe we can blame that on Alan's murder, but I'm worrying about tomorrow. I'd like to see my stock go up—and if Mitch tries to turn himself into United Airlines, it won't happen."

With numbers like this, Gabler tended to thaw.

"Well, Miss Fournier, you may have a legitimate quarrel with management. At least you will have strong stockholder support at your annual meeting."

"Aha! But how much?" she riposted. "That depends on the Sloan."

Everett would not have it any other way. "Therefore, the

76

most useful thing I can do from your point of view is to complete my evaluation. It's going to take at least a week."

"A week?" she said blankly. "You haven't forgotten that next Thursday is Thanksgiving, have you?"

Gabler, rummaging through his briefcase, replied too absently to suit her.

"Wednesday will be a real madhouse. You won't get a thing done," she said.

"Then I am sure that Mr. Gabler will not add to your difficulties on Wednesday," said Thatcher.

"Certainly not," Everett chimed in.

Rapport having been established, Thatcher thought he might get back to poor Rupert Vernon. Before he left, he decided that a cautious word of encouragement might not be amiss.

"I realize that you and your colleagues are impatient, Miss Fournier, but Gabler's time will be well spent. At the moment, there is nothing effective you can do to advance your cause with Scovil, anyway."

He did not add that if Mitchell Scovil were arrested for murder, her cause would take on new dimensions.

His restraint was unnecessary. If Phoebe was listening, it was to some inner voice.

"Then, I'll leave you two," Thatcher said, more loudly.

"Fine," said Gabler, champing at the bit.

Between them, they roused Phoebe Fournier from her trance.

"Nothing we can do?" she murmured, testing each word. "Is that what you just said?"

Without waiting for an answer, she jumped to her feet and marched to the door, pausing only for one buoyant exclamation.

"You've just given me the greatest idea ever!"

Everett was the first to break the silence. "And what precisely do you suppose that meant?"

Thatcher did not have the faintest idea. "But, from the little I have seen of her, I expect we will find out soon enough."

* * *

Joe Cleveland was aghast when Phoebe outlined her latest brainstorm.

"Shut down all Pittsburgh flights on Wednesday afternoon? Have you lost your marbles?"

Phoebe was pleased at this response.

"I knew you'd say that at first," she purred. "Because you're surprised. But think for a minute, and then tell me what's wrong with it."

Joe cast around. "For one thing, it's got to be against the law. Isn't that what they call an illegal work stoppage?"

"How can it be? It's standard operating procedure at Sparrow." Phoebe smiled broadly. "One of us is always pulling the plug on a scheduled flight. If it isn't equipment failure, it's lack of personnel. There was even that foul-up in Albany with fuel."

"But those were all legitimate," Cleveland protested.

"We're expected to use our best judgment for the good of the company. That's what participatory management is all about. Isn't that what Mitch says at every orientation?"

Joe was familiar with the quotation. "That's not the same as asking people to dynamite our own operation just before Thanksgiving."

"Maybe not. But our best judgment is that Pittsburgh should be closed down, and now we've decided to test it. Besides, half the roster there won't know what's going on. They'll just follow orders in good faith. I know this wouldn't work at most airports. But Tom Reardon is the world's biggest incompetent, and we're dead in the water in Pittsburgh, anyway. Come on, Joe, the meeting is in ten minutes and I know that, between us, we can persuade them."

Joe struggled to express his misgivings. "Oh, they'll probably love the idea. In fact, that's what gripes me. Half of them are already dying for action. But that's because they honestly think Mitch killed Alan Whetmore. They're going to get the wrong idea about why we should do this."

"What difference does that make?"

"It makes a lot," he said stubbornly. "We've always managed to hash things out. I don't say it doesn't take time and effort, particularly with some of the dodoes we've got.

But that's the way it's been done—out in the open, with everybody knowing what's going on. And that's the way we should be acting now."

Phoebe was trying to show she understood.

"Joe, nobody would like that better than me," she said earnestly. "But we're not the ones who've changed the rules. Look what happened last time. We never had a chance because of Alan Whetmore."

"And whose fault was that?"

Phoebe flushed. "How could I guess he was going to pull that stunt?"

"We knew what he was like."

"The more I think about it, the more I'm convinced it wasn't Alan's idea," she replied. "Somebody sold him that stuff about capital vetoes, counting on his eye for the main chance. If that's the kind of thing they're doing, we've got to loosen up ourselves."

"Okay, so we get tougher. That doesn't mean we have to con our own people."

Phoebe moved from defense to offense.

"Do you admit we have to get to Mitch before it's too late?"

"Yes," he said unwillingly.

"All right, then," she challenged. "Name one other way we can do it."

When he was silent, she continued her argument. "We're still after the same thing, Joe. Remember the old story about how you can't convince somebody unless you get their attention first. That's all we're doing, we're slapping Mitch with a fly swatter to get his attention."

Within moments a dozen Sparrow employees had become co-conspirators. Their surroundings provided the necessary atmosphere.

For security reasons, the gathering was taking place in an enormous hangar currently housing grounded aircraft. The group was huddled in a shadowy corner, its members perched on rough crates and low dollies. Every word or footfall stirred up ghostly resonances under the lofty roof.

As Joe had feared, everyone's imagination was fired by

Phoebe's inspiration. The enthusiasm, however, mirrored widely differing aims.

There was the subgroup demanding retribution against Mitch Scovil, murderer.

A fledgling pilot made those feelings absolutely clear.

"Look, I know Alan was no big loss. But we've got to take a stand. That's what solidarity is all about, isn't it?"

The romantic in the crowd was convinced that delay was not only cowardly, it was dangerous.

"It's like I said, all along. We should have walked the minute we heard about Whetmore. For all we know, Phoebe and Joe could be next. I say we put guards on them."

Singlemindedly, Phoebe ignored side issues.

"Then you agree about Wednesday?"

"The sooner, the better," the romantic replied truculently.

Then there were those who felt Mitch Scovil's intransigence justified all-out war.

A supply clerk removed a slice of pizza from his mouth to formulate a battle cry. "Mitch wants to throw his weight around, we'll show him who's got the real clout," he said, his ferocity impeded by strings of cheese. "We'll tear his company apart."

"Not his company, our company," Joe growled.

"Joe's right," Phoebe said hastily. "We're not tearing anything apart. This is going to be a neat, restricted operation. We stop flights in and out of Pittsburgh from two o'clock to six o'clock. That's all. Remember, we're just rapping Mitch across the knuckles to remind him we could do worse."

"I'll see that the orders go out to Pittsburgh, all right," said a young woman, making notes. "The shift should leave, but to make sure, we ought to send somebody out there."

"That's no problem. I'll volunteer for a flight to Pittsburgh," said Phoebe, as if wild horses could have kept her away.

"Someone may smell a rat," the romantic said darkly.

There was a chorus of hoots. The extra flights at

Thanksgiving always required volunteers, and Phoebe's record was exemplary.

"What about headquarters on Wednesday?" asked a health-food enthusiast, unwrapping his bean sprouts. "Does anybody know how the brass are splitting it up?"

The Sparrow partners rotated duties every Thanksgiving.

There was a moment's silence and a forest of wrinkled brows. "Wait a minute! I've almost got it," pleaded a young man whose memory was about to erupt to the surface. "Mitch handled Wednesday last year, so it will be Eleanor or Clay."

"It doesn't matter," Phoebe declared. "That's the beauty of it all. If Rita can get the orders transmitted, Pittsburgh will be a fouled-up mess before anyone hears what's going on."

The girl with the notepad was confident. "Trust me for that."

"Attagirl, Rita!"

As every obstacle crumbled, the exuberance was growing. Then a precisionist interrupted the cheers.

"Shouldn't we have somebody in charge at this end? What about you, Joe?"

"I'm off on Wednesday and Thursday," Joe said expressionlessly. "And Betty would kill me if I tried to change now."

Joe's family obligations were too well established for his refusal to cause comment.

"Barney, you can handle it, can't you?" Phoebe intervened, without missing a beat.

"Sure, sure."

They were past the point of no return. Any group that becomes absorbed in technicalities has implicitly made the big decision. The romantic was already looking beyond Pittsburgh.

"What do we do when it's all over?"

"Then we tell Mitch where he gets off," said someone, with immense satisfaction.

"Not just Mitch," Phoebe announced. "Don't you see? We're bound to get some publicity from this. It may not be much, but it does give us a chance to make a statement. And we're not throwing it away."

As might have been expected, there were as many ideas about the contents of the statement as there were reasons for the work stoppage.

"We don't have time to do it now," Phoebe said unblushingly. "I'll draft a press release, and then you can all have a crack at it."

By the time the session broke up, they were ready for anything.

"We'd better leave one by one," the pilot intoned.

He walked to the door and peered to the right and left.

"All clear," he whispered, before sauntering away with ostentatious nonchalance.

But the patch of blazing blue sky now visible broke the spell. Without undue caution, his comrades returned to their normal activities.

"What? We don't synchronize our watches?" Joe asked sarcastically when he and Phoebe were alone.

"Of course they're excited," Phoebe defended them. "After all, they've been wanting to do something for days."

"If you ask me, your fly swatter is turning into a bulldozer. And what's this statement going to say? It'll have to be a dilly if it's going to satisfy everyone."

Phoebe was unruffled. "It will have to be pretty general, but it will say what we want, trust me."

Joe's silence was not reassuring.

"You're making too big a thing out of this, Joe. Pittsburgh's the only place that will be inconvenienced. The real impact at Sparrow will come later."

"You mean after six o'clock? When the mess has to be straightened out?"

Phoebe meant more than that.

"I'm not talking about the work, I'm talking about the worry," she said grandly. "That's where we really score with Mitch. He'll be afraid we intend to hit again and again over the weekend. That's what will bring him to the table. He won't be able to think about anything else."

Joe was much more receptive to badgering Mitch Scovil than to grounding Sparrow passengers. His heavy frown began to lift, and Phoebe continued the good work by laying a coaxing hand on his arm.

"Besides, what could possibly go wrong?"

～ 11 ～

Ruffled Feathers

The Wednesday before Thanksgiving proves that mass evacuation is really possible. Within hours, eighty percent of the population relocates to distant feeding grounds, in a migration with predictable characteristics. Airport parking lots are filled at dawn, highways are jammed by noon, and Amtrak, for one shining moment, actually turns away prospective passengers.

For Phoebe Fournier, the day began with a flourish. Bryan had sent her off in style with a lavish breakfast at the Parker House. They ordered bacon and eggs with the daredevil feeling that they were provisioning Phoebe to go over the top. Then, at ten o'clock they plunged into the subway, embraced passionately, and separated.

By the time Phoebe flew into Pittsburgh at one-twenty, the pace of the day was well established, and she savored the atmosphere like a connoisseur. The signs of pressure were everywhere. All baggage carousels were several flights behind, and the indicator board had lost any connection with reality. The whole overstrained apparatus could be toppled by one small push.

At five minutes to two she was back in Sparrow's quarters, beginning her countdown. Soon Rita's orders should be arriving from Boston. The first would cancel all flights into and out of Pittsburgh. The second would release the Pittsburgh afternoon shift from duty. Would those orders come through? And, if they did, would they be obeyed?

Crossing her fingers, Phoebe stationed herself on the floor, in full view of the world. Waverers might be heartened by the sight of their leader. As she watched the minute hand on the clock, a young male clerk suddenly frowned at his monitor. Turning to consult a colleague, he caught sight of Phoebe. He raised a questioning eyebrow, and she gravely nodded. Instantly a grin broke over his face and then, without hesitation, he left his station. Seconds later, the girl to his right excused herself to a passenger and moved away.

With the awe of Dr. Frankenstein seeing his monster stir, Phoebe witnessed the complete evaporation of the Sparrow staff.

"It's so easy, it's unbelievable," she whispered to herself as she hurried backstage. This was no time to encounter Tom Reardon. She had already chosen the women's locker room as her coign of vantage.

There the prospects looked good. Around her, girls were slipping out of uniform, snatching up purses, and dashing off.

An aide reported within ten minutes. "You can relax, Phoebe. Charlie says three of the pilots have changed and are leaving right now. The computer staff walked in a body. Only one of the ticket clerks tried to make trouble."

"What did he do?"

"Nothing. Charlie pointed out that, if he stayed, he'd have to handle the public alone. So he decided to take the orders at face value."

Only then did Phoebe realize she had been holding her breath. The tide was now irreversible.

Still, Phoebe felt oddly unconvinced. Her aim had been to create chaos and, so far, all she had seen was some people changing clothes. There had to be more to it than that. Even the Sparrow lobby, when she returned to it, was unsatisfying. Instead of havoc, there was empty space. True, the employees had disappeared, but so had most of the would-be passengers. The action, Phoebe discovered by trailing the last stragglers, was over at the main terminal.

There, the turmoil was all that she had anticipated. Bewildered travelers were charging the counters, trying to exchange nontransferable tickets for nonavailable space. Agents who had never before raised their voices to the public were openly snarling.

"Mister, I don't know what's going on over at Sparrow. This is Eastern! Would you get out of the way and let me take care of our customers!"

Nobody paid the slightest attention and the lengthening lines began to twist into knotted coils. Information booths were disappearing, engulfed by howling mobs. Mothers' voices were raised in desperation, fathers were urging calm.

Phoebe took in the panorama with guilty pleasure. It was not what she had foreseen.

"After all, nobody has to go away for Thanksgiving," she had reasoned to herself and others. "They'll simply go back home."

But now, with the carnage spreading beyond Sparrow, her press release was surely becoming doubly important.

Five minutes later, she received a rude shock over the phone.

"What do you mean, you're not interested?" she demanded.

"We've already chosen our travel stories for the day," the voice replied inflexibly.

"I'm not talking about human interest, I'm talking about news!" she protested.

The voice explained that, on this day, chaos at an airport had no news value whatsoever.

After calling every television station in Pittsburgh, Phoebe had to accept the inevitable. Nobody cared about her lovingly drafted statement, nobody was interested in horizontal management. Abandoning her dreams of a press conference, she reminded herself that the walkout was designed to exert pressure on Mitch Scovil.

"And it's worked," she declared. "Publicity doesn't mean a thing."

It is always a mistake to underestimate others. From the outset, Phoebe had assigned the roles in her drama. She was the heroine and Mitch Scovil was the outwitted opponent. Nobody else had a speaking part.

The three men who would insist on writing their own lines were sales engineers holding tickets on the four o'clock flight from Pittsburgh to New York. At noon, they had joined forces over a well-oiled luncheon. By the time they had been poured into the airport limousine, they were the merriest spirits aboard.

Like everybody else, when they found a tomblike void at Sparrow they marched to the main terminal. Unlike everybody else, they soon adjourned to a bar for consultation. During the first and second rounds they merely bewailed their predicament. It was, they agreed, one hell of a note when a man could not share Thanksgiving with his family. With the third round, a tiny seedling of originality emerged. They were all middle-aged men, slow to baseless recrimination. As they watched the angry confrontations outside, they grew censorious.

"That's not right," said the small, dark one, waxing more and more lugubrious. "Those TWA clerks are just poor slobs doing their job. None of this is their fault."

The one with the beefy build and the thick neck was angry, but just. "No, Tony, it's not their fault. And the airport manager didn't do anything either."

The chubby one had been confused even before leaving the lunch table. "Manager?" he echoed, groggily rising. "I'll tell him what a great sale I made."

"No, no, Louis." They hauled him back into his chair. "The airport manager, the one who's pinned to the wall."

With the next round, each continued down his own emotional path.

"I'll tell you what," the ex-athlete declared truculently.

"That bunch at Sparrow has had its fun and, so far, we've been paying through the nose. I say it's time they did."

Tony agreed in principle, but saw practical difficulties.

"There isn't anybody over at Sparrow, Frank. You saw how empty it was. They've all gone home to their families," he reasoned dolefully.

"There's nobody out front," Frank retorted. "They're all in back, laughing while we sweat."

"They shouldn't be allowed to get away with it," Tony moaned.

Lou wanted action, not words.

"Lead the way!" he cried, heaving himself erect with a blind wave that embraced three-fourths of the horizon.

The office on which they were descending was not, as they fondly imagined, a den of malevolent, snickering troublemakers. It contained only two occupants.

Tom Reardon, as Phoebe had anticipated, was making a bad situation worse by nonstop misdirected activity. He had delayed notifying headquarters of his plight as long as possible. Instead, he called his vanished employees at homes they would not reach for hours. Then he tried activating his six o'clock shift only to founder in a bog of baby-sitting and car-pooling arrangements.

In all these efforts he was supported by his assistant, Mrs. Virginia Kaltenbrun. Ginny was a true-blue loyalist. All attempts to enlist her in the ranks of the dissidents had failed, as her personal allegiance was to Tom Reardon, not Sparrow. In the face of outright aberration, the employees had given up.

When the three sales engineers rolled into the office area, spied the door marked MANAGER, and burst through it, she was around the corner at the copying machine.

Being a man of great consistency, Tom Reardon went straight for nonessentials.

"This is a restricted area," he said fussily. "You'll have to leave at once."

"Restricted!" Frank bleated sarcastically. "You mean it's where you're hiding."

This was too close to the truth to be acceptable.

"It's my office. It's where I'm supposed to be."

"Shame on you," Tony cried.

Reardon realized he was dealing with passengers who had some ground for complaint.

"I'm sorry about the mess here today," he said perfunctorily, "but Thanksgiving is always a difficult time and we're doing everything that can be done."

A confused babble about home, families, and the sacred obligations of contract failed to impress Reardon. He was still convinced that he was the chief victim of Phoebe's plot.

"You'll just have to be patient until I can sort things out," he snapped.

This was far from satisfying to his guests.

"That may be quicker than you think," Frank growled.

"What's that supposed to mean?"

"I've got news for you, little man. If we can't go home, then neither can you. How's that for an incentive?"

With these words, Frank planted his broad shoulders across the door, leaned back, and projected a bleary challenge.

Reardon had no intention of engaging in a shoving match.

"Nonsense," he said, sounding like a schoolmaster. "Get away from that door instantly or—"

"Or what? Who's going to make me?"

"Or I'll call the police," Reardon said severely.

"Wanna bet?"

Startled, Reardon swiveled to check on the activities of Frank's accomplices. Tony was no problem. In the corner of the room he was quietly weeping and telling over the names of his loved ones as if they were so many beads. "Won't see Helen . . . won't see the twins . . . won't see Uncle Mario."

But, on the other side of the desk, Lou had quietly carried off the telephone. Collapsed into a distant chair, he was playing with the dial. As his hands momentarily separated, so did the phone. He cocked his head, listening to the dial tone with innocent expectancy.

Reardon had been more exasperated than alarmed by the

invasion. When Frank barred the exit, he remained composed. When Tony began sobbing, he grew disgusted. But, with the desecration of his telephone, something snapped. Let these three spend the night in the drunk tank, he decided vengefully. They richly deserved it.

And, once again, Tom Reardon did the wrong thing.

"Ginny! Call security!" he bellowed without warning. "They've got me in here, and they won't let me go."

On the other side of the door, Mrs. Kaltenbrun never doubted who *they* were. Already convinced that the Sparrow insurgents were capable of any atrocity, she wasted no time responding to this call for help.

"They've broken into Sparrow headquarters," she gasped to the airport switchboard. "And they're holding Mr. Reardon hostage."

She could not have chosen a more unfortunate word. At Pittsburgh, as at every other airport in the world, the staff had been drilled and redrilled. To avoid panic during crisis, they had been turned into automatons who reflexively pushed the right button.

First, additional civilians must be prevented from entering the danger area, so all approach roads were sealed off. Then, all potential victims must be removed, so the guards cleared the terminal. Finally, the danger must be contained, so fire doors were slammed and barred to isolate the Sparrow facility from the rest of the world. As these steps were taken at the airport, a convoy of rescue vehicles set forth from downtown, and the FBI announced that sharpshooters were on the way.

To Phoebe Fournier, who was munching a broccoli croissant at the operative moment, ensuing events were a nightmare. A guard rushed into the coffee shop and ordered everybody out because of terrorists. Phoebe was preparing to obey orders when she heard that Tom Reardon's office was the eye of the storm. Flinging prudence to the winds, she ducked down a side corridor and raced toward Sparrow, only to be brought up short by a barrier of steel. She then made the mistake of deliberately seeking out a guard.

"Don't worry. We'll get your friends out safely," he said, hustling her through the deserted lobby.

Unbelievingly, Phoebe gazed around. Everywhere there were signs of disorderly flight. Counters were covered with half-finished tickets. Luggage lay abandoned in the check-in stalls. One newsstand had several dollar bills lying next to the cash register.

"You're making a terrible mistake," she insisted. "You've got to let me go over there."

The guard had been dealing with hysterical women for a quarter of an hour.

"Through this door," he said, opening it for her.

Outside there were thousands of evacuees, waiting in long bedraggled lines. The lucky ones had their coats with them. But waitresses from the coffee shop shivered in thin uniforms while adults stripped off jackets to wrap around infants. From every direction there were the laments of people separated from their companions.

Compelling as the scene was, Phoebe was more shaken by the silence overhead. She knew at once that the airport had been closed to traffic. Her mind leaped to the inevitable convulsions at other airports. In New York and Washington, there would be Pittsburgh-bound flights cluttering the runways. Philadelphia and Baltimore would have to clear space for diverted flights. Every little ripple would be reducing the day's finely tuned schedules to a shambles.

With one small push, she had triggered an avalanche.

"My God," she gasped. "I've closed down the whole East Coast."

❧ 12 ❧

Helpless on Land

Ever since his winning lottery ticket, Mitch Scovil knew he had been born under a lucky star. The sequence of events that Wednesday seemed to prove he was right.

While Phoebe was watching the clock in Pittsburgh, Scovil was picking up his wife at Channel Three. Thanks to traffic leaving the city and bottlenecks along the turnpike, the drive to Hartford took twice as long as usual. Kate and Mitch occupied the time discussing the changes in her family during the last year. This was part of Kate's master plan. She was determined that, for at least twenty-four hours, Mitch was going to forget all about Captain Lemoine.

When they finally pulled up to the McDermott home, they moved from one hermetically sealed capsule to another. Everybody and everything was circling the swaddled six-week-old packet named Joshua McDermott Haviland. While his proud parents beamed, the grandfather was cooing and gurgling, and Kate's brother was dangling a strange feathered object.

Mrs. McDermott forgot herself so far as to greet the

Scovils with a radiant face and her first uncensored remark since their marriage.

"I'd almost given up hope of a baby," she cried. "I knew it was useless to expect anything from you."

Mitch was somewhat taken aback. Until today he had been under the impression that his mother-in-law regarded him as flawless. Kate, of course, was not surprised, but anything was better than Sparrow Flyways and its unsolved murder.

An hour passed before Mr. McDermott tardily recalled his duties as a host and served drinks. Mrs. McDermott, with a squawk of dismay, remembered there were appetizers to be heated and fled to the kitchen with her daughters. The men, left to themselves, shifted position. Joshua's father stretched his long frame in an easy chair and turned his mind to new matters.

"It's a good thing we weren't coming here by plane," he said, lofting his glass in congratulation. "We'd never have made it."

The remark passed by Scovil, who had surprised himself by remaining with the baby. This tiny scrap of humanity had every moral and legal right to regard him as Uncle Mitch. Bemused by this new conception, Scovil extended a forefinger and was pleased as punch when five infantine fingers curled around it.

Idly Mr. McDermott asked: "What's wrong with the planes? The weather's all right."

"Don't you know about the hostage stand-off in Pittsburgh?" his son-in-law asked incredulously. "It's thrown off air schedules in half the country."

"WHAT?"

Scovil had reared upright, followed by a wail from the crib. "I've got to call my office. I may have to leave right away."

Kate, coming in with a tray of steaming cheese puffs, almost dropped it. "Oh no!" she cried despairingly.

She should have had more faith in Eleanor Gough.

Nobody had ever been tempted to claim that Eleanor Gough was born under a lucky star. She had married early and watched a young husband die of a wasting disease. Driven to the marketplace to support two children, she had been overworked and underpaid. For twenty years, she had cleaned up other people's messes. It was a bad thing for her that she was on duty Wednesday afternoon, and a damned good thing for Sparrow.

By two-twenty she was receiving phone calls from station managers in New York and Philadelphia, querying the cancellation of service to Pittsburgh.

"Why the hell didn't you call me at once?" she stormed when she finally got through to Reardon.

Virtuously he outlined his attempts to secure a staff.

"You should have asked for emergency crews from Philadelphia while there was still time," she raged, before setting to work herself.

When she tried to communicate her results to Pittsburgh, she was defeated by the familiar busy signal. She was still simmering when an excited clerk rushed in to announce that TV was reporting a hostage crisis in Pittsburgh. By four-thirty Eleanor Gough knew what was going on and exactly how much damage she had to contain.

At five-thirty Mitch Scovil's voice was simply another distraction.

"That's all right, Mitch," she said, after explaining to him how Phoebe Fournier's walkout had mushroomed into a national crisis. "I can handle it."

"I could start right away," he offered.

Mrs. Gough gritted her teeth. "That's nice of you, Mitch, but it would take you hours to get here. That's what I told Clay when he called."

"I hate to have this all land on you," Scovil persisted.

The last thing she wanted was another cook at this particular stove.

"Don't give it a thought. The worst is almost over," she lied shamelessly.

Mitch might be persuaded to stay put, but he insisted on talking.

"How could Phoebe do this to me?" he complained.

"I wouldn't worry about it," she said tersely, not mentioning his many rebuffs to Phoebe.

"Not worry?" he repeated. "What about the publicity Sparrow will be getting?"

Mrs. Gough had wasted as much time as she could afford. "The FAA is coming through on another line, Mitch. I have to go," she said, before adding hastily: "And don't bother too much about the publicity. I have a feeling we're going to be luckier than we deserve."

She hung up before he could reply.

The FAA was not on the line at that moment, but it was for the rest of the evening. Sparrow—and every other airline—had to retrieve its passengers. Even with clearances for a revised schedule stretching into the wee hours of the morning, monumental housekeeping chores remained. Mrs. Gough spent hours on the intricacies of connecting flights and vouchers for everything from hotels to taxi transfers.

Unfortunately her decisions had to be effected in Pittsburgh by Tom Reardon. Since his release from captivity, he had adopted a posture of open hostility to all passengers.

"A honeymoon couple?" she gasped, after interrogating him at midnight. "And you just gave them a voucher for dinner? Not on your life."

As she expanded her ideas on the subject, he began objecting.

"This is already costing us a fortune. We don't owe these people an arm and a leg."

Eleanor was adamant. "Now, if ever, is the time for a gesture!"

Mrs. Gough's instincts were right on the money. As she had hoped, the media were not interested in Sparrow—not when they had sharpshooters and police cordons. And, when the Pittsburgh Massacre dissolved into three boozed-up engineers, the cameras left.

On Thursday morning her gesture paid off. Thanksgiving is a slow day for news and the networks are grateful for what they can get. They all decided to tell the world about the honeymoon couple. Who could resist them? They had come to the airport from the wedding reception, planning to spend the weekend at Niagara Falls.

"And you missed your wedding night?" a reporter throbbed.

"We did better," the groom said practically. "Sparrow is sending us to Hawaii for ten whole days."

"Hawaii," the bride repeated, glowing. "And we're staying right on Waikiki beach."

"With Sparrow picking up the tab," the groom marveled. "Isn't that wonderful?"

Most of America thought it was.

Before the sun rose on Thanksgiving morning, airlines on the East Coast had put the whole tawdry episode behind them. Clay Batchelder could not.

Stifling a yawn, he stood and watched the honeymooners extol Sparrow until his wife thrust a mug of coffee at him.

"You have to leave in five minutes," she announced.

Their only daughter was coming home from college. She had been due yesterday afternoon, yesterday evening and, most recently, at the crack of dawn today. As a result, Clay, unlike everybody else at Sparrow, had suffered through long hours of airport turmoil as a member of the general public. He had asked hopeless questions, instead of giving misleading answers. He had paced the floor, checked his watch, and called home until far too late.

And now he was going to do it all over again.

"I still don't see why Jill has to come in to Providence," he grumbled. "At least if it was Logan, I could have helped Eleanor last night."

Criticism of her children was not allowed under Mrs. Batchelder's roof.

"Eleanor didn't need you," she said unflatteringly. "Jill did."

"Sure, honey," he said, despite a novel thought. Why did Jill, world-traveler since junior high school, have to be hand-carried from Providence to Duxbury?

He managed one sip of coffee before his wife started again.

"If you don't leave now, you're going to be late."

"Okay, okay," he said, abandoning the mug.

But he was still thinking like a civilian. "It would have been easier to pick her up at Ithaca in the first place."

"And whose fault is that?" she demanded rhetorically. "The whole mess began with your precious Sparrow."

As usual, it was ten minutes before Clay found the right reply.

"Sparrow didn't cause the mess. Phoebe Fournier did," he said to himself. "And I hope she's happy."

Far from it. On Wednesday night Phoebe had returned home so pale and drawn that Bryan barely recognized her.

Thursday was hard on her, too. They were spending the holiday with Bryan's married brother, his wife, and the television set. It was one defeat after another. First, the wrong football team won. Then, opinion-makers began telling the nation what to think about Pittsburgh and never mentioned Sparrow. Instead, the pundits focused on themes worthy of them. What was wrong, they asked, with a country that could overreact so disastrously? Was our transport system hostage to our own fears?

"Oh for God's sake!" Phoebe exploded. "They've got it all wrong. It was our work stoppage that sparked everything."

Julie Kiley brought to the festive board her own peculiar sympathies.

"I think they're being much too hard on those engineers," she declared, her spoon poised over the stuffing that she was adding to each serving of turkey. "They looked like nice men to me. They just didn't expect people to push the panic button."

A sober and repentant threesome had been interviewed more than once.

"Come on, Julie," Douglas Kiley protested. "They caused a lot of inconvenience to other people."

"Oh, they shouldn't have done it. But you know how maddening it is when you have a serious complaint and the people in charge don't seem to give a damn," Julie persisted. "These men decided the man at the top was going to listen, whether he wanted to or not."

"So they took him prisoner?" her husband asked ironically.

"They were simply trying to get his attention," she said with gentle mulishness as she passed heaping plates.

Both brothers accepted every syllable as more of Julie's muzzy benignity. Phoebe, however, was turned to stone. It was, she told herself, sheer accident that Julie was reproducing, almost word for word, her own justification to Joe Cleveland.

Bryan had another bone to pick.

"They were plastered," he said, from the virtuous heights of one glass of Vouvray. "Even if they'd gotten their plane, they would have been a menace. You know what Phoebe always says about drunks on board."

Before Phoebe could weigh in with an appropriate anecdote, Julie had an even more unfortunate insight.

"I realize that. But this was a childish temper tantrum." She paused to smile affectionately at the high chair containing her own tantrum-thrower. "I've seen little Bryan try to wreck the room because I'm too busy to pay attention to him."

Phoebe gulped. She knew that nobody was equating the Sparrow walkout with kicking and screaming on the floor. Nonetheless, she did not care to risk more of Julie's wide-ranging charity.

"This sweet potato casserole is wonderful, Julie," she said enticingly. "I know about putting marshmallows into it, but there's something else, isn't there?"

Julie forgot all about human waywardness.

"I grated fresh ginger in," she said proudly. "I've always wanted to try it, but the roots were hard to get until recently."

"What a great idea!" said Phoebe, submerging the fact that she had eaten an identical casserole at her mother's Thanksgiving table for twenty-two years.

John Thatcher had worked late on Wednesday and risen early the next morning. By ten o'clock he had driven to his daughter's house in Connecticut. His weekend was going to be spent with his grandchildren and his son-in-law's parents.

Sad to say, his only response to the television bulletins about Pittsburgh was unashamedly self-centered.

"I was right to drive. In fact, it's a mistake to get anywhere near a common carrier at Thanksgiving."

Normally this statement, like almost any other, would have encouraged an outpouring from his fellow father-in-law. After a lifetime teaching classics at Columbia, Cardwell Carlson lectured automatically. But he barely opened his mouth before he was interrupted by a shriek from his wife.

"He's circling," she cried. "Get him into the yard."

The Carlson home, like the McDermotts', contained a new arrival. But, after four children, Laura and Ben Carlson were settling for an eight-week-old Newfoundland puppy. He was not, as the breeder had guaranteed, housebroken.

Between the puppy and the grandchildren, Thatcher did not read the *New York Times* until well after dinner. Page one featured the usual photographs of airport drama. Page twenty-three, however, contained a small paragraph identifying an employee walkout at Sparrow as the primary cause of the subsequent upheaval.

"Phoebe Fournier!" Thatcher snorted, but that was the beginning and end of his reaction.

He had put his professional instincts to rest for a full four days. There were others, he knew, more sternly dedicated to duty. Everett Gabler, for instance, proposed an early return to Sparrow on Friday. But Everett, thank God, had all the old-fashioned virtues. He would not lightly intrude on John Thatcher in the bosom of his family.

Unless, of course, Sparrow had further bombshells to explode.

❧ 13 ❧

Close to Extinction

Along with Gabler, Mitch Scovil was returning to work on Friday. Travel on the day after Thanksgiving was always so light that he had even scheduled some nonroutine activities.

Weeks before Alan Whetmore's murder, Channel Three had planned to showcase Scovil on a forthcoming weekend magazine show. Today they were taping at Sparrow.

". . . and it will make a nice change from the publicity we've been getting," he yodeled from the bathroom.

It was seven-thirty in the morning, and Kate was nervous as a cat.

"No black or white clothes!" she yipped suddenly, remembering another last-minute caution.

"I'm not exactly a beginner, honey. And I don't usually wear a black suit to work, anyway," he said, emerging for inspection.

She grinned at the rebuke, but could not help running an eye over him. He was irreproachable in a light green shirt and dark brown suit.

"Why don't you ever look this good just for me?" she teased.

He had drifted over to his mirror and spoke with his back turned.

"By the way, don't you think we ought to send a present to the baby? After all, we are his aunt and uncle."

Proud of her domestic staff work, Kate replied too quickly. "We sent a silver porringer a month ago."

Her husband was not interested in mere gestures.

"I was thinking of something personal," he said, reproachfully. "Something that Josh would enjoy."

Kate still felt that any extracurricular distraction should be encouraged.

"I think I know what you mean," she said. A life-sized giant panda would be a sure-fire success with her husband, if not with Josh's parents. "I've got the day off. I could stop by F. A. O. Schwarz this afternoon."

"Good," he replied instantly. "I'll meet you for lunch and we'll go together."

By the time he talked himself to the door, he sounded like a man without a care in the world. He rushed off, leaving his wife to ponder the vagaries of men and the unnecessary alarms experienced by their womenfolk.

Captain Gregory Lemoine was also back at work, and he was not satisfied with the progress of his investigation.

"Try and get this through your head, Doyle. One way or another, Scovil is the key to this thing. I've already got him on opportunity and motive. All I need is the means. Let me put that wrench into his hands, and I can crack him like an eggshell. You hear what I'm saying?"

Doyle shifted restively but retained his wooden expression.

"I hear you, Captain. Loud and clear." He then made the mistake of trying to justify himself. "But my team has questioned every single solitary employee who went into that locker room. I didn't stop with the men who were on duty here. I went after the ones who were on stopovers in Boston or the ones who were filling in for somebody. Hell,

I even chased down a guy who's on vacation. Not one of them admits to seeing that damned wrench."

His efforts backfired with a vengeance.

"What did you say?" Lemoine asked savagely. "You questioned all the men? Why the hell haven't you been after the women?"

Doyle stared at him as if he were insane.

"Women don't use the men's locker room," he said warily.

"So what?" snarled Lemoine. "The wrench left the locker room in the morning. It wasn't used on Whetmore until five or so. It was someplace else in between. When a thing goes missing, you don't just try and trace it forward. You try backward, too!"

Under this hail of censure, Doyle stiffened, but he was not convinced.

"Anybody who took that wrench as a murder weapon wasn't flashing it around," he protested.

"It was that meeting of theirs that got them going. Maybe there wasn't any intention of killing before then." The captain's heavily patient voice suddenly cracked like a whip. "Now get out of here and question those women!"

Doyle was only too happy to go, particularly as Lemoine was already baying for his next victim.

"Where the hell is Paretti? I told him to have that court order for Whetmore's safe deposit box first thing this morning."

Sally, the receptionist, was typing dementedly and flinging harried glances at the clock when Doyle entered. He paid no attention to her obvious race against a deadline and began fishing for information. His first two casts produced only blank incomprehension. At the third trial, enlightenment dawned.

"You're not talking about the wrench Mitch brought here from the locker room, are you?" she asked incredulously. "Why in heaven's name didn't you say so?"

He ignored her question in favor of several of his own. When had this taken place? At what time had the wrench come in, at what time had it left?

"Let's see. Mitch must have dumped it on the coffee table just before I went for my break," she said, only to be reminded of a long-standing grievance of her own. "I don't know how they expect me to keep this area tidy. The three of them cart in everything but the kitchen sink. You should have seen how Eleanor left the place on Wednesday night. When I came in, it looked like a war zone."

Doyle was not interested in her housekeeping problems. He was recalling, with new respect, Lemoine's theory about spontaneous combustion.

"What about *after* the meeting? Did you see it then?" he pressed.

This required far more thought. "I don't know about after the meeting," she finally decided. "But it was there when Mr. Islington arrived. I remember because I straightened the pile of magazines, and I put the wrench on top as a paperweight."

Thereafter she had no recollection of ever seeing the wrench again.

And Sally was more exasperated than impressed when Doyle accused her of concealing information. Since she knew exactly what Norman Pitts and Jason Tiedeman had told the police, she failed to see why Doyle was making such heavy weather of her testimony.

"Norman left the wrench in the locker room, Jason was there when Mitch took it, so you should have figured out he brought it here. This is where all the junk ends up. Although," she added fair-mindedly, "Eleanor and Clay are a lot worse than Mitch."

Lemoine's rebuke to his subordinate rankled even more now that it was proving to be well-founded.

"That's a lot of hot air. You know damned well you should have told us about this," Doyle said suspiciously. "And I want to know why you didn't."

"Because nobody had the sense to ask me," she snapped, immediately producing a fusillade of flying typewriter keys to signal the end of the conversation.

Eleanor Gough came strolling into headquarters in a leisurely manner at eleven o'clock. Her only reason for appearing was to sample public opinion at Sparrow. A preliminary reconnaissance told her that employees everywhere were responding to the Pittsburgh shutdown.

The hard-liners, still identifying Mitch as Alan Whetmore's murderer, were the loudest.

"I said all along the shutdown wasn't enough. And look what happened," one of them demanded. "We should've all walked, the way I said. At least people would have known what we were protesting."

Today the water cooler was the nerve center of the moderates.

"Come on, admit it! It was a hare-brained scheme all along," said an excitable programmer.

"You sure aren't going to bring Mitch to the bargaining table by calling out SWAT teams," somebody else agreed.

Down in the cafeteria, they were complaining about lack of prior consultation.

"They want solidarity, they better tell us what they're planning," a stewardess said as she thumped her water glass angrily.

Even Norman Pitts was beginning to raise his voice among his peers.

"I signed the petition, and I'm glad that I did. But I haven't forgotten we're trying to run an airline. You shut down the country's air traffic and you simply encourage people to use their cars instead."

It was better than she had hoped for, Mrs. Gough decided as she finished her circuit. Let splinter groups flourish if they gave Mitch time to mend his ways with the work force.

She was mentally composing the speech that would convert him when she entered the executive suite.

"Oh, Eleanor," Sally called, "there's a visitor in there."

Mrs. Gough paused with her hand on the doorknob and a frown on her face. The calendar, she knew, was clear.

Respectfully, Sally stilled her keyboard. "It's Alan Whetmore's brother," she intoned. "Representing the family."

"Good heavens! I suppose I'll have to take care of him."

Within ten minutes Mrs. Gough realized that she was not

dealing with another Alan. Vincent Whetmore was a dried-up little man who set the record straight at once.

"My mother wants me to bring the body back," he said glumly. "She's eighty-three, and she gets upset."

Nobody had to tell Eleanor what horrors this statement encapsulated. Under her sympathetic guidance, a picture of the Whetmore family in Ohio began to emerge. Alan had disappeared into the Air Force long ago. His annual Christmas card was the chief communication between widely spaced visits.

"We weren't at all alike," Vincent conceded. "Alan was the ambitious one. I just stayed in the same old job, while he was always going on to something better."

Who was Mrs. Gough to dispel this illusion by explaining that Alan's career had been largely downhill? As nearly as she could fathom, Alan had spent those short visits flourishing snapshots of himself and his current companion enjoying Caribbean beaches or world-renowned ski resorts.

While Alan had been chasing the good life, Vincent had married, raised a family, seen his father through a final illness, sheltered his widowed mother, and was now picking up the tab for the nursing home.

Mrs. Gough said something meaningless about different choices.

"Sure, Alan had a right to live it up," said Vincent, honing in on the purpose of his visit. "But he was making big money. The price of just one of his fancy weekends would have been a real help."

Ostensibly, Vincent was here to seek guidance in the air transport of a body. He was naturally hoping for something more and Mrs. Gough obliged.

"You're not to concern yourself with the costs," she said firmly. "Of course the coffin will go by Sparrow. And we'll handle the local arrangements in Boston, too."

Eleanor Gough was a generous woman, and she had been touched by Vincent's plight. She could have gone whole hog and extended Sparrow's largess to the funeral itself. But she had taken the measure of Mrs. Whetmore, Senior, who clearly intended to enshrine the younger brother at the expense of the son who had borne the brunt.

That, of course, was life, and Eleanor was too old to fight it. But Alan's mother was not going to stage an extravaganza—not with Sparrow's money.

Resolutely she turned to technical detail. "There's a considerable amount of documentation that you'll need, particularly as we'll have to transship the coffin in Buffalo," she began. "Now, in theory, the undertaker will supply everything. But you'll be safer if I have Sally type up a master list for you to check against."

It was not the first time that Sparrow had been involved in long-distance obsequies, and Mrs. Gough had the regulations at her fingertips. When she left the room, she expected to be back within five minutes.

But Vincent Whetmore sat patiently waiting for over an hour.

The Channel Three crew had arrived at Sparrow at nine o'clock. By late that morning, Mitch Scovil had been filmed consulting an employee about the day's roster, peering into a computer monitor, and stripping off his jacket to lend a hand with luggage. Finally they had moved outdoors for the ultimate sequence, to film Scovil striding across the compound.

Luckily, his thoughts were invisible. Kate, he decided, should have warned him about this three-ring circus. The men ahead, with video equipment on their shoulders, were not the major culprits. It was the audio expert who was wreaking havoc. Before each sequence it was necessary for him to perform strange rites with his supersensitive devices. He would then make one unreasonable demand after another, all in the name of quelling background noise.

Now he was again bringing the entire operation to a halt. But this time the director of the epic was showing fight. In a feature about an airline executive being shot at an airport, he refused to agree that the sound of aircraft was objectionable.

The audio zealot remained unyielding. "Then you've got to scrap that business of him talking to the foreman outside," he insisted. "Nobody's going to understand what they're saying."

The director's reply was lost in the din of two jets zooming overhead.

While Scovil waited for them to settle the dispute, he realized that they were obstructing traffic in the area. Personnel in greasy coveralls were making wide circles around the group that now included the camermen, the director's gofer, and some flunky whose duties had never been clarified. Loaded dollies being pushed around the corner squealed in protest as they suddenly veered to avoid collision.

In the confusion Scovil failed to notice the police cruiser pulling up.

"Mr. Scovil? Mr. Mitchell Scovil?"

Scovil swung around and scowled at the familiar uniforms. "Yeah, I'm Scovil. What is it now?" he asked unenthusiastically.

"Captain Lemoine wants you to come down to the station for questioning."

To Scovil this was simply another unwelcome intrusion by the police.

"Are you crazy? Can't you see I'm busy? Whatever it is, it will have to wait."

"It can't." The trooper paused. "Captain Lemoine thought you'd rather come down voluntarily than the other way."

Scovil's eyes narrowed. "What's that supposed to mean? The other way?"

"I have a warrant for your arrest, Mr. Scovil. We can *take* you downtown."

There was no longer any room for incomprehension. Scovil stared back, the blood draining from his face. But his voice was steady.

"I've already told Lemoine I'm not answering any more questions without my lawyer," he rasped defiantly.

The trooper could have been soothing a recalcitrant child. "That's all right. Your lawyer's meeting us at the station. So we'd better get started."

Scovil was dragging his feet when he caught sight of other activity.

"Oh for Christ's sake!"

The film unit had become a news team, aiming cameras at him like so many bazookas.

"Let's get the hell out of here," he growled, diving for the cruiser.

❧ 14 ❧

Concealed Nest

Minutes later, when the troopers rushed Mitch Scovil into Captain Lemoine's office, a skirmish was already underway.

". . . no cause to drag my client down here like this," Steven McAllister was declaiming. "Oh, hello, Mitch. I'm surprised they didn't clap you into handcuffs while they were at it."

Unmoved, Lemoine dismissed his men. As they trudged out, Scovil said: "Thanks for getting here on such short notice, Steve."

"It wasn't easy," McAllister told him.

Their byplay glanced off the man behind the desk.

"Sit down, Mr. Scovil," said Lemoine with exaggerated courtesy. "Mr. McAllister has just been telling me what a big shot you are."

"Captain Lemoine, there is no need—"

"Dammit, who cares—"

With heavy irony, Lemoine flattened their protests. "But I already know that. Half the politicians in town keep telling me how important you are—and that includes the State

House. So I can't afford to horse around, even with a warrant. That's why I got you down here so fast. Now's your chance to convince me that you didn't murder Alan Whetmore."

Stubbornly, Scovil shook his head. "I've already told you everything I know," he insisted.

McAllister, careful not to look in his direction, leaned forward earnestly. "Let's stop playing these cat-and-mouse games. I assume you think you've found incriminating evidence, Captain Lemoine. Suppose you go ahead and tell us what it is?"

He got more than he bargained for when Lemoine placed the murder weapon in Scovil's hands immediately before the meeting.

". . . and so, in spite of the fact your client's been swearing he never even saw the wrench, he's the only one who knew where to find it. Anybody else just stumbled on it."

Scovil, his lips tightly compressed, studied a late-season fly buzzing against the window pane. In the silence, Lemoine smiled and waited. Then McAllister chose his tactics.

"So you have witnesses of unknown credibility," he said scornfully. "Captain, after what happened in Pittsburgh the other day, we all know that there are Sparrow employees with grievances against Mitch Scovil. How can reliance be placed in anything they say?"

"You want lie-detector tests?" Lemoine challenged.

But even State Street lawyers know about polygraph machines. Automatically McAllister reeled off a denunciation of circumstantial evidence. He was just getting up to speed when his client cut him short.

"All right," said Scovil. For the first time he was backing down from a confrontation with Lemoine. "I picked up that damned wrench in the locker room. I suppose I must have dumped it on the coffee table without really thinking. But I don't know what happened to it after that. I didn't kill Alan Whetmore, and I don't know who did."

Lemoine was almost kindly. "There you are," he said approvingly. "We've just been here a few minutes, and we're already making progress. Who knows how much we'll dig up after a couple of hours."

"Hours?" Scovil repeated blankly.

"Take it easy, Mitch," McAllister interjected.

"Yeah, relax and make yourself comfortable, Scovil," said Lemoine, dropping honorifics. "We're going to be here for as long as it takes, even if that's the rest of the day. Unless you decide to cooperate. Suppose I tell you how you killed Alan Whetmore and when. If you want to speed things up, tell me why you did it."

"Shut up, Mitch," McAllister said briskly. "Let me take care of this. Captain Lemoine, first I want to say—"

But Scovil barely listened. He was staggered by the implications of Lemoine's flat accusation. The comforting crowd of suspects had just vanished, leaving one man alone in the spotlight.

And Captain Lemoine was inches away from making an arrest.

"Is that you, Mitch?" Kate demanded after being called to the phone at the Magic Pan. "Do you know how long I've been waiting?"

"It's me, Kate—Clay."

Her heart constricted. "What's wrong?" she gasped, visualizing every possible disaster.

"Mitch is all right," Clay said hastily. "That is . . . I mean . . . oh hell, the cops picked him up an hour ago. It's probably just for more of their questioning—but I wanted to get you as soon as I could, before all hell breaks loose. I wasn't there, but apparently your people from Channel Three were right on the spot, taking it all in."

"Oh no!" she murmured, stricken.

Sounding in need of consolation himself, he muttered: "It was bad luck, but the news would have gotten out anyway."

As far as Kate was concerned, he was wandering from the essentials. "What station have they taken him to? Is his lawyer there? You don't mean the police have actually arrested him, do you?"

Her rapid-fire string of questions caught him short.

"Hell, I don't know, Kate," he said. "Everything here happened so damned fast."

"Tell me," she said, determined to extract every possible crumb of information.

"Why do you sound that way?" she demanded when he finished speaking. "You don't think Mitch is guilty, do you?"

"You know better than that," he replied gruffly. "It's just that I'm pretty shook up. Having Lemoine pull a trick like this is the last thing I expected. And I still don't see what makes him think he can do it—"

Once again they were straying, and Kate cut in ruthlessly. "Thanks for calling, Clay. Now I've got things to do."

But two steps into the foyer demonstrated that she was already running late. Bona fide customers were swamped by reporters.

"There she is!"

"Kate, do you know your husband has been arrested?"

The death-beetle click of the cameras made her flinch. Assuming a brave smile, she earned the undying gratitude of the Magic Pan by saying: "Just let me get my coat and I'll make a statement outside. Not that there's much I can tell you. . . ."

". . . every expectation that Mr. Scovil will be resuming his duties shortly," Eleanor Gough dictated grimly. "In the meantime, Sparrow Flyways is maintaining normal operations."

Sally was not sure whether this was a full stop or fatigue. "Is that all?" she asked.

"That's it," said Eleanor. "No, tell anybody who calls that that's all Sparrow will have to say until sometime later."

"Sure," said Sally, making a note. "But you know the employees will be dying to talk."

"Oh, damn the employees," said Mrs. Gough.

To keep Sparrow from lapsing into shock, she had been coaxing and bullying to the point of exhaustion. The press release represented her first step in a more meaningful direction. It came as an afterthought, the result of an urgent call from the business editor of the *Boston Globe*.

"I just hope that will keep everybody quiet," she said in a rare moment of weakness, "until Mitch can straighten everything out himself."

But financial markets do not tarry. The bald fact that the CEO of Sparrow Flyways was being detained by the police hit the newswires early and promptly sped to trading desks around the world. If Sparrow had been one of the blue chips, there would have been convulsions from the Ginza to Leadenhall Street. As it was, most of the disquiet was confined to Wall Street, where it translated into a burst of activity rare on the day after Thanksgiving. A wave of sell orders pounded the price of Sparrow stock down six points in as many minutes. In the lull that followed, a retraction —or news of Scovil's release—could have reversed the decline. When neither came, the tempo picked up again. With the downward spiral threatening to spin out of control, the market authorities stepped forward and halted trading in Sparrow stock.

To the general public, this was a footnote to the story. For Fidelity, Drexel Burnham—and the Sloan Guaranty Trust—it was the beginning of a long wait.

At lesser banks, other agitations were disturbing the Friday somnolence. In Boston, the decorum of the Copley Institute for Savings was being ruffled by Lieutenant Paretti and his court order. However, after Copley's pro forma reluctance, Alan Whetmore's safe deposit box was finally produced.

"Here you are," said the assistant manager solemnly.

"Thanks," said Paretti, raising the long, narrow lid.

Besides three paper clips, he discovered a package wrapped in brown paper. A flick of his wrist broke the Scotch tape and the contents spilled onto the desk.

One-hundred-dollar bills—and lots of them.

"Looks like more than petty cash, doesn't it?" he remarked prosaically. "We'd better count it."

Reverting to type, the assistant manager dealt and sorted the bills with poker player's hands.

"Fifty thousand dollars," he summed up, "in used bills. And I don't think they're marked, either."

"Uh-huh," said Paretti, who had access to experts of his own on this subject. "Now you told me that Whetmore just rented the box three weeks ago, didn't you?"

"I have the date right here," said the assistant manager, consulting his file. Then curiosity got the better of him. "Can you tell me what this is all about?"

But Paretti was on a short leash. "I've got someone else to talk to first," he said. "Where's the nearest phone I can use?"

The Copley Institute for Savings was all cooperation. The resistance came from the police switchboard.

". . . screw Mitch Scovil," Paretti said heatedly. "Lemoine told me he wanted this—or he'd have my hide. You'd better put me through, Foley."

"Greg won't be happy about this," said Foley, complying.

Before the day was out, however, others would be.

❧ 15 ☙

Immature Male

At first, Kate McDermott had been grateful when Clay Batchelder and Eleanor Gough arrived to share her ordeal. But, as the hours passed, Clay became less of a comfort and more of a threat to Kate's precarious self-control.

From the beginning he had been unable to sit still. He had made endless phone calls, he had insisted on helping Eleanor with the coffeepot and, as the afternoon wore on, he had even tried to force drinks on everybody. Kate could forgive his restlessness; it was more difficult to excuse some of his unguarded remarks.

At one o'clock he had said: "Lemoine's crazy—that's all."

By two-thirty, self-interest had appeared.

"How could they do this to us?" he groaned.

And now, as he stood staring over the harbor, he was ready to lash out at anyone and anything.

"If Mitch had only gone home the way he said he did, he wouldn't be under arrest. Why the hell did he need to do his drinking at Logan?"

Kate, closing her eyes, wondered if a shrill scream

would shut him up. It would certainly relieve her own feelings.

"Mitch hasn't been arrested," Mrs. Gough corrected sharply. "And none of this is his fault. How could he know Alan Whetmore was going to be murdered?"

Kate tried to smile. "I know Clay didn't mean it that way."

With a start, Batchelder remembered where he was. Flinging himself into a chair, he began a shamefaced apology. Then came the sound they had all been waiting for. A key was turning in the door.

Kate flew across the living room. Clay, already on his feet, hung back to give her a clear field while Eleanor Gough froze into immobility, her eyes glued to the archway.

For a moment they could hear only indistinct murmurings. Then Mitch Scovil appeared, his arm around Kate.

"That one was a lot closer than I like," he said, tired but unmistakably triumphant.

Clay and Eleanor were bursting with questions, but Kate would not allow Mitch to say one word until he had showered and changed.

"Now, you can make the drinks, Clay!"

Fifteen minutes later Scovil rejoined them in jeans and a plaid shirt. The coffee table, with cheeses at one end and pâté at the other, was ready for a party. Kate, glowing with joy, would have extended her embargo against serious talk, but Mitch was burning to tell his story.

"Lemoine thought he really had me nailed," he chortled. "When he found out I was the one who'd had the wrench—"

Both his partners exploded and, when an explanation was forthcoming, they reacted differently. Eleanor was aghast at the tightrope that Mitch had been walking. Clay, relaxed and beaming, was inclined to be jocular.

"It used to be me and Eleanor always carting hardware around. You picked a great day to start, Mitch."

Scovil acknowledged the shaft with a broad grin. "It was touch and go for a while, there. Then, right in the nick of time, the cops found fifty thousand bucks that Whetmore had salted away in a safe deposit box. Talk about luck! Lemoine didn't know what the hell it meant, but I did."

He looked around his audience, savoring the baffled expressions he encountered.

"You still don't get it?" he challenged. "I figured that one out while I was with Don Islington after the meeting. C'mon, Eleanor, what was the first thing you did then?"

"I rushed out to circulate our side of the story to as many people as possible," she answered, puzzled.

"And why did you do that?"

"If the employees thought we'd stamped out of a normal meeting, the situation at Sparrow would have gotten worse." Eleanor was becoming testy at explaining the obvious. "For all I knew, Alan's little ploy could have been designed to create that impression. So I—"

"Aha!" said Scovil gleefully. "You were already halfway there, you just didn't go far enough. Of course somebody fed that garbage to Whetmore in order to create a ruckus at Sparrow. Whetmore didn't think of it himself, and he wasn't in the habit of doing favors for other people. It's plain as the nose on your face when you think about it. Somebody was buying himself some labor trouble at Sparrow."

Mrs. Gough was shocked. "You mean a competitor? It's hard to believe a major airline would resort to anything like that."

Scovil leaned forward to press home his arguments. As he spoke he began waving a cracker like a conductor's baton.

"Consider your own reaction. You instinctively wondered whether we'd been deliberately suckered. And who else would shell out fifty thou for the privilege of upsetting our applecart?"

Kate had become interested in spite of herself. Wrinkling her nose in thought, she said: "But you can't be sure the fifty thousand was a bribe. Whetmore could have saved it over time. Maybe he was trying to evade taxes."

Far from being a problem to Scovil, this was an opening. "I haven't told you the best part. Whetmore got the cash all at once three weeks ago."

"That's hard to explain away," Mrs. Gough agreed. "And I have to admit Alan would be the ideal candidate for a job like that."

Batchelder had been pondering every word. "You've got to admit more than that, Eleanor," he said slowly. "Mitch's idea covers damn near everything."

"It hit me when I was describing the meeting to Islington," Scovil preened himself. "That list of demands was so phony it jumped off the paper. I knew we'd been set up."

"Anyway, Lemoine must have bought it," Clay answered. "You did say the pressure went off you as soon as he found out about the safe deposit box."

"Well, he sure as hell couldn't come up with a reason why I'd slip dirty money to one of my own pilots to wreck the joint."

Eleanor could see broader grounds for Lemoine's action. "Even if he wasn't completely convinced by your theory, he had to let you go. At the very least, the fifty thousand shows that Alan was into something so fishy it could easily have been the motive for his murder. You're right, Mitch, having the money pop up was a godsend for us."

Scovil examined his drink, decided it required freshening, and moved to the bar. When he next spoke he was almost invisible, bending over his glass behind a barricade of ice buckets and mixers.

"Actually I was able to give Lemoine more than a theory. I finally gave him what I've been sitting on. You see, after Don Islington left, I went out to the parking lot, intending to go home. And guess what I saw!" He paused to let the suspense mount. "Alan Whetmore was having a nice, cozy confab with Fritz Diehl."

The climax fell flat.

"So?" Eleanor said impatiently. "Sally already told us that Fritz came by that afternoon."

Scovil's tone hardened. "But she didn't tell us that Whetmore was reporting results to Fritz."

"Mitch!"

This time Eleanor Gough was outraged. Before she could say anything intemperate, Batchelder asked the question that needed an answer.

"But why did that make you stay at Logan?"

"Seeing them together like that really floored me," Scovil admitted. "I knew, if I followed Fritz in and tackled him right then, he'd have some fancy story up his sleeve. So I decided to bump into him casually when he didn't know how much I'd seen. Since there was only one plane to St. Louis after five, I hung around the gate. When he never showed, I figured I'd catch him the next morning at the gym."

Mrs. Gough had been biding her time.

"Are you out of your mind, Mitch?" she asked stonily.

Scovil, having already extracted half agreements, pressed his advantage.

"Come off it, Eleanor. You realized within five minutes that Whetmore was making patsies out of us. You admit that getting his payoff three weeks ago ties it into our meeting. And you haven't come up with any alternative to a competitor. Now you act as if I'm throwing you something from left field."

"Why don't *you* come off it?" she snapped angrily. "You've been deliberately leaking hints about California for months. And the reason you've been doing it is precisely to needle all the transcontinentals. Well, you've had your fun, you've stirred up a lot of hornets' nests. Now maybe one of them did bribe Alan Whetmore. But you haven't proved a thing against Fritz."

Kate, watching her welcome-home party turn into a pitched battle, tried to intervene.

"Couldn't we talk about this some other time?" she suggested. "The important thing is that Mitch isn't under suspicion anymore."

This remark drew a derisive snort from Mrs. Gough, but it was Kate's husband who ignored the plea for peace.

"Nobody's pulling a stunt like this simply to prevent our expansion. A minute ago you couldn't believe any of the majors would act this way and now suddenly they're all suspects. Fritz isn't piddling around with distraction. He wants to take over Sparrow. That's what he's been after all along."

"And you told that story to the police?" Eleanor cried in horror.

"I could have told Lemoine about Fritz and Whetmore right off the bat," Scovil said defiantly. "But I sat on it, hoping the cops would settle things by themselves. Just how long do you expect me to cover for Fritz?"

Eleanor knew that Scovil had been protecting his own alibi, but she stayed with the main issue.

"Nobody expects you to cover anything," she insisted. "There's no reason you shouldn't tell them you saw Fritz. But spilling out accusations that have no foundation—"

"Like hell they don't. I heard Fritz when he walked out on us. You heard him, and so did Clay."

Batchelder was not eager to leave the sidelines.

"I don't like it any better than you do, Eleanor, but we've got to face facts," he said, appealing to her sense of justice. "Fritz did say he'd take over Sparrow."

"If it comes to that, Mitch said a lot of things, too. They were both furious, but they were talking about normal competition."

"I'm not so sure," Clay continued unhappily. "I learned something during Sparrow's first two years. Fritz plays to win."

"And he's a smoothie," Kate suddenly chimed in. "I remember saying so."

She and Fritz Diehl had barely overlapped in Scovil's life. Mrs. Gough could shrug off Kate, but not Batchelder.

"Do you realize you're accusing Fritz of being a cold-blooded killer?" she demanded, shifting brutally from bribery to murder.

Scovil was ready for her.

"It's a choice between him and me," he retorted. "Besides, we don't know it was all that cold-blooded. Maybe there was a fight about money. It would have been just like Whetmore to try for a second helping. So Fritz lost his cool and beat his brains in."

The graphic description created another hurdle for Batchelder to clear. "I suppose it could have happened that way," he said, only partially convinced, "but it doesn't sound like Fritz."

Scovil, still intent on Mrs. Gough, dismissed Clay's difficulty.

"The trouble with you, Eleanor, is that you buy Fritz's nice-guy act. Just look what's happened to Sparrow in the past couple of weeks. We began at thirty-five, where at least we had a ten-point cushion against the sharks. Then Whetmore's death pushed us down to thirty-three and today I get hauled off by the cops in front of TV cameras. I'm afraid to ask how much we lost this afternoon."

"They suspended trading," Mrs. Gough said briefly. "We won't know what the damage is until the market opens on Monday."

"And you still don't see that Fritz is behind this," Scovil marveled. He shook his head silently at this denial of reality.

"We're going through a bad patch because of Alan's murder. But he wasn't necessarily killed for that reason," Eleanor said, casting around for another interpretation. "You might just as well say that Fritz was responsible for the slide to thirty-five."

The words were out of her mouth before she realized how double-edged they were. It was unwritten law at Sparrow that the stock's slow retreat from its high was due to changing conditions, increased competition, or black clouds over the Persian Gulf. Never, under any circumstance, was it attributed to the loss of Fritz Diehl's managerial skills.

Appalled by her inadvertent clumsiness, Eleanor Gough knew that further discussion would only convince Mitch that she had blurted out a long-held opinion. Deciding that the least said, the soonest mended, she began to gather her belongings.

Kate McDermott, confused by her husband's lowering brow and Clay's open consternation, remained a lady to the bitter end.

"Oh, Eleanor, what a shame you have to run off so soon," she said.

❧ 16 ❧

Note the Bull Neck

Fritz Diehl was not content with simple success. To be satisfactory, his success must appear effortless. Over the years he had honed the image of a man born to control himself and everything that came into his orbit. This was the public Fritz Diehl. In private, he spent hours losing battle after battle with the forces of nature.

His neighbors in St. Louis were accustomed to the ghostly glow bathing his collection of African violets. Every amenity that money could buy had been lavished on those pots. Lighting, temperature and humidity were all ideal. Deadly chemicals were stockpiled to repel blight or mite.

But nothing worked. While humble enthusiasts with one growlight took prizes at the annual flower show, Diehl could not even mount a respectable entry. Without rhyme or reason his charges flourished, withered or, most cruelly of all, maintained a feeble status quo.

When the phone rang on Sunday, Diehl had just discovered that Little Miss Muffet was drooping. Still immersed in his pharmacopoeia, he lifted the receiver.

"Mr. Diehl, this is Captain Lemoine of the Massachusetts State Police," a gruff voice announced. "We met in Boston."

When there was no response, the caller added impatiently: "You remember, don't you?"

Diehl, feeling as if he had been caught in his underwear, was busy transforming himself from one person into another.

"Of course I remember," he managed to say. "What can I do for you, Captain?"

A voice never tells the whole story. To the policeman sitting at Logan Airport, it sounded as if Diehl were being deliberately patronizing.

"For starters, you could tell me why you've been keeping quiet about your meeting with Whetmore the day he was murdered."

But Diehl had prepared this answer over a week ago.

"I haven't been keeping quiet about it. It just wasn't important."

Lemoine was stung, more by the tone of indifference than the actual words.

"Sure. I turn up at your breakfast table asking about Whetmore's movements, and it wasn't important."

The sarcasm failed to ruffle Diehl. By this time he had hooked an ankle around a stool and dragged it to the potting bench. Unconsciously he was re-creating the atmospherics of his office at A&P. Seated at a desk with a phone to his ear, he became a vice-president again.

"You were asking about a murder at midnight," he said reasonably. "What does my seeing Whetmore in the middle of the afternoon have to do with that?"

"Scovil was the one who thought Whetmore was killed at midnight. Actually he was killed around six, and the body discovered at midnight."

"Six o'clock!" Diehl whistled softly. "I can see how that changes things. But you must have explained the timing after I left."

Lemoine's brow creased. He recalled explaining the time discrepancy, he recalled dismissing Diehl from the break-

123

fast table. But for the life of him, he could not pinpoint the order of these events.

"This has been public knowledge for over a week," he said accusingly. "Are you claiming this is the first you've heard of it?"

"A Boston murder doesn't get that much coverage here in St. Louis, and I came back a couple of hours after I saw you."

Lemoine chuckled. "Our little murder may not have gotten national attention before Thanksgiving, Mr. Diehl. But it's gotten plenty since. Or didn't you notice the TV clips of Mitch Scovil being hauled off in a squad car?"

"Oh, I saw them," Diehl admitted readily. "I even heard you released him. But Thanksgiving weekend in the airline business doesn't leave a lot of time for reading the fine print."

Lemoine had no intention of being diverted.

"All right. For the sake of argument, let's say you haven't kept up with the story on Whetmore's killing. Suppose you tell me why you wanted to talk to him that afternoon."

"He wanted to talk to me," Diehl corrected mildly. "I'd just parked when he came over and reminded me that we'd been at Bayou together. So we had the usual exchange. I asked him how he liked Sparrow, and he asked me how I liked St. Louis. And that was it."

"Come on. You don't see the guy for years and suddenly he wants to pass the time of day. Didn't you think that was funny?"

Diehl was patience itself. "It happens all the time with pilots. When they realize they can only fly for another year or two, they start buddying up to every airline executive they can find. If you don't believe me, ask around."

Captain Lemoine knew that Alan Whetmore had barely squeaked through his last physical, but there are two sides to every coin. If Diehl had been looking for somebody at Sparrow to corrupt, then Whetmore would have been a Grade A prospect.

Doggedly the captain plowed ahead. "Where did Whetmore go when your talk broke up?"

"He headed into the parking lot and I assumed he was getting his car. But I went straight into the office and didn't see."

"That's right, you said you were looking for Mrs. Gough."

Diehl sounded bored. "Yes, but she wasn't there. So I asked for Mitch, and the receptionist said he'd just left."

Carefully, so as not to alarm his quarry, Lemoine maintained the same monotonous rhythm.

"You didn't bother asking for Batchelder?"

"I didn't have to. His door was open and I could see his empty office when I looked for Eleanor."

Bingo! The only way Diehl could have seen through that doorway was by advancing into the conference room beyond the coffee table.

"Mr. Diehl, the wrench used to murder Alan Whetmore was lying on the coffee table in the conference room earlier that afternoon. Was it still there when you were in the room?"

The silence was so protracted it was painful.

"Mr. Diehl, I'm waiting for your answer."

"I'm thinking," Diehl said stubbornly.

Like policemen the world over, Captain Lemoine wanted the people he was interrogating to be nervous, flustered, and speaking too quickly. But there was no hope of that with this clever bastard. He was too smooth and too careful.

On his part, Diehl realized that one word could suggest that the wrench had left the conference room with Mitch Scovil. It would also be a statement, admittedly self-serving, that he himself had not been near the weapon. He knew this, and he knew that Captain Lemoine knew it.

Neither man was surprised at the form of the answer.

"I'm sorry, Captain," Diehl said perfunctorily. "I've been trying to picture that table without any success. I have no idea what was on it."

Lemoine had heard this evasion in many guises.

"How very convenient," he observed.

Diehl's shrug was almost audible. "Well, that's the way things are."

"I'll want a signed statement from you. The boys in St. Louis can send a man over."

"Unless you're in a hurry, that isn't necessary. I'll be on the East Coast this week, and I can stop by," said Diehl, making it sound like any other business appointment.

This show of bravado was too much for Lemoine.

"See that you do!" he snarled.

In the world of corporate jostling the man who keeps his cool has won. But police investigators play a different game.

Fritz Diehl returned from lunch on Monday unaware that round two with Captain Lemoine had already begun.

"Mr. Merrick wanted to see you as soon as you got back," his secretary said, causing Diehl's eyebrows to rise.

The president of Atlantic & Pacific knew that his days were numbered, but he did his best to forget that unpalatable fact. At policy meetings he had to face his would-be successors, but at all other times, he tried to ignore their existence. A tête-à-tête instigated by Wilfred Merrick was unheard of.

But curiosity was not enough to deflect Diehl from the rules of in-house fighting.

"I'll drop by his office after I've seen Ben," he said casually, making it clear that he was not a flunky leaping to attention.

When he sauntered into the presidential suite half an hour later he expected to find irritation; instead he met uncharacteristic geniality.

"Have a seat," Merrick invited with a flap of the hand. "Glad you could make it."

The unmistakable gleam of anticipation in those elderly blue eyes was enough to set off alarm bells. Outwardly composed, Fritz Diehl was all wariness as he sank into a chair.

"Something come up?" he inquired with minimal interest.

"We had an unexpected call from the police this morning. They want to go through some of our books."

Merrick paused, relishing every word.

"Of course I could have made them go through a lot of red tape," he continued. "But why bother, I said. After all, if they've got good grounds, they can always get a subpoena."

This was arrant nonsense. Standard procedure dictated that such a request be forwarded to the law department which, at the very least, demanded time-consuming compliance with every formality.

"But you just invited them right in," said Diehl appreciatively.

"That's right," said Merrick, enjoying himself. "It's a shame you weren't around earlier. Did I mention that it's your disbursements that they're checking?"

Diehl nodded as if his approval had been solicited.

"I don't see how you could have done anything else, Will, not with that great Merrick tradition of cooperating with the law."

Merrick winced. Two years ago, during a grand jury investigation, Merrick's nephew had abruptly left A&P to take up employment in Taiwan.

Nonetheless, Merrick was still convinced that he was going to witness Fritz Diehl's discomfiture.

"Of course this is all flow-back from that mess over at Sparrow. The police have found out that someone was bribing their people." Merrick waggled his head solemnly. "And that's not the kind of dirty play I'm prepared to condone."

"If it's going to make the front page, who would?" Diehl asked, like a man miles removed from the storm center.

Fritz Diehl had been playing roles all his life. He was seething with suppressed fury at Merrick's futile vindictiveness. Didn't the old imbecile see he was no longer a contender? Diehl was still too young to realize that, after a certain age, a struggle doomed to defeat is preferable to no struggle at all. But not one sign of his rage was reflected in the polite, attentive expression he presented to the president of A&P.

Merrick, on the other hand, was incapable of sustaining any pretense. He had foolishly imagined his opponent would collapse after the first salvo was fired. As soon as a longer engagement threatened, he reverted to form.

"I'll be reporting this to the board," he snapped. "When the police are combing through our files, the directors have a right to know."

"That'll be a big surprise for them." Steepling his fingers beneath his chin, Diehl looked as if he were gently strolling down memory lane. "Let's see, at the last board meeting you were sure Stevenson had inflated his profit reports. And two months ago Werner was supposed to be playing patty-cake with a supplier. So this time it has to be me or Duvalier. I'll bet the suspense is killing everybody."

It was true that Merrick had been attacking his possible heirs at recent board meetings, but it infuriated him to hear a major felony equated to the misdemeanors of Stevenson and Werner.

With red spots mottling his corrugated cheeks, he shot back: "We're not talking about penny-ante stuff anymore. We're talking about bribery and murder."

Instantly, Merrick knew he had made a mistake. For months he had been trying to sell the picture of Fritz Diehl as an unscrupulous opportunist who wanted to go too far, too fast. Even a hint of shadowy payments in a deserted parking lot would flesh out that image. He should have stopped while he was ahead.

Fritz Diehl's affable smile emphasized the error. "So that's your pitch, is it? That I'm the kind who runs around whipping out his six-shooter and going rooty-toot-toot? I think the board may want a little more than your say-so on that."

"You've been up to something," Merrick insisted stubbornly. "Otherwise the police wouldn't be rummaging through your books."

"But they won't find anything. And you know what? The directors may not be crazy about your blind effort to land A&P with a stink."

Merrick was beyond rational considerations.

"You wouldn't be so sure of yourself if you weren't safe here in St. Louis. I'll bet the Boston cops would pull you in just like Scovil."

"Then they'll have their chance. I guess you've forgotten the bond dealers are meeting tomorrow." Diehl had risen and was drifting toward the door when he added: "You should try to stay on top of these things, Will, even if it is getting a little difficult for you."

This solicitude for failing powers deprived Merrick of the last shred of restraint. His explosion of obscenity came, exactly as Diehl had intended, in time to be overheard by three witnesses in the reception room.

On the whole, Fritz Diehl had every right to be pleased with his own performance. He had not deviated by one hairbreadth from his normal behavior. But the encounters with Captain Lemoine and Wilfred Merrick had taken their toll.

At five o'clock, he paused to give his secretary last-minute instructions and to pick up tickets for the dinner flight to New York. Then, suitcase in hand, he was on his way when she hastily called him back.

Fritz Diehl, the man who never forgot anything, had left his briefcase on his desk.

∿ 17 ∿

Stormy Petrels

Monday was not a wonderful day at Sparrow, either. The CEO was back at the helm, trading had been resumed, and the usual flights were taking off. Unfortunately, too few people had noticed the colorless account of Mitch Scovil's release, Sparrow stock was stalled at a disappointing 29 7/8, and most of the work force was still reliving Pittsburgh.

For the first time since Sparrow's inception, Scovil flinched at the prospect of appearing in public.

"I'm scrubbing my trip to New York," he announced. "You'd better handle the bond dealers' meeting, Clay."

Batchelder hesitated. He was uncomfortably aware that bond dealers were a long way from his usual responsibilities.

"Just your being there would prove the cops let you go," he pointed out.

"And half of Wall Street would think I'm out on bail," Scovil rejoined savagely. "Look, it's just a couple of days, and you could knock off Islington, too. You wanted to see him about the new specs, anyway."

"Hell, it's not the time, Mitch. But I'm no good at talking finances to the big-money men."

Scovil's face cleared. "Forget about that, Clay," he urged. "The important thing now is to make sure that everybody in New York knows that the police are finally moving in the right direction. And it's going to sound a lot more persuasive coming from you than from me."

Batchelder was relieved at this change in emphasis.

"Now that I can do," he promised.

Phoebe Fournier took one look at Joe Cleveland and braced herself.

"So nothing could possibly go wrong," he greeted her.

She flushed, remembering her unequivocal assurances in the airplane hangar. "All right, all right, things got out of hand."

"That's one way of describing it."

"It's not my fault if a couple of drunks went ape."

"There are always drunks at Thanksgiving."

"They don't always run around taking hostages."

At this impasse, they both settled back on their heels and glared at each other. Joe, however, had barely begun his indictment.

"And what about the famous press release? I haven't heard anything about that."

Here Phoebe felt she was on firmer ground. "The release was never central," she informed him. "It was only an explanation for the public if they asked for one. But the main point of the exercise was to put pressure on Mitch. Now that he knows we can shut him down, he'll listen to reason."

"You can forget that tune, Phoebe. Mitch has got bigger things to worry about."

"Are you talking about the police goof on Friday? They let him go right away," she countered. "So that's all over."

"Mitch came within an inch of being arrested for murder, and it could still happen. He has to concentrate on that," said Joe. "We've got to face facts. Pittsburgh was a washout."

Phoebe was not ready to concede this point.

"I suppose you think you could manage things better," she said.

"No, I wouldn't be any good at it. But we'd get a lot farther if you stopped trying to manipulate everybody."

The word was a red flag.

"I am not manipulative!" she snapped.

"Oh yeah? You were going to use Alan Whetmore and he turned out to have ideas of his own. You were going to use Sparrow's passengers last Wednesday, and three of them broke ranks. You're always surprised when other people call their own shots. But worst of all is the way you keep trying to duck Alan Whetmore's murder. Has it occurred to you that if Mitch didn't kill him, someone else did?"

"Of course I realize that," she said loftily. "It's just not our problem."

"Like hell it isn't. It means somebody around here has got an angle we don't even know about, and he's playing for keeps."

While Phoebe searched for a rebuttal, Joe arrived at a conclusion.

"You know what your trouble is, Phoebe? You're great with numbers, but you're lousy with people."

By the time they parted, Joe Cleveland had managed to unload a good deal of his dissatisfaction on Phoebe. There was no disputing some of his contentions. But she refused to admit that the biggest snarl in airline history had yielded no leverage whatsoever. She was still clinging to this comfort when an unkind fate brought Eleanor Gough around the corner.

Mrs. Gough barely glanced at Phoebe. If any confirmation for Joe Cleveland's views were needed, here it was. Eleanor was the apostle of wholehearted devotion to Sparrow. Eleanor had borne the brunt of Wednesday's dislocation. By rights, she should have been foaming. Instead, she was going to pass without a glance.

It was unbelievable and, for Phoebe, intolerable.

"Eleanor!" she called out abruptly.

Mrs. Gough blinked in an effort to refocus her attention.

"Yes?"

Other concerns had not only taken priority over labor disaffection, they had apparently obliterated all memory of it.

"I suppose you've got plenty to say about Pittsburgh," Phoebe suggested defiantly.

She was wrong.

"Wasn't that disgraceful?" Mrs. Gough murmured.

The remark could have been directed toward Sparrow employees or drunken sales engineers or an airport staff that cried: *Wolf!*

"It's disgraceful that we have to resort to that kind of action to get Mitch's attention."

"Oh, do stop being so childish, Phoebe."

There was a weary patience about this plea that was more offensive than any accusation.

"And since when is worrying about the future of Sparrow childish?"

"If it will make you feel better, I admit that Mitch should have taken the time to explain his plans to you."

By now Phoebe was itching for a real fight.

"Look, we're not miffed because Mitch hasn't personally explained his wonderful plans to us. We want him to scrap them."

Mrs. Gough swept on as if there had been no interruption. "But when I finally got Mitch to a meeting, what did you do? You sprang Alan Whetmore on us. Then the meeting blew up, Alan got murdered, and Mitch had a lot of other problems. You have nobody but yourself to blame."

"Oh yeah? You're forgetting that I never saw Alan's precious list. Why didn't you and Clay make Mitch read it beforehand? Or you could have just come to me. You wanted the whole thing to explode in our faces."

"We didn't choose Alan Whetmore. He was your responsibility."

Phoebe did not see it that way. "It's not my fault he got himself murdered. And it's certainly no reason for us to sit by and let Mitch go ahead with plans that spell disaster."

"You've done pretty well out of Mitch's judgment so far," Mrs. Gough said acidly.

"But times have changed, and he isn't changing with them. He acts as if deregulation started last week."

"Don't be ridiculous."

"Oh yeah? Then why have you been complaining about Pittsburgh and Tom Reardon until you're blue in the face?"

Nobody enjoys having his inconsistencies shown up. Mrs. Gough's lips tightened. "I do not necessarily agree with Mitch on every single detail."

"Then why are you pretending he's Mitch the Infallible? And expecting us to swallow it?"

"There's such a thing as loyalty."

"Loyalty?" Phoebe laughed mockingly. "Why don't you show a little loyalty to us?"

"Now what are you talking about?"

"You're the one who developed the employee policy around here. You're the one who preaches team spirit."

"And what's wrong with that?"

"A lot, if you think you're some kind of Lady Bountiful. None of it was a gift. We've worked our tails off while you've dangled the carrot of co-ownership."

Phoebe had the satisfaction of seeing Mrs. Gough's eyes narrow.

"Even on a team somebody has to have the final say. Haven't you learned anything in the field, Phoebe?"

But now that Phoebe had found a crack in the facade, she was determined to split it wide open.

"Crap! That's just an excuse. You've made your pile, and you're not interested anymore."

"That is simply absurd!" Mrs. Gough retorted.

"Do you think we don't notice what's going on? I was here from the start, remember? You and Fritz Diehl came up with a bunch of ideas. What's more, you were ready to fight it out with Mitch if it took months. That's how we got the profit-sharing plan and stock bonuses."

Eleanor Gough was openly snarling. "Is there supposed to be some point to what you're saying?"

"It proves I'm right," said Phoebe, smashing away against her opponent. "When was the last time you were interested enough to fight for anything? Hell, half the time you don't bother to sit in with Mitch and Clay. It doesn't matter to you if Sparrow goes under and takes thousands of us along. Why should it? You know damn well you won't lose out."

"How dare you? You're sitting on a lot of stock yourself."

Now that she had drawn blood, Phoebe was zeroing in for the kill. "But I still care about the others. That's where we're different. For five years you've been conning us into splitting a gut, and now you're opting out."

"You miserable little brat. You have about as much idea of the real world as a baby. Why don't you stick to what you're good at and leave the grown-up decisions to—"

"To Mitch the Pope?" Phoebe cut in. "Forget it, Eleanor. At least I try, which is more than can be said for you."

"Sure you try," raged Eleanor. "While you were trying to wreck Sparrow last Wednesday, I was the one who pulled us through."

"Housekeeping work!" Phoebe instantly riposted. "That's how you put in your time while you're thinking about something else. You're willing to assign new recruits and, if there's an emergency, you'll fool around with refunds and new schedules. But when it comes to the gut decisions, you can't be bothered. I suppose you get your fill of that, building up your estate."

Mrs. Gough had moved so close that she was almost spitting in Phoebe's face. "It beats putting in time by making trouble."

The more furious Eleanor became, the better Phoebe felt.

"You're the one who's been causing trouble. In fact, it's all your fault. Mitch has gotten used to handing down his edicts and having you lap them up. Now he expects the rest of us to roll over and play dead. Well, it isn't going to work. We've got too much at stake."

"Stop sounding like a soap opera! Mitch has more at stake than anyone. Sparrow means more than money to some of us."

Phoebe smiled nastily.

"Sure, Mitch gets his kicks out of being the hotshot who

walked all over the majors," she admitted. "That's why he's so rattled now. The going gets a little rough and—"

"You don't know what rough is," Mrs. Gough scoffed. "Until now you've been on to a sure thing. You may have given a lot. You got a lot, too. And in spite of your smoke screen about responsibility, that's what you're worried about. Your stock has been dropping and you're hysterical with fear. You don't have the stomach for a real risk."

The counterattack threw Phoebe on the defensive.

"At least I'm reacting to cold hard facts. I'm not falling to pieces because of some fantasy about People Express and a takeover by A&P."

"Takeovers happen in the real world."

"They sure do, and sometimes they happen from inside," said Phoebe, trying to regain the initiative. "Maybe Mitch should stop worrying about Fritz Diehl. There are other ways he can lose Sparrow."

But Mrs. Gough had recovered her composure. Stepping back a pace, she examined Phoebe dispassionately.

"Yes, but you couldn't even begin to count them, Phoebe," she said, abandoning an exchange that no longer mattered to her.

❧ 18 ❧

Extremely Long Bill

It was only natural that every airline in the country should be represented at the meeting of the National Association of Bond Dealers. Municipal bonds mean bigger and better airports, as well as improved water supplies and sewage systems. But before the money can be spent, it must be raised—which explained the attendance of another group.

"Today?" John Thatcher asked in pained surprise.

Miss Corsa was adamant. "You're appearing on a discussion panel at two o'clock."

Children are not the only ones who hope the day of reckoning will never come.

"I thought that wasn't for months," grumbled Thatcher. "At least I'm not spending two whole days listening to every mayor in the country. Who have we got covering the meetings?"

In spite of the best efforts of the program committee, those attending did not expect to gain much from the scheduled events. They came to make deals, broaden contacts, and exchange rumors.

"Mr. Bowman and Mr. Yetter are both already at the Hilton," Miss Corsa said encouragingly.

And, indeed, the first person Thatcher saw when he emerged from the elevator was the Sloan's chief of research. Acquiring information was the breath of life to Bowman, a past master at sifting fact from fiction.

"Hello, John," he called, "I was just congratulating Diehl here on the last quarter's earnings. A&P is back in the black."

Diehl's teeth gleamed. "Glad you noticed," he smiled. "If you think that's good, just wait until next quarter. Most of the fat's been trimmed. *Finally.*"

His emphasis on the last word was unnecessary. The fat at A&P had been notorious for years.

As Bowman performed belated introductions, Thatcher studied Mitch Scovil's *bête noire* with interest. On the surface he looked like a thousand other executives. If he had ever been an exemplar of the youth culture at Sparrow, he had wisely shed that image.

Recalling Everett Gabler's assignment in Boston, Bowman nudged the conversation in a helpful direction. "Now that Sparrow's stock is so weak, I suppose all the majors are taking a look at it."

"Not us," said Diehl pleasantly. "We're doing too much reorganization to think about acquisitions."

"Well, I'll bet somebody is. How often do you get the president of a hot prospect in the slammer?" Bowman asked with his usual gusto.

Diehl corrected him. "They let Mitch go right away. It was probably some kind of mistake."

The use of the first name had jogged Bowman's compendious memory. "I forgot. You were with that bunch for a while."

"That's right," Diehl agreed.

Thatcher decided not to waste Bowman's efforts.

"But what you may not know, Walter, is that Diehl sold his stock to Jim Vandervoort."

Fritz Diehl lifted an inquiring eyebrow.

"The Sloan handles the Vandervoort Trust," Thatcher explained.

"Oh, I see," said Diehl. "Of course I knew that Jim's estate went to his son. Then you probably know more about Sparrow these days than I do. I haven't had time to keep up."

Walter Bowman nodded approval. What was past was past in his book.

"You've had your hands full in St. Louis," he said.

But Thatcher decided to make one more cast. "That stock has not been an unmixed blessing," he observed.

"You couldn't expect Sparrow's early rate of growth to continue," Diehl said reasonably.

Thatcher wanted more than generalities.

"No, but we didn't expect their employees to shut down the East Coast, either."

Diehl guffawed. "That's Phoebe for you. Never a dull moment when she's around."

Smiling politely, Thatcher let Walter Bowman return to his real interest, the projected earnings at A&P.

Fritz Diehl was either genuinely indifferent to Sparrow or putting on a very good show. Naturally he was not volunteering the information that he had been on Sparrow premises the day of Alan Whetmore's murder. Thatcher could scarcely blame him for that. Anyone could see that Fritz Diehl was a very prudent young executive.

For the next hour and a half the corridors of the Hilton rang with the professional chitchat so dear to Walter Bowman. John Thatcher might just as well have been in another county. Immured in a small auditorium, he traded bromides with three other men on the subject of Making America Competitive Again. This endeavor was not particularly taxing because Thatcher knew that by tomorrow nobody, including himself, would remember a single commonplace. The sole purpose of the exercise was to generate expensive transcripts which the bond dealers could sell to institutional libraries for dead storage.

With duty done, Thatcher sallied forth to freedom, ran smack into Clay Batchelder, and unwittingly created a social problem.

"God, that's right," said Batchelder after two members

of the crowd pouring into the corridor congratulated Thatcher on his performance. "You were on some kind of symposium, weren't you? I meant to take it in."

"I doubt if it would have interested you," said Thatcher truthfully. "It was mostly about the manufacturing sector. And of course Pulford got off his usual shots about agriculture."

Batchelder did not pretend to be an habitué of these circles.

"Actually this sort of shindig isn't my bag," he confessed. "I'm just here to tell everybody that Mitch is out. But, with Gabler on the spot, you must already know."

"Oh yes, Everett called me on Friday."

"It was such lousy luck," Batchelder lamented. "An hour would have made all the difference."

Thatcher thought he knew what they were talking about.

"The presence of the television crew was certainly unfortunate," he said, suppressing Gabler's opinion about the insensate thirst for publicity.

"That's not what I mean. By an hour later, the cops were finally on the right track. If poor Mitch had just been out of the way on Friday morning, the whole thing would have been cleared up by the time he got to the office."

"Perhaps he should take up golf."

Batchelder was in no mood for jokes. "You know that they found fifty thousand bucks in Whetmore's secret safe deposit box?"

"I hadn't heard," said Thatcher, instinctively scanning a host of possibilities.

"Someone was bribing him to cause trouble," Batchelder continued. "Whetmore deliberately staged it so that Mitch would refuse to budge and all hell would break loose."

"That is certainly one interpretation," said Thatcher, reserving judgment. "But if Whetmore did take a bribe, then it will be important to find out who paid him."

They had reached the limits of Batchelder's frankness.

"The cops aren't saying," he muttered, looking elsewhere.

* * *

" . . .well, the talk around here is that it was Fritz Diehl," reported Kyle Yetter.

Yetter and Walter Bowman were comparing notes when Thatcher ran into them.

"And I suppose Diehl's goal was to drive the stock down for a takeover?" he suggested.

"Actually there are two theories," Bowman expanded. "The first one is the takeover bit. But the other crowd says that it was to block Sparrow's expansion. They claim that A&P would go back in the red, at least temporarily, if a price war broke out. And profits are the only thing that will make Diehl their next president."

Thatcher frowned. "Somehow this all sounds too convenient for Mitch Scovil. I wonder what the police think of this theory."

It was a point of honor with Walter to mine some nuggets that had been overlooked by his colleagues.

"They're buying some of it," he announced with a triumphant smile. "Steve Werner from A&P tells me that the cops are going through Diehl's disbursements back in St. Louis. Of course, Steve's been trying to sink a knife into Diehl ever since he came aboard."

Thatcher dismissed in-house rivalry. "Tell me," he asked, "is everybody assuming that Diehl murdered Whetmore?"

"Well, they're all executives themselves and they don't often bash in brains for the good of the company," said Walter with some contempt. "Most of them would like to think the labor people up at Sparrow executed a traitor. Then there's the gang that really believes Mitch Scovil's PR. They say he goes with his emotions. He just saw red and began swinging. A few of them are sticking with Diehl, to keep things simple. But everybody agrees that the murder was an attempt to cover up the mess."

Yetter was outraged. "What a bunch!" he exploded.

"At least you aren't contemplating a credit accommodation for A&P," said Thatcher, looking on the bright side.

"I wouldn't lend a penny to either one of them," Yetter said roundly. "Not until this is settled once and for all."

Thatcher agreed that credit extensions were out of the

question. "Unfortunately that still leaves the Trust Division with the baby."

"How much of this junk are they stuck with?" Walter Bowman asked.

"Twenty percent of Sparrow," Thatcher said crisply, "and they can't get rid of it."

Bowman produced the only consolation available. "Well, the market's cooled off since Scovil's release. Sparrow didn't go anywhere today."

Grateful for a staff that kept up with the market wherever they were, Thatcher wished his subordinates good hunting and made his way to the elevators. Down in the lobby, where tourists and traveling salesmen replaced bond dealers and municipal authorities, he spotted one familiar face. Fritz Diehl was also shaking the dust of the Hilton from his feet.

Thatcher raised a hand in greeting, but the gesture was not acknowledged. Diehl, his face set in lines of stone, straight-armed the revolving doors that led to the street. As he disappeared from sight, Thatcher realized he was not witnessing a departure.

It was a flight.

Fritz Diehl marched ten blocks at a furious pace, still bewildered by his experience at the Hilton. Shortly after leaving Bowman and Thatcher, he had begun to notice that conversations faltered and ranks closed whenever he appeared. An encounter with Clay Batchelder ten minutes before had been the final straw. Clay, visibly embarrassed, had uttered a few disjointed remarks, then remembered another appointment.

Steve Werner! The sudden idea made Diehl slow down and think. Werner had traveled east, too. Had the S.O.B. done a real job on him? And if he had, how many people in New York thought Fritz Diehl had blood on his hands?

There was only one way to find out.

"Taxi!"

By nine o'clock that night Fritz Diehl was in his hotel room with a bottle. His tour of Wall Street had been a disaster. At two brokerage houses he had been told that the men he wished to see were out. At a third, a stranger had announced that A&P was being removed from the Buy List. At two investment banks he had been informed that now was not the time to make a move on Sparrow. When he disclaimed any such intention, his advisers simply smiled.

Fritz Diehl had taken too much punishment to risk more. He would have faced a firing squad sooner than enter one of the Hilton's bars after dinner at a crosstown hotel.

But solitary drinking affects different people in different ways. Some experience a warm glow and renewed confidence. Others plunge into self-pity and despair. For Fritz Diehl, three straight shots did nothing but leave a bad taste. Emptying his glass down the drain, he decided he had to know what he was up against.

Fortunately there was a way to find out, provided that Eleanor Gough was not working late. He wanted to talk to her in the privacy of her home.

She answered on the third ring.

"Eleanor? This is Fritz. For God's sake, what the hell is going on?"

He made no attempt to hide the strain he was under and she too skipped the niceties.

"Hello, Fritz," she said slowly. "I suppose I should have expected to hear from you."

"Considering that I've had the police on my neck in St. Louis and everybody in New York thinks I'm a killer, you might expect me to be a little curious, yeah. Particularly when it's all coming out of the blue."

The release of his frustration was providing all the warmth that alcohol had failed to achieve.

"Oh, Fritz, I'm so sorry. I thought by now you'd know."

"Suppose you tell me," he grated.

The length of the pause indicated that she was choosing her words with care.

"It was Alan Whetmore's safe deposit box. The police discovered that somebody paid him fifty thousand dollars two weeks before he was killed."

"Go on," he said grimly.

"Naturally that led them back to Alan's recent behavior at Sparrow. They seem to suspect he'd been paid to make trouble. So they've started to look at our competition. That must be why they've landed on you."

As her voice trailed off, Diehl gave a bark of humorless laughter.

"Come on, Eleanor, who do you think you're kidding? I'm not your only competition, but the police aren't ransacking files at TWA and United."

"I suppose it's because you know the setup at Sparrow," she said with an effort.

Diehl sounded desperate. "Eleanor, do you know what this is doing to me? We're not talking about my future at A&P. I'm a murder suspect. Don't I have a right to know why?"

Suddenly she capitulated. "Mitch saw you," she said in a burst.

"Saw me doing what, for Christ's sake?" Diehl yelled.

"He saw you with Alan Whetmore in the parking lot. It looked as if you were getting a report from him."

Diehl had always been afraid it would come down to this. "Just tell me one thing," he said dully. "When did Mitch get this bright idea?"

"He said he got it right away and tried to contact you that night."

Diehl began to see the outlines. "Forget about what he says. When did Mitch take the world into his confidence?"

Mrs. Gough sighed. "Last Friday. When the police picked him up."

"I knew it was something like that! The minute the heat went on, Mitch looked for someone to throw to the wolves. You're lucky I was available, Eleanor. Otherwise it could have been you."

"He only found out about the fifty thousand at the station. He couldn't be sure there was a payoff until then."

"He thought he was wriggling out before," Diehl countered. "But he found out the police had built a strong case against him."

Evasively she said: "That kind of bribe would make anybody furious."

"Furious? He was probably counting his blessings. Mitch screwed things up at Sparrow, then lost his head and bashed Whetmore. He was one damned lucky S.O.B. to have that money come to light."

"Stop it! Stop it at once, Fritz!"

"You mean I shouldn't criticize my old friend Mitch when he's trying to railroad me for something he did."

Mrs. Gough was tired of being backed into corners.

"I mean I'm sick to death of both of you," she decided. "First, Mitch tried to make me agree that you're a murderer. Now you want me to say that *he* is."

Diehl saw only an admission. "Oh, great, he not only snows the police, he's going after you, too."

"That's what you're trying to do, and I've had enough. I don't happen to think Mitch is a murderer, and I don't think you are, either. If you don't like it, you'll just have to lump it."

Diehl was taken aback. "But we're friends—" he began.

"It's been a one-way street long enough, buster! You and Mitch and Phoebe all go hell-bent after what you want. Then you expect me to tag along. Well, forget it. I'm tired of being pulled in all directions by the pack of you."

"Now, wait a minute, Eleanor. Mitch is shafting me and I've got a right to be mad."

"And that's where your rights end. Don't tell me what to do and think and feel. In a way, Phoebe's right. I've been ducking my responsibility. From now on, *I'm* going to decide what I want. Let's see how you all like that!"

Nonplussed, Diehl could only say: "What does Phoebe have to do with this?"

"Oh, I've been a big disappointment to her, too," Mrs. Gough said bitterly.

Fritz Diehl brushed this aside. "Look, Eleanor, I don't know what the hell is the matter up there, but I'm not going to be a whipping boy for Mitch or Phoebe. I've got enough on my plate already. I'll give you a call when I'm in Boston in a couple of days. Maybe you'll have simmered down by then."

"Don't count on it!"

✖ 19 ✖

Readily Identified

In a bar at the Hilton, people were offering bets on Fritz Diehl's guilt. But, in the police cubbyhole at Logan Airport, Captain Lemoine was still studying the field.

"This was no dirt-simple killing," he reasoned to the ceiling as he tilted back in his chair. "Scovil didn't just blow his stack and swing on Whetmore the first chance he got. There's more to it than that."

Ed Crawley liked the alternative. "According to Scovil, it's Diehl who blew his stack."

"Could be," agreed Lemoine. "But the boys in St. Louis haven't found a whisper of a fifty-thousand-dollar payoff in the A&P files. What's more, Diehl's basic story checks out. He does drop by regularly when he's in Boston to chat with the old-timers and take Mrs. Gough out to dinner."

"So? That means he probably knew all about Sparrow's labor trouble."

Lemoine scowled ferociously. "That's not the point. Scovil was used to seeing Diehl shoot the breeze with someone around Sparrow. Suddenly it's so important he scrubs his schedule and starts play-acting over at the main terminal. Why?"

"Scovil claims he wanted to pump Diehl."

"Then how come he never got down to it? By the time I showed up at breakfast, the two of them had finished in the gym and were through eating. They'd been together for almost three hours. That whole rigmarole in the morning could have been a cover-up for what Scovil really did at Logan."

Crawley never abandoned the obvious until he was forced to—which might have explained why he was now outranked by his old friend.

"You can't get away from the fifty thousand in the safe deposit box," he argued.

"Oh yeah? That money was paid before Whetmore was named to the employee committee. How come he was worth so much then? And, even if Diehl was pulling a fast one, why should he kill Whetmore? It would make more sense if Scovil saw red after figuring out what was going on."

"Unless Whetmore was trying to up the ante," Ed pointed out. "He could have threatened to blow the whistle unless he got a sweetener."

This theory did not go far enough for Lemoine. "Whetmore was in no position to go public about Diehl," he said, then continued, "but Whetmore could have been playing both ends against the middle. That's why I sent an accountant over to Whetmore's apartment."

"Did he come up with anything?"

"Belliers says I can forget it. Whetmore didn't have anything out of the ordinary at all."

Lemoine crushed his coffee cup in exasperation. "No matter how you look at it, Whetmore was killed because of something going on in Sparrow. And we don't know that much about the company itself. That's why we're stymied."

"You could hand it over to the fraud section," Crawley suggested.

"There may be a quicker way. The Sloan has had a guy

living with the company books for over a week. I'll bet he knows plenty."

The captain's subsequent instructions to Humphrey Belliers were brief and to the point.

"Look, if I go after Gabler, I'm a cop getting careful answers. But maybe you can cozy up to him as one accounting expert to another."

Nature had blessed Belliers with a look of dewy-eyed innocence totally at variance with his character. "Is that the dried-up little guy I saw with Phoebe Fournier?"

"That's right," Lemoine said.

"Just lead me to him!"

The accidental encounter took place as soon as Everett arrived the following morning. Captain Lemoine withdrew, leaving his subordinate to pursue the acquaintance.

"They tell me you're going through the books," Belliers began cleverly. "I haven't done much corporate work, and I wouldn't know how to begin on a company that's as unusual as this one."

Humphrey Belliers had known instinctively that there was no hope of expert-to-expert intimacy. But teacher-to-student was something else again.

Gabler took a happy breath and for ten minutes Belliers was instructed about Sparrow's peculiarities.

"And while the various stock programs have certain unusual features," Gabler declaimed, "I would have no hesitation in describing their profit-sharing fund as the heart of their remuneration scheme. You know, of course, about their salary policy?"

"Tell me about it," said Belliers encouragingly.

"There is a ban on wide differentials. Even the three partners take home relatively small salaries, with their real compensation coming from large slices of the profits. The philosophy is that everyone has a direct interest in the success of the company's operations."

"Yes, I see that."

Gabler frowned at the neophyte's too-ready concurrence. "But this policy has built-in drawbacks when it comes to reinvestment. Scovil should have realized that major capital expenditures would alarm his employees. Ideally, he should have sold his proposal to them long before a crisis occurred."

"That wouldn't have protected him against Whetmore's demands," Belliers objected. "They weren't about the California run."

Gabler always had some nice distinction with which to prick his opponent's balloon.

"Only in one sense. Whetmore seized on the breakdown in communication to call for mandatory employee input. He never would have had that springboard if Scovil had displayed more foresight."

So far Belliers had nothing to complain about. It never occurred to him there was any question of a quid pro quo. When Gabler interrupted his own lecture to ask about his companion's work, Belliers replied with vague generalities, little realizing that Gabler would require more.

"You say there is nothing in Whetmore's finances to raise questions?" Everett challenged.

"Well, nothing except the fifty K. And, if a competitor slipped him one bribe, why should there be?"

Gabler's face tightened. "That is mere speculation."

"Supported by the evidence," said Belliers, allowing himself to be drawn into specifics. "Whetmore wasn't getting big sums from anywhere, and he was leading a pretty frugal life. Hell, I'm not talking about anything complicated like fancy tax shelters. He had one bank account. At the beginning of every month he deposited his pay check, and it was pretty near gone before the next one came along. Even his credit-card charges were almost nonexistent."

Everett was still an instructor, but he was about to give a failing grade. "I have now been working at Sparrow for over a week, and your picture of Alan Whetmore fails to accord with the view of his co-workers. They say he was a lavish spender with a flashy lifestyle."

Belliers shrugged. "He was probably just shooting a line," he said, out of the depths of his experience.

By now Everett was itching to get his hands on the raw material.

"Then Whetmore was producing a remarkable amount of corroborative detail. In the face of this major discrepancy, surely you agree that further review is necessary. In fact," he announced with magnificent effrontery, "I would be extremely interested to see these records myself."

The automatic refusal that sprang to the tip of Belliers's tongue was held in check by two considerations. First, it was his job to keep Gabler sweet.

Even more important, it would be a real pleasure to watch this old curmudgeon fall flat on his face.

An hour later Gabler was ensconced at Alan Whetmore's desk, surrounded by check stubs and bank statements. Humphrey Belliers was standing at the window, gazing down at the Back Bay and admiring the view. (In fact, he was looking above Gauthier College and, if Rupert Vernon prevailed, that view was doomed.)

The quiet had been undisturbed for fifteen minutes, and Belliers anticipated a confession of failure in short order.

"Aha!" Gabler exclaimed, his head still bent over his work.

Belliers swung around. "What's that for?" he demanded irritably. "There's nothing there."

"Exactly. It's what isn't here that gives the game away."

When Gabler finally looked up, Belliers gasped. He never would have believed that those faded blue eyes could sparkle so brightly.

"There are no checks drawn to cash," Gabler intoned.

"Holy Christ!"

Humphrey Belliers was not as inexperienced as he had been pretending. He recognized the implications of Gabler's find immediately. Alan Whetmore's life had included a source of income that had never been funneled through his bank account.

"I've got to get back to headquarters right away. And I can't even give Greg Lemoine any order of magnitude," he lamented. "It will take weeks of legwork before we know whether we're talking about five thousand or a hundred thousand."

Gabler's mouth twitched, but his reply was as sedate as ever. "I agree this should be reported immediately."

Everett had found more than check stubs in Alan Whetmore's desk. He had also found the certificate of title for a car purchased from a Boston dealer. And there had been no car payments in Whetmore's modest array of monthly charges.

Other men might have walked away from temptation. Everett walked straight to Fine Foreign Cars, Ltd., on Commonwealth Avenue. Here they were not interested in the latest economy marvels from Yugoslavia or Korea. He had to stride past serried ranks of BMWs, Mercedes and Rolls-Royces to reach the office.

After asking for the manager, he flourished his credentials and burst into speech.

"I'm sure you've read about the death of Alan Whetmore and you will realize that his estate is in the process of being settled. I find that among the assets is an automobile purchased here in June, two years ago. It would be a great help if you could bring me up to date on the schedule of payments."

"Certainly," said Mr. Bronson, calling for a file.

As usual, every word that had fallen from Everett's lips was the naked truth. It was not his fault, he thought virtuously, if Mr. Bronson somehow concluded that the Sloan Guaranty Trust was handling Whetmore's estate.

When the file arrived, it triggered Bronson's memory.

"Oh yes, I remember this one. There aren't any payments on it. Mr. Whetmore paid for the Jaguar with his previous car and twenty-five thousand dollars. He had recently moved to Boston, so his trade-in still had Nebraska plates. But everything was in order."

"Splendid," said Everett, unconcerned with motor-vehicle registration. "I didn't realize that he'd written a check for the car."

The manager cleared his throat. "Actually he paid with cash. I'm not likely to forget."

"Good Lord!"

"Well, it's still legal tender," Bronson said apologetically.

As a banker, Everett was forced to agree. "But that's a great deal to carry around. You must have been startled."

"It was bigger than that. I think it's queer if they do anything but finance. A check, cash, what's the difference? Who plunks down twenty-five grand for a car?"

"What you say is very true. And I must thank you for your assistance. It's been a great help."

Gabler thought they were through, but Bronson had different ideas.

"By the way, if the estate is selling the car, you might be pleasantly surprised at our offer. If anything, those Jags have appreciated. If you're looking for a sound investment, I always say you have to go a long way to beat . . ."

Like a good citizen, Everett stopped at the first public telephone booth to report to Captain Lemoine.

~ 20 ~

Sexes Alike

While Gabler waited for his call to go through, Mrs. Gough was nerving herself for an ordeal.

The decision to assert herself had, if anything, become firmer overnight. She could tolerate unreasonable appeals for sympathy, but Phoebe Fournier's accusation still rankled.

For two years, Eleanor Gough had been excluded from policy-making. Knowing how unsolicited suggestions would be received, she had deliberately refrained from a thoroughgoing analysis of Scovil's latest plan. But, the new Eleanor argued, expansion to California represented such a discontinuity in Sparrow's operations that Mitch ought to welcome as many critiques as he could get. Unlike her nagging about Pittsburgh's losses, this kind of opinion could be offered in the guise of admiration for the basic concept. And by the time they were done, she would have her foot in the door.

On this heartening note, Mrs. Gough polished off the day's chores and plunged into the files. By two-thirty, her face was drawn with shock, and she was no longer castigating herself or Mitch Scovil or even poor Clay. She was too intent on averting catastrophe.

But Mitch Scovil was nowhere to be found. When he finally appeared, an hour later, he was striding down the corridor as if he were in a race.

"Mitch," she began, "I've been looking for you. I want—"

He shook his head. "It'll have to wait, Eleanor," he said. "I've got some important things to finish up."

Before he could walk on, she planted herself in his path. She knew her adrenaline would never again be flowing at this rate.

"No, Mitch. Right now."

Then she pivoted and marched into the executive quarters. After a brief hesitation he followed, frowning.

"Okay," he said after closing the door. "What's so bad that we can't talk outside? Don't tell me they've finally arrested Fritz?"

This was not an auspicious beginning, but Eleanor persevered. "I've been going over our financials," she said, rushing to put the first rocky moments behind them. "The expansion, as proposed, could ruin us."

His anxiety was dispelled at once.

"Is that all? My God, from the way you looked, I thought somebody had planted a bomb on one of our flights."

Mrs. Gough had seated herself by Scovil's desk and was spreading out work sheets in a businesslike manner. "This could be worse than a bomb," she said tightly. "I accepted the escalation in our debt burden, but I assumed that your final figures made provision for—"

"Why, Eleanor, you're scared," he teased. "I never figured you for one of our nervous Nellies."

"Scared to death," she admitted.

Scovil was still standing. He smiled down at her, and said: "Let me give you a tip. No matter how scared you are, the big thing is not to let the troops see it."

Doggedly she plowed ahead. "We have to be realistic about the kind of competition we'll be facing. You're projecting a profitable run in the same period as Toronto. But we're not just filling a gap in service this time."

"Damned right! We're leaving the minor leagues behind for good." Perching on the corner of the desk, Scovil let the familiar phrases unroll. "The thing is, Eleanor, we've got to expand or go under. A lot of people afraid to make the gut decisions don't realize that doing nothing is a decision, too."

Grateful for any statement with which she could concur, Eleanor said: "That's very true, Mitch. And I have no quarrel with the idea of expansion. It's how you go about it. For instance—"

"I knew I could count on you, Eleanor. Now, if ever, is the time to keep the faith."

With a valedictory pat on her shoulder, Scovil rose as if they had ironed out their differences.

"We haven't even started, Mitch," she said, without turning her head to follow his retreat. "I said the trick in expansion is how you go about it."

Reluctantly he came back several paces. "You're not wondering why I haven't gone the acquisition route, are you?" he asked, heavily patient. "I shouldn't have to explain to anyone in the business. Look what happened to People Express when they tried it. We'd end up mixing a union force with a nonunion force, and I'm too smart to make that mistake."

"That wasn't the only mistake People made," she said quickly. "They didn't bother to consult their employees beforehand."

This was too close to the bone for him.

"So what? The whole scheme was bound to fail. Getting the employees to ratify it wouldn't have helped."

"Perhaps," she said, still determined to get them to numbers instead of generalities. "But the basic problem at People was overextension. For the past two years we've had enough cash reserves to cover any glitches. But once we lose that cushion, we could be overextended ourselves."

"As if I didn't know that! California is going to need a lot of detail work, and that's where you come in. Remember, Eleanor, you're the one I always count on. And right now I need you to support me, not to start sniping at me."

"But I *am* helping you. All I'm doing is warning you about some of the risks that you haven't insured against sufficiently. If you'll just look at my figures for the first six months' operation, you'll see that—"

Gently Scovil pushed back the proffered notes. "I know all about the figures. It isn't as if I've got a lot of time to spare. I not only have to bring the Sloan up to scratch on the biggest deal Sparrow has ever made, I have to keep the police pointing away from all of us. C'mon, Eleanor, is it so much to ask you to stay off my back now?"

Instead of the pledge of allegiance he expected, he received an answer that confused him.

"That makes three times," Eleanor said drearily.

"Three what, for Christ's sake?"

"I've asked you to talk numbers three times. And what have you done? You've told me to keep the faith, you've accused me of sniping, and you've used the police as an excuse. Mitch, are you afraid to talk numbers?"

"Now, wait a minute," he flared. "You know the way we operate at Sparrow. Starting from scratch and getting where we are today was mostly a matter of faith. I wouldn't have gotten to first base if I stopped to analyze every little detail."

Mrs. Gough's lips had compressed into a thin line. "You didn't do it alone."

Promptly misinterpreting her remark, he forced a smile. "Always thinking of the employees, eh? Look, I'm not denying that the kids came up with some great cost-cutting ideas, but we're way beyond that stage."

"I was talking about your partners," she corrected. "I can remember nights that were nothing but analysis of every little detail. No matter whose idea we were talking about. It could have been yours, or mine . . . or Fritz's."

Today, mentioning Fritz Diehl's contribution was deliberate.

"You want to talk about what Fritz has done for Sparrow?" Scovil demanded savagely. "What about bribing Alan Whetmore?"

Eleanor swept on as if he had not spoken. "I can even remember Jim Vandervoort advancing some criticisms."

"We had to listen to Jim. He was our money man."

"He didn't put in a cent more than anybody else. And," she continued, forestalling his next remark, "we didn't need his name after we got started."

She was stopping up the holes, one by one.

"All right, all right. So we were a wonderful, merry team," he snarled. "That was a long time ago. Why bring it up now?"

"Because your plan needs some changes," she said half desperately. "For heaven's sake, Mitch, calm down and realize I'm trying to help you."

"That kind of help I can do without. And, for your information, every single item has been okayed by Clay."

Mrs. Gough opened her mouth, then closed it. Idle recriminations were not on the agenda. She intended to make every painful minute as productive as possible.

"Clay's an expert on the aircraft market, and he's also a first-rate chief of operations. But financial projections aren't his specialty, so that's why he overlooked some inconsistencies in the profit-sharing. After all, you covered it in one short paragraph."

"Oh, is that what this is all about?" He produced a wry grimace. "Why the hell didn't you say so, and we could have settled this ten minutes ago."

He finally circled the desk and sat down. With high hopes Mrs. Gough reached for the relevant document, only to have him lean back, his hands behind his neck.

"You see, Eleanor, if there's one thing I've learned in these last crazy five years, it's to take your jumps one at a time. We're right on the edge of the biggest one ever, and now's no time to rock the boat."

As he seemed to be straying farther and farther from a balance sheet, she said crisply: "California will require more people on the payroll. But you don't say anything about increased participation in either profit-sharing or stock purchasing."

"Now we've got to keep this under our hat for the time being," he said gravely. "You see, we're not going to enlarge either plan. The new employees are going to be handled on a more rational basis."

Mrs. Gough watched him in mounting consternation. "My God, a minute ago you were saying a two-tier labor system was asking for trouble."

"Well, it isn't going to be two-tier for long," he reassured her. "We'll never have a better time to phase out these programs. And once we've got California under our belt, I'll be thinking about a secondary stock offering. We certainly don't want that confused by the remnants of a lot of amateurism. Besides, there'll be more to come and . . ."

Scovil had almost forgotten that Mrs. Gough was on the other side of the desk. Lost in the pleasure of outlining his goals, he described an airline that not only embraced the United States, but covered the major international routes. Even then he was not done. He dreamily proceeded to innovative tie-ins with resorts and other ground facilities. But she was no longer listening.

He did not notice the lack of response until he had added the last flourish to his elaborate design. Suddenly snapping upright, he leaned across the desk and said:

"I know why you're looking that way, Eleanor. As usual you're letting yourself be overwhelmed by all the minor obstacles. You think Phoebe and her gang are going to raise hell and I should be worrying about that."

"You don't have to worry about Phoebe, you have to worry about me," she said with arctic clarity. "Who the hell do you think you are, Mitch? Wrecking years of work without so much as a pretense of consultation? I will not sit still through one disastrous piece of mismanagement after another."

He was taken aback. "I suppose it's been a shock, hearing about Sparrow's future all at once. But just because you're rattled is no reason to go wild."

"Sparrow doesn't have a future the way you're going. You can't even handle California, let alone the world. The only realistic figures in this whole thing are equipment and hangar costs. Your income projections assume current ticket rates instead of price-war rates. And as for labor!" She sounded as if she were strangling. "You're so far off the mark, it's pathetic. This great new rational approach makes no allowance for lowered productivity or middle-management salaries."

Before she could continue her indictment, he pounced. "Where have you been for the last five years? Sparrow has never—"

"Mitch, it's time you learned there's no such thing as a free lunch. And you'd better learn it fast or Sparrow will be dead on its feet within a year."

Instinctively Scovil fell back on a tried-and-true technique. "I thought I could rely on your loyalty," he said, swallowing his annoyance.

"These days I'm putting my marbles on responsibility. A lot of mistakes have been made, and it's my duty to rectify them."

The annoyance could no longer be contained.

"And since when have I made so many mistakes?" he asked sardonically.

"Oh, your mistakes aren't important," she said, with a flick of the hand that reduced Mitchell Scovil to one of the crowd. "I'm the one who ought to be shot. I've been spending my time protecting Sparrow from the wrong things. I honestly thought Alan Whetmore was a threat, but he was nothing compared to you."

Scovil's jaw had set and he was gripping the edge of the desk. "Would you spare me all your droning about duty and responsibility, Eleanor? And I can do without a lot of hot air about how you shoulder your burdens, too. You can forget them. I'm the one who's going to take care of Sparrow."

"Over my dead body," she said grimly. "I don't know where you got this idea of yourself as the Red Baron winging his way through the clouds, but it's got to stop."

"Whether you like it or not, I'm the CEO of this company," he retorted. "And where do you get off, trying to call the shots around here? Sparrow was your only chance at the big time. If we hadn't let you in on the ground floor, you'd still be back at Bayou."

But a newfound calm had descended on Eleanor Gough. After all the hesitations and equivocations, the stark simplicity of being Mitch's adversary was a relief. In a subdued way, she was almost carefree.

"You didn't just let me in out of goodness of heart. You needed an FAA expert. For that matter, you still do."

"I can go out and hire one tomorrow," he said, probing for soft spots. "They're a dime a dozen."

She was more than ready for him.

"Everybody's replaceable," she agreed. "Including you, Mitch."

White with rage, he lashed back. "Oh, so that's what you're plotting, is it? You think you can get support from the board?"

"Don't be absurd," she said mildly. "They're all your men."

"Well, at least you've got enough sense to see that. Face it, Eleanor, there's no place you can go."

Mrs. Gough could have been correcting a first-grader. "Yes, there is. I can go to Phoebe."

He stared at her for a moment, then burst into a contemptuous guffaw. "That's a good one. I can see you enlisting under Phoebe's banner and becoming her trusty lieutenant. I give it twenty-four hours."

"But then, your predictions haven't been a big success lately, have they?" she said indifferently as she scraped her rejected work sheets back into her folder.

Now that she was rising, it was Scovil who tried to prolong the discussion. "We've been through a lot together, Eleanor," he reminded her. "You don't want to march out of here and do something silly just because your feelings are hurt."

His gibes had fallen wide of their mark and so did his cajolery. Her hand was already on the knob when she replied.

"You know, Mitch, you're a bright boy in some ways," she said judiciously. "But you have as much business trying to go it alone as an amoeba."

For a full five minutes after her departure, Scovil sat slumped in his chair, staring straight ahead. Fritz Diehl had stalked through that doorway after a shouting match whose echoes still haunted Sparrow. Jim Vandervoort had passed through it on his way to a fatal car smash. And now Eleanor, inspired by God knew what vagary, had joined them.

As usual, Mitch Scovil saw it all from one point of view.

"I've always been willing to work with them," he muttered. "They're the ones who keep leaving."

❧ 21 ❧

Hatching Out

Meanwhile the police, primed by Everett Gabler, had begun fanning out over Boston. Alan Whetmore's address book gave them plenty to start with.

The woman behind the desk at the Orion Travel Agency did not have to send for records. "Wasn't it awful?" she cried at the first mention of Whetmore's name. "I could hardly believe it when I read the story."

"He was a customer of yours?"

"We did all his work," she said proudly. "Alan took a trip every five or six weeks. He'd go as far as he could on Sparrow, and we'd ticket him from there."

The officer's head came up alertly. Could Whetmore have been getting his funds out of town?

"Always to the same destination?"

"Oh no. He went to the in place for the season. It might be Acapulco or Vail or Sea Island."

She was in her mid-thirties, and her eyes sparkled as she ran down the list. The agency, only two blocks from Whetmore's apartment, was small and seemed to specialize in inexpensive package tours. Alan Whetmore had brought some cachet to Orion Travel.

"And it was always a trip for two," she continued. "Alan certainly knew how to show a girl a good time."

The hint of wistfulness was unmistakable. Whatever this travel agent did after hours, it did not measure up.

"He must have been running a pretty big account here," the officer reasoned. "How did he pay?"

Again there was no need for research.

"He always paid in cash," she said promptly. "Alan didn't like to run up big bills. He even paid for the hotel in advance."

The officer hated to puncture this anthem to the departed, but he felt obliged to query her tranquil acceptance.

"Didn't you think that was funny?"

"Oh no. It's great to see someone who's kicked the plastic habit."

The restaurant on the waterfront was not yet open for business, but that was all to the good. The manager infinitely preferred to deal with the police while his clientele was absent.

"Of course I remember Captain Whetmore," he said with dignity. "He was one of our regulars. Maurice usually waited on him."

Luckily Maurice was on lunch duty and had already arrived. When he was asked about Whetmore's habits, he put first things first.

"He was a good tipper. Of course I always made it a point to call him by name—he liked to be called Captain—and to give him good service. That impressed the lady with him."

"Was it the same one all the time?"

Maurice shook his head. "Oh no. In fact we rarely saw the same one twice."

Asked about payment and size of bill, Maurice was informative. "He always paid in cash and he never tried to save pennies." His voice lowered. "The wine was usually in the middle range."

* * *

It was more difficult with one of the girlfriends.

"Yes, I went on a ski weekend to Vail with Alan," she admitted readily. "We had a wonderful time."

She was obligingly forthcoming about her meeting with Whetmore—at a tanning salon—her relations with him, and even her disappointment when the calls ceased. But about payment she was blank.

"Well, I never paid attention to that," she said indignantly. "I don't think that would be very nice, do you?"

Mary Lou, the girl who worked at Kate McDermott's television station, had been more observant.

"I met him on Cape Cod over Labor Day," she said, "and then, out of the blue, he called up at the end of October. We had dinner once, and then I took him to a party at Kate's place. You know that Kate's married to the big boss over at Sparrow, don't you? I expect that's what Alan was really after, because that was it."

"He never called again?"

She grinned cheerfully. "That's right. But it wouldn't have done him any good. I got engaged the next week."

"You didn't happen to notice how he paid for dinner?"

"Cash," she said instantly. "I remember thinking I'd never seen anybody carrying a roll like that. He should have had more sense."

The story was the same everywhere. At many establishments, Alan Whetmore was the last surviving cash customer.

"He gave us a lot of business," the florist said. "But even if he ordered over the phone, he dropped by later to pay up."

The liquor store owner had even dropped hints.

"I told him I'd be happy to run an account," the owner recalled. "The less money I have in this place, the happier I am. But he said cash on the barrelhead was his motto. And you can't really argue with that."

The mechanic who lovingly tended the Jaguar had been surprised to receive crisp, new bills for a set of Michelins.

"But it made a nice change from some of the deadbeats I deal with," he growled.

After every interview there was a phoned report to Captain Lemoine complete with ballpark figure for Humphrey Belliers.

Finally the accountant looked up from his calculator.

"It isn't chicken feed, Greg," he said. "If these numbers are typical, we're talking sixty thousand at least since Whetmore's been in town. It could be double that."

Lemoine was beginning to wish he had never heard of Sparrow Flyways. "Did you get on to Nebraska?" he grunted.

"Yes, and Whetmore was normalcy itself out there. He ran up big bills, he juggled three credit cards and always ended up paying whopping interest charges, and"—Belliers, still wincing from Gabler's show of strength, underlined his final words—"and he drew checks to cash regularly."

"When did the break come?"

"Two weeks after he hit Boston. That's when Whetmore canceled two credit cards and stopped getting his cash from the bank. It's also when he moved out of a cheap hotel and took that fancy apartment, to say nothing of buying the Jag."

Lemoine was idly studying his notes of the last phone call. Now he crumpled them into a ball and pitched it in the general direction of the wastebasket.

"Okay, let's see what we've got," he said wearily. "Figuring in the safe deposit box, we're talking about a hundred, a hundred and fifty thousand in the last couple of years. That gives us a rough idea of the amount. The next question is, what did he do to get it?"

Belliers was a policeman first, an accountant second.

"Drugs," he said reflexively.

"No way! I had the same idea at the beginning. I checked back through every job the guy ever held. He was clean all the way—and in places with fatter opportunities. On top of that, these Sparrow pilots never know what run they'll be on. We can forget drugs."

"We can also scratch any sophisticated paper crime," Belliers said disapprovingly. "In that case, the money would have appeared as dividends from a dummy corporation or something."

Lemoine stretched himself like a big, lazy tomcat. "All right, scratch sophistication. There are still a lot of old-fashioned crooks around. I think Whetmore was one of them, working all by himself."

"It's obvious, isn't it?" Belliers was tiring of the game. "One pretty stupid guy being paid off for a year and a half and never having trouble with the police? I'd vote for blackmail."

"Just what I was thinking," Lemoine said cozily. "And it all started when Whetmore came to Boston."

This was undeniable, but Belliers thought they were going too fast. "That doesn't mean it has anything to do with the people at Sparrow."

Lemoine cocked a challenging eyebrow.

"Like hell it doesn't!"

The police were not the only ones moving into high gear. Eleanor Gough was making up for lost time with a vengeance.

"W-wonderful," Phoebe stammered, numbed by Eleanor's abrupt U-turn. "What convinced you? . . . I mean, after all this time . . ."

As her dazed response indicated, it was no longer glad, confident morning for Phoebe. Ever since rumors of bribery began circulating—and Mitch made absolutely sure they did—Sparrow's solidarity had been collapsing around her head. The nonmilitants, bleating in alarm, leaped to the conclusion that Phoebe had been duped. And, despite her heated protests, she was chagrined to find herself and her platform dismissed out of hand. Between wounded pride and frustration, she was already floundering.

Nevertheless, she tried to deal with Eleanor's bombshell. "Tell me, what made you change your mind so radically?"

Instead of answering, Mrs. Gough consulted a scribbled pad. "We're going to be operating on a very tight schedule. There's just enough time to file for a proxy fight."

"A proxy fight?"

Phoebe had never expected to have her bluff called.

"Of course," said Eleanor serenely. "And the annual meeting won't wait. So the first thing is to get the lawyers on to this."

Gulping, Phoebe could think of no immediate objection. "I can ask Bryan," she said unenthusiastically. "One of his friends is bound to do SEC work."

"No." The monosyllable was kind, but firm. "We need a Wall Street firm that knows about the airline industry and specializes in proxy battles."

Phoebe was flabbergasted to be on the receiving end of worldly wisdom from Eleanor Gough. "Well, you're the one who's talking about time pressure," she complained. "How are we going to find somebody like that in a flash?"

"Oh, I have a few contacts," said Eleanor, unconcerned. "I'm expecting Tom Hilyard to call back any minute."

Dimly Phoebe could recall that, in the early days of Sparrow, Mrs. Gough had spent a good deal of time with a Washington law firm. Phoebe had never known that Mrs. Gough had also been the telephonic voice of Bayou Airlines to Hilyard, Amory, and Smythe. So she was unprepared when Eleanor reported victory fifteen minutes later.

"I told Tom we were in a desperate hurry, so he got us an appointment for right after lunch. The twelve o'clock flight to New York will get us there in time. Will you have to trade shifts?"

With the sensation that she was being towed behind a speedboat, Phoebe found herself racing to consult Mavis, changing her clothes, and hurtling down to New York.

When they disembarked from their taxi in front of a towering skyscraper, Phoebe experienced some unfamiliar qualms. For years she had been proud of her ability to deal with the mighty. Before every quarterly report, she welcomed the outside auditor as one peer to another. When she was in charge of a field team, she sallied into banks without a tremor. But then she had been the embodiment of Sparrow Flyways. Now she was simply Phoebe Fournier.

Her sangfroid was never put to the test. From the moment that Chester Longley, senior partner, hailed Mrs. Gough as an old friend of Tom Hilyard, it was Eleanor who dominated the scene. Scrupulously she introduced Phoebe as the leader of the dissident employees.

"We think of ourselves as employee-shareholders," Phoebe proclaimed.

As if she were simply rounding out this statement, Mrs. Gough continued smoothly: "And Miss Fournier holds ten thousand shares herself."

Longley glanced at Phoebe with more interest as he apologized for not having had time to do his homework on Sparrow. He was, he said, only familiar with the gossip on the Street, then proceeded to take away Phoebe's breath with the extent of his knowledge.

"When Tom told me this was about an insider fight, I was really surprised," Longley admitted. "With the stock sliding, everybody expected an outside takeover."

"I know," said Mrs. Gough.

"Some people even claimed that Fritz Diehl over at A&P had engineered the trouble at Sparrow. Then, when Mitch Scovil was actually pulled in by the police, nobody knew what to think."

Eleanor did not spring to the defense of either man. Instead she saw an opportunity.

"Good," she said briskly. "With any luck, all the uncertainty about what's going on and who might be arrested should make the raiders back off. If we win the proxy fight in the interim, we have a chance to bring the stock back to a stronger position."

Rather sadly Longley accepted the fact that Mrs. Gough was not here to supply juicy details about Sparrow's crime wave. And, like all lawyers, he could not resist the chance to deflate a client's expectations.

"That's a damn big 'if.' You may be right about people backing off, but the proxy fight is something else again. You've got to realize that the odds are against you."

"Of course," she agreed quietly. "But most people starting a proxy fight don't have forty percent of the stock already in their corner."

"Scovil's got forty percent, too. And the institutional investors aren't going to get involved. They'll stand pat, and you may find your own support isn't as solid as you think."

This was unthinkable to Phoebe. "I can vouch for the employees," she said with something of her old assurance.

Longley shook his head. "Your people are willing to fight Scovil's policy, but that doesn't mean they're willing to dump him. And that applies even more to the small investors. They figured they were buying a piece of Mitch Scovil with their stock. They can't imagine Sparrow without him."

Phoebe swallowed. It had taken most of the flight to New York to digest Eleanor Gough's astonishing assumption of leadership. Manhattan's skyline was already visible when Phoebe admitted that she had never expected things to go this far. She wanted a Mitch Scovil willing to confess the error of his ways, a Mitch Scovil no longer imperiling the safety of Sparrow. But she, too, could not imagine a Sparrow without him.

"He could always stay on as president," she suggested.

"With a hostile board looking over his shoulder?" Longley snorted. "Forget it!"

"Then maybe he'll come to his senses," she faltered.

Mrs. Gough was dispassionate. "I wouldn't bank on it," she advised. "I expect it will be a fight to the death."

One of the wonders of this day of wonders was that Eleanor Gough did not share the general identification of Mitch Scovil with Sparrow. Fortunately Phoebe's bemusement was interrupted when Longley, having completed his formal warning, turned to the business at hand.

"I assume that you and Miss Fournier will be on the slate as inside directors. But some of the current outside directors are Scovil men, aren't they?"

Mrs. Gough agreed that they would have to be replaced and began to consider the claims of a well-known economist.

Phoebe, however, was lagging a step behind. "Me? A director?"

"Naturally," said Eleanor. "Given our kind of horizontal

management, it's absurd that we don't already have an employee on the board."

"I never thought of myself as a director. What a title!"

"And what a salary!" Mrs. Gough said with amusement. "Think about that, too."

After this Phoebe had to enter into the spirit of things. By the time the ladies had descended to the lobby and Eleanor had stepped aside to make a telephone call, Phoebe was reconciled to the new era in her life and congratulating herself on the caliber of her two allies.

Mrs. Gough was all smiles when she returned. "We're in luck," she announced. "John Thatcher can give us a few minutes. Let's see, the Sloan is on Exchange Place, so it must be two blocks down there."

Phoebe came to a dead halt. "Now wait a minute! We just bought ourselves a high-powered lawyer who told us the institutional investors won't budge. Why did we hire him, if we aren't going to listen to him?"

"That's the same mistake you made the first time you met Thatcher," Eleanor said reprovingly. "The Sloan is not an investor. It's a trustee."

John Thatcher had never lost sight of this distinction. It was the reason he had forced his secretary to squeeze twenty minutes from an already overcrowded docket. Miss Corsa deplored this cavalier imposition on his time, but she had not heard the latest bulletin from Everett Gabler. Now that blackmail had been added to the stew boiling away at Sparrow, Mrs. Gough's request for a meeting could be the harbinger of almost anything.

In spite of this open-minded attitude, Thatcher was surprised to learn that Eleanor was the new champion of the anti-Scovil forces.

"Considering the Sloan's very heavy position in Sparrow—and the rumors circulating on the Street—I thought it only right that you be informed before the official announcement of our SEC filing," she said sedately.

Phoebe was still clinging to the only constant in a shifting world. "That means forty percent now, with Eleanor's ten."

Mrs. Gough's methods were not so crude. "A great deal can happen between now and the annual meeting," she acknowledged. "No doubt some stockholders will change their minds and, of course, we hope that there will be a gain in our favor."

"Naturally," said Thatcher.

"It would be a help if the police resolve Alan Whetmore's murder, but we may not be that fortunate. In the meantime we'll be preparing a schedule of financial proposals which we'll send to you. Luckily Mr. Gabler will have completed his analysis by then."

As she continued, Thatcher inspected his guests with burgeoning irritation. They looked as if they were in church. Did they know that a short forty-eight hours ago, both Clay Batchelder and Fritz Diehl had been adding fuel to Wall Street's speculations? Was Phoebe aware that a good deal more than numbers had changed? And most important, did Eleanor Gough realize that, at this very moment, Captain Lemoine was waiting to cross-examine her? Sitting there in an attractive jacket of some rosy purple tweed with a wide silk bow at her throat, she certainly did not seem an appropriate subject for blackmail. But then, Thatcher reminded himself, neither had the last blackmail victim to surface at the Sloan. For the first time in his life he realized that an expression of ladylike attentiveness is the feminine equivalent of a poker face.

"I can certainly promise you that your material will receive very close consideration," he said noncommittally when Mrs. Gough had finished.

A stranger would have counted three poker faces in the room.

"That's all we can ask," she said, rising gracefully. "We realize that institutional investors hesitate to become embroiled in an insider battle. Phoebe and I only hope that the force of our arguments may persuade you."

Thatcher appreciated the tact with which Mrs. Gough had avoided telling him his business. She was simply making it impossible for him to forget the Sloan's anomalous position.

On the way to the airport, Phoebe felt honor-bound to bestow an accolade. "You handled that beautifully. I couldn't have done it. You managed to remind him that the Sloan is a trustee without ever coming out and saying so."

"We don't have to remind Thatcher of much. And he's the only one left who can pressure Mitch into backing down. Just in case you're still hoping for a peaceful solution."

Eleanor ended on an inquiring note, and Phoebe flushed.

"I'd prefer not to tear Sparrow apart."

Even to her own ears, this sentiment came poorly from the woman who had polarized Sparrow in the first place. Either Mrs. Gough was too generous to say so, or she was more interested in their meeting with Thatcher.

"Even if Thatcher doesn't oblige, the Sloan can still be very useful to us," she said reflectively. "I thought it was worthwhile to stop by, and I'm glad you agree now."

"Actually I meant more than just your tactics," Phoebe admitted. "It's the way you handled both Longley and Thatcher. You went ahead and got exactly what you wanted. I didn't know you had it in you."

"It's always been there. It just took a while to come out."

Phoebe was making a discovery. "You know what, Eleanor," she said in tones of congratulation, "you've become liberated."

Mrs. Gough did not agree.

"Rich women have always been liberated," she replied coolly. "Some of them were born that way. The rest of us have to adjust. I've never had any reason to throw my weight around until now. But, if Sparrow is going to be maintained in a form we recognize, it's going to take every ounce we can muster."

A hideous suspicion dawned on Phoebe. "Is that why you told Longley about my ten thousand shares?"

"It certainly didn't hurt."

But Phoebe was true to her generation. "I earned those shares," she said rebelliously. "I didn't have them handed to me on a platter."

Mrs. Gough, with one eye on the taxi meter, was fumbling in her purse for a billfold. Without looking up, she said:

"Chester Longley doesn't care."

22

SECRETIVE HABITS

Back in Boston, Clay Batchelder wanted to move on to Don Islington's latest concessions. Scovil, however, continued to gnaw another bone.

"Where does Fritz get off?" he demanded. "I have to lie low because of all the stinking publicity and I haven't done a damned thing. Meanwhile he gets to parade around as if he's Mr. Clean."

"Take it easy, Mitch. The police are working on it."

Scovil shook his head angrily. "We haven't got all the time in the world. You saw what happened to the stock when Lemoine pulled me in."

"It was just a blip." Batchelder sounded as if he were trying to persuade himself more than Scovil.

"One more little blip like that and Fritz will have his opening."

Batchelder was more optimistic. "Fritz has plenty of problems of his own. He can't have much clout at A&P anymore."

"I'd like to be sure of that. And what the hell are the police doing? For two weeks they've been all over the place. Now, when they could do some good, they disappear."

"That's because they've quit concentrating on Sparrow," Clay insisted. "They're probably digging away at A&P."

"Maybe so, but I'd like to see some action from Lemoine."

The opportunity came sooner than Scovil expected. After a final round of arithmetic by Humphrey Belliers, Captain Lemoine was back at Sparrow.

"We're going to send in the fraud squad and pull this place apart," he announced.

"That's crazy," Scovil retorted. "I told you where Whetmore was getting his money."

"For two years?" Lemoine asked ironically. "Talk sense, Scovil. Whetmore had somebody around here by the short hairs."

"Diehl was here two years ago. Maybe Whetmore had something on him."

"Like what?"

Scovil was only sure of one thing. "Whatever it was, it had nothing to do with Sparrow."

"Like hell it didn't." Lemoine hunched forward aggressively. "That ploy by Whetmore at your meeting was pure extortion. He was on to something so good, he thought the sky was the limit."

"Well, he didn't get it!"

"No," Lemoine agreed softly, "but somebody had to kill him to shut him up."

For once, Scovil was silenced.

If Mitch was rocked, Clay was belligerent.

"Send your bloody accountants in," he invited. "We run a clean shop. You won't find a damned thing."

"Oh yeah? I suppose somebody forked over a hundred and fifty thousand for the fun of it."

This was the first time Clay had heard Belliers's final estimate. "A hundred and fifty thou?" he repeated.

"Starting from two weeks after Whetmore got to Sparrow," Lemoine said remorselessly.

Batchelder's weakness had passed.

"So? We've got a whole mob of people working here. Maybe he recognized somebody who didn't want to be recognized. Maybe he saw somebody in Boston. It could be anyone."

"You're forgetting one little detail. The killer could put his hands on a hell of a lot of money. That narrows the circle as far as I'm concerned."

Batchelder's chin shot forward. "We're not the richest guys in Boston."

"Maybe not, but then Whetmore's price got too stiff for somebody, didn't it?"

Scovil and Batchelder had both been willing to lock horns with Captain Lemoine. Mrs. Gough was another proposition altogether. When she finally returned from New York, her thoughts were elsewhere.

"I've been waiting for you for hours," Lemoine complained.

Mrs. Gough was laying down an attaché case. "I had to go to New York," she said unapologetically.

The captain was not feeling reasonable.

"You've been here steadily ever since Whetmore's murder. It's funny that you should go missing the minute we find the real motive."

She was more pleased than alarmed by his disclosure.

"I always said suspecting Fritz was nonsense."

Her complacency irritated Lemoine. "It's a lot closer to home than that," he said. "Somebody around here has been blackmailed by Whetmore for two years."

"Blackmail?" She considered this, then rejected it. "That's absurd."

And when Lemoine thundered the facts at her, she promptly counterattacked.

"What could possibly be a reason for blackmail at Sparrow?"

He lashed back: "I don't know yet. But if Whetmore could find out, so can I."

"You didn't know Alan Whetmore, Captain," she replied, unimpressed. "It's inconceivable that he unearthed any company secrets. Even if there were any, he was too stupid."

"He was stupid enough to back a killer into a corner. There I'll go along with you." Lemoine was almost yelling at her.

"Besides, we all know what's going on at Sparrow."

"I wouldn't put it past the three of you to be in this together."

She shrugged her shoulders with the same exasperating indifference. "We're not that much of a team."

"Okay, you're such an expert, you tell me," he snarled. "Come on, make a guess. What could there be that's worth that much hush money?"

Her eyes finally met his.

"Absolutely nothing," she said flatly.

That was not the line they were taking in the employee cafeteria. There speculation was running rampant.

"But everything here is open to our inspection!"

"Inside the company," said someone shrewdly. "But what about outside?"

"Such as?" demanded a skeptic.

"Taxes!"

"Insider trading!"

"Supplier kickbacks!"

The chorus was a credit to their general knowledge more than anything else.

"Ah, use your heads," the skeptic said disgustedly. "Somebody murdered Alan Whetmore after paying him off in a big way. Why do all that if you could waltz down to the IRS and pay back taxes and a penalty?"

There was a brief silence, broken at last by a new, thoughtful voice. "You're right. Those things wouldn't cause enough grief to be worth killing for. But I'll tell you one thing that would blow this place sky-high."

Everyone looked expectant.

"What if there was monkey business with the profit-sharing plan?" asked the genius.

The silence was almost reverent.

"Oh, God, we'd be the ones committing murder," someone said, awe-struck.

Norman Pitts wanted to get everything absolutely clear. "You mean, if management was skimming a slice off the top?"

"You've got to admit that'd be something worth covering."

But now the voices of reason made themselves heard.

"I don't believe they could get away with it. We keep an eagle eye on that fund."

"And Alan Whetmore is supposed to have found out? Act your age. He couldn't even read the financial page."

"It'd be too big a risk. Why should they do it?"

The genius went that one step too far. "Suppose it was just one of them? Somebody with a fancy lifestyle to keep up?"

There was instant protest.

"Come on, that's Mitch you're talking about."

They were still arguing when Everett Gabler, at an adjoining table, quietly left the cafeteria.

Normally, after Captain Lemoine removed himself from Sparrow, the three partners would gather to plan a common defense. When Clay Batchelder appeared on schedule, Scovil realized he had to reveal the breach with Eleanor.

"What the hell can have gotten into her, Clay?" he asked for the third time. "I think Eleanor's gone bananas. When she left, she was talking about joining Phoebe. If I weren't so fed up with her, I'd feel sorry for her."

Like most men baffled by the intransigence of a woman, Mitch expected automatic support from his fellows. But Clay had no sympathy to spare.

"You two picked a beautiful time to square off with each other," he said apathetically. "Don't we have enough to worry about?"

"That's exactly what I told her," Scovil replied. He was quartering the room, flinging his comments at Batchelder from every corner. "Of course, she can't do any real harm. Phoebe doesn't need help to lob her grenades. What can Eleanor add?"

"Ten percent," Batchelder grated.

Scovil paused in midstride. "What?"

"Eleanor owns ten percent of the stock."

"Well, of course, in a manner of speaking . . ."

Clay summoned the energy to bellow: "No, Mitch! There's no manner of speaking about it. Her ten percent is counted just the same as yours or mine."

Scovil did not really believe it. "All right, all right. What difference does it make?"

"A lot. After all, Phoebe's been hinting about a proxy fight."

Scovil brushed this away. "That's not really Phoebe's style. She's just letting off steam."

"Maybe so, but what bothers me is the Sloan's reaction. Thatcher won't make any decision until he sees the final report and Gabler doesn't seem to be in any hurry."

"There are other banks."

Clay Batchelder closed his eyes briefly. "You think they don't read the papers, too? For God's sake, Mitch, Phoebe tied up half the air traffic in the country and your picture with the police made television. Do you suppose the Bank of Boston is going to fall over itself to get our business?"

"Then there's another way out. You said it yourself. The Sloan holds twenty percent. They back us and that more than evens things up."

"I don't know." Clay was dubious. "There's a big difference between a temporary labor grievance and a management split."

"So what?" Scovil said with undiminished confidence. "I'll get Thatcher back here and really sell him."

"God, I hope so. Just see to it that Eleanor doesn't give him an earful."

Mitch Scovil had been so astonished by Mrs. Gough's defection that he had never considered the practical problems involved. Now he stood staring down at the bare surface of his desk as if there were words of wisdom inscribed on the walnut.

At last he came to a decision. "I think you should talk to Eleanor, Clay."

Batchelder gaped at him. It was received truth at Sparrow that Scovil was the one with the magic touch.

"Just what did you two fight about?" Clay asked suspiciously.

"How can you call it a fight?" Scovil temporized. "I barely got a word in edgewise. You know what it's like when Eleanor gets all windy and uplifted. There was something about not working together."

The atmospherics were familiar to Clay. When Mitch was revising history, getting the truth was like pulling teeth.

"Employee democracy again?" Clay hazarded.

"Not really. Oh, there was a passing reference, but there was a lot of yapping about shouldering responsibility."

Clay tried again. "Was it the Pittsburgh mess?" he asked.

"Pittsburgh wasn't mentioned. She was so damned elevated I couldn't tell what she was talking about." Carefully omitting all reference to California, Scovil retailed some of Mrs. Gough's more generalized statements.

Batchelder was looking more and more uneasy. "Let me see if I've got this straight," he said slowly. "Eleanor made a big mistake, she got Sparrow into a mess, and now she's got to atone?"

"And her idea of how to do it is a real beaut! Splitting Sparrow apart!" For the first time Scovil noticed his partner's dismay. "Now what have I said?"

"Nothing, nothing." Hastily Batchelder changed the subject. "You haven't given me a lot to work on with Eleanor."

"God knows what'll do the trick. The way she's going, I'm beginning to think she's reached the age when they all go flaky."

"That could be it."

Scovil wheeled.

"I was joking, Clay," he said shortly. "Why don't you try the old line about pulling together for the good of Sparrow?"

"From what you say, she's not so keen on team spirit right now."

Like everyone who has passed the dirty work to someone else, Scovil was now brimming over with useful tips.

"Look, I know how you can get to her. For Chrissake, we've got the police back on our necks. Tell her this time they're going after both of us. Tell her they're accusing us of paying blackmail."

Batchelder shook his head. "She already knows, Mitch. Lemoine grilled her, too."

"He did?"

"Why shouldn't he? Eleanor's got as much at stake as we have, and she's a rich woman." Batchelder produced a wry smile. "She's probably richer than I am. After all, her kids were off her hands when we started."

Scovil blinked, then rapidly changed his argument. "Then we're all in the same boat. We thought we'd gotten rid of Lemoine, and he's after us again. She's got to see that."

"Sure, she just loved the way you fingered Fritz Diehl. If you ask me, that's probably what set her off."

Batchelder was rising stiffly as if he had aged twenty years in a day.

"Maybe I'd better just play it by ear," he suggested from the doorway. "But, Mitch, don't expect any miracles."

After he had left, Scovil sat down to the task of organizing his thoughts. He had to establish some priorities. There was the Sloan Guaranty Trust and a potential proxy fight. But above all there was Eleanor Gough.

"Oh my God," exclaimed Scovil, horrified. "That can't be it."

By six o'clock John Thatcher was announcing a decision to Charlie Trinkam.

"There really isn't much choice. I've received pressing invitations to Boston from Scovil, Everett, and Rupert Vernon."

Charlie had no doubt who counted. "What did Ev say?"

"He has not only finished his review of the financials, he feels the police investigation is reaching a critical stage."

"As soon as the cops stopped messing around with alibis

and wrenches and started concentrating on money, Ev was bound to get interested," Charlie observed.

Thatcher recalled Gabler's modest account of his triumph with Alan Whetmore's checkbook.

"More than that, I'm afraid. Everett has become a participant. In any event, he will be making considerable demands on my time. So, while I am at Sparrow . . ."

"While you're dealing with the gloom and doom, I'll be holding Rupert's hand. Good!" Charlie completed the sentence.

Trinkam was a complete professional who could handle any necessary chore, but he made no secret of his preferences. "I like Rupert's style," he continued. "There's always plenty of action when he's around."

Thatcher also valued Rupert Vernon.

"But you may be getting the short end of the stick, Charlie," he murmured. "Murder cases have been known to generate fireworks too."

✃ 23 ✄

A MODEST FORAGER

The man John Thatcher listened to was Everett Gabler. This might be a humdrum fact of life for Charlie Trinkam, but Mrs. Gough regarded it as a rare opportunity. Her campaign began with lunch the next day.

Predictably, Gabler was still doing research of his own.

"I understand that you have broken with Scovil, but I'm not altogether sure why," he said as soon as the salad arrived.

"The financials," she said briefly. "You've been examining them, too, so I don't have to explain my reaction."

"You've left it until quite late, haven't you?"

Her apology came in the form of an explanation. "Yes, but after Fritz Diehl left, Mitch began shouldering me aside, and I actually let him get away with it." She smiled wanly. "I thought, because Mitch and Clay had been executives, they must be the experts. When you consider how long I worked for so-called experts, that's pretty silly, isn't it?"

"That would depend on the people you worked for," Gabler said cautiously.

She laughed aloud. "I was personal assistant to the president at Bayou when old Mr. Perkins retired and Bill Johnson was promoted. Poor Bill! He couldn't run a corner gas station without help. I ended up doing his job and covering for him. You know the sort of thing I mean."

Everett did, indeed. Currently, two overpaid incompetents at the Sloan were being kept afloat by their secretaries. He had always accepted the situation as a special dispensation from Providence, without wondering how it seemed to Mrs. Molineaux and Miss Teague.

"Yes," he said minimally.

Fortunately Eleanor was more concerned with Sparrow than the Sloan.

"Has it ever occurred to you, Everett, how much you don't see when things are going well?" she asked philosophically. "Mitch was freezing me out, he was alienating the employees, he was turning Clay into a yes-man, and I never noticed because Sparrow was leaping from one success to another."

Gabler wondered if she were deluding herself. In Thatcher's account of the early days at Sparrow, Scovil and Batchelder had remained behind the scenes while Jim Vandervoort and Fritz Diehl cast an Ivy League gloss over the partnership. Mrs. Eleanor Gough had not figured in those reminiscences. Of course, this could have been a distortion by Scovil's memory, rather than hers.

Ignoring such thoughts, he resorted to homily. "Success is no excuse," he said sternly.

Mrs. Gough had already learned this lesson. "How right you are," she agreed. "I didn't wake up until we ran into snags. Even then, all I did was try persuasion. It took me far too long to realize Mitch is incapable of effective action."

She paused to sip her wine, waiting to see if Gabler would rise to the bait. Everett, however, seized on something else.

"By snags, I suppose you refer to the major carriers retaliating with price cuts?"

Somewhat disappointed, she began again. "Yes, Pittsburgh was just a symptom. But Mitch was too stubborn to drop the route."

"If it was symptomatic, then surely a similar battle would have to be fought elsewhere."

"Under more favorable circumstances. We can afford to pick where we'll fight, and that should be where Sparrow has an advantage."

Finally Gabler gave the response she wanted. "That sounds like an elementary managerial decision. Why didn't Scovil make it?"

Mrs. Gough wanted to ensure that the Sloan understood not only what should be done, but who should do it. "Mitch has been running in circles ever since People Express collapsed."

Gabler knew there was more to it than that.

"Isn't he also worried about a takeover threat by A&P?"

"Oh, for heaven's sake," Mrs. Gough said impatiently. "Yes, Fritz Diehl said something like that—two years ago. I had forgotten the whole thing, and I'm willing to bet Fritz had, too. Then airlines began folding all over the place and Mitch remembered. That's why he sees Fritz's dark hand behind everything."

Everett disapproved of runaway emotions. "That sounds very close to paranoia," he sniffed.

"Mitch isn't paranoid, he's schizophrenic," she shot back.

"Oh?"

Mrs. Gough was not pulling her punches. "He's promoted this image of himself as a lone wolf and now he really believes it. Actually Mitch was a lot happier when he had partners sharing the responsibility."

Scovil's countless public appearances during the last two years flashed before Gabler's eye—television panels, Wall Street talks, magazine profiles.

"He certainly gives the impression of being happy with his lot."

"Like me, he didn't feel it until recently," Eleanor said tellingly. "He's noticing now, all right. That's why he goes through the motions of conferring with Clay about everything."

"And your defection must be adding to the tension in the office."

Mrs. Gough was honest enough to admit that she had not been tested.

"Mitch still thinks I'll come around, so he's being very polite. Even under provocation." Her lips twitched. "This morning, when he asked me to take care of something, I told him to do it himself. And he even tried to smile."

Gabler was not surprised at Mrs. Gough's malice. Turn-about, in corporations, is often more than fair play.

"And what does he think will bring you around?"

"He has two strings to his bow. First, he's got Clay Batchelder sweet-talking me. Poor Clay, he's more likely to drive me up a wall. Then there's the police investigation. At the moment we're all suspects. When that's over, Mitch expects things to be normal again."

Her overview of Sparrow had inevitably arrived at murder. Quite soberly she continued:

"I don't think it's occurred to him that things could be even worse."

Her realism made it possible for Everett to ask his next question.

"Does the blackmail theory seem sensible to you?"

The answer she had given Captain Lemoine would not do for Everett Gabler. "Sometimes it does, and sometimes it doesn't," she said slowly. "There's been a lot of talk and you've probably heard most of it. But I know what's going on at Sparrow—and so do the employees and the outside auditors."

Everett had encountered too many auditors mortified by the skulduggery that had eluded their inspection.

"So you think it's impossible?" he asked skeptically.

"Not impossible, but very difficult. Captain Lemoine may think that Alan was saying to Mitch: *Make me a director or I spill the beans*. But I don't believe it for a minute. First, Alan couldn't catch something that the rest of us missed. And Mitch may have his faults, but he doesn't steal from employees. Not now, and not five years ago."

Unenthusiastically Gabler moved on to a broader arena.

"Everybody has a life outside the office."

"True. Both my children have phoned to say the police are checking my background. But it's not as if we were three mysterious Cubans who created Sparrow to launder Mafia money. The way we started Sparrow is history, and our lives are open books."

Gabler, who believed in original sin, retreated.

"Yes, but your proxy fight has introduced a time dimension for Scovil," he pointed out. "He has to deal with it before the annual meeting."

Mrs. Gough was ready to call a spade a spade. "That's why Mitch wants John Thatcher here, and," she continued with impeccable precision, "it sure as hell is why I dragged you to lunch."

It was, Everett acknowledged, a salient reminder. Before he could agree that the ball was now in John Thatcher's court, his companion's attention wandered.

"Good heavens," she said, genuinely amused. "So much for Mitch doing his share of the chores. He's shoveled it off onto Clay."

Her glance was fixed over Gabler's right shoulder. Resisting the temptation to swivel, he asked: "A luncheon obligation?"

"Something like that. Clay is towing around Alan Whetmore's brother, and it looks like heavy going. Do you mind if we ask them to join us?"

Clay Batchelder was visibly relieved as he came to rest by their table.

"We're only here for a drink," he announced. "Vince has an appointment in town."

Mrs. Gough competently ran through the social niceties, ending with: "We didn't expect you back in Boston so soon, Mr. Whetmore."

"I wasn't planning on it," Whetmore explained. "But, when the police told me about Alan's fifty thousand, it was worthwhile getting a lawyer to start probate here. Maybe that sounds callous, but you don't know what it's like when money's tight."

Eleanor Gough had been through this before, and she had no intention of letting Whetmore establish the rest of them as plutocrats.

"Don't be too sure of that," she said cheerfully, then turned to explain to Gabler. "Mr. Whetmore is a mailman back in Ohio, but he doesn't know that Clay's brother is a mailman, too."

Vincent Whetmore shifted tactics.

"Of course I'm thinking of Mother," he said virtuously. "At her age she needs all the help she can get. I can't do as much as I'd like because I still have one in college, and you wouldn't believe what that costs."

Although it had not been his intention, Whetmore had stumbled onto the one topic capable of uniting the group. Clay had been putting a son through college during the first lean year at Sparrow. Mrs. Gough still shuddered at the thought of tuition. By the time Vincent Whetmore had been given a resume of every cent spent by the Batchelder and Gough families for higher education, he was on the defensive.

"It would be great if there was more than just the fifty thousand." Sheer disbelief took over. "My God, Captain Lemoine told me Alan got through a hundred thousand in walking-around money. He must have stashed something."

As a man who had reviewed Alan Whetmore's checkbook, Everett could speak with authority. "Don't raise your hopes too high," he said. "Your brother seems to have regarded money as something to spend rather than to save. He did, however, acquire at least one salable asset. Perhaps you don't know about the car."

"A car?" said Vincent Whetmore, in tones conjuring up a rusted-out Ford Escort.

"A Jaguar. Fully paid for. What's more, I think I can give you the name of a man who'll be interested."

Gabler never threw away business cards. This necessarily meant that he had to shuffle a sizable deck before he came to Fine Foreign Imports.

"According to them, the car has appreciated since your brother's purchase. But I'm sure you will wish to obtain several offers before you make any decision," he said, tactfully proffering advice.

When Vincent Whetmore left, he was still clutching the card, bemused by the form Alan's estate was assuming.

Clay Batchelder seized the opportunity to express his thanks. "That was a help, Eleanor. It wasn't easy finding something to talk about."

"You should have made Mitch do his own dirty work," she told him. "That's what I did, and it could become a habit."

Clay grimaced. "It wasn't the ideal time. Lemoine was practically accusing Mitch of murder when the victim's brother walked in on us. I'm too old-fashioned to suggest they go out to lunch together."

She saw the difficulties.

"By the way, Eleanor," Clay continued diffidently, "Lemoine wants to go over our personal finances. I don't know how you feel about it, but Mitch told him to go to hell, said he wouldn't see a thing without a court order."

Under Gabler's clinical scrutiny, Mrs. Gough flushed, but she never hesitated. "Certainly not. I don't think Captain Lemoine—or anybody—should be encouraged to go on unlimited fishing expeditions."

⮟ 24 ⮞

GROUND FEEDERS

When Everett Gabler left the luncheon table, he went directly to his hotel, where he found Thatcher and Charlie Trinkam unpacking. They both fastened on Mrs. Gough's rationale for deserting Scovil.

"If she were in politics," Thatcher said, "she would simply be following a great tradition. She'd be distancing herself from Mitch Scovil."

"Before he gets sent up the river, you mean?" Charlie considered this prospect, then went beyond it. "If that happens, she's sure positioning herself to grab the reins."

"Yes," Thatcher agreed. "But what eludes me is whether she's doing it to ensure continuity for Sparrow or whether she's been waiting for the ideal moment."

Charlie waved expansively. "Well, Ev should know. He's just been pumping her."

Gabler, however, shook his head. Women, in his opinion, were always incalculable. "That's impossible for me to say. You have to realize that everybody was apprehensive about Sparrow long before Whetmore's murder."

"That's a pretty shaky bunch there," Charlie observed.

"One quiver in their P-E ratio and they start falling to pieces."

"Their uneasiness has a more fundamental basis than that," Gabler pointed out. "Sparrow is moving from one plateau to another. Each faction—whether it's Scovil or Miss Fournier or Eleanor Gough—claims to be the only one grasping this. Quite the contrary is true. They all realize what has happened. Where they differ is in their response."

Thatcher could almost hear the earnest voices ringing in his ears.

"You're absolutely right, Everett," he said. "Scovil wants to transform Sparrow into a major carrier. Phoebe's solution, on the other hand, is to hunker down and weather the storm. What is Mrs. Gough proposing?"

"She didn't tell me." Everett smiled thinly. "I thought she might have been more forthcoming with you in New York."

Thatcher recalled the scene in his office. "Hardly. You see, she wasn't alone with me. My guess is that Phoebe Fournier is simply assuming they agree on the future of Sparrow, and Mrs. Gough is not rocking that boat until she has to."

"She's a clever woman," said Gabler, clearly with mixed emotions. "At lunch she let Sparrow's record speak for itself in order to underline Scovil's shortcomings. Her theory is that he is unbalanced about Fritz Diehl."

Charlie had always been the Sloan's expert on women. "That settles it," he said decisively. "She's out to snatch the company."

"Always assuming there's still a company to snatch." Thatcher turned to Gabler. "Don't keep us in suspense, Everett. What are your conclusions?"

Scrapping mountains of preliminary material, Gabler answered: "Sparrow is in a precarious situation, and Scovil is the last man to be in charge."

Charlie whistled. "That's telling 'em, Ev!"

It never pays, thought Thatcher, to force a prolix man into brevity. "Perhaps we should turn our attention to the background data for these views," he murmured.

"Sparrow's financial position is intrinsically sound," Gabler began. "Naturally they face the problems associated with spectacular growth. They need to regroup and reorganize their operations. Their earnings will again be disappointing at the end of this quarter, but an executive willing to cut his losses could handle this."

"That's scarcely as ominous as I expected from your resume," Thatcher remarked.

If anything, Gabler was pleased. "Wait! Scovil's plans for a transcontinental route include a fleet of new aircraft and executive-class service."

"Phoebe doesn't think the public will buy the new image," Thatcher remembered.

"They may not have the opportunity," Gabler retorted. "Before he starts, Scovil will deplete Sparrow's cash reserves and incur substantial interest charges."

Charlie Trinkam was saddened. "And I thought he was one of our boy geniuses."

"He is neither." Gabler always deprecated hyperbole. "When deregulation came along, Scovil had the imagination to create a new kind of airline. But he seems unable to adjust to further changes."

"You shouldn't be surprised at that, Charlie. It's the human condition," Thatcher observed. "All revolutionaries become conservatives in the end."

Charlie always enjoyed the larger view. "Okay," he said amiably. "So we need a Maoist to run Sparrow. Do we import him?"

Ignoring all distractions, Gabler forged ahead. "Even more threatening is the absence of structure at Sparrow. Say what you will, the corporate form has provided American industry with useful guidelines."

Charlie Trinkam could see the lecture coming. "I remember hearing something about that," he said vainly.

But there was no way to hold Everett down.

"Sparrow, with its horizontal management and its stock programs, has blurred the distinction between the stockholders, labor, and management."

"Come on," Charlie objected. "Lots of companies sell

stock to their employees, and the unions are beginning to demand a voice in management."

Gabler insisted Sparrow was quite different. "This stock program represents more than a drop in the bucket. As Miss Fournier discovered, it amounts to thirty percent and can be voted as a block. Furthermore, these same young people routinely make management decisions and implement them without any consultation whatsoever. They do not know whether they are working for an hourly wage, a stock bonus, or capital gains. In fact," he concluded, "Sparrow has no guidelines and I doubt if it should be called an American corporation at all."

"Very well, Everett, it can be a miserable mongrel," Thatcher conceded, "or anything else you please. The question is, does this hybrid form pose a danger?"

"In one sense it does. Almost nobody at Sparrow understands the accommodations that may be required. Scovil has surrounded himself with thousands of investor-managers. Yet he's incensed when his policies are challenged. Even your Miss Fournier, John, has not assimilated the implications."

From the tone of Gabler's voice every time he mentioned her, Thatcher had expected, sooner or later, to be held responsible for Phoebe's existence. "She has some unusual accomplishments to her credit, Everett," he said mildly.

"Possibly. But I have spoken with her at some length," said Gabler, suggesting that no investigative stone had been left unturned. "She signally fails to comprehend that she has been paid with the capital gains on what began as penny stock. She presents herself as a role model without ever wondering if such rewards are still available."

"Fat chance!" Charlie said. "The only way you get a return like that is by starting at zilch."

Thatcher was less interested in truisms than in an earlier remark.

"You said almost nobody at Sparrow recognized the situation, Everett. Is there an exception?"

Gabler pursed his lips. "Mrs. Gough admits that from the beginning, she had no idea how the system would develop. Her attitude has been that it should remain infinitely flexible. If that woman is to be believed, she is happy with perpetually fluid arrangements." He did not conceal bewilderment. "They say there really are people like that."

"A lady Maoist," said Charlie, pleased.

Thatcher, thinking of the neat silk bow and the rosy tweed jacket, was kindly. "She's not exactly what you're visualizing, Charlie."

But as he spoke, he was foreseeing that if, by any miracle, Mrs. Gough emerged victorious at Sparrow, the ideal person to deal with her would be Charlie.

"Well, Everett," Thatcher continued, "you've told us about the financial and institutional land mines lying ahead. What about the criminal ones? Are the police still talking blackmail?"

"No evidence has emerged about any other source of under-the-table money for Whetmore."

Charlie liked the sound of it. "That's some mess they have at Sparrow. There isn't a single thing they've missed —murder, strikes, and now blackmail. And the cops have got to be thinking in terms of the three partners. Who else has that kind of cash to put in a brown paper bag?"

"There is no logical necessity for the culprit to be at Sparrow. There is all of Boston too," Gabler said fairmindedly.

"Where, according to you," Charlie riposted, "Whetmore spent all his spare time with third-rate models, not with millionaires."

Thatcher pointed out that any policeman in his right mind would dispatch three conspicuous suspects before sifting through an entire city population.

"What bothers me is the underlying cause for blackmail. When it emerges, it could be devastating to Sparrow. Whetmore put a high price on what he knew, and somebody was willing to pay it."

"It could be anything," said Charlie cheerfully. "Let's say that Whetmore recognizes Clay Batchelder as part of the gang that kidnapped Patty Hearst. Or he knows Scovil's marriage is bigamous, because there's a wife and four starving children in Seattle. Or Eleanor Gough's kids are by-blows of the Ayatollah. Or—"

"Thank you, Charlie," Thatcher interrupted. "In summary, we seem to have storm clouds threatening Sparrow from every direction of the compass."

Nature had never intended Everett Gabler for benign and sunny conditions.

"Very true," he said with quiet satisfaction, "and therefore I have a suggestion. In view of these circumstances, can the Sloan secure judicial relief from the prohibition against selling the stock?"

Thatcher always welcomed an occasion to show his talented staff that he was far ahead of them.

"Not without the support of the family—which is why I phoned Jim Vandervoort's widow yesterday."

Everett nodded approvingly. The guardian of the juvenile beneficiary was the appropriate person to consult. "Did she tell you how strongly her husband felt about Sparrow?"

"No, she didn't tell me anything. In fact, she could barely remember Vandervoort," Thatcher reported. "A year ago she became Mrs. Keith Rossiter. More important, two weeks ago she gave birth to triplets."

Some men can be diverted by trivia; others are made of sterner stuff.

"So?" Gabler demanded.

Thatcher could have described the background noises he had encountered. There had been the clatter of falling objects, there had been questions and counterquestions, and —easily audible above the general din—there had been the piercing shrieks of dissatisfied infants.

"She says she isn't organized yet," he said evasively.

"The poor girl is probably worn to a thread," said Charlie with ready sympathy.

A reminiscent smile played over Thatcher's lips. Mrs. Rossiter had certainly sounded harried and distracted, but the predominant impression had been exultation.

"I wouldn't say that. But it comes to the same thing, because I have waived my claims to any of Mrs. Rossiter's attention for at least another month."

"Why didn't you tell her this is essential?" Gabler persisted.

Charlie Trinkam now repaid the lecture on corporate function.

"And you call yourself a trust officer, Everett," he said reproachfully.

"What does that have to do with it?"

"Trusts are created to facilitate the orderly transfer of property from one generation to the next," Charlie intoned. "If they closed the stock market tomorrow, we could still get along. The only absolute essential to our function is a next generation. Without that, where would we be?"

Gabler, who knew that Mrs. Rossiter's efforts could not possibly outweigh his own, glared. "Do you realize that we have spent the better part of this last hour discussing three women?"

Charlie's mock applause was not intended as balm.

"And you never even noticed," he said. "I do believe that somebody has been raising your consciousness."

"Tcha!" said Everett Gabler.

❧ 25 ❧

INLAND HABITAT

Humphrey Belliers, who had been so scornful of Alan Whetmore, would have approved of Sparrow's partners. They believed in elaborate stratagems for increasing income and lessening taxes. At the first threat of surveillance by Captain Lemoine, they all decided to heap complexity upon complexity.

The Batchelders had succeeded in life beyond their wildest dreams, and usually when Clay produced papers, Mrs. Batchelder silently reached for a pen. Today the act stirred memories.

"Didn't you shift everything around just a couple of months ago?" she asked suspiciously.

Batchelder realized that, for once, the federal government was going to be useful.

"Tax reform, Marjorie," he said as if that explained everything.

Marjorie never admitted ignorance.

"Oh yes," she said wisely. "They talked about it on 'Donahue.'"

Kate McDermott was more knowledgeable. As she signed, she frowned at Mitch's explanation. "A new depreciation schedule? You left it pretty late, didn't you? It's December."

"Just some last-minute details," he said, pocketing the papers.

Mrs. Gough did not have a spouse, but she did have a family.

Her son, an assistant museum curator in San Francisco, posed no problem.

"Sure, Mom," he said incuriously.

As a taxpayer she smiled; as a mother she frowned. If Martin ever rose in his profession, he was going to discover that fund-raising was an art form too.

Her daughter in New Orleans was more troublesome. Jennifer had spent several years nursing a new mail-order business.

"But, Mother! I thought everybody wanted to get out of irrevocable trusts."

"They can't. That's why they're called irrevocable," her mother said in a tone that brooked no argument.

Fortunately Jennifer was not really interested. She had something else she wanted to talk about. "Say, Mother, when we all get together at Christmas, I'm bringing someone along. Someone I want you to meet."

Mrs. Gough had made it clear, years ago, that she was not interested in mere transients.

"Oh yes?" she said hopefully.

The subsequent conversation was protracted and personal.

It took Fritz Diehl over half an hour to get through.

"Eleanor? I was beginning to think your phone was out. I've been trying since two. Thanks a million for your tip yesterday."

The lilt in his voice told its own story.

"I knew you could straighten things out with the police now that they're concentrating on blackmail, not bribery," she said.

"I just signed a statement for Lemoine. He's going to call off his dogs in St. Louis, which will make a nice change. How about having dinner with me?"

Mrs. Gough nodded to herself. In line with her new policy, she had plans for Diehl.

"I have a better idea, Fritz. Why don't you come out here?"

Phoebe Fournier was young, but four hours of Christmas shopping can flatten the strongest.

"Ouf!" she said when she returned home and collapsed into a chair.

The phone immediately rang.

She did not welcome Mrs. Gough's suggestion of a trek to the western suburbs. "I just got in," she protested.

"I think you'd better," said Eleanor.

Ever since New York, Phoebe had accepted her role as junior partner. Eleanor was simply better qualified to deal with the world of Wall Street lawyers and proxy fights. But Phoebe was damned if she was going to be outstripped in stamina as well.

"Oh, all right!"

Ten minutes after arriving in Newton, Massachusetts, Phoebe decided there was no end to the surprises about Mrs. Gough.

In the first place, there was the house itself. Gleaming hardwood floors, oriental rugs, a Hepplewhite library table —all proclaimed lavish expenditure. And a card table with its mahogany flap against the wall, the ample seating arrangements, and a brick barbecue glimpsed through a window suggested regular entertaining. Eleanor, it seemed, did not creep home to a monastic cell when she left Sparrow.

Even more unexpected, however, were the occupants of the room.

Fritz Diehl, his jacket tossed aside, lounged on the sofa with his hands locked behind his neck. Eleanor was sitting at a grand piano, belting out jazz.

"Hi, Phoebe," Diehl caroled. "You a jazz buff?"

Phoebe, whose musical history began with "The Yellow Submarine," said that she was not.

"You don't know what you're missing," he continued. "I'll never forget the first time Eleanor took me and Libby to Basin Street right after I joined Bayou."

Phoebe was slowly absorbing the fact that Eleanor and Diehl shared more than office camaraderie. How could this be? It was received truth at Sparrow that Mitch and Clay and Fritz had been as one with their employees. Ma Gough was den mother at best, and fussy schoolteacher at worst.

As Diehl beat time to the piano, Phoebe examined his receding hairline and did some arithmetic. Fritz was older than she had thought.

Mrs. Gough, who had deliberately staged this demonstration, decided that her point had been made. Leaving the piano, she opened a cabinet and dispensed hospitality, while Diehl continued to chat.

"I've been following your campaign, Phoebe," he said. "I liked your style in Pittsburgh."

Phoebe grinned. "You'd like anything that kept Sparrow away from California," she replied.

"You'd better believe it. Keep up the good work."

Mrs. Gough placed a glass in his hand and casually changed the subject. "What a shame you had to come all the way to Boston to make your police statement. Although, of course, I'm delighted to see you."

After a quick glance at her noncommittal expression, Diehl laughed.

"All right, Eleanor, I surrender," he said ruefully. "I heard a rumor that you're filing with the SEC. Satisfied?"

"I thought that might be it."

Now that the cat was out of the bag, Diehl relaxed. "When I left Sparrow I wondered if you'd ever really go to the mat with Mitch. Well, it took you long enough, but you're doing it with class."

"And, as Phoebe just remarked, in a way that vitally affects your interests."

Diehl nodded. "If Sparrow goes to California, I'll lose my job. Of course, I may be out on my ear anyway."

He did not receive a rush of womanly sympathy.

"Yes," Eleanor said, settling herself midway between her guests, "and you understand the position here, Fritz. If Phoebe and I lose this fight, we'll be out on our ears."

This conclusion was axiomatic to Fritz Diehl, but not to Phoebe.

"What makes you think that?" she gasped.

Eleanor regarded her sternly. "Why do you think Mitch hasn't already fired you? He doesn't want to force the issue. But once we do exactly that, he has nothing more to fear. And there won't be any place for us at Sparrow."

This explanation should not have been necessary. But Phoebe had lived so long with special privileges that she had forgotten pink slips. Suddenly hereditary fears surfaced. Where could she find another job like this one? What employer would provide scope for her talents? Could she be blacklisted?

"In fact, Fritz," Mrs. Gough said decisively, "if the proxy fight goes against us, and we want to perpetuate the principles of Sparrow, we'll have to found another airline."

Phoebe could only goggle. Fritz Diehl, however, burst into a loud guffaw.

" 'You've come a long way, baby,' " he quoted merrily.

Unmoved, Mrs. Gough continued her Napoleonic tactics.

"And, if things go sour at A&P, you might do worse than join us."

"I've got to hand it to you, Eleanor. This is the last thing I expected." Suddenly he sobered. "But if I can go to the top at A&P, I'm staying."

Mrs. Gough nodded. "If we can go to the top at Sparrow, we're staying," she rejoined. "And I'm not denying that the difficulties would be greater now than five years ago."

She knew her man. When other people saw problems, Fritz Diehl instinctively searched for solutions.

"What do you mean? Sure the competition's tougher, but remember the trouble we had raising the seed money. This would be a piece of cake. And we've got a proven track record."

It was no part of Eleanor's plan to disagree. "I was

thinking in terms of available routes. On the other hand, there are possibilities in the Northwest that haven't been exploited."

In spite of herself, Phoebe joined the game.

"And we'd have a head start on key employees. I know Joe Cleveland is itching to head his own shop."

"If Mitch starts swinging an ax, you could pick and choose," Diehl remarked. "But you'd still need an equipment man. Were you thinking of Clay?"

Eleanor now sounded more like a reluctant follower than an instigator. "I hardly think that's possible. Clay is standing behind Mitch every inch of the way. In fact, that's why I invited Don Islington to join us for a drink."

Diehl eyed his hostess appreciatively. "Got any other tricks up your sleeve?" he inquired.

Bit by bit, Phoebe was catching up. "Islington is the one who's trying to unload that overpriced fleet on Mitch," she said. "Why should he come out here?"

"Because aircraft sales are slow. He'll be affected by what we do, too," Eleanor explained absently.

An hour later Fritz Diehl was expanding on this topic to Islington.

"It's a funny situation, Don," he mused. "If Sparrow goes to California, I'll be unemployed and you'll be on velvet. But if Eleanor and Phoebe squash the deal, then you're the one in trouble."

"That's why I've got a real interest in how things turn out." Islington looked expectantly at Eleanor.

She did not give him a satisfactory answer. "It's too early to say. California may not be out of the question. Our main goal is to rationalize Sparrow's operation. The only firm decision is termination of the Pittsburgh route."

Islington waved Pittsburgh aside.

"What I'm interested in is your schedule. If you folks are going to horse around for months, it's not going to do me much good. My people are just about ready to scratch the possibility of this deal, and when they do that, they'll probably scratch me, too."

Mrs. Gough cocked her head. "I hadn't realized you were that close to the edge," she said untruthfully. "If we can't be any help with the sale, I suppose we might help in a different direction."

"There isn't anything else that's going to help."

Blandly she swept on. "This will be public information in twenty-four hours anyway," she began as if just reaching a decision. "Phoebe and I are filing for a proxy fight with Mitch."

"There's been talk," Islington admitted as he drained his glass.

Mrs. Gough rose and began to fix him another drink. Her subsequent remarks were tantalizingly dropped as she busied herself with bottles and ice.

"The fight could go either way," she announced, reawakening Phoebe's misgivings. "If we get bounced, we'll be starting up on our own and we'll be looking for an equipment man."

Islington could hardly believe his ears. Involuntarily he looked at Fritz Diehl.

But Fritz shook his head, smiling gently. "I just heard myself. Aren't they something?" he asked with ironic admiration.

Don Islington clearly did not share this sentiment, but he confined himself to his own predicament. "Even supposing you get this thing off the ground, you'd never pay me the kind of money I'm making now."

Executive relocation calls for tact, but it calls for realism as well. Fritz Diehl decided to make amends for his earlier withdrawal.

"Will anybody?" he asked baldly. "Like you said, no one's buying airplanes."

Islington swallowed. "Probably not. So I take a cut in income. I don't say I'm crazy about it, but at least it's not pie in the sky. Hell, if I have to, I can go into business for myself as a consultant. With new airfleets costing a small national budget, every line in the world is going to need equipment counseling."

The art of persuasion does not lie in forcing people to the wall.

"You can always get by, you have a good many options," Eleanor said soothingly. "But most of them don't lead to anything bigger. Actually I wasn't talking about hiring an executive. I was talking about finding a partner."

Islington recoiled. "You mean you're looking for an investor? No way! I'd have to be out of my mind."

"Thanks, Don," Fritz said cheerfully. "For that frank appraisal of what we did when we started Sparrow."

"You were a bunch of kids without responsibilities."

"Like hell!" Diehl retorted. "I had two children at the time."

"So you had some babies," Islington said dismissively. "That's different from me. I've got kids who go to orthodontists and drive their own cars. You think I'm going to scrub my salary, throw away my savings, and hope for a miracle? Forget it!"

Phoebe was drinking in every word. Until today she had believed that success like Sparrow's was due to inspiration, intelligence, and dedication. Miracles should have nothing to do with it. Fritz Diehl and Don Islington were both mirroring astonishment at the audacity of Mrs. Gough's proposal. And Phoebe had a sneaking suspicion that they were the voices of prudence—which led to the most disconcerting insight of the day.

Eleanor Gough was willing to gamble recklessly when she saw something she wanted.

⅋ 26 ℰ

PREFERS COASTAL WATERS

For all Americans, December involves a shopping blitzkrieg and the end of the tax year. Breadwinners face something else as well. Like it or not, Sparrow Flyways was saddled with its annual Christmas party. This year there were no triumphs to report, and employee morale was at a record low. To make matters worse, formal notification of Mrs. Gough's proxy battle had reached Mitch Scovil that very morning. With prospects like these, everybody would have liked to cancel. Instead, they rushed around, looking for dilution.

Mitch Scovil ran into Fritz Diehl on State Street. Midway through an awkward apology for his misguided accusations, Mitch suddenly saw a way in which Diehl could be useful.

"Oh, come on, Fritz," he urged. "To show there's no hard feeling. It'll be like old times."

Diehl, who recognized the motives for this invitation, smiled enigmatically. "When you put it like that, how can I refuse?"

Relieved, Scovil punched him in the upper arm. "Great!"

"To show there are no hard feelings," Diehl murmured.

Eleanor Gough also realized that outsiders might be what she needed that evening.

"Just the men I'm looking for," she announced, when she came across Everett Gabler conferring with Humphrey Belliers.

Police accountants rarely receive invitations in the course of their duties. Humphrey blinked, then accepted immediately. Gabler, an old hand at company hospitality, agreed on the condition that John Thatcher had not made previous plans for him.

"Well, that's blown it," Thatcher said philosophically when he heard. "I told Batchelder we'd come if you hadn't made other plans. He was so pressing, they must want every neutral body they can find."

Needless to say, this reading of the situation did not encourage optimism. When they returned to their hotel at the end of the workday, Thatcher headed firmly for the bar.

"If we are attending the social donnybrook of the year, I need all the fortification I can get," he said.

He was not the only prospective guest whose thoughts had taken this direction. No sooner had they passed through the archway than Fritz Diehl waved them over to his table and explained that he, too, was attending the festivities.

"It may be better than we expect," he declared happily. "The way things are going, somebody may clobber Mitch."

Gabler was not prepared to encourage fisticuffs. "Even if such an eventuality occurs," he said stiffly, "we will be long gone by then."

Thatcher was with him every inch of the way.

"Courtesy may require us to put in an appearance," he reasoned, "but we can circulate a modest length of time and then discreetly leave."

Diehl's spirits were rising higher and higher. "You mean the bastards didn't tell you where the party is?"

Gabler, an ascetic in private life, was accustomed to the perquisites of visiting firemen.

"What difference does that make? They're sending a car for us."

Diehl was now grinning broadly. "Not exactly. The car only takes you to the pier."

"The pier?"

"Then you board a harbor cruiser and take to the sea. The idea is to spend the evening dining and dancing and admiring the city lights."

Gabler stared at him in stark disbelief.

"In the middle of December!"

"The kids always love it," Diehl assured him solemnly.

This was no recommendation to Everett. "So we can look forward to an interminable evening of pitching decks and open dissension. What else, for heaven's sake?" he snorted.

"Quite a lot," said Thatcher. "If the radio in the cab was accurate, you can include falling temperature, gale winds, and driving sleet."

Thatcher's words were not wasted on his companions. When they foregathered in the lobby to await their driver, Fritz Diehl was dashing in a cossack hat and fur mittens, while Gabler had supplemented his gray overcoat with buckled galoshes and a scarf of conspicuous length and brilliance.

"Princeton colors, Everett?" Thatcher inquired after absorbing the orange and black.

Gabler, a loyal son of Haverford, was not abashed. "The shop had a limited selection and, this evening, I feel that warmth outweighs other considerations."

Any fears that Gabler might be a sartorial eyesore were laid to rest when their limousine deposited them. The young people mounting the gangplank had enveloped themselves with enough winter gear to scale Mount Everest. There were down parkas and après-ski boots, foam-thickened gloves, and knit headwear of all descriptions.

The red pom-pom bouncing along in front of Thatcher suddenly swiveled to reveal Phoebe Fournier.

"Oh, Mr. Thatcher, I'm so glad you're going to be here," she cried with unmistakable sincerity.

Things must be bad indeed, Thatcher reflected, when even Phoebe was daunted by the prospect of a Sparrow gala.

"We're looking forward to it," he replied without a quaver.

A moment later he was regretting his powers of dissimulation.

"I'll tell you what," she caroled over her shoulder as she passed on to the deck, "I'll save you a dance."

To a man of Thatcher's generation there was only one reply when a pretty girl offered a space on her crowded card.

"Splendid," he boomed, inwardly resolved to flee whenever she was in the offing.

The beginning of the evening, however, proved painless even by Gabler's exacting standards. The cocktail hour was brief and without peril. Although hard liquor was available in the usual serried ranks, the drink of choice with the young people seemed to be an innocuous wine cooler, and they were more than ready to charge the dining room as soon as the doors were flung open.

Conviviality at dinner was encouraged by the use of small tables. Thatcher and Gabler were sitting with Clay Batchelder. He was not an accomplished host but his deficiencies were offset by the warmth of another old acquaintance.

"Hi, Mr. Thatcher," said Joe Cleveland. "This is a lot better than our last meeting, isn't it?"

When Batchelder had difficulty getting the party going, Joe swam smoothly into action with an explanation of the Chinese waiters.

"It all goes back to the first Christmas at Sparrow," he said. "Mitch wanted to have some kind of celebration before the holiday rush, but I guess he was pretty broke. So he took all twenty-five of them to the local Chinese hash house for chow mein. Now we get catered by the ritziest gourmet restaurant in Boston. Here, try some of these black mushrooms."

Gabler, after one bite, agreed that it was a welcome change from the usual soggy fare.

"Well, some lobster and a few scallion pancakes are a small price for him to pay," said Joe, who combined a healthy zest for the good things of life with an understanding of how they were acquired. "After all, everybody here has busted a gut for the company."

But one of his colleagues did not wish to fly under false colors.

"Actually I'm not a high achiever," Norman Pitts said conscientiously. "They have a dozen rookies at the party every year, and I drew one of the lucky tickets."

"Then I assume you have not been with Sparrow very long," Thatcher said kindly.

It was like opening the floodgates.

"I got out of orientation four weeks ago, but I already feel at home. Everybody's great at letting you into the action but, of course, I haven't been on a team or come up with a cost-cutter yet."

Batchelder roused himself to do his duty.

"There's plenty of time for that," he encouraged. "You've barely gotten your feet wet. You're in reservations, aren't you? Well, there's room for improvement there. Maybe you'll be here again next year."

Batchelder was simply being a leader of youth, but Pitts had succumbed to the Sparrow virus more than most. "I've already got an idea," he said instantly. "Most of the time we wouldn't have to make the reservation at all."

This was riveting enough to freeze Batchelder as he was helping himself from the waiter's tray.

"What's that?" he said, spoon in midair.

"It's the old home-computer gimmick," Joe Cleveland said disparagingly.

Norman was indignant. "Why do you call it a gimmick?" he demanded. "Travel agents tap into the computer bank for airline reservations. There's no reason why our customers can't. If you think that's impossible, you're just not keeping up with the times."

"I never said it was impossible." Cleveland was immensely tolerant. "When you first told me about it, I said you had to put some meat on its bones and then write up a proposal."

"But the thing speaks for itself. Sparrow must be spending a lot of money on reservations. And home computers have been selling like hotcakes. A big percentage of those sales are probably to yuppies who'd be on to something like—"

"Hold it right there!" Cleveland directed. "You say we must be spending a lot. You've got to find out how much. And what percentage of home computers have this capacity? Above all, how many people use them to do anything but play games? You can't expect to get credit for a proposal like this unless you're willing to do the gut work."

Thatcher was amused by the exchange. It reminded him of an experienced herd dog training her puppy, while the herdsman idly looked on. But, when he glanced at this particular herdsman, it was apparent that Clay Batchelder had other preoccupations. Of course the scene could scarcely hold much novelty for him. Nonetheless Thatcher thought that Sparrow's management should be leaping at any opportunity to emphasize those aspects of their system that worked. They were few and far between these days.

If Batchelder was blind to these considerations, Joe Cleveland was not. For the next hour he did the honors for the company, leading the discussion to the special achievements of his colleagues at the table. With the arrival of dessert, Batchelder's abstraction was explained.

"Now, if ever, is the time to support Mitch." He turned apologetically to his guests as he rose. "He has to give the financial projections for the year and announce the bonus. I know he's not looking forward to the next fifteen minutes."

But Mitch Scovil, loyally flanked by Batchelder and Mrs. Gough, did a very creditable job. He was forthright about the situation, while managing to convey an air of sturdy optimism. His only departure from business was an obligatory reference to Alan Whetmore's death. He deplored the murder and the convulsions it entailed but looked forward to a speedy police resolution. In finale he announced that the band was already warming up and invited everybody to have a good time.

An hour later Thatcher cast a surreptitious glance at his watch and congratulated himself.

"This isn't half as bad as I expected, Everett," he commented. "And we only have another hour or so to go."

His comfort was largely due to the physical layout of the party. The dining room was approximately midship. When Mitch Scovil had concluded his remarks, the young people had surged forward to the dance floor. Their elders had made their way more decorously aft to the lounge. The usual small talk was occasionally punctuated by a blast of music as a couple, red-faced with exertion, entered and fell on the refreshment tables. Thatcher had even been beguiled by Mrs. Gough into a brief excursion to the deck where he had peered through the scudding sleet to view the lights of the waterfront before hastily returning to shelter.

"The evening is not yet over," Gabler replied automatically, but he, too, was so off guard that he absently steered a course past the bar without first checking its occupants.

"I wish you'd tell Fritz he's got rocks in his head," Mitch Scovil genially invited the newcomers. "He's trying to claim that there's no difference between being a cog in a mammoth corporation and running your own show."

Thatcher would have evaded the issue, but Gabler fell prey to his passion for accuracy.

"I would scarcely describe a vice-presidency at A&P as being a cog in a machine," he said severely.

"Call it what you like," Scovil said with an expansive wave. "You've still got a lot of other people trying to second-guess you."

Thatcher felt that, of all the subjects available, it was unfortunate that Scovil should have hit upon one that struck a spark from Everett.

"Surely that is unavoidable in any substantial enterprise," Gabler said with that heavy reasonableness guaranteed to provoke resistance.

"Not at Sparrow," Scovil insisted grandly. "This is my baby, and what I say goes."

"That's a fine line coming from you," Diehl retorted. "You've got the Sloan living in your accounting department, and your employees launching a proxy fight."

Scovil was unimpressed. "Ah, but you've missed the real difference," he said as if uncovering a hidden subtlety. "In your position, you've got to listen to the kibitzers. I don't."

"Why don't you wake up, Mitch? You're still trying to bowl over the grown-ups by being a young hotshot. It's about time you realized you are one of the grown-ups."

Scovil shook his head with a pleased expression. "You're jealous, that's your problem, Fritz. Face it, you're not a born entrepreneur, you have the soul of a wage slave."

By this time, Thatcher realized that both disputants had had too much to drink. Fortunately neither of them was displaying symptoms of pugnacity. Scovil was encased in complacent superiority. Fritz Diehl, blinking owlishly, was becoming more judicious by the moment.

"The trouble with you, Mitch, is that you don't realize we could call the tune the first couple of years because we were the only ones with anything at stake. As soon as you become big and successful, that's over. A lot of other people have something riding on Sparrow now."

"Sure they do. I'm carrying them all, just the way I have for five years. That's why I make the decisions." Scovil squared his shoulders, either as a symbol of his burdens or as a sign of departure. "I promised the gang I'd be on deck by nine-thirty. I've got to go now."

A few minutes earlier the blast of discordant percussion had announced the arrival of yet another group of dancers, but Thatcher had been too intent on the discussion to identify them. Now he saw Phoebe Fournier advancing.

But Phoebe had things on her mind other than dance partners. "I heard that last crack," she said, watching Scovil's retreating figure with simmering disapproval. "Mitch isn't listening to anybody these days. He's put in earplugs for the duration."

"Can you blame him?" Joe Cleveland had loomed up behind her, carrying a saucer of sushi. "Half the company is saying Whetmore blackmailed Mitch for skimming the employee profit fund."

His remark was not overly loud, but it reached Eleanor

Gough, who was bearing down on Everett for the mandatory trek outside.

"Joe, how can you make an accusation like that?" she demanded sternly. "That fund is the core of Sparrow's operations. Mitch would never attack it."

"You don't have to jump down my throat," Joe defended himself. "Hell, you could look on it as an improvement. Two weeks ago they were all saying Mitch was a murderer."

"That's not funny," she snapped. "It's bad enough to say Mitch lost his head in his anxiety to protect Sparrow. But it's simply insane to think one of us could have been deliberately undermining Sparrow for years."

Her fervor made everybody uncomfortable, but Joe rallied.

"Look, Eleanor, I don't really think anybody is playing games with the profit fund. After all, Phoebe monitors that fund and nobody's putting anything past her."

This tribute left Phoebe unmoved. She was still concentrating on Scovil's intransigence.

"God damn him. He's got no right to behave like this," she muttered.

Fritz Diehl was amused. "Calm down, Phoebe. Right now, Mitch is being his own worst enemy."

"Like hell!" she shot back. "If he pushes us into a proxy fight and wins, he's forcing us out into the cold where we have to start a new company. That makes him my worst enemy."

For Thatcher, this reference to a new company put a different light on Mrs. Gough's expectations from the Sloan.

"You know, Phoebe, Mitch would say you don't have the soul of an entrepreneur," Fritz Diehl said teasingly. "You're not willing to take the risks, so you're not entitled to anything."

"Big risk he took," Phoebe scoffed. "Mitch got a lucky win on the lottery. It was easy for him."

Diehl was not prepared to have his own contribution undervalued. "Well, it was damn hard for some of us. I couldn't have done it if my father hadn't died then. And I still had to go into hock."

"All right, I'm not saying it was as easy for you as it was for Mitch. But at least you were older than I am. You'd had more time to save."

This outrageous statement was too much for the bankers.

"Increased age usually brings increased responsibilities and expenditures," Thatcher informed her.

Everett was more statistical. "On the whole, you will find that discretionary income falls after the twenties, virtually disappearing until after the children are grown."

Phoebe, thrown into momentary disarray by this introduction of unborn children, was silent, and Fritz resumed the attack.

"You remember what Don Islington said? He couldn't take a cut in income, let alone fork out assets." Diehl turned to Thatcher. "Don's an equipment man that Eleanor and Phoebe were sounding out in case they go it alone. But he's got a slew of adolescent kids, and obligations from here to eternity."

Mention of Mrs. Gough embarrassed Phoebe. "Oh, Eleanor, I realize you took an almighty risk when you sold your house to invest in Sparrow. I suppose," she said, taking her hurdles bravely, "I should stop complaining about how hard it will be for me. No matter how I slice it, it was worse for you."

Mrs. Gough seemed to be having second thoughts.

"You always think you have a right to take your own risks," she said somberly. "But half the time, what you do affects other people. When you're building something together, you have a moral responsibility to each other. Because, win or lose, everybody is stuck with the consequences."

Phoebe was taken aback. "Eleanor, I didn't mean I'm not willing to go through with it. But it's all so needless, if only Mitch would see sense."

"Why should Mitch see things any more clearly than the rest of us? In spite of what he thinks, he's not infallible. He's . . . oh, hello, Clay."

Batchelder had materialized at Mrs. Gough's side, his wristwatch conspicuously to the fore.

"It's nine-thirty," he began briskly, then stopped as he saw she was still elsewhere. "We said we'd be on deck by then."

She shook herself briskly. "I almost forgot. I'll get right up there."

The spell had been broken and she bustled off, leaving Clay and Phoebe with puzzled frowns.

"I don't know where Eleanor picked up this guilt-and-atonement talk, but I could sure do without it," Clay groaned, before he hurried to catch up with her.

Diehl burst out laughing. "That's Sparrow all over. Mitch pretends he's in charge of things. Then he'll end up leading a cheering section while Clay and Eleanor get things done. You want to see the show, Phoebe?"

He linked his arm with hers, but Phoebe stood stock-still.

"We weren't talking about the same thing at all," she said in a gust of discovery. "Eleanor's still trying to find some justification for Alan Whetmore's murder. That's what she meant by other people getting involved."

"Eleanor's always windy at these affairs," Diehl said impatiently. "Do you want to come or not?"

Slowly Phoebe began to move. "I'm coming, I'm coming. But I wish I understood Eleanor better. I don't like the way she sounds."

"Phooey!" Ruthlessly Diehl bore her off, shouting an invitation to Joe over his shoulder.

"In a minute," said Joe, providentially turning to reload his saucer.

Everett Gabler was beside himself with indignation. "Do you realize what that young woman was doing? Now I am the first to admit that Mrs. Gough may have some peculiarities, but she is a woman of principle! More principle, I daresay, than anybody Miss Fournier's age has ever heard of. I consider—"

It was well known at the Sloan Guaranty Trust that Everett Gabler, once launched, could continue indefinitely.

But few monologues are proof against a sudden explosion overhead.

"Good Lord, what was that?" he exclaimed.

Joe Cleveland was chuckling as he left them. "We're passing Logan," he explained. "We always fire off rockets to salute the staff on duty."

He grinned mischievously.

"You've got to admit, we do things differently at Sparrow."

His remark stirred to the surface too many disturbing images.

"You certainly do," Thatcher rejoined.

❧ 27 ❧

A PLAINTIVE WHISTLE

Thatcher and Gabler were not talkative as they made their way ashore and waited for their limousine to nose its way along the pier. But once the doors were safely closed, Gabler was prepared to voice his concerns.

"I have been thinking, John," he began.

Since Gabler had fallen into a brown study at the bar and remained mute for the remainder of the evening, Thatcher had surmised as much.

"I noticed," he said.

"Of course you remember what Miss Fournier said just before she left us. That girl was making a deliberate and not particularly subtle attempt to direct suspicion toward Mrs. Gough. In my case, at least, her tactics have backfired. Her uncalled-for innuendos opened up an entirely different possibility for me."

"I agree about the tenor of Phoebe's remarks, but I'm not so sure they were uncalled for, Everett," Thatcher objected. "Mrs. Gough's discourse about the unforeseen consequences of one's own actions was certainly odd."

Gabler was close to snarling.

"There is not one jot of evidence to suggest that she was referring to herself as the perpetrator of these consequences," he retorted. "Her reaction would be identical if any principal at Sparrow were responsible."

"Perhaps," said Thatcher, who was anxious to proceed. There had never been any doubt which of the two ladies Gabler would choose to support. With Mrs. Gough, Everett mounted only the same wariness he extended to any Sloan customer. With Phoebe, he acted as if he were dealing with Che Guevara. "You said something about a new possibility?"

But now that Gabler had discharged some of his steam, he reverted to type. With a silent nod toward the limousine driver, he said darkly: "Later."

"Oh, very well."

Enemy ears, for Gabler, included room-service waiters as well as chauffeurs. When Thatcher ordered coffee and sandwiches, Everett could barely contain his impatience.

"I very much fear that both I and the police are guilty of overlooking an elementary fact," he said the moment they had been served. "Simply because of the size of the sums paid to Whetmore, we have focused our attention on the three partners, forgetting Phoebe Fournier's net worth."

Thatcher frowned. "Just a second, Everett," he objected. "It's improbable that Captain Lemoine has the slightest idea how wealthy Miss Fournier is."

Gabler ducked his head in agreement. "In a very real sense, Sparrow has four principals, not three."

"I'll pass on that one, but of course you're right about the resources Phoebe has."

"Or *had*," Everett said emphatically. "Has it occurred to you that her reluctance to invest in a new venture is entirely out of character? She is always portrayed as leading the way, not lagging behind. Isn't it possible that, after major disbursements to Whetmore, she could have difficulty raising the money? Particularly when she can't afford to let anyone know she's short? And, to my mind, she presents the most easily explained target for blackmail."

Thatcher nodded slowly. While Gabler had fastened on Phoebe's remarks at the bar, he himself had been riveted by

Joe Cleveland's. "It's Phoebe who's supposed to oversee the profit-sharing fund for the employees, theoretically to prevent hanky-panky by management. But nobody seems to keep an eye on her."

For a moment both bankers contemplated this violation of basic security maxims.

"There is far more to it than that," said Everett, returning to the matter at hand. "You don't know how these Sparrow field teams work, John. They set up everything needed to implement a new facility, which means that the possibility for kickbacks from contractors is self-evident. Good heavens, she could have created her own supply company."

"She wouldn't be the first," Thatcher agreed, rather startled at the sweeping opportunities presented to Phoebe.

"Wait!" Gabler instructed remorselessly. "I'm not finished. She is also the in-house liaison with the independent auditors. It cannot be denied that she has had temptations on every side. I also think it striking that her chosen second-in-command should be Joe Cleveland."

Gabler was conducting a shameless, no-holds-barred, defense of Mrs. Gough. But now Thatcher, himself, experienced a wave of partisanship. Joe had made tonight's dinner endurable. Furthermore, he was the only participant at the ill-fated meeting with Whetmore whose contributions had been valid and cogent.

"What about Cleveland?" Thatcher growled.

He was promptly disarmed.

"On the whole, a young man with very sound instincts for his age," Gabler said indulgently. "He is clear-sighted about the goals of the employees, sensitive to the needs of people, and inclined to stick to the point. But . . ."

With Gabler almost any commendation ended in *but*. Thatcher waited to hear what the fatal flaw was this time.

"But he is entirely lacking in any financial or accounting skills."

Now that they were both degenerating into champions, Thatcher thought it right to reestablish some impartiality. "You just said that Mrs. Gough's remarks could be interpreted in different ways. So could Phoebe's choice of adjutant. Maybe she wanted a balanced employee representation."

"Or maybe she wanted someone incapable of double-checking her work. What's more, her selection of Alan Whetmore as committee spokesman defies justification. It was so strange that when his safe deposit money was found, Cleveland and others jumped to the conclusion that she had been unknowingly manipulated by a competitor."

By this time Thatcher was interested enough to lay down his half-eaten chicken sandwich. "You're not maintaining that Phoebe thought she could pay off Whetmore by negotiating his idiotic demands, are you? Because, believe me, she is far too knowledgeable about Sparrow to think she could have succeeded."

"Exactly," said Everett. "But Whetmore was not knowledgeable. She could have maneuvered him onto a collision course with Mitchell Scovil. Even more compelling, it explains that meeting. You said yourself, John, that Whetmore was thunderstruck when his list was brushed aside without a hearing. Perhaps he was waiting for Phoebe to throw all the weight of the united payroll behind him."

"I admit that might explain Whetmore's behavior at the meeting, but what about before?" Thatcher murmured. "He deliberately changed his schedule to evade Phoebe, and he certainly made no pretense that his list had been endorsed by other employees. Quite the contrary."

Everett was so engrossed by his argument that he absent-mindedly helped himself to a potato chip.

"John, why don't we stop speculating and look at what has actually happened?" he suggested. "Scovil's control over his work force has almost disappeared. Things have reached such a pass that a proxy fight seems inevitable and, wonder of wonders, Phoebe Fournier is now on the insurgents' slate of directors—a position she repudiated in front of Alan Whetmore. To sum up, everything has worked out to her advantage."

"Not quite, Everett. The leadership of the anti-Scovil forces has passed to Mrs. Gough. You're not forgetting that, are you?"

Now Gabler sounded like a hanging judge.

"Far from it. But now that Mrs. Gough has emerged as a power factor, Miss Fournier is casting her in the role of murderess. Viewed in one light, all these events make a coherent picture of Phoebe Fournier advancing her own interests at any cost."

After some consideration, Thatcher shook his head decisively.

"You may be right in your reading of Phoebe's character. She may be a cold-blooded thief and killer. Or she may be aiming for Sparrow's front office. However, you cannot combine the two. I can believe that Whetmore was blackmailing someone who finally decided to kill him. I can't believe that the murderer was also thinking about corporate advancement."

Everett Gabler had a long and successful career in the art of persuasion, but his tactics were always of the water-dripping-on-stone variety. He was still going strong when Charlie Trinkam rolled in from a night on the town with Rupert Vernon.

"I've got to hand it to Rupert," he said cheerfully, tossing his coat over a chair. "When it comes to enjoyment, he's got the right approach. Someday I'd like to see him in a place worthy of his talents."

"In Rupert's book, that's probably Edinburgh," warned Thatcher.

"Don't you believe it. I'll bet it's a toss-up between Paris and Hong Kong." Charlie surveyed his companions with bright interest. "So how did your bash go? Did they start swinging on each other?"

"Remind me to introduce you to Fritz Diehl, Charlie," Thatcher said dryly. "You both seem to have the same yardstick for the success of a social event."

Gabler was impatient with these diversions. Instead, he tried to enlist Charlie in his cause by a careful recapitulation of his suspicions.

"There!" he concluded. "You have to admit that it covers the main facts."

Charlie's response dashed Gabler's hopes.

"The trouble with you, Ev, is that you don't understand girls like this Phoebe," Trinkam said authoritatively. "I haven't met her, but I'm willing to bet that she comes from a background where she didn't know a damn thing about money."

"She taught elementary school for a year after college," Gabler admitted.

Charlie nodded sagely. "And she was bored stiff. Then she was lucky enough to get a job with a company just getting off the ground, and found herself doing things she'd never dreamed of doing. Before you know it, she thinks she's the smartest thing that ever came down the corporation pike. She doesn't realize that she got the rewards of other people's risk taking."

Gabler was swift to point out that this appraisal did not cover everything.

"If Miss Fournier had simply been reluctant to join a new venture, I would have accepted your explanation," he said. "After all, true entrepreneurs are relatively scarce. But why the sudden attempt to cast suspicion on Mrs. Gough?"

This, too, posed no insuperable problem for Charlie Trinkam.

"How old is this lady?" he asked, hitching himself forward like a consultant reviewing the patient's medical history.

Everett sniffed. "I have, of course, not inquired. But she has two grown children, a married son and a daughter."

"Mother-of-the-bride stuff. I thought so." Charlie had spotted the symptom that explained everything. "You've got to realize that these girls all think they're a new breed, striking out where no woman has ever gone before. Your Phoebe's burned up that some dame in pastel chiffon and a little flowered hat has got more of the right stuff than she has."

Floundering in deep waters, Gabler thought he saw an opportunity to score. "When last seen, Mrs. Gough was far from wearing the clothes you describe."

Specialists are accustomed to interjections from the untutored.

"When her daughter's going down the aisle, she will be," Charlie said simply.

"So you think Miss Fournier is acting from some form of jealousy?"

"Not exactly." Trinkam pondered briefly. "Your Phoebe has been knocked off her little pins. She thought she knew all about good old Mrs. Gough. It turns out she hasn't even scratched the surface. So she's beginning to wonder how much more is lurking down there. As far as she's concerned, it could be anything—including murder."

Everett was a past master of minimal retreat. Instinctively he surrendered outlying ground to maintain his center.

"You may be correct about Miss Fournier. I agree that Mrs. Gough's performance these past few days has been sufficiently unexpected to startle any colleague," he conceded. "But I still believe that the Whetmore meeting must have been contrived. That is the only explanation for its incongruity."

Thatcher always enjoyed the spectacle of Charlie instructing Gabler in the way life is lived outside an accounting ledger. While his subordinates clashed, he quietly demolished the remaining edibles on the tray. He was about to pour himself another cup of coffee when Everett made his final declaration.

As the words penetrated, Thatcher froze. The pot remained suspended, the cup stayed dry, while vignettes from Sparrow flashed before his eyes. There was Eleanor Gough stubbornly insisting that Scovil could not evade the employee meeting; there was Clay Batchelder hustling Joe Cleveland away from contact with Alan Whetmore; there was Fritz Diehl comparing Phoebe to Don Islington.

"You've put your finger on it, Everett," he said. Then, with mounting conviction: "Good God, it's been staring us in the face all along."

❧ 28 ❧

SIGHTED IN LOUISIANA

The solution to Alan Whetmore's murder was staring far too openly for Eleanor Gough's peace of mind. Late as it was when she returned from the party, she began packing a suitcase immediately.

Phoebe Fournier, on the other hand, enjoyed a night of untroubled repose, waking to sunny blue skies and a feeling of buoyant optimism. Her misgivings of the previous evening did not survive the light of day. Eleanor had simply been reacting to the strain of simultaneously confronting Mitch Scovil and maintaining Christmas cheer. Today would be business as usual, Phoebe promised herself, and the first item on the agenda was a lunchtime huddle with Eleanor. Mitch had already been shaken by the official notice from Chet Longley. This afternoon he would be meeting with John Thatcher and Everett Gabler. After these two body blows, he should be ripe for compromise.

This happy mood lasted until Phoebe's coffee break took her to the cafeteria, where she found the central table crowded with the early morning shift. From their midst rose the despairing accents of Joyce Wrigley, who was notorious for the lamentations that accompanied her well-intentioned career of mistakes, miscalculations, and mishaps.

"You know what a madhouse the 6 A.M. shuttle was," she keened.

"It always is," a fellow sufferer groaned.

But Joyce was merely painting in the background. "So there I was, snapping the head off this poor schnook who hadn't made out his boarding pass. And wouldn't you know it? Eleanor Gough was next in line!"

She paused dramatically while her colleagues gasped in pleasurable dismay.

"What did she do?" they asked.

"She just had time to board. But she won't forget, not our Eleanor. When I think of what she'll say to me when she gets back, I could just die."

It was nothing new for Joyce to prepare to meet her maker. While everybody else produced rival episodes, Phoebe thumped down her coffee mug and stalked over to the table.

"Are you saying Eleanor's gone to New York?" she demanded, cutting across anecdotes about other lapses.

Joyce was puzzled. "Of course she was going to New York. That's why people take the shuttle."

"Dammit!" said Phoebe as she saw her hopes of seizing the psychological moment fade.

But there was worse to come. Two hours later she was preparing to go out to lunch when the locker room was inundated with a flight crew coming off duty.

"Hi, Stephanie!" she said, moving over at the mirror where she was brushing her hair. "Through for the day?"

"Finally," said Stephanie triumphantly. "These morning shuttles during the Christmas season are living hell."

Phoebe looked at her with new interest. "Say, I hear you had Eleanor on board the dawn flight."

Stephanie was leaning forward to apply her lipstick with pinpoint accuracy. Only when the operation was complete did she reply. "That's right. And was she ever in a tizzy when we had to circle for twenty minutes at La Guardia. She was so uptight I thought she'd scream."

"She probably had an appointment in New York."

"Not New York," Stephanie corrected. "She was afraid of missing her connection with Delta. You know she always flies with them when she visits her daughter in New Orleans."

"New Orleans?" Phoebe stammered.

Clicking her cosmetic case closed, Stephanie turned for a final word. "And if you ask me, something's wrong down there. Eleanor looked really grim."

"Oh no!"

"A family emergency, for Chrissake," Phoebe reported indignantly. "That's all I need."

Joe put down the ketchup bottle and looked reproachful. "It probably isn't what Eleanor needs, either," he pointed out.

"Oh, I know it's not her fault," Phoebe grumbled. "But it couldn't have happened at a worse time. From the look on Mr. Gabler's face when he finished the books, Mitch should be pulverized by their meeting."

"Have a heart, Phoebe. It must have been pretty bad if they called Eleanor in the middle of the night. She could be sitting around some hospital by now."

"Just coffee, Eleanor? Sure you don't want to try the pastry cart?"

Mrs. Gough was not maintaining a deathbed vigil. Instead she was lunching, a good deal more grandly than Joe and Phoebe, in one of New Orleans's renowned restaurants. Her host, in another world and another life, had been her boss.

Unlike her colleagues at Sparrow, Eleanor Gough had never lost touch with New Orleans. There, Fritz Diehl and Mitch Scovil had been itinerant executives, holding down their first jobs after business school. Clay Batchelder had been an outside consultant, destined to live intimately with Bayou Airlines for several months and then disappear forever. Mrs. Gough, however, had spent twenty years sinking roots into the community. It was not unusual for her to be catching up on company events with Bill Johnson, and he never suspected that this time his reminiscing was being artfully steered. Like all stay-at-homes, he assumed the returned traveler was as engrossed by local gossip as he was.

"That was Ramon Estevez, Eleanor. You must remember him."

Eleanor's face was a polite blank.

"He ran our charters to Mexico," Johnson amplified.

Now her expression correctly mirrored dawning memory. "A little, dapper man? Rather flashy?"

"You could call it that. The customers ate up his gallant hidalgo act."

She nodded. "Of course. I just didn't place the name."

"How could you forget him? He and Whetmore were our men of the world. Everybody else at the club played golf, but the two of them were always toweling down after squash and telling us how they'd chartered a boat to go out after the big ones. You must . . ." Johnson's voice died away in a tide of embarrassment. Then he coughed and began again. "Of course you weren't at the club in those days."

"No, I didn't move in those circles," she agreed calmly, then continued with a twinkle, "and I still don't. No power on earth would get me out on the Gulf in one of those boats."

Johnson smiled gratefully. Trust Eleanor not to take offense at a little slip. She was still the same, he thought. Just as unassuming and comfortable as ever.

The men of the Sloan were not quite so content with their lot. The previous evening John Thatcher's dazzling insight had been subjected to a punishing critique by his subordinates. This had failed to reveal a single flaw. But where, they asked, was the proof?

"Nowhere that I can see," Thatcher had admitted ruefully. "What's more, there's still one unanswered question. How does a stupid, uninformed man like Whetmore discover things that have eluded everyone else?"

This was no mystery at all to Charlie Trinkam. "Somebody tells him."

"What difference does it make?" Gabler had snapped. "We are still left in an untenable position."

As the hour for their meeting with Scovil approached, Everett became more militant.

"It is inconceivable that the Sloan should support either of these factions at Sparrow until this entire matter is resolved," he trumpeted.

"If it ever is," Thatcher said. "We're talking about five years ago."

Gabler snapped his fingers at this bagatelle and narrowed his eyes. "With sufficient persistence and the cooperation of relevant financial institutions, an investigator could surely produce evidence."

Things were bad enough without Everett Gabler disappearing from the East Coast on a search for the Holy Grail.

"Given enough time, the police can probably do it," said Thatcher, sternly directing his colleague's attention to their primary interest.

"But Mrs. Gough, you may have noticed, has carefully arranged a scenario that forces the pace."

"And no wonder!" Everett snorted.

It took two cheeseburgers for Joe Cleveland to reason Phoebe into a realistic frame of mind, and his good work was almost immediately undermined.

"How should I know when she's coming back?" demanded Sally, the receptionist. "I didn't even know she was leaving."

"But she always calls in," Phoebe protested, her voice unconsciously rising.

Over the years it had been well established that, during any emergency, the phone might ring forever in Mitch Scovil's apartment, it might be answered by an unhelpful adolescent in the Batchelder home, but Eleanor Gough was always available.

"If you ask me, that's just it," Sally grinned. "I'll bet she's told Mitch and Clay that they can carry the can for a change. She sure enjoyed telling Mitch to run his own errands the other day. Anyway, until she tells me different, I'm holding her mail here."

It did not help that Phoebe, automatically following Sally's gesture, spotted an envelope bearing the letterhead of Chester Longley's law firm.

Phoebe was outraged. This was no time to be playing games. If Eleanor was simply twisting Mitch's tail, the least she could do was keep her partner informed.

With her jaw set and her spine stiff, Phoebe stalked into the corridor just as Mitch Scovil rounded the corner, ushering John Thatcher and Everett Gabler to the executive suite.

"Oh, Mitch," she blurted. "Did Eleanor tell you when she's due back from New Orleans?"

She regretted her impulse immediately. The smile was wiped from Scovil's face and he stopped in his tracks, leaving his guests to forge ahead.

"New Orleans?" he repeated, his eyes wide and fixed.

"That's right," she said impatiently. "I want to reach her."

Scovil merely shrugged his shoulders. "How would I know?" he asked, then added tauntingly: "If you're having trouble figuring out what Eleanor's up to, Phoebe, there's a lot of that going around."

Bent on extracting information from Scovil, Phoebe never noticed the startled glance exchanged by his visitors.

Two hours later, even Mitch Scovil could not convince himself that he had succeeded in winning the Sloan's support. Characteristically his report to Clay Batchelder placed the blame on other shoulders.

"I never thought Eleanor would play so dirty. How the hell can I get the Sloan to see reason when she's letting off one land mine after another?"

Clay was still one day behind. "We always knew that it might come down to a proxy fight."

Actually Mitch had never believed it for a minute.

"It wouldn't have, if Phoebe was still running the show," he grated. "Eleanor's the one who's charging around like a wild bull. Yesterday we hear from her lawyers and today she lights out for New Orleans without a word to anybody. How do you think it looks to Thatcher when we can't even keep track of our top management?"

"What the hell did she go to New Orleans for?"

"I don't know. I suppose it's something to do with her daughter." Catching sight of Batchelder's expression, Scovil went on less confidently. "Well, it has to be something like that, doesn't it?"

"Sure," said Clay too quickly. "That's bound to be it."

"What else could it be? It's been five years since we moved to Boston. She doesn't have anything left down there except family," Scovil persisted.

Clay had his second wind by now. "We don't know what kind of interests she's got down there, and we're not going to find out by talking to each other," he said firmly. "Besides, nine chances out of ten, it's her daughter, just like you said."

The ensuing conversation was not much comfort to either man. Scovil was unwilling to break down and admit that the Sloan had blasted his grandiose plans. Batchelder was determined not to voice his forebodings about Eleanor Gough's disappearance. Both men wanted unqualified reassurance and sympathy for anxieties they refused to specify. Neither of them got it.

In an attempt to end their session on a positive note, Scovil had to cast far afield. "At least there's one good thing," he remembered. "The stock has inched up to thirty and change."

"Great," said Clay dully.

"Well, now we know where the evidence is located," Thatcher said as soon as they rejoined Trinkam. "It's at Bayou Airlines."

"Or *was*," Charlie rejoined. "That's one enterprising lady you've got there."

She was even more enterprising than Charlie gave her credit for, as Phoebe discovered the next day. Upon being told by the Sparrow switchboard that there was still no word from Mrs. Gough, Phoebe realized there could be

230

only one logical explanation. Eleanor planned to spend the day in transit. Fortunately Phoebe was in the right business to verify this conclusion. It was the work of a moment to dial a number in Delta's New York office and make her request.

"G-O-U-G-H?" her acquaintance double-checked. "First name, Eleanor? Sure, Phoebe, I'll have someone on the reservations computer find out and get back to you."

"I owe you one, Hilary," Phoebe acknowledged.

"Forget it."

Hilary's performance was flawless. It was not her fault that computers are remorseless in their display of data.

When Phoebe answered the phone twenty minutes later, she heard an unfamiliar gravelly voice.

"You the party inquiring about Gough, Eleanor?" it rasped.

"That's right," she said eagerly. "I want to know if she's reserved space back yet."

"And just where is back?"

It was a measure of Phoebe's confusion that she had descended to amateurism. "Boston, Mass.," she corrected herself crisply. "She flew down to New Orleans and I want to know when she's coming back."

"Something's wrong somewhere." The voice had become perceptibly more cheerful. "New Orleans was just a stopover. Gough, Eleanor, transferred to Aero Mexico. She left the country on their two forty-five flight yesterday afternoon."

~ 29 ~

ENDANGERED SPECIES

Phoebe was so stunned that she distinctly heard a click and renewed dial tone before her frozen lips produced an automatic acknowledgment. Every subterranean suspicion of the last twenty-four hours revived. Eleanor had discarded the behavior patterns of a lifetime. Eleanor had been talking about guilt and responsibility for days. Was this her atonement? Was her flight supposed to be Sparrow's salvation?

Wildly looking around the accounting department, Phoebe was not reassured. Instead of old friends, she saw too many members of Captain Lemoine's fraud squad. Heads bent, fingers poised over calculators, they were sandwiched into every square inch of the already crowded facility.

Like a zombie, she rose to seek more neutral surroundings. As her thoughts stopped whirling, she decided this was no time for old cronies. It was too late to share discoveries under a pledge of secrecy. For once, Phoebe yearned to shift her burden to other shoulders. Somebody would have to inform the police, but it was not going to be her.

Not on your life! Management pulled down the big money. Let them do the dirty work.

This effectively directed her to one man. Clay Batchelder had been disturbed about Eleanor even before the party. More important, Clay would instantly confer with Mitch. After that, it was out of her hands. Mitch, as they already knew, was perfectly capable of pointing the finger.

Phoebe finally ran Batchelder to earth in one of the storage sheds, barely noticing in her progress across the compound that the skies had darkened and were filling with pendulous gray clouds.

The weather, however, was uppermost in Batchelder's mind.

"They're forecasting freezing rain tonight," he grumbled upon her entrance. "I just hope it holds off until after dinner."

Phoebe made no pretense of replying. Instead she baldly repeated Delta's announcement.

"I'm worried, Clay," she concluded.

But he was unwilling to meet her halfway. "Come on, Phoebe. I admit Eleanor's been acting weird these past couple of weeks. But that's no reason to think what you're thinking. There are probably lots of explanations."

"Name me one."

Clay winced. "How do I know? Sure, I'm worried about Eleanor. But only because I think the strain's getting to her. She hasn't been at all like herself. That's why she walked out on Mitch."

"That's got nothing to do with bolting to Mexico."

"Maybe not." Clay sounded almost desperate. "Look, Lemoine wants to comb through our personal finances. Eleanor stopped in New Orleans first. Maybe she's moving some investments out of the country."

Phoebe eyed him stonily. "Don't treat me as if I'm a child. I'll bet you and Mitch are moving assets, too. Neither of you has to leave the country to do it. You just call your broker or lawyer."

"Eleanor's got family down there," Batchelder said doggedly. "She may need their signatures."

"There's another explanation," Phoebe said.

Batchelder was not encouraging. "You're full of them today. And I don't like any of them."

"You know the way we're always hearing that story about the start of Sparrow? I mean, Fritz getting his inheritance and then Mitch hitting the lottery just when he needed it?"

By now Clay was deeply suspicious. "That's just part of Mitch's PR."

"And then Eleanor tells us how she sold her house to get her stake?" Phoebe pursued relentlessly.

"So?"

"Well, she has to say something. But does anybody really know that's how she came up with a hundred thousand? From what you all say about Bayou, Eleanor was in an ideal position to pull off some quick embezzlement."

Batchelder had sunk onto a stool to listen to Phoebe. Every time she made a point, he shifted as if he were squirming under a physical onslaught. The look he flashed from under his heavy eyebrows was not friendly.

"You're making this up out of thin air, Phoebe," he charged. "There's nothing to support it."

"Oh yes there is," she insisted, determined to voice every one of her fears. "The fraud squad hasn't come up with one single irregularity in Sparrow's books. There's not a damned thing anybody could be blackmailed about. But Alan Whetmore was in New Orleans when Eleanor was supposed to be selling this famous house. He had friends and contacts, he could have heard a lot after the rest of you left. Maybe the police are looking at the wrong company's books."

Clay was heaving himself to his feet. "Your trouble is an overactive imagination, Phoebe."

"I could go on."

But he was already on his way to the door. "Well, I don't want to hear it."

"Then give me one good reason why Eleanor's in Mexico," Phoebe challenged his back.

"I don't know, and I don't care!"

* * *

A distant onlooker could easily have decided that Eleanor Gough had come to Acapulco to work on her tan. Like any other vacationer, she was sitting on a patio, gazing at the sea, with a marina spread immediately before her and the world-renowned cliffs to her left. Wearing a short-sleeved blouse and a cotton skirt, she reclined at ease with a cigarette in one hand and a glass of iced pineapple juice in the other. To Ramon Estevez, sitting directly across the small table, she did not seem so relaxed. Her voice was tight with control and the knuckles grasping the glass showed white in the unforgiving sunlight. But, even at close range, certain telltale signs escaped him. He did not know that the cigarette was the first after a three-year abstention, and he could not see the lines of tension concealed by wide wraparound sunglasses.

"I never thought it would come to this," he snarled.

"You've been well paid."

Her indifference flicked him on the raw.

"It was peanuts. By rights, this should all be mine."

He waved his arm angrily in a gesture that encompassed the bar, the clubhouse, the marina.

Mrs. Gough fastened on only one aspect of the scene—a sign suspended from a cross post, reading: ESTEVEZ MARINA AND YACHT CLUB.

"In one sense it does," she pointed out.

"Don't give me that. The bank owns ninety percent and they're nervous about the payments."

"It's not my fault if you've botched things."

Ramon would have liked to deny this, but it was all too clear where the fault lay.

"My one regret is that Whetmore did not die by my hands, preferably wrapped around his miserable throat. He could have saved us all much trouble."

"That wasn't Alan's big aim in life. Forget him!" she directed. "He is no longer a factor."

Despite himself, Ramon agreed. Magniloquent threats of vengeance are not really satisfactory after the corpse has been buried.

"It is curious, is it not?" he mused. "In the old days,

who would have expected this? Then, Alan and I were friends and men of substance. You were a menial nobody."

He peered at her, hoping that she would be stung. But he was disappointed; she was not even interested.

"The only important thing about the past is that it does not prejudice the future," she said. "But that's very easy to forget, when the past is still the present."

Ramon, like Mitch Scovil and Clay Batchelder, found Eleanor tiresome when she soared into loftier realms. He himself was equally unmoved by past and future. The present had always been difficult enough.

"I have not made as much out of this as I should have," he said, reverting to his original grievance.

Eleanor merely murmured something about a plane to catch and put down her glass. As she reached for her capacious straw bag, Ramon's eye rested on it speculatively. Possibly there was still hope of further profit from his association with Mrs. Gough.

"When will I see you again?"

As the only occasion on which this was likely to occur was a joint courtroom appearance, Eleanor checked in her preparations for departure and involuntarily grimaced.

"With luck, never!"

Ramon did not share her desire to put distance between them. Frowning against the brilliant light, he let his glance follow her receding figure until a clump of palm trees obscured it.

Inevitably the police fraud squad had reached the conclusion already arrived at by both Everett Gabler and Phoebe Fournier.

"The place is so clean it squeaks!" Humphrey Belliers reported at the conclusion of the audit.

When Captain Lemoine remained unresponsive, Belliers feared that his past blunder was rising to haunt him.

"That's not just me," he hastened to add. "That's the fraud squad and even Gabler, too."

Finally Lemoine roused himself from his trance. "I know. Thatcher and Gabler were just in here. They've got a theory that explains everything. But to get the evidence means going back over five years."

"Sparrow wasn't in existence then," Belliers protested.

"Not Sparrow. They're talking about personal finances."

"Well, the court's already rejected a fishing expedition with the three of them."

"It's just one now. But the court's still going to say no when all I have is a theory."

Belliers would have liked Lemoine's confidences to be more specific, but he had other grounds for dissatisfaction. "What difference does it make? If you were just doing one, there wouldn't be anybody to arrest when you were finished. These people run an airline. They know all about hopping a plane to leave the country."

"I thought the same thing," Lemoine said placidly.

Common sense was Belliers's outstanding characteristic. "I'll bet the old curmudgeon could do it under the table," he suggested. "The Sloan swings a hell of a lot of clout with other banks."

The captain recalled his recent visitors. Everett Gabler had been wearing his usual expression of stern disapproval. But under the disapproval there had been disappointment.

"He not only could do it, he wants to do it," said Lemoine, thoughtfully examining his fingernails. "But Thatcher is calling the shots. He intends to shovel the whole mess into our lap and go home."

"Ha!" Belliers snorted. "The Sloan is in the hot seat, too. Why don't you apply for another court order? When you get thrown out, Thatcher's not going to like it at all."

But Lemoine was sinking deeper and deeper into his thoughts. "Somehow I don't think it will come to that. I think those crazies at Sparrow are raising such a head of steam that they'll blow themselves to bits."

On the whole Phoebe was satisfied that she had done the right thing. She had not failed to note the signs of Clay's discomfiture. In front of her he might profess skepticism, but by the time he had analyzed and reanalyzed her suspicions with Mitch, they would both be convinced.

For that very reason she took care to stay beyond their

reach. The next three hours she spent penetrating nooks and crannies of the Sparrow compound whose very existence she had forgotten.

It did not lighten her mood of sober resignation that the day's roster included too many people who had been on duty when Alan Whetmore was murdered. As the weather worsened, she overheard many people draw the same comparison.

"God, will you look at that fog rolling in. It was just like this the night Alan got killed."

At the third repetition, Phoebe's defenses crumbled, and she finally admitted what she had been avoiding as late as her conversation with Batchelder. The fraud squad might examine books, and she could use words like embezzlement and blackmail; but the crime that had convulsed Sparrow was not a wrongful transfer of money. Alan Whetmore, however contemptible, had been a living, breathing entity until he was lured to that desolate, fog-shrouded spot and battered into a bloodied shell.

Shivering, she continued to wander until she found herself in the outpost that received fresh laundry. It was here that a persistent caller, who had been trying to reach her for some time, finally succeeded. The voice was unmistakable.

"About Gough, Eleanor," it began.

"You mean you're still tracking her?" Phoebe gasped.

She could have bitten her lip in vexation. She did not want to follow Eleanor to Costa Rica—or Havana, for that matter.

"You're the one who asked about her return," he reminded her.

"Are you saying she's coming back?"

"She's probably there by now. Her ETA in New York was three fifty-five. If you ever answered your phone, you would have known sooner."

This time, at least, Phoebe managed to beat the dial tone with her dazed thanks.

She could not begin to imagine what Eleanor was up to now, but this unexpected return did not allay her suspicions. She was, she realized, honor-bound to report the

238

development to Clay. With dragging steps, she made her way back to the main building, oblivious to the fact that night had fallen and the first spitting showers of icy pellets were delicately rebounding from every surface. Her determination carried her to Batchelder's office, but he was not there.

"Clay's left," Sally answered her question.

"He's already gone home?" Phoebe echoed, wondering what to do next.

"Well, actually, not home. He was asking Francine the quickest way to get to Newton."

Phoebe made no attempt to conceal her dismay.

"But he mustn't do that!" she cried.

Blind to Sally's amazement, Phoebe castigated herself. After the twin debacles of the employees' meeting and the Pittsburgh shutdown, Joe Cleveland had said she was good with numbers and lousy with people. And he was right! In spite of a week learning that she had failed to read Eleanor Gough entirely, she had had the colossal arrogance to assume that she could predict Clay's actions. Deliberately working on his earlier fears, she had been so sure that he would rush straight to Mitch. Instead he must have checked Sparrow's passenger lists and now, out of some stubborn sense of loyalty, he was going to give Eleanor a chance to explain. The ghost of her belated realism about Alan Whetmore's murder rose to haunt Phoebe. It would never occur to Clay to be on his guard.

"And it's all my fault," she said bitterly, completing Sally's confusion before she dashed away.

She was heading straight for those police accountants she had been so anxious to avoid a few hours ago. None of this would have happened if she had gone to them in the first place.

But, unnoticed by Phoebe during her soul-searching, the magic hour of quitting time had come and gone. Both the police and the Sparrow regulars had departed, leaving only two men in the office. John Thatcher, already in his overcoat, was waiting while Everett Gabler shoveled stacks of notepads into an ancient buckled briefcase.

Thatcher looked up at Phoebe's tumultuous entrance and

smiled. "You'll be glad to hear you're getting at least one desk back, Miss Fournier," he said. "We're leaving on the next shuttle and—"

She never let him finish. In a torrent of words, Phoebe relieved herself of her suspicion, fear, and guilt.

"I'm going out to Eleanor's house right now," she ended on a surge of nervous desperation. "They think they're old friends with nothing to be afraid of, and that's dangerous. But if somebody else is there, I don't see how anything can happen."

Even as the sentences tumbled out, Phoebe realized she was not provoking the reaction she had expected. Thatcher and Gabler did not reject her ravings out of hand; they did not plead with her to reconsider her plans; they did not even seem to be surprised. Instead they nodded as if she were merely confirming what they already knew.

There was, however, the beginning of a frown on Thatcher's face. "I had not considered the possibility of additional violence," he confessed. "You may be right about that. In any event this seems the ideal moment to try to wrap this whole thing up. What do you say, Everett?"

But Phoebe, like Captain Lemoine, had no doubt who was calling the shots, and she had no intention of waiting for pro forma consultations.

"My car's right outside and we don't have any time to waste," she said, urging them toward the door. "Clay left half an hour ago."

Following her lead, Thatcher and Gabler were grateful for a guide across the parking lot. The overhead lights were almost useless, each one a pale nimbus regularly obscured by drifting tendrils of fog. At ground level every object— cars, railings, stanchions—was weeping with moisture, and the metallic ping of ice crystals had swollen into a steady background accompaniment.

"This may take longer than you think," Thatcher warned as he closed his door.

The words popped out of Phoebe's mouth before she could stop them.

"It was just like this on the night Alan was murdered." Shaking her shoulders angrily, she gunned the motor into life and continued firmly: "We'll leave the fog behind as we head inland."

In one sense, she was accurate. As they swept westward along the Massachusetts Turnpike, they passed through the unseen barrier of the freezing mark. Fog and icy rain gave way to increasingly heavy snow. By the time Phoebe circled onto the Newton exit and headed into a maze of side roads, the windshield wipers had created two semicircles in a thick mantle of white.

Outside, houses and shrubs were fast losing their individuality, and every turn seemed to reveal the same vista. Phoebe was muttering over and over, like an incantation, the directions from her earlier trip to Mrs. Gough's home.

"Third right, then second left, then fourth right."

Her memory was all that stood between them and total disorientation.

Everett Gabler was sitting in the inadequate backseat, his bony knees hunched under his chin. With the side windows blanketed and the rear defroster fighting a losing battle, he could have been squatting in a black cave. Always distrustful of any competence other than his own, he stared past the two shadowy silhouettes ahead of him and despaired of ever reaching their destination.

Thatcher, on the other hand, was congratulating himself. He had expected the normal nighttime suburban phenomena of invisible street signs and nonexistent house numbers. But now, with even major landmarks obliterated, he was grateful they had not entrusted this expedition to a city cab driver.

His confidence was vindicated when the fourth right brought them to a short cul-de-sac permitting no further progress. Gabler sighed fatalistically and Phoebe, peering intently beyond the wipers, emitted a grunt of satisfaction.

"That's Clay's car!" she cried, swerving sharply into a driveway behind a Lincoln.

With the agility of practice, she wriggled out of the car and began crunching up the walk before her passengers had extricated themselves from unfamiliar seat belts and door locks. Driven by the fear that their trip had taken too long when every second counted, Phoebe was in no mood for formalities. Finding the front door unlocked, she ignored the bell and tumbled into the hallway, crying loudly:

"Eleanor! Clay! It's me, Phoebe."

Her boot heels clicked on the waxed floor as she made straight for the living room, marching boldly into the silence until she was brought up short by the scene before her.

Mrs. Gough was directly ahead, her back to the fireplace, her arm outstretched along the mantel, her fingers touching the base of a heavy silver candelabra. Unresponsive to the intrusion, she continued looking downward at the chair facing her.

Then Phoebe heard an agonized groan and her horror-stricken gaze fastened on Clay Batchelder, slumped forward, his hands cradling his head as if shielding it.

"What have you done to Clay?" she demanded.

Mrs. Gough finally looked up and Phoebe gasped. This was an Eleanor never seen before. Like an avenging fury, she stood erect, her shoulders back and her head high. But it was her face that had undergone a transformation. The dead skin was so taut that the deep lines and hollow shadows seemed chiseled from some gray, unyielding stone. Mrs. Gough had not aged; she had desiccated.

With incredible relief Phoebe heard footsteps behind her, then a reassuring voice at her shoulder.

"Batchelder's all right, he's just sobbing," John Thatcher explained. "Confession doesn't come easily to some men."

∾ 30 ⊁

A WELL-FORKED TAIL

"I should have realized that it was unnecessary for us to race out to Newton," Thatcher said to Phoebe Fournier, two days later, when they were all waiting for a plane to New York. "Mrs. Gough was capable of handling Batchelder in any showdown, and she knew exactly what she was dealing with."

Phoebe was even more apologetic. "I had it the wrong way round. When I saw the two of them in that living room, I thought Eleanor had just bashed Clay."

Everett Gabler snorted.

"No doubt I should have explained more clearly," Thatcher said hastily, to forestall a clash. In reality, he still did not understand how she could have been so mistaken.

"You shouldn't have had to," Phoebe echoed his unspoken thought. "I guess what really bugs me is that I was the one who brought everything out in the open at the Christmas party, and I never realized what I was doing."

"Well, I didn't either," Joe Cleveland said handsomely.

"I wouldn't expect you to," Phoebe replied with more candor than tact. "But what the hell happened to me?"

Joe was more than ready to tell her. "You got thrown off balance when Eleanor was willing to tear up more of the pea patch than we were."

"I really didn't mind Eleanor's being gung-ho," Phoebe insisted. "But she was capable of so much more than I bargained for that the possibilities began to include murder."

"You talking about the murder?" demanded Fritz Diehl, as he and Mrs. Gough returned from the newsstand. "Good. The papers haven't told me a thing except that Clay confessed. Why in God's name did he do it?"

Phoebe reddened with embarrassment at this indication that her words had been overheard, but Thatcher, ignoring her social gaffe, answered Diehl's query as succinctly as possible.

"Whetmore was blackmailing Batchelder. So Batchelder killed him, using the employee dissension as a smoke-screen."

"Are you telling me that Clay had some dark secret in his past?" Diehl found this the hardest part to believe.

"He certainly did. You could all have saved yourselves a good deal of grief if you had asked, five years ago, where Batchelder got a hundred thousand to invest in Sparrow."

"It never occurred to me." Diehl scowled as he tried to reconstruct ancient history. "Back then, when Mitch and I were scratching around for some seed money, Clay was very sympathetic. He never acted as if it was a problem for him and, of course, we didn't know much about him. He wasn't a paid hand at Bayou, he didn't live in New Orleans, and he had his own business."

Eleanor Gough was rueful. "These days we know more about the Don Islingtons of this world. We weren't surprised when Don refused to consider investing in a new company because he has expensive family responsibilities. We should have remembered that Clay had the same kind of obligations when we started Sparrow, and he went right on meeting them."

"Catch that wife of his letting him cut costs in the home," Diehl chuckled. "But if Clay didn't have a cent, what did he do?"

Mrs. Gough's equanimity vanished. "The same thing everybody at Bayou did who wanted easy money," she said caustically. "He agreed to a drug run."

"The goddam idiot! I always knew Clay was limited, but I didn't realize he was a jerk."

John Thatcher shook his head sadly. "I expect he was consumed by envy at seeing two young men miraculously enabled to live a dream. Batchelder wanted to share the golden opportunity."

"Didn't he realize he'd have it hanging over him forever?" Diehl protested.

"Clay's strong point is daily operations. He's not very good at anticipating long-term developments," Mrs. Gough said temperately. "According to Clay, he only considered the immediate risk. The drug-enforcement people keep an eye on repetitive patterns. So he thought a one-shot effort would be safe, particularly as his partner in crime was just as deeply involved. Once the run was over, Clay never gave the matter a second thought. That is, not until Alan showed up at Sparrow, having found out all about Clay's past."

"God, for a minute I thought you were going to say Alan had been the partner," Joe Cleveland exclaimed. "And I knew he didn't have that kind of moxie."

Mrs. Gough's pride at not employing pilots in the drug business had suffered a setback. "No, Joe," she agreed, "Alan didn't believe in taking risks."

"Then he should have been more adept at recognizing them," Gabler remarked. "Blackmail can be a dangerous pursuit."

"Clay says Alan was greedy from the start," she reported, "but it was the physical exam that put the fat in the fire. Alan knew his days as a pilot were numbered."

Thatcher was all too familiar with this line of reasoning. "So he decided to emerge as a senior executive with a seat on the board and access to the firm's assets. Whetmore thought it would be easy for Batchelder to arrange, and Batchelder knew it would be impossible. That's why he kept everyone in the dark before the employees' meeting and sat back to watch the sparks fly."

"And we obliged," Phoebe groaned. "Imagine playing patsy to Clay Batchelder!"

"Remember that you were a disappointment to him," Thatcher said hearteningly. "He wanted you all to go for Whetmore, not each other."

Gabler was barely able to contain himself. "What good did all that nonsense at the meeting do? As soon as the money surfaced, the police knew they were dealing with a more complex situation."

"I think Whetmore's legendary stupidity was to blame for that," Thatcher argued. "Batchelder probably didn't dream that the cash was being dissipated on simple bachelor thrills. If it had been steadily absorbed into normal investments, the police might never have noticed. After all, Everett, you were the one who established the magnitude of the under-the-table payments."

It is difficult to be critical of praise, but Gabler came close.

"My intervention should not have been necessary," he said ungraciously.

"Even the emergence of the fifty thousand was no real threat to Batchelder," Thatcher continued. "Whetmore's outlandish behavior at the meeting could easily be attributed to an inept *agent provocateur,* and Batchelder snatched at the theory of Diehl's responsibility."

Eleanor was obliged to demur. "Clay wasn't that quick to agree when Mitch first raised the idea."

"Perhaps not in front of you," said Thatcher, who could imagine Mrs. Gough's reaction to such an accusation. "But in New York it was quite a different matter. He did everything but name Diehl directly to me. And when I checked back yesterday with some of my men, they said that a Mr. Werner from A&P contented himself with describing police activity in St. Louis. It was Batchelder who was filling in chapter and verse for all comers."

"Between the two of them, my old pals Mitch and Clay did a real job on me," Diehl said unforgivingly.

Thatcher refused to pander to this single-minded view. "Not for long. As soon as Everett went to work, the list of suspects narrowed to a handful," he said, skillfully eliding

Gabler's preference for Phoebe as First Murderer. "By that time Batchelder was desperate, and he fastened on Mrs. Gough as the only acceptable scapegoat."

Phoebe still did not realize how docilely she had danced to Clay Batchelder's piping. "I agree that he made all Eleanor's talk about guilt and atonement sound suspicious, but he was just using the material at hand."

"Not precisely. Mrs. Gough spoke in terms of duty and responsibility. As soon as she left, he paraphrased her remarks to give them a more sinister gloss. What's more, from Scovil's uneasiness about Mrs. Gough during our last meeting, I suspect he may have been subjected to the same subtle poisoning by Batchelder."

Mrs. Gough was more interested than disturbed. "I noticed that Mitch was leery of me, but I felt the same way about him. You see, I knew there were no irregularities at Sparrow. If Captain Lemoine was right about blackmail, something had happened when we were all at Bayou, something that Alan could have found out about. I wondered if it could have been as simple as a drunken-driving accident with Alan sitting in the passenger seat. It wasn't difficult to visualize Mitch just stepping on the accelerator and speeding away. When disaster strikes, he does tend to . . . to . . . ."

"To panic," Diehl said baldly. "Face it, Eleanor, Mitch can't take pressure."

But Eleanor had no trouble with the concept. She had simply been searching for the right word.

"To go hysterical, is what I was going to say," she corrected calmly. "It wasn't until the party that everything straightened itself out. Only twenty-four hours earlier, I'd been talking to Don Islington about his financial problems. Then Phoebe started in on how we all got our stake money, and I realized that Clay had never told us where his came from. And if I was looking for a little irregularity at Bayou, I didn't have to think twice. The only logical course of action was to go to New Orleans and make sure."

It did not seem quite that simple to Thatcher.

"But how did you get results so quickly? We had been

thinking in terms of a laborious financial resurrection," he admitted.

"That's because you didn't work for Bayou," Eleanor retorted. "I merely encouraged Bill Johnson to tell me anecdotes about who had been picked up for drug-running after we left. When he told me that the biggest bust involved one of Alan Whetmore's buddies, I knew I was on the right track. Then all I had to do was locate Ramon Estevez and go ask him."

"And he just told you?" Thatcher made no attempt to hide his skepticism.

Mrs. Gough smiled. "For a price. Ramon was having trouble meeting the payments on his marina. I wrote a check and he confirmed what I already suspected. Shortly after Ramon came out of prison, Alan turned up in Acapulco on one of his fancy weekends. In the course of a long, boozy reunion, Ramon told him about Clay's solitary fling. At the time it didn't mean anything but, when Alan came to Sparrow, he realized it was a gold mine."

"He was right," said Thatcher, speaking as an expert. "Ramon didn't know about Batchelder and Batchelder didn't know where Ramon was. In effect, Whetmore was offering protection."

"That's certainly how Ramon saw it. When I told him Alan had gotten a hundred and fifty thousand, he went wild. As far as Ramon was concerned, it was his personal property that Alan had exploited. He was still trying to find some profit for himself when I left."

All of Gabler's confidence in high-minded ladies was proving to be justified. Beaming, he said: "When it was learned that you were in New Orleans, there were fears you might be engaged in a cover-up. I knew that was out of the question."

"Clay didn't. That's why he came out to Newton, to persuade me to keep quiet. And, if I'd found out two years ago, I might have been tempted," she confessed, proving that she had more of the old Adam than Gabler recognized. "That kind of publicity could have killed Sparrow. But after Alan's murder, silence was unthinkable. Clay didn't understand my moral objections at all. He didn't give up until I reminded him that I was now a prime suspect. That's when he started crying."

Fritz Diehl was still riding his hobbyhorse. "I'm surprised he didn't suggest serving Mitch up on a platter."

"Oh no," said Eleanor instantly. "He needed Mitch to run Sparrow. Clay even tried to ensure that Mitch had an alibi for the time of the killing. And he never would have touched that wrench if he hadn't assumed I'd brought it to the office. In fact, Clay had the nerve to be quite indignant with Mitch for nullifying these protective efforts and getting himself hauled off to the station."

"He should have remembered that Mitch always hogs the limelight." Joe Cleveland reviewed his own statement, then added a rider: "But that doesn't mean Clay hasn't been central at Sparrow."

Phoebe burst into derisive laughter. "Now that you're taking over some of his work, it's going to be the mainspring of Sparrow," she jibed.

When Thatcher raised an eyebrow, Mrs. Gough explained.

"While Clay is out on bail, he's giving us as much help as he can for the California expansion. Joe and I are going to New York to see about some secondhand planes, with Joe taking care of the technical end."

Thatcher was carefully expressionless. "Then you've agreed to Scovil's proposals."

"No, Mitch has agreed to mine," Mrs. Gough replied without batting an eye. "We're canceling Pittsburgh and going transcontinental on our tried-and-true system—used aircraft, economy facilities, and no frills. Phoebe has been right to insist on that, as I am sure you see."

Thatcher saw more than that. On the surface it appeared that everyone had gotten something. The truth, he suspected, was quite different. Eleanor Gough had gotten everything she wanted.

"So everybody's happy. Right, Phoebe?" Fritz Diehl asked challengingly.

But Phoebe was beginning to learn. "I didn't realize Eleanor saw so much merit in the California idea," she said sedately. "And if I find space at the right price, that makes a real difference."

They were saved further constraint by the public address system, which burst into life. A voice, distorted enough to be almost unintelligible, informed them that Flight 235 was ready for boarding. Galvanic upheavals began at every bench as passengers crammed themselves into overcoats and snatched up shoulder bags and carry-ons.

"Don't bother," said Mrs. Gough as the first ripples began in her own group. "I've told them to keep seats for us. It will be easier to let the others fight their way through."

Even at economy rates, Thatcher thought, it paid to travel with the management. It also gave him more time to satisfy his curiosity.

"You say that Batchelder is out on bail?" he asked.

"Yes, Clay has agreed to plead guilty to a lesser charge of unpremeditated murder. With time off for good behavior, he should be out in seven or eight years."

"Wonderful," Diehl said ironically. "What you mean is that your lawyers worked their tails off to avoid a public trial featuring drug smuggling and blackmail. So Sparrow gets off the hook, the DA's office gets a conviction, and poor old Clay pays the price."

It was Joe Cleveland who took up the cudgels.

"What's with this poor-old-Clay business?" he rapped out. "Clay bashed in Whetmore's brains with a wrench. That's way out of line in my book."

"And he put the rest of us through the wringer," Phoebe chimed in. "For three weeks we've been wondering if we had any company left."

At this point Everett Gabler was inspired to air his own uncompromising views. "What you say is very true. It is outrageous that a comparatively light sentence should be the judgment for a cold-blooded murder which was motivated by sheer self-interest."

"You both make me tired," Eleanor Gough said trenchantly. "Fritz thinks it's deplorable that Clay should go to jail at all. Everett wants an eye for an eye. You're both enjoying the luxury of demanding the impossible and being affronted when you don't get it. What happens to Clay isn't all that important. What is important, is minimizing the fallout on innocent bystanders. As Phoebe says, we've been put through the wringer, and we don't deserve to have Sparrow fall apart under us."

"Attaboy, Eleanor!" Joe applauded.

John Thatcher was not far behind him. Defining absolutes has always been easy. Thatcher reserved his approval for those willing to forge a decent compromise between things as they are and things as they ought to be.

"I certainly agree that Batchelder's sins should not be visited on others."

Fritz Diehl was more than ready to change the subject. "Sure," he said, and continued without missing a beat: "But what I'd really like to know, Thatcher, is how an outsider like you tumbled to Clay. It can't have been just Phoebe's review of how we all got a hundred thousand."

"No, that simply provided the missing motive. And, after Everett had given Sparrow a clean bill of health, we needed one. Of course we had no idea what crime Batchelder had committed at Bayou to obtain his original stake. But we started at the opposite end from Mrs. Gough. For weeks I had been puzzled by that extraordinary meeting with Whetmore and its consequences."

"Oh, that!" Joe flapped a nonchalant hand. "We're different at Sparrow."

"Not to the point of lunacy," Thatcher said dryly. "When Everett insisted the meeting must have been rigged, I realized there was only one person who could have done it. Why, for instance, didn't Scovil read the list beforehand?"

All four of them tried to explain at once, but Fritz Diehl's baritone easily prevailed.

"Because Mitch is such a lazy S.O.B. he never reads his in-basket."

"Exactly." Thatcher was willing to accept any phrasing that took them in the right direction. "But his shortcomings were not allowed to interfere with the operation of Sparrow. You yourself pointed out at the party that Mrs. Gough and Batchelder would both go on deck to make sure the rockets were fired properly. Similarly, when there was anything important, they thrust it on Scovil's attention. But, in spite of the fact that Whetmore could easily have been scotched before the meeting, Batchelder did nothing. His tactics almost backfired when my arrival jeopardized Scovil's attendance. Then Batchelder had to abandon passivity and weigh in with the deciding vote."

Mrs. Gough was shaking her head at her own blindness. "I never even thought of that," she admitted.

"As soon as you looked at Batchelder twice, the situation was obvious," Thatcher insisted. "Once the hostilities at the meeting started, he tried to prevent you and Miss Fournier from attacking each other and encouraged you to go after Whetmore. He wanted as many people as possible to tangle with his intended victim."

Joe Cleveland thought he saw another nice touch. "I suppose that's why Clay pretended I was about to deck Alan."

"Only partially. The most damning thing of all was the timetable."

"Now wait a minute," Diehl objected. "Nobody had an alibi. Mitch himself was roaming around Logan."

"And while Clay may have been running all over the Sparrow compound before dinner, so was I," Mrs. Gough added.

Not to be outdone, Phoebe made a contribution, too. "And Joe and I were both stuck in the tunnel."

Thatcher regarded them all severely. "You're looking at the wrong time period. Consider Whetmore's movements before the murder. He left the conference room, consulted the work roster for his next flight, then took his car to a restaurant several miles away. While there, he checked his watch and rushed off so as not to be late for something. As he was never seen again, it's safe to assume that something was his meeting with the killer."

"So?" Diehl asked, puzzled by Thatcher's air of completion.

"That appointment must have been arranged before Whetmore left the Sparrow compound. When and where was it made? Scovil was closeted with Islington, and Mrs.

Gough was making a speech at the water cooler. But Batchelder was alone with Alan Whetmore."

Joe Cleveland looked thunderstruck. "You mean when Clay pretended he had to hustle me out of the building, it wasn't just to throw suspicion on me?"

Relieved that someone had grasped his meaning, Thatcher nodded. "Alan Whetmore had just received a nasty disappointment and might easily have said something rash. Batchelder started to soothe him while we were still there, by attributing Mitch Scovil's rage to lack of preparation. As intended, Whetmore interpreted that as a suggestion there was still hope. Then Batchelder had to get all of us out of the room—under the pretext of keeping the peace —and set up his victim for murder. He was the only one who had the opportunity to do so."

"Imagine Clay doing all that," said Phoebe. "When I chose Alan as our spokesman, I gave him just the scenario he needed."

Unwittingly Thatcher probed a sore spot. "Batchelder was ingenious in some ways, but he made critical miscalculations about people. First there was Ramon Estevez, chatting too freely about the past. Then Mitch Scovil wandered into the line of fire. But worst of all was the money. Batchelder obscured the payments at his end without troubling to learn if Whetmore was exercising similar caution."

"Clay made a real balls-up of the whole thing, didn't he," murmured Diehl. "He should have stuck to what he knew about."

"Well, that's what he's doing now, insofar as he can without leaving the jurisdiction," Eleanor replied. "If we can just defer his court date for four or five weeks, our proposals for California will be ready. And that, of course, is why Fritz would like to see us all embroiled in a messy trial."

"It would help," Diehl acknowledged cheerfully. "But don't overrate the innocents in St. Louis. When I explain how Sparrow will be running a real cheapie, they'll think the threat has receded. Some of them still haven't grasped that price is a competitive factor. Hard to believe, isn't it?"

His insouciance led Thatcher to infer that Fritz Diehl could not yet be counted out in the power struggle at A&P.

"And now, I've got to be off," Diehl continued. "Have a good flight, everyone."

"You're not traveling with us?" Thatcher enquired, for once forgetting reality.

"Are you crazy?" Diehl replied with mock ferocity. "I do my flying on A&P. I just dropped by to get the dirt." Having shaken hands with everyone else, he bent to peck Eleanor Gough's cheek. "I'll give you a ring sometime this week, Eleanor, and let you know how things are."

"Fine," she said absently, "if I don't get to you first."

The frenzied mob that had been filing through the gate was now reduced to a tail of eight or nine people. Automatically everyone began to check belongings.

"I gather from this agreement with Scovil that the proxy fight is a thing of the past," Thatcher ventured, "and we won't be seeing you back at the Sloan."

"Only for financing," she replied calmly, "after we decide what aircraft to buy."

Thatcher blinked at this indication that the impossible had, indeed, happened and Mrs. Gough was supplanting Mitch Scovil without a battle royal. Perhaps this was the moment for the Sloan to send in its own designated hitter. That is, if Charlie Trinkam could ever be extricated from his current assignment, now that Rupert Vernon was offering to make Boston the winter home of the Edinburgh Festival.

Meanwhile, she was sweeping on: "And there's one more item in our agreement that will interest you. Mitch needed no persuasion to see that Phoebe was the ideal replacement for Clay on the board."

Phoebe unsuccessfully tried to smother a giggle. "Alan must be turning in his grave," she finally yelped.

During the congratulations, Joe directed a conspiratorial wink at Thatcher.

"That's just great, Phoebe," he said artlessly. "Now, whenever anything comes up, we can get together and tell you how to vote."

The merriment vanished from Phoebe's face like dew before the desert sun.

"Like hell you will!" she snorted.

Seizing her duffle bag, she marched toward the plane. Joe Cleveland instantly fell into step beside her, initiating what was bound to be a spirited debate.

Thatcher was delighted to have Mrs. Gough to himself. "Has Scovil retired from active participation in Sparrow?" he asked bluntly.

"Of course not. Mitch just has some other problems right now."

"You mean, beside Batchelder?"

"Kate McDermott, his wife, has been offered a spot as anchorwoman on a network morning show," she explained, obscurely amused. "It's a wonderful opportunity, but, of course, it's based in New York."

Tucking a portfolio under her arm, Eleanor Gough rose and briskly shook herself. The gesture was a simple act of physical adjustment but Thatcher, overcome by a sudden fancy, saw her as a tigress waking from a long sleep and stretching luxuriantly. With a chill prickle at the nape of his neck, Thatcher realized how many potential big cats there were in his own life. He did not want to be around when his secretary, Miss Corsa, and his daughter, Laura, began to flex their muscles.

Oblivious to his premonition, Mrs. Gough gazed at the boarding desk where Joe and Phoebe were still at it, then at the corridor down which Diehl had disappeared. Thatcher knew without being told that she was considering Mitch Scovil and his marital problems, Phoebe and her new status at Sparrow, Fritz Diehl and his struggle at A&P.

Eleanor Gough, rapt in some sibylline overview of the past few weeks, took several seconds to achieve the summation Thatcher was waiting for.

"These young people," she said with affectionate scorn. "They don't have a clue!"

About the Author

EMMA LATHEN is the nom de plume shared by Mary Jane Latsis, an economist, and Martha Henissart, a lawyer. The authors met at Harvard, where they were doing graduate work. Miss Henissart went on to practice law for twelve years, and Miss Latsis worked as an agricultural economist for the United Nations and the United States government. Their first book written together, *Banking on Death*, was published in 1961. *Something in the Air* is the twentieth novel by Emma Lathen.